Three Cats Publishing

This book has been written in an attempt to provide accurate and authoritative information regarding the subject matter contained herein. It is a work of fiction. It is therefore offered for sale on the understanding that neither author nor publisher can be rendered responsible for any errors, whether cultural, political, legal, factual, or statistical. The reader should seek the legal and professional assistance of appropriate experts when dealing with some of the situations that are covered in the book.

All statistics and facts quoted are those that were relevant and available at the time of writing. All research was made with the intention of presenting an unbiased portrayal of the various subjects as seen through the eyes of the author. Some of the content of this book is the personal opinion of the author and should be treated as such. Any misrepresentation or offence that may be made or caused is completely unintended and is therefore apologized for, unreservedly.

ISBN: 978-0-578-20526-7

First Edition

(May 2018)

Publisher:

Three Cats Publishing

Printed in the UK & USA by:

BookPrintingUK &Amazon

Also available as a digital eBook at Amazon Kindle, Nook Press, Xlibris, Lulu, CreateSpace, Apple iBooks, Kobo, Ingram Spark and many others.

Nick Robson can be contacted by email at:

nickrobson7@gmail.com

www.nickrobsonbooks.com

Cover design by Nick Robson

Interior design by Nick Robson

Interior art by Jodi Whitby

Lucy's Cats by Lucy Robson

The Sea Glass

a novel

Nick Robson

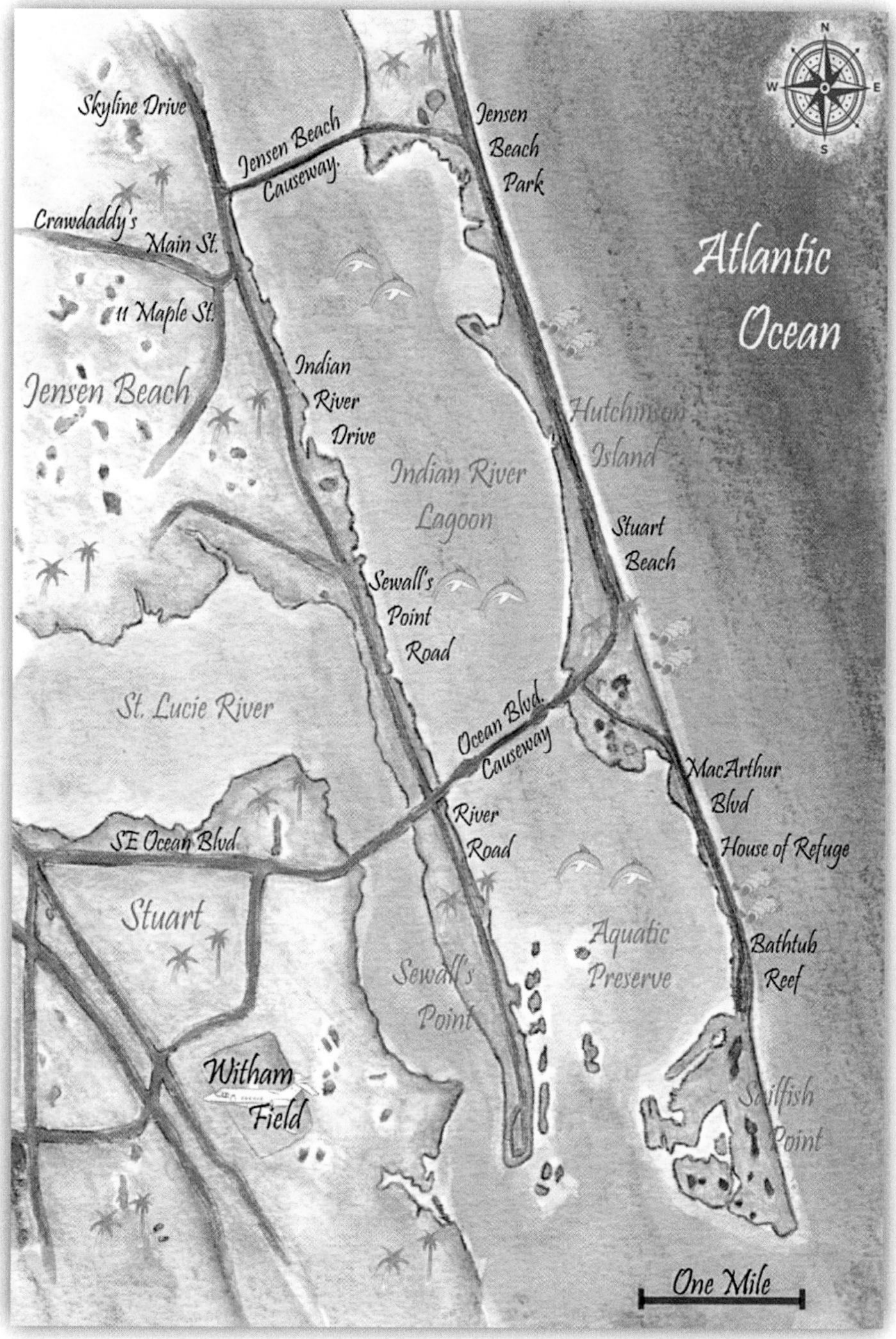

Skyline Drive
Jensen Beach Causeway.
Jensen Beach Park
Crawdaddy's
Main St.
Atlantic Ocean
11 Maple St.
Indian River Drive
Jensen Beach
Hutchinson Island
Indian River Lagoon
Stuart Beach
Sewall's Point Road
St. Lucie River
Ocean Blvd. Causeway
MacArthur Blvd
River Road
SE Ocean Blvd
House of Refuge
Stuart
Aquatic Preserve
Bathtub Reef
Sewall's Point
Witham Field
Sailfish Point
One Mile

Chapter 1

My mother was a good looking woman, a natural blonde with all the right bits in all the right places. Her only real problem was her predilection for fine looking gentlemen, an infinite list with whom she dispensed somewhat quickly and frequently. Until she got reckless with the condoms and that was where I entered the world. Kind of sperm of the moment, I guess, but I'm not complaining. I never knew my dad but I'm guessing he was a reasonably good looking man with a razor-sharp sense of humor. But to echo the words of the inimitable Jack Nicholson, when my mother called me a son of a bitch, which was a frequent administration, I really don't think she saw the irony in what she was saying.

My name is Jake Delaney and I have a story to tell, a story of love, of unrequited love. Please sit back and listen…

Part One

November 1984

Have you ever fallen in love with someone you shouldn't have fallen in love with? No, I don't mean the song by The Buzzcocks, but have you ever actually fallen for forbidden fruit?

Summer Cantrell was one of two daughters of a vaguely hippie, new age family in Jensen Beach, Florida. Naturally, her sister had been christened Autumn and both were extraordinarily pretty South Florida girls. You couldn't make this up. Their parents, Joe and Reyna, were the kind of couple who could only produce angels of daughters. Summer was the youngest at 16. Summer was who I fell in love with. The problem? I was 24.

~

The Cantrells lived high up on Skyline Drive, their house a pretty Cape Cod style frame home with staggering views across the Indian River Lagoon and then further out towards the Atlantic Ocean. Jensen Beach is one of those quaint old Florida towns that have managed to stay unique, individual and unspoiled even with the southern Floridian sky-rise cities like Miami, Boca Raton, Fort Lauderdale and West Palm Beach not too far away. The three-story height limit on new buildings in Jensen Beach meant that as yet, there were no hideous blots on what remained a beautiful landscape.

The town had a potpourri of budget beach-style restaurants which catered to the snowbirds in the peak season of November through April, but settled into a gentle rhythm for the locals in the off season. It had one well respected restaurant called 11 Maple St. which resembled a Swiss chalet style eatery with a sumptuous menu and wine list. This was where I first laid eyes on Summer Cantrell.

It was like I was watching myself. I was ambling down Maple Street, two of my friends with me, when a flurry of activity at one of the restaurant's deck-side tables caught my attention. Four teenage girls, clearly lost in their own world, laughing out loud and enjoying themselves on a balmy Florida evening. As I neared the table, she looked up and our eyes locked. It was like slow motion; a thousand frames a second, six steps seemed to last for hours. The world around me seemed to come to a standstill like a scene from one of those special effects movies where the camera keeps tracking but everyone is frozen in the frame. I couldn't take my eyes off this girl. Blue, blue eyes and a mane of wild sun-bleached hair, her eyes looking straight back at me. Teenagers, I thought; how I'd love to be in their world again.

The moment passed but as I walked by, I had to look again. This girl was staring right back at me and as she broke into a smile, I was dazzled by the whitest teeth highlighting the purest and most joyful face I’d ever seen. Frankie Goes To Hollywood’s “The Power Of Love” was playing on a tannoy system over at a restaurant on Main Street which for some reason felt incredibly poignant. What was going on with me?

Come on Jake, get it together, she’s a kid!

My friends and I continued on to a live music bar around the corner but for the rest of the evening, I couldn’t concentrate, I felt a ridiculous dizziness that I couldn’t escape from, and foolishly, I realized that I didn’t want to escape.

Chapter 2

I was born and raised in New York, not the nice parts that everyone sees on TV and in movies, but in a somewhat less enviable section of The Bronx. But I have always been, if nothing else, a grafter. I worked hard at high school, played soccer, and before graduation, I had somehow managed to secure an athletic scholarship to a college in South Florida, Stetson University. Strange name; I always thought that it belonged in Texas or somewhere vaguely cowboy and cattle, but it was a great school and I enjoyed my time there.

I was wary of the costs involved living away from home, even though the college picked up my tuition fees, so with money tight I never stopped working, I would never stay out late partying like my buddies did; I just needed to get things done and graduate so I could go to law school. I managed to achieve a four-year degree in three tough years while balancing my soccer scholarship obligations with my academics.

Although I am a New Yorker, I developed a fondness for Florida; South Florida in particular, notwithstanding its mostly octogenarian and blue-rinsed demographic. But Florida was a happy state; no one seemed to have too many worries in life. And I also loved the younger crowd I'd met whilst at college; a truly blessed bunch of kids who must have thought that everyone grew up near the beach and surfed all day. Those films you've seen of American kids enjoying life in their daddy's Corvette? Well, it was real and I kind of had the good fortune of becoming a peripheral part of it.

After graduating, I decided to stay in Florida and signed up at Stetson University College of Law. By the time I was 24, I was a bonafide lawyer with a new job in a big New York law firm and ready for the world. In retrospect, going straight out of college into law school isn't always the best route. You're still a kid trying to be something important in a man's world. But I was in a hurry and I needed to work. I just needed some money.

What I said about my mother at the start of this story may paint an unfair picture of a woman who didn't seem to care much for her kid. I may also have portrayed myself as an unwanted irritant in her social calendar. But that's so far from the truth. She worshipped me as a son, she loved to talk about my nascent achievements, but she had a whiplash tongue sometimes.

She wasn't broke either, she was a businesswoman with many fingers in many pies, although I'm not absolutely certain that all of them were legal or even ethically correct. From what I understand, my father was one of New York's finest on Ladder Company 9 in the NYFD. He died a young man so thankfully never witnessed the atrocities of 9/11 but his job meant he spent a lot of hours on shifts waiting time out. But it also gave my mother plenty of free time, particularly in her nocturnal moments.

There were many evenings when she would say, "Jake, I'm going out, but please don't wait up for me..."

So here I was, this naïve new lawyer, gearing up to take on the dizzying cocktail called New York City, with a spring in my step, ambition in my heart. I'd been lucky enough to secure a position at Newman, Hart, Stratton, Turnbull, Glass & Finnicombe – try saying that when you've had a few drinks. I was the newbie, I got the scut work to do and for sixteen or more hours every day, that's exactly what I did. But any weekend I didn't need to go into the office, I would make the thousand-mile trek down to South Florida to see my buddies, Talbot and Perryman.

Chapter 3

Joe and Reyna Cantrell had a happy marriage. They had met when Reyna transferred to Martin County High School for her sophomore year after her parents had relocated from San Diego. Reyna felt very much out of her comfort zone when she arrived. She'd left behind all of her teenage friends in Carlsbad and felt like a fish out of water. But when she met Joe, a baseball player on the high school team, she immediately fell for this gentle giant of a boy.

Joe was born and had lived much of his life in Miami and he had been equally despondent when he arrived in Jensen Beach at the age of fourteen. He was an only child too, the son of two proud parents who worked at Florida Power & Light. He was a freshman when he joined Jensen's local high school but fortunately, his athletic abilities allowed him to make friends easily through his success at playing baseball.

The two relocated and dislocated teenagers found common ground in each other and after a couple of unlikely meetings with mutually shared friends, the pair started dating. This was Florida in 1958 and at the time, there weren't a whole lot of places to take a girl on a date or to just hang out. So invariably, Saturday nights would find Joe and Reyna taking the thirty-five mile trip down to Palm Beach to watch a movie in one of the many drive-in theaters that had sprung up all over Florida in the early 1950s. By the time they arrived at the theater in Joe's father's Chevy Bel Air convertible, they felt truly alive and Reyna's hair wasn't even affected by the blustery journey because of the many cans of hairspray she went through each week. The only negative was that when they parked the car to sit back, hold hands and watch the movie, there would be countless other high school friends from their home town doing exactly the same thing. But it had the strange effect of building relationships and creating a wider circle of friends that neither Reyna nor Joe had experienced before in Carlsbad and Miami, and a love affair was born that would last a lifetime.

After graduating from high school together, they were inseparable. Four years at the University of South Florida was followed by a private wedding on Captiva Island with only their respective parents present. Fortunately, both had planned ahead for life after college and they each had jobs to go to once their brief honeymoon on Sanibel Island was over. Joe had managed to find a position as a trainee engineer at nearby aircraft company, Pratt & Whitney and Reyna had fulfilled her ambition to become a primary school teacher in the neighboring town of Stuart.

Once they had become reasonably established in their respective careers, the couple tired of paying rent for their two bedroom apartment and yearned to find the perfect idyllic home where they might one day raise a family. The offer of a deposit from both sets of parents shocked them – they didn't realize that their collective parents had sensed Joe and Reyna's desperation to buy a home and had colluded together to raise enough money for a deposit. Reyna's feeling of euphoria was short-lived when they began to search for that perfect property. Everything was just too expensive. The $50,000 mortgage offer they had, along with the $2,500 deposit from their parents was just not enough to find that dream home they had been envisioning.

But one day, just as Joe and Reyna were beginning to give up hope of ever finding anything, something happened to change everything. An aging uncle of Reyna's who lived locally, died at the age of 94. Having no children or other family in his will, he had decided to leave his home to Reyna and her sister, Clare. It was in poor condition and selling it would be a task, given the $65,000 price tag that had been suggested by their selling realtor. After realizing that the money would be useful to both sisters if it sold quickly and easily, the pair agreed that Joe and Reyna should buy the house for $53,000, thereby making a quick and painless sale and also avoiding the hefty 6% realtor's commission.

When Joe and Reyna first toured the property on Skyline Drive, they started to understand the task at hand of making this a modern 1960s home. Built in 1924, and although kept impeccably clean by Reyna's uncle, it had seen little or no updates and maintenance in the preceding decades. But Reyna had fallen in love with the house on first sight and all she could imagine was what they could do to it to make it their perfect paradise, overlooking a sparkling lagoon on the Indian River.

In the ensuing years, Joe, with his engineering knowledge and expertise in do-it-yourself, slowly transformed 3775 Skyline Drive into everything that Reyna had ever dreamed about. The plank sided home received a new paint color scheme, pale baby blue siding with bright white trim and the old jalousie windows were replaced with updated versions that included the necessary hurricane shutters that were at that time being widely installed throughout Florida. The couple painstakingly sanded the original cypress floors, varnishing and restoring them to their former glory. Not a single weekend went by when Reyna didn't have a paintbrush or a screwdriver in her hand and Joe wasn't up a ladder or on the roof. Eventually, after working on the property with every spare day and hour they had when they weren't working at their own respective jobs, they finally completed their monumental task and set about making it feel like a home, somewhere they really could start a family.

When Reyna gave birth to their first child, a daughter, it was the 21st September, a day that both Joe and Reyna had always assumed to be the first day of fall. The couple was also hugely fond of the band, Earth, Wind & Fire so the lyric to one of their biggest hits flowed naturally back to them, *"Do you remember, the 21st night of September..."* The baby girl was named appropriately, Autumn. Twenty-one months later, they were blessed with a second daughter, a child born in the Florida heatwave of 1969, a tiny blue-eyed blonde girl who inevitably inherited the name, Summer. Summer Cantrell, a miracle baby who survived an early birth due to complications that Reyna had experienced towards the end of her third trimester.

The two sisters grew up in a state of Floridian bliss. Every day, they would swim in the pool that their dad had eventually installed, spurring their love for everything aquatic. Summer's bedroom had a picture window and every day she would gaze mesmerized, out to the Atlantic Ocean beyond the Indian River, her love of the water adequately fed by her irresistible and enviable view. In the late afternoons, she would clatter out of the bedroom when she and her sister heard the throaty roar of their father's Ford Bronco coming up the driveway.

"How are my two perfect seasons?" he would ask as his daughters clung to his legs before he'd barely stepped across the home's threshold.

"We were just waiting for you, Daddy, can we swim now?" they yelled in unison.

"Of course, let me find Mom first to say hello and I'll get changed into a costume. Actually, I really need a swim this evening, it's hotter than hell outside!"

Joe lived for evenings like this when he could indulge in downtime with all of his girls. He gazed adoringly at the two little girls in the pool, swimming like dolphins. Even though he and Reyna had never taught them to swim, they were just natural water babies. He had to pinch himself sometimes, he just couldn't believe what a lucky man he was to be here, living in a literal paradise, with a beautiful, witty and intelligent wife and blessed with these two exquisite daughters.

And so, as the years passed, Joe made the house bigger and better, the family remained in a state of bliss and their two daughters grew into the kind of teenage girls with whom a father had to be particularly protective. He became more and more aware of the teenage boys whose heads did a one-eighty spin as they turned to stare at his girls every time they were out together as a family.

Might need that shotgun one day…

But Autumn and Summer were remarkable in spite of the attention they received. Either they were blissfully unaware of the stir they were causing or they were just very adept at dealing with unwanted suitors.

Chapter 4

April 1985

I pulled the rental Camaro up to the dockside and could see Talbot already setting up on his boat.

"Hey Talbot, what's happening?"

He looked up in amazement to see me standing on the dock with a cooler in my hand.

"Jake! I had no idea you were coming this weekend! You made perfect timing though, we're going out on the boat in a few so get your ugly butt onboard, fella!"

I'd had the most incredible week at the office but it had exhausted me and I was so ready for some recharging on the Florida waters.

"So what's the big occasion?" I said, "Is it just us and Perryman or is someone else coming? You look like you're stocked up for a party." I was looking down at an array of pre-made sandwiches and lobster rolls, crab claws on ice and a giant cooler filled with every type of drink imaginable.

"Oh, I don't know if you know them, but the Cantrell family is coming out with us today. I got to know them recently when I was playing in a restaurant downtown. They're ultra sweet and super cool."

Talbot usually splits his time between working as a real estate lawyer in Jensen and in the evenings as a guitarist and singer in local bars and restaurants. He makes friends too easily.

"No, I don't think I've met them but then again, you've got so many friends, Talbot, I can't keep up with you," I said.

"Perryman's coming too but you'll like the Cantrells, great people and they have two lovely daughters. But make sure you keep your hands to yourself, those girls are way too young!" he replied.

"Oh God, how old, Talbot? I thought we were going to have a boys' weekend with some grown-up girls! Now we're babysitting?"

"Trust me," he said, "You're gonna love this family, they've adopted me, so maybe they'll adopt a big ugly oaf like you too."

Talbot is one of those wiry guys who eats like a horse but doesn't put on an ounce of weight. His stomach should be pot-bellied by now at the ripe old age of 24, but instead, it's almost concave. He has a thin musculature running throughout his entire body but he's immensely strong, although he looks pretty much like a stick. His sun-freckled face which rarely loses its grin is topped by a shock of unruly and wavy dark hair. In short, this boy is charm personified. People love him. So do I.

As I listened to the songs playing on the boat's radio, I couldn't know then that 1984 would turn out to be such an incredible year for music. In many ways, it felt like the second coming of the Brit Invasion, Tears For Fears, Duran Duran, Culture Club, Frankie, Billy Idol and Wham! But I guess we also had Madonna, Prince, Bon Jovi, Bruce and Michael amongst our own homespun U.S. talent.

"What's up dudes!" yelled a voice, interrupting the silky tones of Sade's "Smooth Operator".

Perryman, could only be Perryman...

How's it hanging, homeboys!" he continued.

Perryman is one of those surfers you might've thought you'd seen in magazines and on television shows. He's a good-natured, tall, muscular hunk of a man with the requisite chiseled face and straw-colored hair. He would be at home on South Beach or Santa Monica Beach. Every inch of him is a tanned golden color, even the soles of his feet. He is also ridiculously good looking but penniless. I hate him.

Well not really, I love this man too. Everyone loves Perryman. Should be his slogan.

“Saturday!!! And the Perryman’s here!” he said, “I didn’t want to let you down and have you cruise this beautiful weekend without me so I forced myself away from some babes over there on the beach just so I could be with you guys. And, I can see how excited you are to see me!”

“Perryman, you are the veritable icing on an otherwise perfect cake, welcome aboard, buddy,” said Talbot.

“Good to see you Pez, but I think we’re on our best behavior today as we have a nice family joining us. Two teenage daughters, so we’ve been warned,” I said.

“Unless it’s just Talbot’s little ploy to get a girlfriend before she realizes what a moron he is,” laughed Perryman.

“Love looks not with the eyes, but with the mind; and therefore is winged Cupid painted blind,” quipped Talbot, quickly seizing the opportunity to practice his beloved Shakespeare quotes.

“Some Cupids kill with arrows, some with traps,” I responded, digging deep into my own reserves from England’s Bard, not realizing the potential of my words.

Chapter 5

As I looked towards the dockside, I noticed a very cool, vintage Ford Bronco pull up and park. Must be the Cantrell family, I thought. Super cool car, they must be a super cool family in a ride like that. As I watched, the doors opened and the Cantrells stepped out of the truck. Mr. Cantrell, Mrs. Cantrell, a daughter.... and another daughter. My heart suddenly began to race. I couldn't believe what I was seeing. It was the girl I saw on Maple Street back in early November.

Surely not, maybe my eyes were seeing things?

But sure enough, as the group meandered down the dock, it was her, it was the same girl!

Not today, it couldn't be, not on this boat with us?

They climbed aboard and Talbot was his usual enigmatic and boisterous self, asking them what they'd like to drink, even before they were fully aboard.

"Perryman, Delaney, I want you to meet my very good friends, the Cantrells. Joe, Reyna, Autumn and last but not least, the lovely Summer!"

I was bewildered. I once again had that November feeling of dizziness, I was feeling almost nauseous too. As my hand went out to Mr. Cantrell to introduce myself, I was drawn, in fact was pulled to Summer just in the way she was casually staring at me. I tried to ignore it and continued to introduce myself to Mrs. Cantrell, who herself was as beautiful as her girls. What do they say, look at the mother to see how beautiful her daughters would turn out to be? In this case, there was no shortage in the gorgeous stakes.

After introductions had been made and everyone had a cool drink nestling in their hands, Talbot took the wheel and expertly navigated out into the channel. To be fair, it wasn't as though he was a novice sailor; the boy had been in and on the water his entire life. Although he wasn't exactly enamored with his job as a lawyer, he loved the water, loved playing live music, and he loved his buddies and his endless carousel of girlfriends, well, potential girlfriends anyway.

As Talbot navigated the channels, Perryman adopted his usual role of entertainer-in-chief, his audience adoringly listening to his tales of diving and surfing, astonished when he revealed the zipper-like scar on his left calf, given to him by a passing nursing shark as he'd been waiting for the big wave. I'd seen and heard his whole shtick before but I didn't mind hearing it again because the man was so charismatic, you couldn't not be attentive or interested. He was superb with the two girls as well, serving them Shirley Temple 'cocktails', painfully aware of their desire to be treated as adults and also of their parents' wishes that they remain teenagers for as long as possible.

I decided that my main role of the day would be to ensure we had a constant feed of decent music. Talbot had installed an 8-track player on the boat years ago when they were fashionable and he had invested an unhealthy amount of his hard-earned money on the ridiculously expensive 8-track cartridges. Searching the shelf where he stored them, I found a Greatest Hits album from the end of the previous year, a collection from 1984.

So what do we have here? I asked myself. *"Careless Whisper", "When Doves Cry", "Like A Virgin", "Last Christmas", "One Love", "Drive" (oh, I love The Cars), "Relax"....*

I could see I didn't have my work cut out to keep the ambiance flowing with the treasure trove of music that Talbot had provided.

Once I'd set the mood with the music, I decided to kick back and enjoy the spray at the back of the boat with Mr. Cantrell while Perryman continued his expert and easy repartee with Mrs. Cantrell and her daughters. The three were simply entranced with the man.

"Hi again, Mr. Cantrell, it's a real pleasure to meet you and your family today, how long have you known Talbot?"

"Oh please, Jake, call me Joe, everyone else does and I don't like formality. I guess living here in Florida has just taught me to be relaxed and chilled."

"Do you get out on the water much?" I asked.

"Not nearly as often as I'd like. When you have two teenage girls with all the constant needs they have in life, my funds won't stretch to buying a canoe! But Talbot's offer of a day out today was more than welcome."

"Well, given the beautiful family you have, I guess it's not too much of a sacrifice to go without a boat."

We chatted for ten minutes or so, just shooting the breeze and eventually I lay back on the rear seat, casually sipping a Red Stripe, my head gratefully cradled on the boat's cushions. Duran Duran's "Wild Boys" and George Michael's "Father Figure" played on the boat's speaker system and I felt like I was floating in heaven. The cruise out to the sandbar was uneventful, but peacefully serene.

"How tall are you?"

"I....."

I sat up, my eyes blurred from staring at the sky and confused at the dislocated voice asking me questions.

"Where do you work, what do you do for a living?"

"I.... um..."

The girl, it was Summer. For my own reasons, I'd been desperately trying to avoid her for the last hour but here she was, standing in front of me, pummeling me with questions, a sly smile spreading across her pretty visage.

"Is that your car?"

"I... I'm six two"

“So why are all the tall guys the good looking ones?”

“I... I.. don’t know,” I stammered, “Me? Look at Perryman, he’s an Adonis!”

She smiled that smile. She was playing with me, just teasing. But I felt stupidly drawn to her.

“I’m a lawyer. I work in New York City. And the Camaro, it’s just a rental,” I said, trying unsuccessfully to sound mature to this far too young but mischievous girl.

“Nice car, Mr. Big Shot lawyer!”

“As I said, it’s just a rental, it’s not mine. I live in New York, people don’t have cars in New York, they take taxis or the subway.”

“I’d like to ride the subway one day,” she said, “I’ve never been on a train.”

“Well, I’m sure you will – maybe I can show you the city when you’re older.”

What did I just say? Come on Jake, she’s playing with you, she’s sixteen, for Christ’s sake.

“I’d like that, I may hold you to that promise, Jake Delaney.”

“How do you know my last name?”

“We Cantrell girls do our research, Mr. Delaney; you score high on the old guys charts.”

“Summer!” Perryman oozed, “You be careful of that boy, Jake. He may not be the best looking fella in the hood, but with those dark, brooding looks, that boy’ll charm the skin off a snake!”

Oh great, Perryman, I’ll use you for references when I need them, remind me to call.

“It’s Jake, call me Jake, and if it’s okay with you, Miss Cantrell, may I call you Summer?”

"Jake… hmm, well, that's a name I think I'm going to enjoy saying, Mr. Delaney."

Was it humid today or was I just feeling a little uncomfortable with a teenage girl?

"Is my daughter bothering you Mr. Delaney?"

Reyna Cantrell was a welcome interruption to a one-sided conversation between a flustered 24-year-old and a precocious teenager.

"Not at all, Mrs. Cantrell, your daughter is both inquisitive and charming. Please call me Jake, I always get the feeling I'm about to be arrested when someone addresses me formally," I replied.

"I don't think there's any danger of that, Jake, but I might have to arrest you if you call me Mrs. Cantrell again, I sound so old! Please, it's Reyna," she said.

Summer saw an excuse to head up to the front of the boat when her mother joined us. I watched as she slinked away, my gaze not wanting to leave the stunning beauty of her standing at the bow of the boat, her Daisy Dukes revealing long, tanned and perfectly shaped legs and her blonde mane blowing effortlessly in the wind. She was really quite beautiful and I had to remind myself that I was being ridiculous even looking at this vision.

"Thank you, Reyna," I said, quickly averting my eyes from the idyllic scene on the boat's bow, "It's a pleasure to meet you and your family today. May I ask what you and your husband do for a living here in Florida?"

"Well, I'm a teacher here in Jensen and my husband works in the aerospace industry. I'm never sure exactly what it is he does, but something pretty technical."

"Your daughters are very special girls, I can see where they get their looks from," I offered.

"They are special, Jake. And thank you for your comment; I'll take that as a genuine compliment! My daughters are lovely girls and although Autumn is almost two years older, Summer comes across as the older one sometimes. She can be a little precocious and I worry about her intentions sometimes. If she bothers you, please let me know and I'll take steps to rein her in."

"No, no, not a problem at all, she was just being very nice and flattering me, and I'll take flattery all day long from anyone," I replied, laughing nervously.

"Tell me what is that you do, Jake, I heard from Talbot that you're from New York. Is that where you work?"

"I was born there and although I went to school here in Florida, I decided to go back to work for a big firm just to get the kind of experience I doubted I'd be able to find here. But I don't plan to stay in New York for too long; I can't contemplate living in a three room apartment for the rest of my life so at some point in the next few years, I need to relocate to somewhere more permanent."

"Well, don't be a stranger, Jake - you're always welcome to stay over at our house in the future. Any friend of Talbot's is surely a friend of ours," she responded.

I detected a little sparkle in her eyes as she said it and I sat back to contemplate what she had just offered.

"Thanks Reyna, maybe I'll take you up on that offer one day…"

Chapter 6

Back in New York a couple of days later, I was replaying the memory of the boat trip over and over in my mind. I was finding it difficult to focus on work and I was worried that people in the office might start to notice so I tried hard to delete the weekend from my brain.

It was Monday morning and I looked outside at the view from my 35th floor office window. Manhattan was its usual hive of activity below, the people scurrying about looking like ants, beavering away in their own little ant hill. *This can't be the rest of my life*, I thought, memories flooding back to me of my last conversation with Reyna. *This can't be all I'm here for, can it?*

My thought process and general malaise about life was interrupted by Serena Hogue, our general office assistant.

"Jake, Mr. Turnbull wants to see you, he's in his office waiting for you," she said.

"Oh thanks Serena, I'll be right there. By the way, you look wonderful today, something happening to give you that glow?"

"Maybe Jake, potential new girlfriend. I'll keep you posted," she said, slyly winking at me as she sashayed away.

I knocked and entered Arthur Turnbull's corner office, the view beyond his panoramic window revealing a complete picture of Central Park. Arthur was one of the company's original founders but his work rate didn't falter as he approached his 80th year. The man was a dynamo, he didn't see the need to slow down and spend more of the working week taking it easy at his home in The Hamptons. He used to tell me, "When I'm dead, Jake, I'll have all the time I need."

He was speaking on the phone but when he saw me, he motioned me over and pointed to one of the chairs in front of his desk. I took his cue and sat down waiting for him to finish his call.

I guess this office could be mine one day if I put the leg work in. Problem is, I'm too impatient...

"Jake, thanks for sparing me your time."

You're paying for it Arthur, no skin off my nose. Knock yourself out, I've got all day in here.

"This tort we're working on for the smokers who died of cancer. It's getting bigger every day, every minute in fact. We need all hands on deck for the next month so I'm afraid weekends are going to be out for a while. You'll need to be here to deal with the paperwork, affidavits and depositions. You're doing a sterling job here and I appreciate the effort you're putting in so if it interrupts any plans, I apologize in advance."

Shit, I had plans to fly down to Florida in a month's time, maybe we'll get the work done before then? Yeah, of course Jake, take a look at that pig flying past...

The thing about Arthur is that unlike most names above the door, he doesn't abuse his authority and doesn't disrespect his staff. He's one of those men who still remembers where he came from to finally become a partner at one of the biggest law firms in New York City. Arthur is a gentleman. More like your dad than your boss.

"It's okay Arthur, your wish, my command and all that. Frankly, I think I need to get my head down because I'm being distracted elsewhere, so in a way it's a bit of a relief," I said.

"I had noticed, Jake, is there something on your mind, maybe something I can help with?" he said.

Yes, Arthur, you can come and bail me out of jail when I get arrested for dating a teenage girl!

"No, I'm fine, Arthur, I just have a few issues going on down in Florida but nothing I can't deal with on my own."

Back at my desk, I thought about the long hours ahead and that I would likely not be making the trip back down to Florida any time soon. But there was nothing to do about it except get my head down and earn my way out of New York City.

Chapter 7

Summer was an unusual girl. She'd grown up in a family that was not religious, didn't impose many boundaries and was cradled with love and pure devotion by her parents but she had secrets that she couldn't tell anyone. Not yet anyway.

She wasn't the same as the other girls in high school. She'd noticed that her dad was on alert for boys giving her attention when they passed by, but in truth, she really wasn't interested in them so on that front, he had nothing to worry about. Autumn was different, she loved the attention, was already secretly dating one of the boys in her class. But Summer just wasn't interested in pubescent teenage boys, they didn't hold much excitement for her, whatever salubriously salacious effect she was having on them. In fact, they slightly irritated her and she was beginning to be labeled 'lesbian' by her peers at school just because of her lack of interest. She didn't care though; her thoughts were on other things.

"Why don't you want to come to the school dance tonight?" Autumn asked.

"I don't know, I suppose I just find it all a little stage directed. You know, girls on one side of the hall, boys on the other, it kinda feels like you have to hook up with one of them and most of them make me feel sick. Don't any of those boys think that maintaining body cleanliness might make a difference? An occasional shower would help. Most of them are so spotty anyway, sometimes I just want to gag!" Summer replied.

"Maybe your standards are set too high. It might help if you lower your sights a little."

"My sights are carefully aimed right now, sis, I have a perfect aim in fact."

They were topping up their tans on a hot June Saturday afternoon on one of the many beaches over on Hutchinson Island. Now out of tourist season, the beach was mostly empty except for a dozen or so likeminded teenagers keen to maximize their tans for the evening's dance.

Summer reached into her bag and pulled out her Sony Walkman. She had seen the new Sony CD Walkmans that had come out at Christmas but they were ridiculously expensive so there was no chance of getting one of those anytime soon. Dipping back into her bag, she retrieved a cassette of an album she'd been given at Christmas by her mom and dad, *Rattlesnakes* by Lloyd Cole & The Commotions. It wasn't something she'd asked for but it had been an unexpected pleasure of an album to listen to. It was a band she knew little about, only that they were yet another group of musicians from Great Britain making inroads in the USA.

If I didn't have music to get me through some of this stuff, she thought, *I think I'd lose my way.*

A particular favorite for her was the album's title song, "Rattlesnakes". It just seemed to sum her up in so many ways…

Jodie wears a hat although it hasn't rained for six days

She says a girl needs a gun these days

Hey on account of all the rattlesnakes...

She listened to side one before flipping the cassette and listening to the rest of the album. The last song though, "Are You Ready To Be Heartbroken?" made her think about the secret she was keeping.

"Come on, sister, we're going to look like lobsters if we stay out here much longer!" Autumn shouted through the music in her headphones.

Back at the house, Summer lay on her bed and stared out at the lagoon and at the ocean beyond. It was odd, but every time she spent just a couple of hours at the beach, she came home feeling like she'd just come back from a vacation. It was so energizing, so cleansing, but such a shame that she couldn't spend it with someone other than her sister. It wasn't that she didn't enjoy Autumn's company, it was just that she had her eyes on another prize right now. And it definitely wasn't at the school dance tonight.

Chapter 8

The weeks passed quickly as I ploughed on with the workload I'd been assigned. In fact, for me it was a benefit to be this busy because it was the perfect remedy for burying the futile emotions I'd been feeling since that weekend down in Jensen.

I don't have a steady girlfriend but that's only because I've never really met anyone yet who I want to be with more than I want to be without. If you get what I mean? Girls don't rush to go on a date with me, well not all of them anyway. And I'm not an unattractive guy I suppose, but not typically hunky or chiseled like Perryman for example. I'm 6'2", pretty lean and fit, dark hair, brown eyes, standard issue American twenty-something. I like to think my humor is my biggest attraction but some girls say it's my mouth. No idea what that means but whatever works is fine with me.

I don't have many vices, I guess. I don't smoke, and drugs scare the crap out of me but I like a half decent glass of wine, well a cheap glass of wine anyway. I like most sports, love watching movies too. But I prefer romantic comedies as opposed to action movies. I choose to see them in theaters, just in case I'm caught crying, so no one sees in the dark what a wuss I am. I can cook well enough but I prefer to eat out. I'm not even averse to eating in a restaurant on my own; it's kind of therapeutic and apologetic. But if I can find a beautiful, witty and intelligent dining companion, I'm all in.

I don't have a car because I live in Manhattan and there's just no point, but I do like cars. I live in a three room apartment, if you can call it an apartment, more a rabbit hutch with a bathroom and minor cooking facilities. My neighbors like me because I live quietly and I'm reliable for feeding their cats when they're away.

That's me, pussy man...

I'm more a saver than a spender but I like nice clothes. Motto being that it's better to buy one amazing item for a higher price than ten cheap ones from the bargain bin. I don't have the time or the money for vacations right now although I do enjoy my R&R down in South Florida. It de-stresses me and sets me up for the daily, weekly, monthly assault in New York. I'm not sure if I ever see myself relocating to South Florida permanently, but it certainly does have its attractions. I think the west coast might be cool to try too.

"Jake, can I get you some coffee?"

This was Charlotte Acosta, our firm's leading femme fatale. She stood in front of my desk, sheer fitting red cashmere dress seemingly displaying road markers to guide you through each exceptional part of her body. Shapely, stocking-clad legs highlighted by the precariously high Manolo Blahniks that caressed her feet. I looked up at her 'come get me' face, her long black shiny hair ending at breast level. For some reason, I was picturing her naked wearing just the Manolos. Call me weird, but I just like shoes.

"You know what, Charlotte? I could really use one right now. But I'll come with you to the kitchen; I need to stretch a little. I think my back's seized from being slumped at my desk every day," I replied.

Ordinarily, I didn't like being in the office on a Sunday but actually, right now it was pretty nice because of the lack of people there at weekends. Except for the grunts. Like me.

Actually, why was Charlotte in today? A woman who has a pair of Manolo Blahniks for every day of the month doesn't need to be working weekends!

In the kitchen, we are privileged to have an outstanding Simonelli Program V Espresso Machine, It cost more than I make in three months but I would crawl naked over broken glass to beg for the java gift that oozes from this lady. The Simonelli, I mean.

"How do you take yours, Jake?" Charlotte asked.

"Oh, black with two sugars, thank you."

As Charlotte manhandled the Simonelli, I couldn't help but admire her landscape. This woman was a masterpiece in design, function and sheer sensuality. The dress was so fine that it was facile to assume she'd bothered with panties this morning, her ass a testament to why women will always be so much more physically alluring than men could ever be. As she turned back from the espresso machine, I could see that *all* lingerie today had either been abandoned or forgotten. The woman was heaven on legs. Helmut Newton would have had a field day.

"Charlotte, you have succeeded in making the perfect espresso, I can already feel the effects. Thank you," I said, sipping a little more of the delicate juice.

"How's your back feeling now, Jake? Any improvement with the caffeine medication?" she asked.

"Unfortunately, this nectar doesn't seem to reach that far but at least the head is happier," I responded.

"I could try massaging your coccyx for you, if that would help?"

What did she just say?

"I'm pretty sure it would but I'm reasonably certain we don't have a massage table in the building!"

"Well, why don't you stand facing the wall there, lean in and support yourself with your hands?" she asked.

"Are you serious, Charlotte? I replied, a little astonished at her suggestion.

"Serious as a heart attack, I actually did massage therapy as a sideline once upon a time. Come on, stand up and lean in, I know what I'm doing," she ordered.

Now, I'm a pretty compliant person so I did as instructed. In fact, when she started probing deeply into the bottom of my spine, it really did begin to help. I could already feel a tension dissipating. The woman wasn't lying, she'd definitely done this before. She was amazing.

Fuck me, what was that? Either she's found a tension spot I wasn't aware of or she's feeling my ass!

"Hey Charlotte, I'm not sure that area requires attention," I said.

"Sometimes, the cause of the pain isn't in the same site as where you're feeling it, Jake. Just bear with me and let's see what I can do…"

She was right; whatever she was doing to my buttocks was having a hugely positive effect on my lower back. There was no arguing with her so I decided to let her use her expertise on me.

And then I felt her hand slide between my legs and gently take my balls in her hand through my suit pants. I was frozen stiff, as now was my manhood. I was instantly hard and she knew it as her hand crept up to my shaft and gently caressed it.

And then it all stopped. I waited a moment to see if she was going to continue but after a few moments, I realized she wasn't. But as I turned around, Charlotte was sliding her dress up to her navel, revealing stocking tops and a triangle of black, smooth and perfectly trimmed pubic hair. She was smiling as she realized that my gaze was working my way up her body to her chest, where proof was no longer required about the missing bra. Her exquisite breasts moved like sand dunes across a desert, they were hypnotic.

She looked down and I realized that she was staring at my own little friend, eager to escape its shackles. Reaching forward, she gently undid by belt, released the zip on my pants and reached in to free me.

"Charlotte, I'm… I'm not sure what's going on here, have I missed something?"

"I have needs, Jake and right now, you're about to fill those needs, so to speak. Take your pants off and lose the shirt too," she ordered.

She's gorgeous! No part of my body felt inclined to disagree either. Well, it is the weekend…

I slid my pants off and unbuttoned my shirt. Charlotte was doing a little preliminary work to ready herself, her hand disappearing approvingly between her thighs.

I was naked now, fully engorged too. I leaned in to her to kiss her stunning mouth but her hands came up and cradled my head before I could even begin tongue dueling with her.

"I don't need your mouth up here, big boy, you've got a little something to take care of down there. Don't be offended, Jake, but I'm not a kissy girl, I just need your tongue in the area that needs it most right now."

Big boy? Wow!

My head was getting as swollen as my member now; I felt a canter turn into a gallop. I did as instructed, a little offended that she didn't want to kiss, but who was I to start feeling sorry for myself as I moved south and began to devour her elegant thatch. The woman didn't just look insanely good, she smelled good too. I was in seventh heaven when she abruptly pushed my mouth aside and instructed me to change tactics.

"I need you inside me, Jake, I need it now. I need *you* now!"

I entered her, deeply relieved and honored to be sliding in and out of her. I gazed across her mostly naked body, her silky skin punctuated by cherry red nipples that were clearly aroused by our passion. I reached up towards her lips, longing to kiss them, desperate to taste her oral fruits.

"Unnecessary, Jake, don't waste time, I'm not in this for love and affection."

Like I said, I'm pretty compliant so who was I to argue?

I was finding a gentle rhythm now and Charlotte was moaning a deep guttural growl now. I wasn't sure if it was unbridled pleasure or I was killing her with my weapon. Unlikely.

"Jake, don't even think about spilling your load in there, I'll take care of you right now."

She slid off me and went to her knees, feverishly grabbing my chap and surrounding him with those perfect lips, pulling me hard into her mouth. I dared to glance down at her attacking my part like a hungry savage. I hadn't died and gone to heaven yet but I think I was just about to. Sensing my new found swollenness and my body quivering, she took me out of her mouth and expertly ended my torment, exploding my pent up seed and scattering it through the air.

Oops...

"Charlotte, that was unbelievable. I... I don't know what to say. I had no idea you felt this way about me. I think I might be falling in love!"

"Don't get all lovestruck on me, Jake, I'm not the dating type. I just have certain requirements at inappropriate times and you were there. Sorry, don't want to burst your bubble. Although I am super impressed, big boy, because you almost burst mine today. Almost."

There it is again, 'Big Boy', Jake and his unfeasibly large penis...

I'm sorry Charlotte, I wasn't assuming anything, I'm just feeling a little overwhelmed by what just happened. It was incredible! And I've never done all of the things we did today on previous dates with other girls."

"I can see that, Jake, but some boys just need a little teaching and a little coaxing, don't they?"

I watched as she slinked out of the kitchen, delicately smoothing her dress down her body, the clicking of her Manolos fading away as she disappeared from view.

Man, I love those shoes...

Chapter 9

Reyna Cantrell lay back on the sun lounger. It wasn't every day she could have a 'me day' but with her school closing down because of a power cut, she found herself luxuriating by the pool area. Florida kids can't survive in school without power to run the air conditioning system. It was June, already into hurricane season in Florida and there had been a tangible change in the weather from a couple of weeks earlier. Gone were the bright, breezy days of spring, replaced now by high humidity days in the 90s and evenings filled with heavy moisture and breathless air, the sound of the cicada chorus permeating the evenings. She actually liked the summers in Jensen; her body had long ago learned to cope with the humidity and heat. And the peace that followed the exodus of the snowbirds was incredibly welcome.

She gazed around the garden, her eyes dwelling momentarily on a single but harmless Black Racer snake, slithering quietly through the lush grass. A pair of cardinals flitted from tree to tree, their vivid red coloring iridescent in the sunlight, an impossible pair of birds to photograph, their rapid movements far too quick to frame in a lens. Two geckos lay slumbered, one aboard the other, a reminder that the skink and lizard population was ever expanding in this subtropical state. A white ibis dropped in, not to say hello but to see what tasty grubs might be found buried deep in the Cantrell lawn.

Reyna's eyes surveyed her own body, hot droplets of perspiration glistening in the midday sun. She took time to check each of her still athletic features. Her legs were without doubt her best assets. They remained slender and fat free, aided by their enviable length, toned musculature and golden tan.

She rose from the lounger and softly padded into the house, quickly climbing the stairs to her bedroom. As she stood in front of the full-length mirror, she removed her bikini and as it fell to the floor, she admired what she saw. Her breasts, although larger due to childbirth, had remained firm and still very attractive. Her stomach too was stretch-mark free, a gentle concaveness that highlighted her femininity. Considering that she'd borne two children, she was inwardly contented and pleased with how her body had evaded wrinkles and cellulite. Even her mane of sandy blonde hair remained lustrous; an asset that she'd thankfully managed to pass on to her daughters. All in all, Reyna Cantrell was pretty happy with herself. Her husband must have felt the same way too because he certainly never complained about her body and their lovemaking remained a bi-nightly constant in the Cantrell home, once the girls were asleep.

In the kitchen, now fully covered in her robe, she put the kettle on the stove top to make some English tea. She didn't know where her passion came from for the Ceylon leaves that were produced for the tea drinkers in England, but she couldn't even start the day without a cup. Must have some English roots in her somewhere.

Sitting down at the kitchen table, as she waited for the tea to brew, her mind wandered, thinking about all the things that made her happy in her life in Jensen Beach. She and Joe were the golden couple in many respects. A love affair at school that had blossomed through college and remained as strong as the day they'd first laid eyes on each other during her sophomore year. She loved her job; it was what she'd always wanted to do, to teach young children. Joe was exceptional in his career and earned a pretty good salary too. And with the money that she also brought in, the Cantrells were financially in very good shape. They still had a mortgage but they could pay it off easily now if they chose to do so. But they liked the idea of retaining money in the bank for rainy days.

They owned their cars too; Autumn had been given an older 1977 Jeep Cherokee for her birthday. Reyna's was a 1985 Buick Riviera

Convertible which she just loved; she felt like a queen when she was driving it with the roof down, and Joe still had his beloved Bronco. She didn't know if he loved that stinky old gas guzzler more than he loved her but she guessed she was probably safe as he spent every night in bed with her and hadn't yet opted to sleeping in the back of the Ford.

They shared many friends in Jensen Beach, it was one of those towns where mostly everybody seemed to know everyone else and theirs was a tight-knit community. Their home was never without a gaggle of kids running through the house, many of them seeking out the kitchen to see what was on offer that day. Her daughters made friends easily and attracted quite a crowd at weekends, boys as well as girls. She was fully aware of the attraction for the boys when it came to her daughters, they weren't just beautiful teenagers and they were growing into highly attractive and alluring young women.

The interesting thing about growing up in a climate that was permanently warm, was that all the kids dressed for the temperature. Florida's children lived their lives in swim shorts and bikinis. Jeans and sweatshirts only made an appearance on maybe three chilly days in January. Even Christmas was a rare occasion to have any logs burning in the fireplace. For Reyna, this life of semi-nakedness was a good thing because it meant her children stayed healthy and they attuned their minds to a body uncovered so that as they grew into adults, it really wasn't such a big deal.

Autumn was the oldest and she eschewed admirers in the main, although Reyna secretly knew that one particular boy at school had shown more intense feelings towards her than any of the others. She'd have to keep an eye on Caleb Campbell, just in case he thought that Autumn was easy prey.

Summer was a different story altogether. Reyna didn't have a favorite child, but Summer required much more monitoring than Autumn. It wasn't that Summer was a problem in any way; she just had something about her that attracted the entire male species, men as well as boys. She was extremely attractive and not yet even seventeen but she also had a maturity factor about her that was unusual in a girl her age, in fact in anyone her age. Added to that, she had a sense of mischief about her; she was precocious in all the best aspects of the word but that precociousness may prove to be a problem with some older men who had taken notice of her looks and maturity. She wasn't certain how much of a problem it might be but even when they'd been on Talbot's boat that Saturday a few months back, she had been well aware of the spark that had formed between Summer and Talbot's nice friend, Jake Delaney.

And Jake wasn't even a kid, he was an adult, fully developed with a career. What was he, 23 maybe, 24 even? And even though their first introduction had been brief, nothing escaped Reyna's attention when it came to Summer. The look on Jake's face when he'd been peppered by Summer's questions was priceless. Rarely had she seen a man of that age completely floored by a teenage girl. His lingering look as he watched her walk away to sit at the front of the boat had not been lost on Reyna either. This was definitely a situation she'd need to keep an eye on. If she wasn't mistaken and had correctly interpreted the whole scene, the thought occurred to Reyna that young Mr. Delaney had been immediately smitten. If she was not mistaken, he'd fallen in love with her precious daughter.

Chapter 10

The phone rang on Talbot's office desk.

"Hey Talbot!"

"Hi Jake, it's so good to hear your dulcet tones on this ridiculously humid morning in South Florida. How's The Big Apple treating my buddy? I'm assuming you're getting laid on a daily basis with that endless train of ladies in the city?" he asked.

"Well not quite, but there have been one or two interactions, one of which was particularly interesting, I guess."

"Pray tell, my liege, what light through yonder window breaks?" Talbot asked with his unique love of all things Shakespearean.

"Talbot, you know I don't kiss and tell! You should also know that for me, the better part of valor is discretion," I feebly replied, desperate to match his inimitable grasp of The Bard.

"But I can tell you that I did have one rather odd experience at the hands of a lady in red, something that still makes me quake in my shoes to this day," I continued.

"Misery acquaints a man with strange bedfellows," said Talbot.

Oh Lord, is there no end to his quotation notation? He's like a library on legs!

"Alright Talbot, let's end this and just say that in this particular instance, I am a man more sinned against than sinning," I responded, hopefully with finality.

"Good job fella, you are a worthy opponent today! So, what do I owe the pleasure of this call?" he said.

"Well, I've been slammed at the office recently."

God, I hope he doesn't reinterpret that figure of speech.

"And I really need to get away from the city. I was wondering if you had any plans for the weekend?"

"Well actually, there is a music festival going on here in Jensen this weekend, so your timing is perfect. There are some pretty major acts coming, considering Jensen is such a small town. You can stay at my place if you like. But if, by the time you arrive, there're other people crashing, you know the Cantrells said you'd be welcome to stay at their house," Talbot said.

I hadn't forgotten the invitation that day on the boat from Reyna Cantrell. Actually, it had never really left my mind. For all the wrong reasons though.

"Sure, that sounds like a plan, what's the festival all about though?"

"Well, the Jensen Beach Chamber of Commerce has come up with this idea of a Summer music festival, mainly to showcase the town but also to bring some current music acts to this part of the state. It's a grand effort on their part to give something to the local kids during the Summer, something for them to look forward to, I guess," Talbot replied.

"When you say current acts, what sort of artistes are you talking about?"

"This year, which of course is the inaugural festival, we've got Marie Osmond performing, amongst others. And there's talk that Alice Cooper is going to play," Talbot said.

"Alice Cooper would be great, but Marie Osmond? Not so sure about that! I mean, wasn't her time back in the 70s?"

"Don't worry, Jake, it's going to be a great weekend anyway, whoever's performing. When can I expect to see you, are you coming down Friday night or early Saturday?"

“I’ll be there late Friday, I should be on the 7pm flight out of LaGuardia so by the time I’ve picked up a rental car, I should be with you before or around midnight.”

“Okay,” said Talbot, “We have a plan. See you Friday, the beers will be cold and plentiful!”

I put the phone back in its cradle on my desk and thought about the conversation I’d just had. I wondered if Talbot was aware of what he was saying when he mentioned my staying with the Cantrells for the weekend. Had he sensed something between Summer and I on the boat back in March or was I just being over-sensitive?

The truth was that I really hadn’t managed to get the image of that sixteen-year-old girl out of my head since then. In fact, not really since I first saw her in November last year on Maple Street. I had been having terrible thoughts in my head that just didn’t sit easily in my conscience. Thoughts of guilt, pleasure, love and lust and not necessarily in that order. Things that I wasn’t terribly comfortable with having on my mind.

Chapter 11

Summer stretched back on her bed. School was now over for the year and she was so ready for the Summer break, three months of sheer bliss. Looking around her bedroom, she took in all the things that made her the typical American teenager. Posters filled the walls, pop stars like Boy George, Adam Ant and Duran Duran. Movie stars too, Rob Lowe, Brad Pitt, Johnny Depp. Her closet was pretty bare for most teenage girls but she lived and died in the same kind of clothes all year round, cut-off jeans, crop tops, flip flops and a couple of items for more special occasions. But even flip flops weren't always necessary as she spent most of the time barefoot, her feet perennially prone to being lacerated on stray glass and splinters.

On her dresser, she kept little bowls full of seashells and pebbles that she'd found on her many exploring days on the beach and bangles cluttered every available hanging space on the mirror trim. Looking further around, she eyed her music center which was her lifeline. If she didn't have that, escaping into her own private world would be so much more difficult. And her bed, she loved her bed. She could lie there for hours, just thinking about life, where it might take her, who she would meet.

She gazed out of her window, thoughts of the long and seemingly endless Summer in her mind. The beach, her friends staying over, music… the Pineapple Festival this weekend. The Pineapple Festival…

I wonder if Jake will be coming down for that?

Since she'd first seen him on Maple, she hadn't been able to get him out of her mind.

He probably didn't even notice me then, but I noticed him. But on the boat, there was a genuine connection, right? Was I too pushy? Will he remember me if he does come down at the weekend? Does he even care?

She was fully aware of her effect on boys and of their basic instinctual attraction but Jake wasn't a boy, Jake was a man. She also knew she was young and that sometimes teenage thoughts are exaggerated beyond all reality. Her fondness for Jake would be put down to a teenage crush, she knew that. But Summer didn't see it that way in her mind. She didn't go on dozens of dates with boys, in fact she mostly avoided them as far as dating went. She wasn't sure if maybe she just had a leaning towards older men or if she was perverse in some way.

It wasn't something she ever dared discuss with her mother, or even Autumn. She liked boys well enough but her idea of any kind of relationship with the ones at high school was really just that she enjoyed joking around with them and talking about music and surfing and goofy stuff. In her mind, she didn't see or even want to see beyond the surface. She'd kissed a couple but they had bad breath and both of them were spotty. Not their fault but it just made her heave. She realized that her dad had made some mental notes when they'd been out and she guessed he was on the lookout for the wrong attention but she also knew what he didn't know. He had nothing to worry about. At the moment, anyway.

Autumn would just say I'm a freak and she'd probably be right...

She got up from the bed and picked out a cassette to put in her tape deck. Autumn had taped a selection of Top 40 records off the radio and put them onto a cassette for Summer, a prized possession that was now getting worn out. As she inserted the cassette and hit 'Play', she instantly mellowed. *Wham!*'s "I'm Your Man" pumped out of the speakers:

And I know I'll make you happy

With the one thing that you never had...

"How is it," she said aloud to herself, "that every song I hear seems to be talking about me personally? I mean, that could be Jake singing to me..."

Wanna take you, wanna make you

But they tell me it's a crime!

"It doesn't stop!" she cried, almost giddy with laughter now. "George, did you write this with me in mind or are there thousands more teenage girls out there just like me?" she yelled at the top of her voice.

As Summer danced in her bedroom, out in the hallway, Reyna paused by the door to listen. She recognized the song immediately; in fact it was one of Reyna's current favorites too. Summer was clearly enjoying herself so she walked away as George Michael continued to serenade her daughter:

I'll be your first, I'll be your last

I'll be the only one you ask...

"Oh Jake!" she yelled, "Please come down this weekend, I need to play this song to you!"

By this time, Reyna was out of earshot, which was probably a good thing because it was something that she definitely didn't need to hear right then.

As the song ended and the click of the 'pause record join' sounded in the speakers, *Dead Or Alive*'s "You Spin Me Round (Like A Record)" blasted from the stereo system.

"I'm right, every song has a meaning in my life," she said aloud once more, "Jake Delaney, you *do* spin me round like a record so please come to the festival this weekend because I can show you that you're definitely going to be my man!"

Chapter 12

After my phone conversation with Talbot, I could suddenly see the wood from the trees, a light at the end of the tunnel in my job at Newman Hart. A weekend in Jensen was exactly what I needed right now. I didn't think that I could ever be more exhausted than when I was trying to nail four years in three at college but this was a workload on another scale altogether. A lot of it was so new to me that I constantly found myself seeking advice from others in the office, taking care not to engage again with Charlotte. She'd passed my cubicle on a number of occasions, giving me a cursory glance on each pass but the truth is, the woman just scared the crap out of me.

It was Thursday evening and I'd just finally returned home to my apartment and had quickly fed Hercules, my next door neighbor's Siamese cat. He seemed pleased to see me but once I had dispensed his evening meal, he summarily dismissed me and went off to find somewhere to sleep for another twelve hours. What is it about cats? With a dog, the owner is definitely the master but with cats, they're totally controlling.

Selfish little bastards…

Back in my own 'hutch', I showered and changed into sweatpants and t-shirt, happy to wash away the stench of the city. I went to my kitchen which is a short journey of around three steps from my 'lounge'. My main cooking device these days seemed to be my trusty toaster oven, and tonight was no different, a classic Italian favorite. Pizza. I needed to cut down on these things because I could almost feel a little bit of a belly forming and I was too young for that. Okay, salad tomorrow.

So how do you cook salad in a toaster oven?

Settling down to munch my carbs on my enormous two-seater loveseat, I leaned back for a couple of minutes and thought about the coming weekend. I got up and switched on my television hoping to catch the latest news. I was in luck, Peter Jennings was delivering the main stories on ABC. It was an interesting selection of headlines tonight. Apparently, the Coal Miner's Strike in Britain was finally over, being reported as a victory for Prime Minister Margaret Thatcher over the union leader, Arthur Scargill. Russia had a new president, someone called Gorbachev. Shiite Muslim gunmen had hijacked a TWA jet flying from Greece to Italy and in Africa, the Sudanese and Ethiopian populations were facing starvation according to relief agencies. It was all a little distressing to see what was happening outside of my own comfortable little universe.

But Jennings also reported a huge concert in aid of these poor souls in Africa, apparently the brainchild of the singer from the Boomtown Rats, Bob Geldof. I was only too aware of how successful BandAid had been the previous Christmas with the record-selling single, "Do They Know It's Christmas?" which was number one all over the world for weeks and weeks. So this new idea Geldof had had of something called Live Aid should be an amazing event and generate huge sums for the starving in Africa.

As I was staring into space, contemplating what was happening in the world, I was aware of a green flashing in my peripheral vision. I'd recently bought and installed a fancy new answering machine for my telephone. Not that I ever received any messages. The only people who knew my number were pretty much Talbot, Perryman and my mother, and mostly they called me at the office. I didn't have any siblings, choosing to believe that my mother had got it right first time. So, who could be calling me?

Hey Jake, why don't you press 'Play' and find out, numbnuts?

Sliding down onto the floor where my telephone and answering machine ruled the carpet, I hit 'Play'.

Nothing. Well, not nothing exactly, I could hear tape hiss and the sound of what I could only describe as someone exhaling. I rewound the cassette and played it again, but not entirely sure why I was expecting a different result.

So I get my first phone message and it's a heavy breather. Great.

An hour earlier, around 996 miles south of Jake, a shaking teenage finger was dialing his number. As Summer stood at the gas station's payphone, she heard the connection being made at Jake's apartment. She'd found his number easily as he was listed in the phone book. A quiver of panic and excitement spread through her as she heard his voice… *"Hi, this is Jake, I'm either out or at work, so please, whoever you are, leave a message!"* She waited, not knowing what to do, breathing out the plume of smoke that she'd been holding in from the Marlboro cigarette she'd lit to give her the courage to make the call.

She listened to the silence that followed the message, hoping that his voice might come back again or that he'd pick up. But all she heard was a shrill beep which she guessed marked the end of the message. Her cigarette was now burnt down to the butt and she quickly dropped it to the ground and stamped it out.

Leaving the gas station and walking back to her house on Skyline, Summer was relieved that she hadn't left a message for him. She needed to somehow keep her cool and whatever message she managed to garble out would only have sounded like a kid not knowing what to say, a silly girl who had a ridiculous crush. She badly wanted to see Jake again but she knew she had to try and avoid being precocious, which was her natural defense strategy, and maybe get to know the man a little. She just wanted to talk to him. She wanted to kiss him too, but right now, just seeing him would make her world…

I reset the answering machine and pulled a cassette tape from a messy pile that lay strewn across the corner of the room and inserted it into his tape deck. As The Eurythmics' "There Must Be An Angel

(Playing With My Heart)" filtered out from the speakers, I stretched my 6'2" frame across the five-foot sofa and wondered who would have called.

Must be a wrong number, I guess...

Chapter 13

Talbot had a particularly interesting dinner planned for the evening, a menu he'd been researching for weeks. And he'd also just received some excellent news from Jake that because of all the hours he'd been putting in, his boss, Arthur, had given him the afternoon off work, so he would be arriving at around 7.30pm.

"Perfect!" Talbot said to himself.

"What's perfect, Talb?" a voice echoed as Perryman came striding through the hallway into Talbot's lounge.

Talbot lived in a quaint and quintessentially charming old Florida style home that he had inherited from his parents two years ago, when they had sadly perished in a car wreck. He'd been born there and loved the tiny house with its nooks and gables, postal stamp sized cottage garden and single car garage. He could never sell it and move somewhere new because it still gave him a connection to his parents and to a storybook childhood that he still cherished. If he could, he'd spend the rest of his life there and even the mortgage was paid off with the insurance settlement so there was no reason he couldn't stay forever.

"What's perfect, Pez, is that I have a wonderful dinner planned for tonight and I just heard that Jake is going to be able to make it too," Talbot replied.

"Outstanding, bro! Who else is coming or is it just the three of us, assuming I'm invited?" Perryman asked.

"Well I wouldn't be going to these lengths just for you two indigents. We've got Reyna and Joe coming, my friend, Cheyenne is coming too and I thought I'd ask Tara to come because I think she might be Jake's type," replied Talbot.

"Cheyenne's a babe, I'd turn up just to see her. But Tara for Jake? Do you really think so? She's hot but I just don't see those two as an item. Would be great to see the Cantrells again though, I love that family, way cool," said Perryman.

"Yeah, me too, I always look forward to seeing them, but I think you're wrong about Tara, I think she might be a great fit for Jake. I mean, she's loaded, right? Well, her family is but she's gorgeous looking and so nice. What's your problem with her as far as Jake goes?" Talbot asked.

"You know Jake. He's uncomfortable around wealthy chicks, he thinks most of them are spoiled and live in fantasy lands. He prefers low key, sensitive types with deep feelings. Just like him!" Perryman laughed.

"Well I think you're so wrong, Tara's a fabulous girl and I'm playing Cupid, so butt out," said Talbot.

"Whatever. Do what you gotta do. But listen, d'you mind if I crash here tonight? I'm guessing we'll be drinking pretty late and I don't want to get a DUI driving back to my place. My wagon makes a lot of noise driving back in the dark along Indian River Drive and it'll be dead quiet that time of night. I'd be a sitting duck for the cops."

Perryman lived rent-free in a small guest house in the grounds of some wealthy family friends in the nearby town of Sewall's Point, an affluent community that chose to remain as anonymous as possible. But he drove a desperate-to-be-restored, 1950 Ford 'Woody' Wagon which according to its history was apparently finished in a color called Sodium Green, although you'd never know. He hadn't bought it himself as he rarely paid for anything, mostly due to his precarious lack of cash. But he gave surfing lessons and had been talking to a student about trying to get a truck one day to carry his various surfboards around and she'd told him about a wagon she knew of in the neighboring city of Stuart. After schlepping across town to find the owner, he managed to barter a dozen surf lessons in exchange for the old clunker. But Perryman loved this car because it was his and it was everything he needed. Occasionally, he even slept in it on cool nights.

"You can stay over, but I only have one spare bedroom and Jake's going to need to stay somewhere. I already spoke to Reyna and she said Jake can definitely stay at their place and they've got plenty of spare space. I'm not sure she'd be exactly copacetic about you staying though," said Talbot.

"Why, what's Jake got that I haven't?" Perryman replied.

"It's just that they have teenage daughters Pez, and you're a good looking and distracting surfer boy but Jake's a lawyer, he has principles. Who'd'ya think Reyna's gonna trust more? Do the math!" laughed Talbot.

"All that glitters is not gold…" Perryman said tellingly.

"I can't believe you of all people just quoted Shakespeare at me! Tip of the hat, buddy, proud of you," Talbot laughed again.

"Anyway, I plan on serving the first course at 8pm, so you need to arrive at 7.30. I know you'll be late, you always are, but try and arrive before we start eating, can you?" Talbot continued.

"You give me a bad rep, Talbot. I'm hardly ever late and if I am, it's because it's unavoidable. The surf's only there when it's there. And when it's on, I need to grab me some moola! But don't worry, I'll scrub up clean, brush my hair and I might even bring a bottle of wine. What are we eating, by the way?"

"Ah, well that is a very fine question," Talbot replied. I'm actually serving five courses, most of them quite small and delicate but I also have some excellent wines to match each one," said Talbot.

"So c'mon Chef, enlighten me," replied Perryman, hunger already snapping at his stomach.

"Well, the first course is a very small one although it may not sound that way. I'm preparing a *Ceviche with Salmon, Bay Scallops, Wahoo, Hamachi, Pickled Ginger and Lemon.* Followed by a Floridian themed dish of *Pan Fried Caicos Conch with Balsamic Vinegar and Lime...*" Talbot continued.

"I'm salivating already, have you got any bread so I can make a sandwich?" Perryman asked.

"No, wait, I haven't finished yet. Then we move on to *Blue Crab Cake & Fried Green Tomato with a Carrot Reduction* followed by the main course of *Sautéed Maine Spotted Skate wing with Baja Scallops, Tomatoes, Capers, Olives, and Herb Beurre Blanc*. How does that sound?"

"It sounds amazing, Talb, but have you got just two slices and a jar of peanut butter? I'm famished."

"I'll put you out of your misery then and just tell you what the desert is… a *Trio of Crème Brûlée, Amarula, Ginger and Chocolate.* And that's it," Talbot said with pride.

"That's it? I'm going to be trying to hold my stomach together!" Perryman exclaimed.

"Come on then, I'll get you a sandwich..." Talbot said as he glided off towards the kitchen.

Chapter 14

"Fuck, fuck, fuck, fuck, fuck!"

"What's wrong, kid?" Arthur asked, standing at the door of his office which was only yards from my desk.

"I'm sorry, Arthur, I didn't see you standing there," I responded.

"Spit it out, Jake, tell me what the problem is," Arthur said.

"Oh, it's just that I've been phoning the airlines trying to get a ticket down to South Florida this afternoon and there just aren't any seats available. I guess everyone's leaving New York for Independence Day weekend. My fault though, I should have tried to book sooner," I replied.

"Well… I may have a solution. We have a home down in Palm Beach and we're traveling down in my plane at around 4pm. You're welcome to hitch a ride with us if you like. Whereabouts in South Florida do you need to get to?" Arthur asked.

"Wow, are you serious, Arthur? That would be incredible. If I can get to Palm Beach airport, I can find my way up to Jensen Beach in a rental car. Thank you so much, this is fantastic!" I answered.

"Well, maybe I can do better than that for you. I keep the plane at Witham Field in Stuart because it's much cheaper than using Palm Beach International so you'll only be about three miles from where you need to get to in Jensen."

"Even better! I won't even need a rental car. I can get my buddy Perryman to come and pick me up," I said.

"And don't worry about trying to get a return ticket either, Jake, you can come back up to New York with us when we head back Monday, which is a holiday anyway."

"Arthur, as always, you're a life saver," I said, the glee clearly imprinted on my face.

"Jake, you're like the son I never had so don't worry about it. I appreciate everything you do here even though I don't always say it, so if I can help, it's my absolute pleasure, son."

Later that day, I hopped into a cab with Arthur and we made the trek across Manhattan to Teterboro Airport which is actually across the state line in New Jersey. And although only around ten miles away as the crow flies, we had to make a fairly circuitous stop-start journey across the Hudson River to get there which took just over an hour in the taxi.

When we finally arrived, we stepped out of the car and made our way towards Arthur's gorgeous and brand new Gulfstream III jet which was idling silkily on the tarmac. As I dragged my weekend duffel behind me, I could see through the jet's porthole windows that the other passengers were already onboard.

So this is how the other half lives. I guess I'm in the wrong half then...

As we climbed the steps and were greeted by the crew, I spied Arthur's wife already holding her arms out to give me her welcome hug. The lovely thing about Dolores, actually the same with Arthur too, is that even though she's richer than God, you'd never know it. She's one of the kindest, most hospitable and charitable souls I've ever known. She's also almost eighty years old but she could get away with late fifties. Good breeding I guess.

"Jake, I'm so glad you could join us! You must be parched, come, sit down and let's get you a drink!" she said.

Yep. Definitely another world, Jakey boy, and you're not a member of this club.

"Thanks Dolores, you and Arthur are my saviors so I should be buying you a drink but I don't mind if I do. Gin and tonic would be perfect!" I replied.

Chapter 15

Autumn was a pretty safe and sensible girl, even though she was loathe to admit it. There were obvious physical similarities between her and her sister but their thoughts traveled in quite different paths and in many varied directions. Whereas Autumn was fairly acquiescent most of the time, Summer was less yielding and more nonconformist in her approach to most things. Particularly boys.

Even though Autumn was older than Summer, it didn't always feel that way. Summer was different; she wouldn't let you see completely inside of her. She wasn't closed off but she was infinitely more guarded. Autumn realized that the boys at school didn't much interest Summer either. She also thought that something had clicked between Summer and that guy, Jake, back on Talbot's boat in the spring. Autumn had her secrets too though. And Caleb Campbell was one of them. She hadn't gone all the way yet but she could see it coming sometime soon. And he was cute.

Meanwhile, as Autumn lay thinking about Caleb and all the things he might do to her and her to him, Summer crept out of her bedroom window and sat on the pitched roof to watch a gradually setting sun. She picked up a packet of Marlboros and retrieved a cigarette. Shielding the flame from the breeze, she lit up and sucked in its hot nicotine, slowly exhaling a plume of blue-gray smoke.

It was growing dark now and she knew she was safe up on her secret hideout, but this always remained a magical moment for her most days, when the lights of the town came on and the glow from the sun was ebbing. She imagined herself in a movie and would sometimes play out scenes just to take her into a zone of her own. Her parents had gone to Talbot's for a dinner which looked to be a late night from what her mom had said. She was pissed that she couldn't be there too; she had hoped to find out if Jake was coming for the holiday weekend. But it wasn't as though she could ask her mom because it would be too obvious and she didn't want to draw any attention to how she felt.

"God, I need to pee," she said out loud.

She didn't want to risk going back in to use the bathroom because she wasn't even sure if she could make it in time, so she carefully pulled her shorts down enough and let her bladder free of its warm liquid.

"I'm so disgusting, what the fuck would Jake think if he could see me now?" she said aloud again to no one in particular.

As she watched the stream trickling down the roof and into the gutter below, she breathed a sigh of relief as she took another draw on her cigarette.

"I need to give this up, it's gonna kill me and it stinks, Pretty certain Jake doesn't smoke either," she thought.

Back in Autumn's room, a dense cloud of smoke thickened the air as she breathed out the smoke from her joint. Her parents had no idea that she occasionally smoked weed but she'd opened the window to get rid of the evidence. She also knew Summer's secret place to smoke and decided to creep out of her own window to see if she was there.

"Hey sister!" she whispered.

Summer jumped at the words but when she realized it was Autumn, she relaxed again.

"I knew you might be out here, sneaking a smoke. I thought I'd join you and see if you wanted some of this," she said, offering the tiny joint to Summer, "There's not much left but I can tell you're a little jumpy today so it might do you some good."

"Am I that transparent? I thought I was hiding it well but I guess you probably realized a while back where my head's at right now," Summer said.

"I'm guessin' it may have something to do with the arrival of a certain person from New York? But don't worry, sis, I've got your back. Your secret's safe with me. C'mon baby girl, give me a cuddle," whispered Autumn, as the two sisters hugged each other tightly and gazed out at the dark ocean, oblivious to the tiny beads of perspiration that gathered on their bodies in the intensely humid air of July.

Chapter 16

After my journey back from Stuart Airport to Talbot's cottage in Perryman's 'ride', I was welcomed like a long lost brother by my old friend.

"Jake, let me introduce you to everyone," Talbot said. "You know the Cantrells, Reyna and Joe, of course. This is Cheyenne who I think you've heard me talk about before."

I shook hands with Joe, exchanged a warm hug with Reyna and said hello to Cheyenne.

"And this is Tara, Tara Fitzgerald, she lives up at Sailfish Point," Talbot continued, "I thought you two might get along together."

"Nice to meet you, Tara, I'm Jake but don't believe a single word that Talbot may have said about me," I said.

"Actually, Jake, he hasn't told me much at all, you seem to be the mystery man of the party," Tara replied.

Well that's a big relief then...

Talbot had good taste in women. Tara was nothing short of savagely beautiful. Flaming golden hair framed an exotic Eurasian face, her honey-toned skin, smoother than molasses and her visage, glowingly enhanced by her vivid green eyes. They were almost cat-like in their shape and intensity, and bored into me as I privately toured the rest of her shapely real estate.

The woman is obscenely sexy but she's way out of your league, Delaney...

The evening hummed along; Talbot had prepared a magnificent feast and like the great chef that he is, he hadn't overdone the portion sizes on any of the courses. The man was a master host, a genuine bon viveur toward whom, people seemed to naturally gravitate. He was born with charisma, soaked in charm.

Must be gay...

So Jake, tell me what's been going on in your world. We haven't seen you since the boat trip," Reyna asked.

There were seven of us at the table, three of us either side with Talbot at the head. I was seated between Reyna and Cheyenne, and Tara sat opposite, flanked either side by Perryman and Joe.

"Truthfully, Reyna? I feel like I haven't seen daylight in months. This is the first time I've come up for air, pretty much since I last saw you. Coming here is like manna from heaven for me," I replied.

"I'm so pleased that you could make it down here tonight, it's the Pineapple Festival this weekend, so coupled with the Fourth of July celebrations and Summer's birthday, it's a pretty busy weekend. And I'm so happy that you're staying with us, I've prepared a lovely room for you," Reyna said.

"Thank you so much, that's really kind of you. Did you say it's also your daughter's birthday?" I replied, deftly avoiding saying her name.

"Yes, Summer will be seventeen on Sunday. She's growing up so quickly now. Another year and she'll be going to college. In fact, Autumn starts in September, just a couple months from now," she replied.

I thought about this new information for a moment and decided it would be appropriate to buy a little gift for her. But I just couldn't think what on earth I could get for her.

What do *you buy a seventeen-year-old girl?*

Talbot's courses kept coming and we made small talk at the table, a genuine peacefulness settling over the evening. I was feeling a little trapped though and needed some air so I excused myself to take a breather out back.

After retrieving a month old, half-full pack of Marlboro from my jacket pocket, I lit up and enjoyed the solace of the July air. I'm not a smoker which I guess is what all sneaky smokers say when they're in denial. But I really don't crave nicotine; I just enjoy a pleasurable moment of it, either when I'm alone in a perfect moment or sometimes when I'm under extreme stress. Other than that, I can really take them or leave them. But for some reason, I was in need of the crutch of a cigarette to help me through the evening tonight. It wasn't that I wasn't enjoying the dinner party, I just wasn't used to so many questions, particularly from Reyna. Some form of silly guilt on my part, I suppose.

"So what makes Jake shake?" a voice whispered behind me as my sphincter tightened one notch.

I hadn't heard a thing until then. I thought I was alone in the silence of Talbot's tiny garden but I guess the game was up and I'd been found out. I turned around to meet those cat-like almond eyes of Tara's.

"Oh, I'm sorry Tara, I just needed a break from table chatter, I'll be fine in a moment. I get a little claustrophobic sometimes, is all," I said.

"Well, now that we're out here, can I share it with you?" she asked, her mouth opening with her luscious smile, showing that she was genetically blessed in every area of her body, including her teeth.

"Of course, my pleasure," I said offering her the pack.

"No, I mean yours, I'd like to share yours with you," she giggled.

I passed my cigarette to her and watched as her crimson lips drew on the filter.

This woman could make putting out the garbage look sexy...

"Thank you, I needed that," she said.

Yeah, so did I. Thank you...

As I put the cigarette back to my lips, I could taste the lipstick she'd left. Definitely expensive. But this girl had expensive written all over her. Way out of my league but my attraction to her was probably obvious even though I was trying to suppress it. Any man would want her.

"So Jake, I hear that you're a lawyer? In New York? Does that do it for you or are you looking for more excitement in life?" she questioned.

Well, now that you mention it...

"I am a lawyer, although a pretty green one at the moment. And for now, it takes most of my time. Does it excite me? Not really, but it pays the rent and I'm hoping it might be long term employment for me. I can't see me staying in that city for too long though, it just wears me out. I have simpler needs that don't require enormous earnings," I replied. "But what do you do for a living, if you don't mind me asking?"

"I don't, is the simple answer. I'm one of those dreadful people whose family ruins them with copious amounts of money. I'm a spoiled rich kid but I do appreciate what I have. I don't flaunt it but I do thoroughly enjoy it!" she laughed.

"But you don't buy your own cigarettes? I asked.

"I don't really smoke, Jake, I just wanted to have an opportunity to get you on my own. I wanted to find out a little more about you first-hand, if you like. You don't seem like a regular guy and I mean that in a good way. You don't look like your dick leads your mind," she said.

Say what you mean, Tara, I'm all ears...

"Is your question, 'Do I chase women in order to bed them?' No, I'm no lady killer. I guess I must have certain attractive qualities and I adore women but chasing them isn't my thing. In most cases, it only really works for me when there is love or something close to it. You know, when there is a much deeper connection than just achieving an orgasm."

Fuck, where did all that come from, Jake? Next thing you know, you'll be bleeding your heart out to her...

"Wow! You're very direct and outrageously honest, Jake. I'm not sure I've ever heard that from a man of your age before. I'm impressed! But listen, I know the evening is almost at an end but I'd love to chat more with you at a later date. Could I call you if I'm in New York City one day?"

"Absolutely, it would be my pleasure," I said.

We exchanged telephone numbers and I assumed it would probably be the last I saw of her. But she seemed nice. Nice and rich.

Chapter 17

It was two o'clock in the morning by the time we'd bid goodnight to Talbot and it was even later when the Cantrells and I had finally stumbled back to their house. Reyna showed me the guest bedroom she'd set up for me. I hugged her and thanked her and wearily undressed and collapsed onto the bed. Sleep came quickly.

I slept late, for me anyway, and after showering and brushing my teeth, I made my way downstairs to the kitchen where I could hear voices chatting and my nose quickly caught the perfect aroma of bacon being fried.

"Good morning, sleepy head!" Joe said, offering me a glass of orange juice. "You must be ready for breakfast by now and Reyna is the queen of Saturday morning breakfasts."

"I am, sir, that would be wonderful," I replied, "Did everyone else already eat? I don't want to put you all out."

"No, no, you're just in time, I'm serving up, just waiting for the girls to come down," said Reyna, simultaneously calling up the stairwell to her daughters.

I took a seat at the breakfast table and as I sipped my juice and began to tear into the plate of bacon and eggs that Reyna had just set in front of me, I was startled by the almost seventeen-year-old girl who'd just entered the kitchen.

"Hi Jake, I didn't know you were staying over but Mom just told me earlier that you're here for the whole holiday weekend. Will you and your friends be going to the Pineapple Festival here in town?" Summer asked.

"Good morning!" I said.

“I’m sorry, I didn’t mean to bombard you with my questions so early,” Summer replied sheepishly.

“I’m joking, you’re fine, I’m just teasing. And yes, if your mom and dad will have me, I’ll be here til Monday. And Talbot told me about the festival so yes, I definitely plan on seeing some of it. Are you going too?” I said, smiling at her youthful spirit.

“Yes, it starts at around 2pm today and goes on well into the evening and we’re all going so maybe we can all go together?” Summer asked.

“It would be my honor and privilege,” I replied.

“Then it’s a date!” she said excitedly.

I wasn’t exactly certain what she meant by her last words but she seemed pretty keen on going as a group and that suited me. She was a lovely girl for sure. I may have misread our last meeting and actually, part of me was rather pleased; hopefully any romantic illusions were just entrenched in my own thick skull. I also didn’t want to dampen her spirits by telling her that I’d mostly be hanging with Talbot and Perryman because it didn’t seem fair. Besides, as long as the guys were with me, it wouldn’t look like anything awkward or untoward.

“Reyna, that was a wonderful breakfast, thank you so much. If you don’t mind though, I promised Talbot I would go with him for a run on the beach this morning but can I do anything to help? I’m an expert at washing dishes.”

“No, Jake, you’re fine, we have a dishwasher now, no need to worry. Just go and enjoy yourself and treat our home as your home. You’re a very welcome addition to our family, even if only for the weekend. Mi casa, su casa!” Reyna replied.

As I got up to leave the table and get ready for my run, I couldn’t help notice a brief glance from Summer, a subtle glint in her young eyes. But I was equally aware of her father peering over his newspaper.

Chapter 18

As Talbot and I ran through the shallow surf, I felt all of my tension quickly disappear. There's nothing like a few hours at the beach to make you feel like you've just had a vacation.

"I need this run this morning, I think I ate for a week last night and you did an amazing job with the food, Talb," I said as he struggled to keep up.

"I know I cooked it, but I have to give credit to the amazing menu I stole from 11 Maple St. I don't go there often but Chef Michael is something special, as is his lovely wife, Margie," he responded, "But can we slow down and have a break though, I've got a stitch."

The beach wasn't crowded considering it was Saturday but I assumed that this was because the vacationers only really came during the peak season, November through May.

"It's Summer's birthday tomorrow, what do you buy a seventeen-year-old girl these days? Music cassettes? Cologne? Some type of clothing?" I asked.

"No, why don't you just go all out and buy her some lingerie! That should do it," he laughed, "But seriously, you don't have to buy her anything, Jake. Won't it look weird? You'll look like the creepy relative, Uncle Chester, child molester!" he continued, laughing hilariously at my expense.

"Forget I said anything, idiot, but I still have to get something. I'm staying at their house, for Chrissakes! I'd feel a bit of a cretin tomorrow morning when she's opening gifts and I'm standing there empty-handed," I replied.

"I'm just sending out a warning shot," Talbot said, "Unless you're hiding guilty inner thoughts, Jake? But I wouldn't go down that road, if I were you."

"No, nothing like that, I just want to do the right thing, that's all," I replied, "Anyway, what's the deal with you and Cheyenne? Are you an item? I couldn't tell last night but you seemed to like each other."

"Just good friends really. She's a great girl, really sweet, actually. You may have guessed that she's part Native American, just from her name if not her looks. But I don't ever seem to be able to find the 'right one' even though I know a lot of lovely girls. Sometimes, because I mostly prefer the company of men, I think I might be gay!" Talbot said.

"I doubt it, just gotta meet the right one, you'll find her someday. Hey, is that Perryman?"

Perryman was further down the beach, six of his surfboards lying close to the water, a group of teenagers surrounding him. Saturday mornings were clearly his cash cow when it came to his surf business. I loved the way he had these kids' attention though, this master of surf knowledge. They just seemed to naturally gravitate toward him.

We waited for about fifteen minutes as he dispatched the kids with their new instructions and watched as they swam out into the ocean, hugging their boards as they crossed the incoming waves. Perryman looked like a proud father with his flock.

"Pez, you're like honey to the bees!" I shouted.

He looked round, spotted us and jogged over.

"Oh, you know what? I love this. There's nothing much makes me happier than teaching kids, they're just so willing to learn and they actually listen to me. During the week, I mostly get a bunch of bored housewives to teach but if they ain't gonna listen to their husbands, they sure as hell ain't gonna listen to me!" Perryman laughed.

"You realize most men would kill to lead your life, don't you?" I asked.

"Yeah, but most men have more cash in their pockets than I have!" he added, "Anyway, thanks for a rad evening last night, Talb, you are the man. I had to run six miles here on the beach this morning just to wear it off. And that chick, Cheyenne? You dating her?" he asked.

"No, I just told Jake, I think it's always going to be just good friends. But she is a jewel of a girl," Talbot replied.

"You're going to the Pineapple Festival, right?" I asked Perryman. "We're planning on chaperoning the Cantrell girls if you're cool with that?

"Absolutely, it'll be fun and there'll always be a bar to find afterward," Perryman replied.

Perryman: surf, women, booze; a recipe for life…

"But Jakey boy here, Uncle Chester to his friends, feels he needs to buy a gift for Summer's birthday tomorrow. He's fresh out of ideas for his teenage girlfriend. So bearing in mind that you surround yourself with pubescent adulation most of your life, what do you think she'd want, surfer boy?" Talbot grinned.

"I don't have one clue. But she's kind of a free spirit, right? Sort of a back to nature kid? I doubt she's big on material things but I've got one idea that might work. I was running the beach this morning and came across some pieces of sea glass. Most of them aren't that great and they're pretty small but I found one piece which is really cute and all the sharp edges have been worn away. Super smooth now, looks like it's been honed. Maybe you could give her that? Better still, have it mounted on a chain and she could wear it as a pendant?"

He dug into his board shorts and produced a light green piece of sea glass. It had been smoothed out through years in the ocean and to me, it almost resembled the shape of Africa. He offered it to me, and I appraised the little sea gem.

"Wow, that would be a very cool present for her. Having it mounted with a neck chain would be great too but there's no chance of getting it done in time for her birthday in Jensen. Maybe I'll just wrap it up and give it to her like this"

"I have a man," Talbot replied, "He's a jeweler and he works from home right here in Jensen. Leave it with me, Chester, I'll take care of it for you."

"Thanks Talbot, you're a star. But quit with the fucking Uncle Chester name, I'm getting a complex!" I said.

"Just teasing Ches, but be warned, don't get yourself into a situation you can't get out of. Or one that finds you locked up in jail!" Talbot teased.

"Fuck you, Gaylord, I'm just trying to be a well-mannered guest, something I thought you'd know about!" I said, launching a homophobic missile at Talbot's rarely mentioned last name.

"Anyway, what do I owe you for this, Pez?" I asked.

"Nothin' man, nothin' at all. Buy me a beer later tonight, they have a new brew at Crawdaddy's which has got my name all over it, it's called 'All My Tomorrows'!"

"Better than all your yesterdays!" Talbot laughed.

Boy, you're a laugh a minute today...

We left Perryman to his adoring students and idled back to town. It was a sultry hot day and the breeze was welcome.

"Joking aside, can you really get that sea glass mounted for me in time?" I asked Talbot.

"Jake, have I ever let you down? Leave it with me, I'm your man, I've got you covered," he winked back at me.

Chapter 19

Later that afternoon, I walked down Skyline Drive with the Cantrells, headed into town to watch the opening acts at the Pineapple Festival. The place was packed, the town's commissioners having seemingly stumbled on something that was proving to be immensely popular with its residents. And by the size of the crowd, people had come from some distance away to see the event.

As we mingled with the other attendees, Joe and Reyna snagged a spare table on the sidewalk at Crawdaddy's, a very popular Jensen restaurant, and the girls and I continued on towards the end of the street where an enormous stage had been erected. I spotted Talbot in the crowd and shepherded Autumn and Summer towards him.

"Ladies, we are your official dates today!" he exclaimed.

Easy tiger...

"What happened to Perryman?" I asked.

"You know Perryman, if the offer's better somewhere else, he'll take it. But joking aside, he's probably on his reserved bar seat inside Crawdaddy's by now, supping all his tomorrows!" Talbot replied, laughing at his joke as he said it.

The girls were super excited at the atmosphere manifesting during the build-up to the start of the show. All teenage angst had disappeared as pre-show music exploded from the Tannoys on the stage at the end of Main Street. The sound of Billy Idol's voice singing "White Wedding" snarled from the giant PA system.

Talbot took the lead in trying to get us as close to the stage as possible, Autumn tagging along beside him. Summer and I struggled to keep up close behind them but the crowd was growing thicker and it was difficult to stay with them.

I felt fingers curl around my upper arm and realized Summer was holding on to me.

"Good idea," I said, "I don't want to lose you, your mom and dad will never forgive me."

"Don't worry, you won't lose me, I'll be holding on to you!" she said loudly, the music drowning our voices.

Finally, we caught up with Talbot and Autumn and squeezed ourselves close to them, a perfect position to see the first acts. Summer continued to grip my bicep and I could sense her excitement at the upcoming action on stage. She was delightful, her laughter infectious. I could only imagine how boys must have been drawn to her at school.

"Ladies and gentlemen, boys and girls, welcome to the very first Pineapple Festival," the MC's voice echoed from the stage. The crowd responded loudly, fully expectant of what was about to happen, cheers confirming their excitement.

"Are you ready? I can't hear you!" he yelled.

A massive chorus of screams and shouts responded in the affirmative.

"It's my pleasure, my great pleasure, to introduce to you, here for the very first time in Florida, direct from London…." Whoops and yells punctuated his words. ***"Please give it up for…."*** The crowd was going wild now, they were hot and excited and craving the first band. ***"Please give a warm Floridian welcome to… TEARS FOR FEARS!!!"***

The crowd erupted now, surging forward, carrying all four of us with it like a gigantic wave whose force was impossible to battle against. Summer's hand lost my arm and I reached out quickly to hold on to her, just to keep her safe. My claustrophobia was beginning to kick in but I tried to stifle it to make sure I kept hold of her. Tears For Fears opened the show with a crowd favorite:

We will find you acting on your best behavior

Turn your back on mother nature

Everybody wants to rule the world...

The band had the crowd singing along before the singer, Curt Smith, could complete the first line of the song. I tried to keep hold of Summer, but she was dancing now, and the task was akin to holding on to a slippery eel. Talbot was a few feet away, himself caught up in the euphoria of the music and the band. Autumn was writhing to the rhythm in front of him and his hands were clamped onto her shoulders, the relentless beat of the music gelling them as one.

"Everybody Wants To Rule The World" was followed in quick succession by more crowd favorites; "Change", "Shout" and the monster hit "Mad World".

I was perspiring badly now, a combination of the July heat and my stupid claustrophobia and panic attacks. It brings on Hyperhidrosis, something I've suffered from since I was a kid and which results in impromptu sweating from heat and stress.

"Are you okay if I take a breather over there at the side of the stage?" I yelled into Summer's ear.

"Yes!" she cried. "Don't worry about me, I'll come and find you afterward!"

I left guiltily and slowly made my way through the crowd to the area left of the stage where I gratefully collapsed onto a vacant bench. As I sat there, I reflected on the notion of what a sad old twenty-something I'd become. Couldn't handle the crowds, couldn't stand the heat, a man seemingly fast approaching middle age before I'd barely left my teens behind. Minor crush on a teenage girl who was probably blissfully unaware of my secret feelings anyway…

What a douche bag...

Sitting closer to the ocean now, I could feel the soothing coolness of the breeze coming in off the water and my heart rate began to subside. An hour later, I felt normal again and began to people watch, another of my insidious habits. I imagined what people did for jobs, what their passions were and how they lived. I'm nothing if not inquisitive. My reveries were interrupted when I heard a familiar voice.

"There he is, the old man of Jensen!" Talbot yelled as the three of them made a beeline towards me, each of them drenched in sweat. In fact, Talbot must have been hotter than Hades, still wearing a linen jacket and a cheesecloth shirt.

"That was amazing!!" shrieked Summer, "Tears For Fears were awesome and even Marie Osmond was good!"

"Well, I'm glad you had a good time while this old man got his breath back. Shall we go and find your parents now?" I suggested, desperate for something to drink.

We made our way back through the crowd and found Reyna and Joe still sitting at the table outside Crawdaddy's, not a bead of perspiration to split between them.

"Just in time," Joe said, "We're about to order some food. You boys must be thirsty, pour yourself a glass," he continued, offering a giant pitcher of beer, "And Summer, Autumn, mom's drinking some chilled pineapple juice, shall I get you a glass each?"

The girls sat down while Talbot and I finished our beers in one straight hit.

"Jake, have you ever had oysters before?" asked Joe.

"Umm… no, I don't think they're really my type of thing…"

"Nonsense! If you haven't had oysters and got down and dirty with a bucket of crawfish, you haven't lived! Take a seat, boys, this is going to be an experience and Talbot knows what I'm talking about!"

"Okay, well I guess I'm in your hands then. But if you'll excuse me, I need to hit the men's room first," I said.

"Make that two of us, Jake, I'm coming with you," Talbot added.

After we'd relieved ourselves in the acrid smelling restroom and dutifully washed our hands, we made our way back to the front of the restaurant. But before we got back to our table, Talbot stopped me, pulled a box from his pocket and offered it to me.

"What's this?" I asked.

"Don't I always come through on my promises? It's the sea glass, numbnuts!" he laughed.

"Man, I'd almost forgotten about that!" I said, opening the box to reveal the little piece of glass, mounted on a delicate silver chain.

"It's perfect, she'll love it. Thanks buddy, I owe you!"

Chapter 20

It was 2am and I was hungry. I hadn't really eaten all day since breakfast, apart from the oysters and crawfish which still seemed to be swimming in my stomach and for some reason, that same piriform sac was now demanding to be fed. I got out of bed, pulled on a t-shirt and pajama bottoms and crept out of my room, treading deftly on the floorboards as they creaked their noisy welcome back to me.

Finally, having navigated the stairs in the dark, I found the kitchen and pulled open the fridge to see what snacks I could pilfer. Unfortunately, there was nothing there that I wouldn't have to cook, apart from some cheese and salami and I didn't want heartburn for the rest of the night.

Never mind, there's always the old midnight favorite...

I grabbed a carton of milk and searched the kitchen cupboards for the inevitable pack of cornflakes. I remembered where the plates and bowls were from this morning and lucked out when I pulled open the first drawer and found a dessert spoon.

Retreating to the family couch at the end of the kitchen, I greedily munched on my simple meal, laying the bowl down once I'd finished. Feeling happy and contented, I stretched out across the sofa and pondered my visit so far.

What a day, a fantastic festival, and the girls had been seriously charming and quite lovely 'dates'. I mulled over all of the guilt I'd been feeling about Summer, my silly attraction to her, the age difference, her intoxicating personality and charm. But having spent the afternoon with her, I realized that it was all in my head and I inwardly chastised myself for even having those kinds of stupid thoughts. This was a girl who loved life and who easily attracted attention from men and boys of all ages and I was an arrogant fool to think it was something else for her.

Jake Delaney, stud muffin to the female race. Dickweed...

The house was peaceful, my eardrums still thrumming as I snuggled down to try and ease the sound of the afternoon's music that was continuing to reverberate in my head. As the minutes ticked by, I began to relax and could feel myself slipping away, aware that I shouldn't fall asleep on the couch for the rest of the night.

"Are you awake?" a voice whispered.

Startled, I sat bolt upright. Asleep to fully awake in half a second. I turned to where I thought I'd heard the voice, expecting to be admonished by Reyna for camping out in her kitchen.

"Are you okay?" the voice said again.

My eyes focused and I made out a shape in the semi-darkness. Summer stood there. The light from the full moon cast a glow over her, like an angel standing before me, barefoot and wearing what I could only assume was one of her dad's shirts, its fullness hiding her modesty. Her long hair cascaded down from her sweet young face.

"Can I sit with you?" she said.

"Of course, it's your home after all," I replied, "But if your mom came downstairs right now, she'd be less than thrilled. And if your dad came down, I'd be left less than a man."

I shrugged my body up and folded my legs towards my chest as she sat close to me on the loveseat. I could feel the warmth of her bottom as she nestled by my feet. I didn't know if she was aware of this but I also didn't want to make an issue of it.

"Did you enjoy today?" she whispered, aware that our voices might wake other people in the house.

"It was unbelievable," I whispered back, "I never knew that such an amazing event could go on in sleepy little Jensen."

"Thank you so much, you and Talbot, for taking care of us. I don't think I've ever felt that kind of excitement and fear in a crowd before. My mom and dad are really grateful to both of you."

"This may sound corny but really, the pleasure was all ours."

"Do you think you'll be coming down again soon?"

"I'd love to but I have to concentrate on my career right now and it takes a lot of my time. As far as being a lawyer goes, I'm still a freshman so I need to put in the hours and pay my dues. Also, I was lucky to be able to tag along on my boss's plane yesterday otherwise I wouldn't have made it."

"Don't misread me, Jake, but I was hoping and praying the last two weeks that you'd get here and my dreams were answered. I know I probably come across like some stupid little teenager but I need to tell you, that when I first met you on Talbot's boat, I suppose I had a crush. In fact, that wasn't the first time I saw you. You won't remember this, but I saw you and your friends on Maple Street last November."

How could I forget?

"I thought your face was familiar when you stepped onto the boat. Maybe you stayed in my mind from the time you're talking about," I whispered back with a grin.

My eyes couldn't help but be drawn to her exquisite legs, bathed in a golden tan that covered her delicate feet and perfect little toes.

"Do you think I'm attractive," she asked, looking into my eyes.

Averting her gaze, I responded, "Summer, there's probably not a man alive who wouldn't find you attractive. You're a very lovely girl and you are your mother's daughter after all!"

At that, she leaned toward me, with the intention of kissing me. I reacted quickly but tactfully, gently cradling her face in my hands.

"Summer, please don't. You're so lovely but this is so wrong. Don't you see? This would be terrible, I'm twenty-four and you're just sixteen!" I said, slowly pushing her back.

"I'm not, I'm seventeen now, it's officially my birthday!"

"It doesn't matter, It's just not right, I already feel so guilty now. I apologize if you've been interpreting anything between us as anything more than caring on my part. I would never have wanted to mislead you," I said.

Her face had changed from elation to crestfallen in seconds.

Nice, Jake, why don't you just burst this girl's bubble?

"I'm sorry too, Jake, I just got carried away with the moment. I feel so embarrassed now! Please don't tell anyone!"

"Listen, beautiful girl, your secret is safe with me, my lips are sealed. And don't apologize; it's me that probably caused the misunderstanding. My radar isn't always that accurate."

She collapsed into me, sobbing. I put my arms around her and stroked her hair, lightly kissing the top of her head in an attempt to soothe her. After a few moments, I eased her away and smiled. She smiled back, with that face that was almost bound to become addictive.

"So listen to me now. You have to go and get some sleep because tomorrow, well today now I guess, is your big day. Are we good?"

She grinned and got up to leave.

"Thank you, Jake, thank you for everything!"

As she crept away, I figured I'd just dodged a huge bullet. But the feeling lurking deep inside of me, was that I hadn't really wanted to dodge it at all.

Chapter 21

The following morning, Sunday, I entered the kitchen and realized that Reyna had been up early in preparation for Summer's big day. There were balloons, string lights and birthday banners covering the entire kitchen. Joe was reading the Sunday paper on the couch and Reyna was making fresh coffee. Foreigner's "I Want To Know What Love Is" drifted lazily from the radio.

"Good morning, guest of honor!" Reyna said, brimming with excitement at the impending celebration of her youngest daughter.

"Good morning to you too! Are the girls up yet or is this a big sleep in day for them?" I replied.

"I think they're just getting ready. I can't believe Summer is only a year away from being an adult. It seems like only yesterday that we brought her home from the hospital, a perfect and tiny baby," she continued.

"They all have to grow up, Reyna, just like you did!" Joe said from the sofa.

"I know, I just don't like it, I suppose," Reyna responded, her face filling with sadness.

I helped myself to coffee and snagged one of the newspaper sections that Joe had discarded and began to read about the previous day's events at the festival.

"Here's the birthday girl! Happy birthday, sweetheart!" Reyna sang as Summer and Autumn came into the kitchen.

Summer looked lovely, as fresh as a daisy and all trace of sadness from the previous night had vanished, replaced by a smile and was I imagining things, or did she possess a certain new air of maturity?

"It's too early for cake, Summer, but I do have a birthday breakfast planned for you. I decided that rather than me make it, we could do something special and go out for pancakes, waffles or Eggs Benedict. What do think?" Reyna asked.

"Sounds perfect, mama, we could go down to the restaurant on the boardwalk, it's my favorite place to go!" Summer replied, pure joy beaming across her young face.

"But first," said Joe, "We have a present for you."

Looking around the kitchen, Summer couldn't see any obvious gift-wrapped presents.

"Where is it, I'm so excited, Daddy!" she squealed.

"You need to come outside, I think," Joe responded, winking at me as he got up from the couch.

We trooped outside and there on the driveway, was Joe's Bronco, repainted in baby blue with a huge pink bow tied on top of it.

"I don't understand, this is your car." Summer said, a quizzical look on her face, "Except that it's not the same color it was when I last saw it."

"Summer, this is yours now, your dad had it restored and repainted for you. Didn't you realize it hasn't been around for the last two weeks?" Reyna beamed.

"Are you serious, Daddy? Is it really for me? But you love your Bronco, you said you'd never part with it!" said Summer.

"Well, I'm not really parting with it because I'll still see it even if I don't drive it. And the fact is that Autumn already has her Jeep and you've had your license for a year now. You're going to need a car when you start college next year and it's time for me to grow up I guess, and get something sensible, maybe a Volvo!" he laughed.

"I can't believe it, I love this car, this is my dream car, thank you so much, Mom and Dad!" she shrilled as she embraced them both in a hug. Tears were streaming down her face as she eventually broke away from them and turned to look at me. She rushed over and flung her arms around me too.

"And thank you so much, Jake, for being here on my birthday. It means the world to me," she whispered in my ear.

"Well, I have a little present for you too," I said, "But it's not as grand as a car, I'm afraid."

I handed her the jewelry box and watched as she unwrapped it.

"Oh my goodness! It's *beautiful*! It's exactly what I wanted, Jake. Thank you, thank you, thank you!"

Her parents and sister looked over at us, not knowing what the gift was. I didn't sense any kind of suspicion on their part but they were definitely curious as to what had Summer so pleased.

"Mom, Dad, Autumn, look! It's sea glass! My favorite!" she giggled.

"You shouldn't have, Jake, you know that it wasn't necessary, we enjoy having you here so you shouldn't have wasted your money," Reyna said.

"Honestly, it wasn't all my doing, I had some help but it is my pleasure anyway. I'm very pleased that Summer likes it," I replied with a grin, "So how about the birthday girl driving us all to breakfast? And I'm paying, no arguments!" I said as the five of us headed towards the ribbon-clad Bronco.

Chapter 22

After breakfast, at a simple café overlooking the ocean, I wished that the weekend would never end. I paid the check after battling for it with Joe and as we got up to leave, Autumn decided that she was going to meet some friends on the beach.

"Summer, do you think you could drop me off at Talbot's house? I need to pay him some money I owe him," I asked.

"Of course I can, let's go," she replied.

After they dropped me off outside Talbot's cottage, I said goodbye and promised I'd be back later in the afternoon to share cake with them.

As the Bronco drove away, I walked up Talbot's path and before I could ring the doorbell, the door flew open, Talbot's face a picture of panic, clearly distressed by something.

"Where've you been? I've been looking everywhere for you! I kept calling the Cantrell house but there was no answer on their phone!" he shouted.

"Hold on Talb, what the heck is wrong with you? We just went out for breakfast to celebrate Summer's birthday!" I replied.

"It's Perryman!" he yelled, "He's in the hospital, he's been beaten up!"

"Oh my God, what happened? Which hospital?" I asked.

"Last night, it was late, he'd been drinking, I think, and got into a fight somewhere out of town. They took a baseball bat to him and his car! He's in Martin Memorial, we have to get over there now!"

We jumped into Talbot's battered '65 Plymouth Satellite and sped across town to the hospital. When we finally managed to locate where

Perryman was, the horror on our faces matched the sickness we both felt in our stomachs.

Perryman's arms were both in castes as was his right leg. His fingers were puffed up and bruised too. But his face told the full horror of what had befallen him the previous evening. He was unrecognizable from the beautiful surfing man we both knew and loved. Both eyes were so swollen, they were closed shut. His face was a canvas of lacerations and black and red welts. His lips were enlarged to twice the size and when he opened his mouth, we could see that most of his front teeth had gone.

"Hey… guys…" he tried to say, pain etched across his face as he tried to speak through massively swollen lips, "Don't… look… like the… surfer boy…now… I guess…"

Both Talbot's and my eyes filled with tears at what had happened to our friend. This was not what I had envisaged happening on this happy weekend. The question now, was why?

Chapter 23

"We don't know what happened yet," I explained to a distressed Cantrell family, "But he's in pretty bad shape, no… he's in a terrible state. He'll be in the hospital for some time. His lungs were also punctured as well as the three broken limbs and multiple lacerations."

We were seated in the Cantrell's family room, a weathered but supremely comfortable space that was furnished with large, heavy sofas and chairs, recovered in varying damask materials, with enormous throw pillows scattered throughout the room. Reyna wasn't the type to go and buy new furniture, preferring to repurpose older items that people no longer wanted. For her, the motto was 'one woman's trash is another woman's treasure'.

"Oh my God!" said Reyna, "Perryman, of all people, he wouldn't hurt a fly! Who would want to hurt him?"

The rest of the Cantrell family just sat motionless, too stunned to even speak. I could see tears streaking both Summer and Autumn's faces.

"I know, he's like the gentle giant who loves people and is loved back in equal amounts," I said. "He was able to make a statement to the police, although he's missing teeth so it was hard for him with the swelling all over his face."

"Does he know who did it? Did he recognize them?" Joe asked.

"He was driving cautiously back to his place in Sewall's Point, you know, the guest cottage he uses there?" I replied, "And he stopped when he saw a stranded motorcycle at the side of the road. He couldn't tell if it was a male or a female because the rider had a helmet on which is odd for anyone around here, I mean, when did you last see a biker with a helmet on? Anyway, when he approached the rider, this person pointed down at the engine of the bike and Perryman bent down to look. That was when he was hit from behind with something. The doctor believes it was something similar to a baseball bat. After he went down from the blow, more blows rained down on him in a frenzied assault. He doesn't remember a lot of details but he thinks there were at least three people, and again he couldn't say whether they were men or women," I continued.

"This is awful, Jake, things like that just don't happen around here, it's usually so peaceful and the motorcycle crowd is not a violent one. I've never heard of any violence from them in all the time I've lived here. This sounds so premeditated to me, like someone knew where he would be at that exact time and set out to ambush him. They almost killed him, for God's sake!" Reyna cried.

"I know, I know… but even though he survived the attack, it will be a long road to recovery. The doctor said possibly six months before he's fully rehabilitated and that's only because he's such a strong guy. And I'm not even going to be around much because of work. At least Talbot can stop in and check on him regularly," I said.

When I mentioned not being able to be around much, I noticed a palpable look of disappointment in Summer's face. She didn't think I caught it, but it was there.

"The good news is that we're all nearby and Perryman is our friend too so we'll be visiting him as much as possible, whether he likes it or not," Joe volunteered.

"I know, and I'm grateful, really I am. The other thing is that if you thought his car was beaten up before last night, you should see it now. They totally trashed it. So I'm going to try and set up a fund to get it fixed up for him for when he gets out. I suppose it seems a strange thing to be thinking about but it's all I can do for him now and it takes my mind away from the distress he's in."

Well, we'll be glad to help in any way we can," replied Reyna.

I said to Summer, “This is not fair, right? I mean, on your birthday and everything? I’m so sorry it’s gone downhill.”

“My birthday’s not even relevant with what’s gone on with Perryman. And in any case, my birthday was fantastic and I loved my presents so I’m fine, really, more than grateful,” she replied.

She wasn’t fine at all, none of us were. Talbot was in a bad way too but he’s pretty resilient and when I left the hospital to come and tell the Cantrells what had happened, he’d already started busying himself, arranging things, taking his mind off the here and now.

“I suppose that now isn’t the time to suggest we cut some cake?” Joe asked, just to break the silence.

“You know what, Joe?” I said, “Now is exactly the right time and I’m going to eat a piece for our friend too as he’s in no shape to celebrate at the moment.”

Chapter 24

"I don't get it," muttered Sewall's Point Police Officer, Sofia Brunson, "No one dislikes Vaughn Perryman."

Sofia was a petite natural blonde. Her hair was always tied up under her hat when she was on patrol but once out of uniform, her tresses went down to her collar bone. She had an almost pixie-like face and although she was athletic in her build, she was short for a police officer, standing a mere 5'3". But she was tough, a seasoned veteran of martial arts which she'd learned as a child and maintained to this day. And although she was extremely pretty with high cheekbones and taut facial skin, her aquiline nose gave her a look that indicated she shouldn't be messed with. So no one did.

As she sat at her desk in her tiny cubicle in the Sewall's Point Police Department, she gazed at the crime scene photos and reread the single witness statement from Perryman. From everything she had seen and heard, this wasn't just a random mugging, this was a premeditated act of violence, a crime that appeared to verge on hatred or revenge.

She knew Perryman pretty well, not to date him, but she often saw him around in the area. She liked him because he always had a smile and always had time for everyone he met. The SPPD also chose to overlook the fact that he probably drove home over the limit most nights because the alcohol didn't seem to affect his mental or physical capacity. He also crawled home in his old Woody at around fifteen miles per hour. Or less. Basically, most of the time when he drove back to Sewall's Point, he was usually the only car on the road.

She couldn't work out who would possibly want to hurt him though. The man was an Adonis to look at but he didn't act like one, he just wasn't like most other guys, he was almost too good to be true. Even she had a thing for him and she mostly preferred girls, although not openly. Homosexuality, even bisexuality, was not widely accepted in U.S. police forces so she chose to keep her identity a secret for the time being.

But thinking on, she wondered if he had spent too much time with one of the bored housewives who frequented his spot at the beach, maybe offered extracurricular services other than surf instruction. She couldn't be certain though, but this was a man she cared about and she was going to make whoever caused him so much pain, pay for what they'd one.

Chapter 25

Fortunately for me, I didn't get a repeat visit from Summer that night as had happened during the early hours of Sunday, and Monday morning saw me getting in a cab bound for Stuart's airport at Witham Field. Arthur was heading back at noon to New York because they had decided to celebrate Independence Day in the city. The holiday weekend had been tragically blighted by the events of Saturday night and in some ways, I was grateful for the early departure. At least I was leaving Jensen with Perryman in safe hands and tended to by Talbot and the Cantrells.

I also needed to put Summer out of my mind. She was a unique individual, mature for her age in so many aspects, particularly the emotional side of her. She didn't seem to be a loner but she was vaguely insular, maybe more as a protective mechanism. She seemed to care deeply about anything that was truly important to her. I was beginning to think that I might be one of those things and although the temptation was intense, it would be morally and ethically wrong to entertain the thought of anything carnal or emotional.

When I'd arrived back in New York, I opened my weekend bag to do the weekend's laundry and an envelope fell from one of my shirts. It was addressed to me. I opened it and pulled out a card but as I opened the card, a lock of hair tied with a thread of cotton, tumbled from it.

Dear Jake, I'm so sorry about what happened to Perryman, I know how much you love him and care for him. I'll be sure to visit him often with my sister and Mom and Dad.

I'm also sorry about what I did when I came downstairs during the night. It's not like me, I promise! I'm not some delusional teenager lusting after an older man either, I just felt we had a connection but I made a mistake and I'm really, really sorry!

But I also wanted to tell you that I love the pendant you gave me, it was my best birthday present ever! I'll wear it every day, I'll never even take it off so thank you so much.

Please don't tell anyone I sent you this note as they'd just get the wrong idea about me.

Love,

Summer xxx

I was astounded by the note. It was innocent and beautiful and written from a lovely place. I could never hurt this girl but I still struggled with what her true intentions were and how weak my own defenses might turn out to be.

~

Over the next few months, my workload increased intensely, which in some ways was a blessing because it took my mind off events in Florida. Perryman was making improvements every week and I called as often as I could and Talbot kept me fully updated on his condition.

Not much had changed in the office during this time except for one little surprise.

"Good morning, Serena," I said as our PA scurried past my cubicle.

"Hi Jake, sorry, in a rush!" she replied, her legs taking her as fast as she could towards the kitchen.

As I watched her disappear, I suddenly realized I was in need of a caffeine fix myself and decided to go and drink from the font of the Simonelli Program V, so I got up, stretched and sauntered towards the kitchen too.

When I arrived, the image that hit me would need more than espresso to erase it from my mind. Serena was there, as expected, but what wasn't expected was the sight of Charlotte Acosta, gripping Serena's butt and playing tonsil hockey deep inside Serena's mouth.

"Don't mind me," I whispered, quickly retracing my steps back to the entrance.

"Haha! It's fine, Jake, it's no secret!" Charlotte laughed, "We've been dating for a couple of months now!"

Oh yeah, I must have misinterpreted that last event in this very same kitchen...

"But I didn't know you were the dating type, Charlotte," I said snidely, "Although I know Serena here is."

I also didn't know you swung both ways but who am I to question anything?

"I told you that there was someone new in my life a few months back, Jake. Don't you remember?" Serena said to me.

Yeah, wasn't that right before your new best friend raped me in this very room?

"I do, actually. I remember the exact moment and the look of excitement in your eyes, Serena, and I couldn't be happier for you," I replied.

Charlotte had gone remarkably quiet during this exchange, a trait somewhat foreign to her razor-edged personality.

"You owe me, Charlotte," I said to her as I took my coffee and turned to leave.

"What for," she asked, clearly worried that I'd spill the beans on our own Sunday stroll in this room.

"I bought you a hot Pastrami on Rye sandwich from Second Avenue Deli, I left it on your desk.

"But I don't eat meat, Jake," she said.

“Really? I didn’t know that. I thought you were a regular meat-eating kind of girl. My mistake…” I replied, winking at her as I made my way out of the door.

Chapter 26

After work that night, I decided to take a walk before heading home to my hutch. The weather was still beautiful in New York and as I headed down 5th Avenue and onto Central Park South, I could see the first few leaves falling, a sign that the seasons were changing as fall began to overshadow Summer.

"If You Love Somebody, Set Them Free", Sting's latest single wafted from the open door of a café opposite Central Park.

I couldn't help but sing it to myself as I continued my stroll around the perimeter of the park. There were a number of Hansom Cabs still parked up next to the sidewalk, their exhausted horses readying themselves for another evening of unpaid work before they could go back to their stables.

I recalled a line that I'd recently read in a book,

"From the Great Lakes to The Hoover Dam, from the Mississippi Delta to a small piece of granite called Manhattan, this country is more magical than even Disneyland could dream."

And it was true, it was hard to rationalize how this country had raised itself to what it had become in such a short space of time, but as I stroked one of the horses, I couldn't help feel for these poor ponies almost exhausted from sunstroke during the day and then doing overtime at night.

I sat down on one of the park benches that lined the sidewalk outside Central Park and looked down at the peaceful serenity that existed just a few steps from this hive of activity in the cauldron called Manhattan. The idea of making a park on this tiny island was a masterstroke in 1957, even though at the time, its conception by the upper echelons of Manhattan society was an attempt to emulate the parks of Europe, an unveiled attempt to prove that Americans had their own societal class structure.

When I'd checked the history though, I'd learned that although the idea was intended as a benefit to the growing New York community of the 1860s, it had involved the seizing of thousands of black and white families' homes and land in Seneca Village, in order to create the space for the park. So in some ways, I had contradictory feelings on the subject. But now it was a haven for a population that had grown from 800,000 residents in 1857 to almost eight million today.

What's with all the mellow, Jake? Getting soft in your old age?

It was approaching 10pm now and I was hungry so I headed home to cook something exotic in my 'kitchen', a wasteland where culinary dreams lay eternally unfulfilled.

In my apartment, before showering and changing out of my city attire, I glanced quickly at my answering machine and the flashing green light told me that I had at least one message.

"Hi Jake, it's me, Perryman. I just wanted to let you know that I'm making great progress and my doctors are all really pleased with me. I'm even getting out of here in a week's time so I'm hoping I'll see you down here soon. Oh, and you remember the cop? The lady cop who was investigating the incident? She's been amazing, she's here almost every day at some point, brings me food, books, beers, keeps me company, generally cheers me up. Who'da thought that could happen? Anyway, her name's Sofia and she's cool. Well, I won't go on in case the tape runs out but I just wanted to touch base and let you know how I'm doing. Over and out, buddy."

Although I'd been in fairly constant contact by phone with Perryman to keep abreast of his recovery progress over the last few months, this was amazing news. Too late to call back though, I'd wake the whole hospital if his telephone started ringing now.

The message ended with a long beep and a second one played.

"Hi Jake, do you remember me? It's Tara. I'm going to be in town next month and wondered if we could meet up? I heard about your friend, Perryman, of course, and I know he's making good progress. I even popped in a couple of times to see him. I brought him some surf and custom car magazines which he seemed to really appreciate. Anyway, if you're free, call me. My number is 582 976 2766. Bye."

Well, that was a blast from the past...

After I'd showered and changed, I prepared a couple of grilled cheeses in my faithful old toaster oven. I thought about that last message from Tara. What could she want from me? After all, she came from a family of squillionaires, her grandfather apparently making a mint from designing part of a gun or something. All the family did these days was to find new ways of disposing of their continually increasing income. She was so out of my league but she also seemed really nice. At least she was when we chatted at Talbot's dinner party. I mulled over whether I should return her call but decided what the hell, at least she was good company. And I still vividly remembered her first words to me in Talbot's back yard, *"So what makes Jake shake?"*

As I sat back on my enormous loveseat, I dialed the number, realizing that whoever's house it was, I might be calling a little past the approved cut-off time amongst the middle and upper classes.

It rang, and kept on ringing as I waited for someone to answer. And then, just as I was about to hang up, a familiar voice answered the call.

"Hello? This is Tara," she said.

I froze, her voice was one of those that seemed to take command and I felt like a small fish in a very large pond.

"Tara, this is Jake, I got your message," I said, "I hope it's not too late to call."

"No, no, not at all! I'm so glad you returned my call!" she said, "I just wanted to see if you were going to be available when I'm in New York in October? I'm spending a few days there, meeting up with old friends and doing a little shopping and would really love to see you again."

"Um… October? Next month? Well, I don't have any plans to leave the city so I guess I'm going to be around. What dates to you have planned?" I said, checking my invisible and somewhat empty calendar.

"I arrive on the 14th and head back on the 18th, so any time between those dates is good for me. How about Wednesday, the 16th? Does that work?" she asked.

"It's a date," I replied, "And I'm sorry to have called so late, I'd lost track of the time."

"No problem at all!" she said, "A call from the lovely Jake Delaney is welcome anytime!" she continued.

"Thank you. Where did you want to meet?" I asked.

"Do you know Chelsea Pier, just off 14th St.?" she asked, "I'm staying in that area for the week if you want to come to me. I'll even make you dinner."

"Sure, I know it well. So I'll see you there on the 16th, say around 7pm?" I said, "I'll bring wine."

"Lovely!" she said, "Then it's a date. I look forward to seeing you again, Jake. Bye for now!"

The call ended fairly abruptly and as I sat in my box, I tried to understand what this could be about. Was she interested in me or just super friendly?

I guess I'll find out…

Chapter 27

Caleb Campbell was a good boy. He was no innocent but most people saw him as being a nice kid. What they didn't know was that he was still a virgin at eighteen and most of his friends had already done the dirty so he presented an image of himself to everyone that he was not exactly a stud, but that he wasn't inexperienced either.

He knew he was punching above his weight when he first tried to date her but he'd lucked out when Autumn had agreed to go out with him back in July and had done even better when she chose him to be the one to take her virginity. It wasn't ideal, the back of his pickup truck was fairly cramped and twice he'd fumbled with the condom and picked up dust and hair when he's retrieved it from the floor in the back of the truck.

But Autumn had been incredibly caring, almost in a way that he suspected she may know the truth about him and that she knew this was his first time. They'd kissed awkwardly and he'd tried valiantly to unhook her bra, abandoning the task after several unsuccessful attempts and instead pushing it up above her breasts so he could fondle her.

The interesting thing for him was that she seemed to know exactly what she was doing and expertly unzipped him and removed his throbbing part from its hiding place. She had removed her top too and taken off her bra, revealing to him a perfect tanned body, something that he'd only ever visualized in his mind, but the reality was so much better.

She hadn't taken her skirt off but she'd quickly removed her panties and once he'd managed to secure his rubber, she guided him into her. He was in heaven; he never dreamed it could feel so good. Unfortunately, the feeling only lasted for about thirty-four seconds as he prematurely let go of his cargo way before they'd even begun to enjoy it. Embarrassed at his lack of experience and his obvious naivety, Autumn quickly assured him that it had been fine. But he wasn't sure…

~

"I did it, sis!" said Autumn.

"Did what?" Summer replied.

"As of this evening, I'm no longer singing the Virginity Song, what did you think I meant?"

"Wow! You did it? Who with? Caleb? What was it like? Was it incredible?" asked Summer.

"I'm not sure I would say it was incredible and yes, it was with Caleb but it was okay… I guess."

"You mean you didn't really enjoy it?"

"Not that. Just that I guess I was expecting so much more. In my head for the last couple of years, I thought it would be like fireworks going off but it wasn't really like that at all. I don't want to say 'disappointing', but I've had a lot more fun on my own!" Autumn said with a giggle.

"You're so bad! But at least it's over with. I sometimes think it's never going to happen to me," said Summer.

"It's not a race, sis, whenever that perfect time comes along, you'll know it. Tonight just happened to be right for me and Caleb was nice," said Autumn.

"Does this mean that you'll be doing it with him at college?"

"Nope. That was a one-off, there're plenty more fish in the sea!"

"I know that. But who wants a fish!" Summer replied as they both exploded into laughter and collapsed on the floor.

Chapter 28

A week later, while sitting at the desk in my office, a call was put through to me from the company switchboard.

"Hello?" a familiar voice said.

"Summer?" I responded.

"Jake? It's really you?"

Last time I checked, yes...

"Summer, it's so good to hear your voice, how have you been? I asked, "Have you managed to go and see Perryman very often?"

"I'm great, thanks and yes, I try to get to see him a couple of times a week. He's really improving quickly, up and walking around with sticks but he's got so much more strength now."

"I got a message from him recently, and it seems to confirm what you're saying. I'm hoping to get down to Florida shortly so that I can see with my own eyes," I replied, "And how's that Bronco of yours?" I asked.

"It's great, I love it. Dad was generous to give it to me but you won't believe what he's bought as a replacement," she said.

"Last I remember, he was joking about getting something sensible like a Volvo?" I said.

She laughed raucously at the other end of the line, almost hysterically.

"Hahaha! No, He's gone one step further, much further! He went out and bought himself a genuine mid-life crisis car! A Chevy Corvette!!" she laughed, unable to control herself now.

"I don't see much wrong with that! I think you're being a little hard on your dad," I said, wondering if the same fate awaited me in thirty years' time.

I hope so...

"It's not that, Jake, it's just that Dad is such a cool guy so I never expected him to need a prop like that as he got older. Just a bit of a surprise is all!" she replied.

"Now I feel sorry for the fella, but if it makes him happy, you should be happy for him. But changing subject, to what do I owe the pleasure for this call, a lovely surprise by the way, but I'm guessing it wasn't just to tell me about your dad's new toy?" I asked.

"Well... I don't know if you remember, but when we first met, I said I'd like to ride the New York subway one day," she said.

Oh Lord, here it comes...

"But the truth is that I've seen it in movies and it all looks a little grubby to me so I crossed it off my 'to do' list," she continued.

Oh!

"What I'd really like to do is to ice skate at The Rink in the Rockefeller Center. I've seen so many shows about it on television at Christmas and I really want to experience it myself. Do you think you could let me come up and see you so we could skate there? One of my ambitions is to see snow in New York at Christmas. I've never even *seen* snow before!" she laughed.

"Well, I don't have a problem with you visiting but what about your parents? I'm not sure they'd be too happy about it." I said.

"They're cool, really cool actually. The only stipulation is that I have to pay 50% of the plane ticket so I've been working weekends to earn some money," she replied.

Well, that should delay it a little, tickets ain't cheap...

"I'd need to talk to your mom and dad first but it's okay with me if they approve," I said.

"Fantastic! Listen, I have to go now, I've got a shift at the Jensen Diner but is it okay if I call you at work again?" she asked.

"Of course, Summer, but don't be late for work," I replied.

After I'd ended the call, I sat and thought about my own plans for the next few months, including Christmas. In many ways, I hoped Summer didn't come because of all the associated emotional issues that might arise, but the girl was so incredibly excited about it and I didn't want to crush her dreams.

It suddenly occurred to me that now was a perfect time to try and call Perryman.

"Vaughn Perryman here, Pez to his friends, Vaughn to his enemies," his voice came back to me on the phone.

"Perryman! I got your message. Fantastic news about your recovery," I said.

"Well if it isn't my main man, Delaney, the champagne cork from New York, the man who put the long in Long Island, how the fuck are you?" he asked in his own inimitable style.

"I'm good, but right now it's all about you. I just spoke to Summer and she said you're making an amazing recovery. Can't wait to see you again, buddy," I said.

"Okay, quick summary. The broken bones are healing well, doc says I can get the casts taken off in a couple of weeks. All bruising has disappeared and the lacerations are pretty much invisible now. My nose has a new shape since it was crushed but I'm still gorgeous and next week, I'm seeing the orthodontist about getting a bridge made for my missing front teeth. All in all, I'm in pretty good shape considering the mess I was in when they gurney'd me in here!" he laughed.

"I'm checking off the boxes right now, you've pretty much answered what I was going to ask you. But, what was that in your message about the cop? What's that all about?"

"Oh, you mean Sofia? She's lovely, she's here most days and still trying to find out who was responsible," he replied.

"Umm… so how does that work, then? It's not a relationship then?" I asked carefully.

"You mean, are we intimate? Me and her?" he asked, "No! But I think she might be bisexual."

"But does she know you're gay?" I asked.

"Honestly? I have no clue. But she's such a cool girl. If she wasn't bi, she could probably turn me straight!" he laughed, in hysterics now.

"Now I wish I hadn't asked," I said.

"No, you're cool, Jakey, you know it ain't exactly common knowledge around here and I'm happy to keep it that way, but she and I? Well, we just get along, not sure what to do about it but I'm enjoying whatever it is we have," he responded, calmer now.

"You know, not all relationships have to follow the same path so if you're good for each other, it makes me happy," I said.

"I totally, totally agree, man, I'm right with you on that. But listen, I gotta go, one of my nurses is going to foolishly attempt fellatio on me again! See ya!" he replied, the call disconnecting in my ear.

"Everything okay, Jake?" asked Arthur as he hovered nearby.

"It's all hunky dory, Arthur, totally copacetic…" I replied.

Chapter 29

Sofia Brunson wasn't a detective, she was just a lowly patrol officer. But the detective in charge of the investigation at the Martin County Sheriff's Department had so far drawn a complete blank on Perryman's beating and it appeared that he had pretty much closed the case without new evidence surfacing. She'd grown to love the surfer boy and couldn't let the investigation die and become a cold case so she continued trying to put the puzzle together on her own dime.

Her best guess right now was that a jealous husband had been responsible, maybe not for the act itself but for arranging it. Even though she knew Vaughn's secret sexuality, she was aware that most people didn't, maybe everyone in town in fact. She was also aware that he had been the target of several threats from jealous lovers who could never have guessed that he was gay and was never a threat to their women in any way. In most instances, because of his imposing size and enviable physique, he was perfectly capable of taking care of himself but the planned hit on him was almost undefendable, even for him.

She had made discreet inquiries and discovered that the owners of the house where Perryman rented his guest cottage, had been having marital issues recently. The Steiners were going through a bad patch, not aided by the fact that Krystal Steiner had been spending every Monday, Wednesday and Friday mornings prior to the beating, taking surf lessons at Stuart Beach with Perryman. Apparently, Emerson Steiner had become more than a little frustrated with her activities, the assumption being that Perryman was boning her. It was probably a long shot but she needed to either exclude him from the investigation or make an arrest. Or something…

Chapter 30

Stupidly, I'd forgotten to note down Tara's number to confirm where to meet, so with destination unknown, the evening of the 16th October saw me arriving in a cab at Chelsea Pier, not knowing where I should be meeting her.

As I stood on the pier and looked hopefully around, I heard a voice calling out my name.

"Jakey!" the voice shouted.

Jakey?

I turned around, still unaware of where the voice was coming from, when I heard it once again.

"Jake, up here!"

I looked up, and there on the starboard end of a magnificent ocean-going motor yacht, stood Tara, a picture of elegance in a long, sleek and figure-hugging silver dress.

My, my…

"Come on up, everything's arranged!" she said as I made my way toward the gangplank that led up to the boat.

"You look like a princess," I said, realizing too late what a corny line I'd just used.

"And you like a prince!" she replied.

Okay, not that corny then…

Tara greeted me like a long lost friend rather than someone she'd barely spent an evening with. She hugged me, kissing me on the cheek as she took my hand and led me into the boat's gigantic stateroom. If I had ever thought I'd seen opulence, I had clearly not even scratched the surface. Gleaming wood paneling, gold fixtures and white leather was everywhere I looked, an abundance of ridiculous wealth on display for all to see. Even crystal chandeliers that hung from the ceiling didn't seem out of place.

From nowhere, a waiter appeared and offered me a glass of something, a pair of flutes sitting gracefully on a silver tray.

"Champagne, sir?" he asked.

Sir?

"Don't mind if I do," I said, awkwardly offering my fifteen dollar bottle of Merlot to him in some token of polite exchange.

"Thank you sir, I'll be sure to take care of that," he replied, as I envisioned it being tossed over the port side of the vessel in around thirty seconds.

"Tara. I knew your family was wealthy but I don't think I quite comprehended how ludicrously so," I volunteered.

She laughed, "It's not as though I summoned the captain to sail me to New York, Jake! It just so happened that the company is using the boat as a base for client entertaining and I hitched a ride."

"You can sugarcoat it any way you like, but you've got me, I'm impressed," I replied, "This is the swankiest boat I've ever been on, if you count Talbot's."

"Why don't you sit down for a minute, while we toast Perryman's recovery? I've not been a stranger at the hospital and he seems to have a lot of people popping in," she said.

"To Perryman," I said, offering my glass to hers.

"So tell me what's been happening in your life, Jake, tell me about the dazzle of the Manhattan girls who must chase you night and day," she asked, a sparkle in her eye as she posed the question.

That's me, Jake Delaney, Double-0 stud-like…

"Nothing much really, a whole lot of work and not a lot of play. I've been with the company I'm working at for around eighteen months now and if you know anything about the legal business, you have to earn your way up, which involves countless unpaid hours," I replied, "How about you? Do you spend your time shopping and traveling or do you ever work for the company at all?"

"I don't actually travel that much. Most of my days I spend at the estate in Sailfish Point and I occupy myself with golf and tennis much of the time. Occasionally, like now, I help out with the client entertainment which is dreary," she replied.

I don't think I have the pay grade to be considered 'client entertainment'!" I laughed.

"Oh no, Jake. This is strictly playtime," she smiled.

How very convenient...

"But first," she continued, "Let's eat."

My sentiments entirely. Oh right, sorry...

As she rose to head into the dining room, she picked up a remote control from the coffee table and pointed it at something.

Phil Collins' "One More Night" began to play.

"Swanky," I mumbled.

No sooner had we taken our seats at the dining table, than two waiters appeared, again seemingly from nowhere.

What is this, a fucking magic show?

Simultaneously, the silver lids were lifted from the platters they carried, and we were served the first course.

"Don't want to appear ignorant," I whispered to Tara, "But what is this?"

"This Jake, is pan-fried Foie Gras, you're going to love it," she replied.

Pan fried what?

As I deftly loaded my fork with whatever this was, I was thinking once again that I was out of my league. I couldn't even recognize what was on my plate. But once I'd tasted this delicacy, I was hooked, I couldn't eat it fast enough so I consciously made an effort to slow down.

"I can see your appetite is wonderfully healthy," said Tara, "You look like you haven't eaten in a week!"

If you count three pizzas, you'd be about right...

"No, no, it's just that I tend to survive on a somewhat less exotic diet than this. The height of my week is a bagel with lox and cream cheese from my favorite deli," I said, "And if I'm really honest, apart from what Talbot sometimes prepares, I'm a bit of a Neanderthal as far as culinary knowledge is concerned."

"Well, it's time to give you an education then," she cooed, "And I'm the girl to give it to you"

Exactly what I was thinking...

Fifteen minutes after the Foie Gras had been delivered, another course arrived which once again left me mystified.

"Ummm...." I mumbled

"She laughed, "Don't worry, Jake, I don't recognize half of what I'm served the first time, I just learn as I go along too!"

"I'm clueless on this one," I said.

"This is, for want of a better name, Snail Porridge!" she said, but don't let its name put you off, I think you might like it."

I think I might like stabbing myself in the eye with a hot needle too...

I gingerly dipped my spoon into the black mess, reluctantly offered it up to my lips, and tasted it.

"Actually, it's unbelievably good," I said, "It tastes nothing like it looks."

"Don't you find that with so many things in life though, Jake, you need to taste something before you dismiss it?"

Are you reading my mind?

"This is like an adventure, Tara, I'm so glad you asked me along. My taste buds are being educated, my palate is being charmed."

Oh stop it!

"Honestly? Well, in that case, it's my pleasure. I really was hoping that this week would be a perfect time to meet again," she said.

We chatted about everything and nothing until we realized that the disappearing/reappearing waiters were anxious to grace our table with more inexplicable dishes.

I looked down at what I assumed was the main course.

"Not a clue,' I said.

"Pigeon."

"Good enough" I replied.

"Saving All My Love For You" oozed from the sound system.

Behave, Whitney...

~

By 9pm, we had finished dessert and adjourned to the lounge, which was about twenty times the size of my apartment.

Tara picked up yet another remote control, pointed it at something and the lights dimmed.

"I hope you don't have to be up early in the morning, I'm really enjoying tonight," she said.

"Actually, I have to work early tomorrow, I need to be in by seven, but that's okay, my apartment isn't too far from my office building," I replied.

"If you wanted, you could stay here, you'd be much closer to the office than if you went home," she said.

Bring it on...

"There are eight bedrooms on the boat," she added.

Oh...

That's really kind of you, Tara, but it's probably best if I sleep in my own bed," I replied.

"I was hoping you'd sleep in my bed," she said, rising from the sofa, teasing the straps from her shoulders and letting the gown fall to the ground.

She stood naked in front of me, wearing only her Manolos and a smile.

"Oh. My. Goodness." I said.

"You like?

"What's not to like?" I replied, my little friend apparently in vehement agreement, struggling to escape my pants.

"I'm not normally this forward, Jake, but I've wanted to have you since the moment I met you," she said.

"But… what about the staff?"

"They've been dismissed," she said.

Of course...

I'd never seen a body like Tara's before. Yes, she was tall, but raised up in the silver pumps she was wearing, it made her look even more impressive. I kind of felt like I was in a James Bond film because her skin was flawless, looked like it had been painted on and the golden triangle I was at eye level with, truly matched her hair. This was a genuine collar and cuffs girl.

As she moved closer to me, I began to remove my shirt and gently put my hands on her behind and pulled her forward. I lay my cheek on her rounded abdomen and my lips hovered over her mound, enjoying her luscious scent, before slowly running my tongue up further, between her breasts and onto her neck. I felt a shiver run through her as I lightly nuzzled the side of her neck, beneath her ear, nipping gently at her lobe and then the back of her neck.

"Ohhh…" she moaned, her almond eyes closed now, enjoying this delicate moment.

I turned her so that her back was to me and pushed briefly against her so that she could sense my own arousal. I kissed her back, ran my tongue down her spine to the valley between her cheeks and then gently bit into each of them. I turned her again, raised myself to standing and took her face in my hands, pulling her to my mouth.

"Oh, Jake, please don't stop…" she whispered.

Our lips met and I could feel myself drowning in her soft and receptive mouth, our tongues slowly exploring each other. Her lips were like miniature pillows and I couldn't stop myself from gently biting them, running my tongue over and over them.

This was such a different experience to a previous one that still remained and played havoc in my mind.

Tara took my hand and led me to a vast master suite and being the compliant man I am, I followed willingly.

She sat on the end of the bed and expertly but not hurriedly, removed my pants and my boxers. She lay back on the bed and invited me to join her. I looked down at her thighs, golden, smooth and almost Amazonian. I hovered above her, bending my arms so my mouth found her breasts, taking little bites at each nipple until she was fully erect.

Her head had tipped back by now and I moved once again down her stomach until I found a different but much warmer oasis.

I breathed in the scent from her lustrous golden triangle and sank deep into her yielding lips, time seeming to stand still as I pleasured her.

"Please, Jake, I need you so much…" she panted, her body now writhing on the crisp cotton sheets.

Rising up, an ache developing in my now throbbing appendage, I caressed her body as I moved up to her delicious mouth. She took me carefully into her hand and guided me slowly into her.

"Fuck, fuck!" she yelled, "Take me, Jake, take me now!"

Rhythmically and gently, I glided in and out of her, her back arching with every thrust, squeezing me as I pulled further out and relenting as I pushed back in. I kissed her, now harshly, her breasts growing visibly larger as we became one moving, writhing, living entity.

It was too much, this woman was a thing of beauty, a picture of unwrapped and exotic lust. I exploded within her, her body stiffening as though electricity had passed through her entire being, sucking me in, drinking every last drop of me.

I collapsed on top of her, hugging her and rolling us on to our sides, entwined now and breathing hard like we were taking our last gulp of air.

"Amazing, Jake, simply amazing…"

Chapter 31

Sofia Brunson had decided that she needed to question Emerson Steiner. She knew she was stepping dangerously outside of her boundaries but the task of finding whoever had committed this act of violence on Perryman, preyed on her mind, every minute of every day. The closer she got to Vaughn, the more anger she felt for the fact that he'd almost been murdered. The Steiners, for no better reason than that they had a strong connection with Perryman, seemed a good place to start.

Arriving at the Steiner residence on River Road, she eased her patrol car up the driveway towards their mansion.

"Nice digs, if you can afford it" she muttered aloud.

Ringing the doorbell eventually brought a short, heavy woman to the door. She was Hispanic and dressed in maid's attire so Sofia guessed that it wasn't the wife, Krystal Steiner.

"Buenos Dias, 'ow may I 'elp you," she said in perfect Spanglish, her eyes darting from Sofia's uniform to the patrol car parked on the driveway.

"If it's possible, I'd like to speak with Mr. Steiner, if he's home," Sofia said.

"Let me see. Wait 'ere," she said, closing the door on Sofia as she withered in the late Summer heat.

Two or three minutes later, as perspiration gathered on her forehead, the door opened again and Ms. Spanglish beckoned Sofia to come inside.

"Mr. Steiner will see you in the library," she instructed as Sofia followed the woman into the vast entrance hall.

It was an enormous home, cathedral ceilings towered above her, crystal chandeliers lighting the way as she followed the housekeeper across the endless marble floors towards the rear of the house. Although it was a huge house, there was a distinct lack of taste, in that gold seemed to be the prevailing color and texture that featured everywhere she looked, and a shitload of appalling but probably horrendously expensive art covered every inch of the wall space.

They approached two giant oak doors that formed a Gothic style entrance to what she assumed must be Steiner's office. Ms. Spanglish opened them up to reveal a quite extraordinary view out across the St. Lucie River, the waterway sparkling and glistening in the late morning sun. She took in the dozens of motorboats, yachts and catamarans, all enjoying a mid-week nautical stroll on the Florida waters.

Lucky bastards...

"Señor Steiner, zees is the police lady I tell you 'bout," Spanglish announced, her accent becoming more pronounced.

"Well, good morning, Officer… Brunson?" Steiner said, examining her lapel badge and extending his hand in welcome.

Tiny hands, ugh!

Steiner was a tall man although his portly demeanor suggested he didn't use the gym that was undoubtedly located somewhere deep in the caverns of this Disneyland of a home. His hair, which resembled more a tangerine color than straw blond, was carefully combed over his scalp and lacquered in place to hide a balding pate. As he smiled an alligator-like welcome, his teeth gleamed white, likely a recently added purchase at his orthodontist.

I'm gonna be sick...

"To what do I owe the pleasure of this visit from our local constabulary, Ms. Brunson?" he asked, his eyes circumnavigating Sofia's body, darting from one area to another.

"It's Officer Brunson, sir," she said, "And I'd like to ask you a few questions relating to the attempted murder of Vaughn Perryman."

She had to be careful here, she wasn't officially in charge of the investigation but she would need to let him assume she was. She didn't even know if the Martin County Sheriff's Office had already been here and interviewed Steiner.

"Perryman, yes, what a terrible occurrence," he replied.

Occurrence?

"Attempted *murder*, you say? I thought it was merely a case of him being in the wrong place at the wrong time after too many late night drinks?" he continued, "Not that that would be any surprise to most people around here, he was never a stranger to a bar."

His smirking character assassination of her friend did nothing to change her prejudgment of what an arrogant prick this man was. But she was determined not to be baited by his arrogance.

"From what we can ascertain, sir, this was a planned attack, and we are treating it as attempted murder. I'm sure you can understand, as you've known Mr. Perryman for many years, that it was only his physical size and strength that saved him from certain death and is allowing him to recover as we speak," Sofia said.

"Yes, I'm sure he was a big hit with many of the women in the area. No brain to speak of but he's a pretty boy. Although not so much now, I would think."

She really didn't like this man. He was typical of the autocratic and stupidly wealthy egomaniacs that lived in this particular part of the country. He had the air of someone who enjoyed looking down at the little people and without needing to delve too deeply into his charmless character, she assumed racist, misogynistic, xenophobic, homophobic and sexist traits, although not necessarily in that order. Like many of the other repugnant demagogues who hid quietly in Sewall's Point.

"Well, what can I do for you?" he continued, "I'm not sure how I can help, other than to say that Perryman lives in the guest cottage further down the driveway at the end of the property. But I'm assuming you already know that, *Officer*," his tiny mouth pinching out the words, like a dog taking a dump on your lawn.

Cocky little fucker...

"Yes, I'm fully aware of that, Mr. Steiner, just a couple of questions if you wouldn't mind?"

"Of course, please sit down, Ms. Brunson," he said, pirouetting away from Sofia to take a seat behind his gargantuan but hideous desk, his throne-like chair centered between the enormous glass windows that framed the opulent view of his daily vista.

I wonder if you get bored with seeing that every day? Probably not...

"Thank you, sir, but hopefully I won't take too much of your valuable time," she said, "If I could just start by asking your whereabouts on the night of the attack?"

"Me? Why on earth would my whereabouts have anything to do with Perryman? Surely you don't suspect that I had anything to do with it?" he blurted.

Well, yes...

"We have to close all avenues in the search to find out who might have had the motive or even the means to arrange such an attack, sir," she replied, "At the moment, I just want to exclude all possible suspects and obviously you have a relationship with Mr. Perryman and you may be able to offer information that we aren't yet aware of."

"I don't have a relationship with Vaughn, the only reason he lives on the property is because of my wife, Krystal," he said, his face reddening with little disguised rage boiling beneath.

"So your wife has the relationship?"

"Too much of a relationship, if you ask me," he replied.

"I see. So this is a problem in your marriage?"

"No! It's not a problem in my marriage! And my marriage has nothing to do with you! My wife and I are perfectly happy, thank you. Stop reading something into my words to make me sound like a jealous husband!" he blustered, clearly becoming unraveled.

"I understand that Mrs. Steiner spends a lot of time with Mr. Perryman, taking surf instruction with him? Or I should say, used to spend time," Sofia probed.

"My wife spends too much time at the hair salon, at the beauty parlor, at the golf course, at the tennis club as well, but it doesn't make me a murderer!" he bellowed, now squirming on his throne, like a child desperate to get to the bathroom.

"He's not dead yet, Mr. Steiner," Sofia replied.

A voice cut through the toxic air that had so quickly erupted.

"I can do what the hell I like when I like, Emerson, and I don't need your fucking permission for anything, you ignorant bastard!"

Krystal Steiner marched across the polished office floor, her pumps clicking on the marble like a woodpecker savaging a tree. She was the owner of an enviable figure, a movie star face too and she was probably a frequent visitor to her plastic surgeon, her breasts seemingly attached without gravity affecting them in any way whatsoever. All in all, she was the veritable trophy wife.

Sofia stood, not knowing if she should introduce herself but immediately recognizing the opportunity to gather unforeseen information between the husband and wife. But it was already clear that there was no love lost between the Steiners.

"Don't fucking flatter yourself that you're paying for my life because it's not your fucking money, Emerson! Everyone knows that! You sit here in your little ivory tower, playing at being the successful businessman but you're such a fucking loser!" she yelled.

"Er…, honey, we have company. Can we talk about this some other time? This is Ms. Brunson, from the police," he quivered.

Officer fucking Brunson! Are you deaf or just fucking stupid?

Krystal was stopped in mid-flow, like a 35mm projector catching a single frame in its sprocket, and she spun on her heels towards Sofia, like a panther assessing its prey.

"I'm Officer Brunson, ma'am, pleased to meet you," Sofia said quietly, standing and offering her hand in friendship.

"I'm so sorry, Officer, it's just that sometimes we have fights and my husband is forgetful about where our money comes from. I apologize, this isn't the image I usually present to outsiders."

Outsiders…

"Has he offered you a drink of anything?" Krystal asked.

"No ma'am, but it's okay"

"Nonsense, come outside onto the terrace and we'll have some iced tea. And please, it's Krystal. And you are….?"

"Sofia… pleased to meet you," she replied.

Adjourning to the balcony and leaving a fuming and somewhat verbally castrated Steiner behind in his office, the two women took a seat outside, the fresh air from the breeze a welcome relief for Sofia. Krystal poured two glasses of iced tea that had been delivered earlier by Ms. Spanglish, and sat back in her chair.

"Vaughn is a lovely man. I truly love him, Sofia, but probably not in the way you're thinking or even the way my husband imagines. For me, he has become a part of the family, I suppose you might say he's the son I never had but I can assure you that there is no romantic notion between us and for a very good reason. I have plenty of other men who service me in ways that my husband could never do," she laughed.

Sofia was momentarily taken aback, a little shocked even. This woman was airing the dirty laundry to someone she'd never met until five minutes ago.

"It's not that Emerson is a terrible person and once upon a time, believe it or not, he was quite good looking. Well, passable I suppose. But the money all comes from my family. Emerson has been bankrupt three times but we live here in this arena of moneyed families and he likes to pretend that he's something he really isn't. But although he's stupid, he's pretty harmless," Krystal continued.

"I understand," said Sofia, "I was just trying to account for everyone that Mr. Perryman knew at the time of the attack. Perhaps if you could tell me where you and your husband were during that evening, I can be out of your hair?" said Sofia.

"That's an easy one, Sofia, we were at a charity gala at my golf club in Palm Beach. Emerson was with me all the time."

"Can you tell me what time you returned home?"

"Probably around 2.30am, it was a lengthy evening and we danced til late. Well, I did anyway," Krystal replied.

"I think I can exclude you from the investigation then, Krystal, I'm sorry to have taken your time today," said Sofia.

"It's really no problem at all. If I can help in any way, please don't hesitate to call me. In the meantime, as Vaughn looks like coming home soon, we're hoping his car will be back from the restorers shortly. One of his friends, Jake Delaney, called me and asked if I could contribute to the cost and for Vaughn, well I'd help in any way I can, so I've paid the bill in full. None of those boys have enough left over each month and I have more than enough to cover everyone."

"You really do like Vaughn then," said Sofia.

"Yes I do, Sofia, more than you can imagine," Krystal replied.

That makes two of us then...

Chapter 32

Summer slowly ran her finger up the side of the glass, catching the droplets of water trickling down.

"Why does that happen?" she asked herself, "Why does a dry glass suddenly have water running down the outside? Does the glass leak?" She guessed there must be a scientific reason for it but she didn't dwell on it.

Sitting on a sidewalk table outside the café, she leaned back in her chair, gazing into the afternoon sun. Prince's 'Little Red Corvette' played inside the restaurant but Summer was oblivious to music today. She picked up a newspaper that had been left behind by the previous customer and began to flick through the headlines of *USA Today*.

"God, it's so hot," she said, but no one heard her.

On the front page, the big story today was that Rock Hudson had died of AIDS.

"Don't get that at all," she thought, *"Are all the best looking guys gay? What is this disease anyway? They say it comes from monkeys..."*

On the second page was the announcement that Billy Joel had married Christie Brinkley.

"Like that's gonna last," she thought, *"I'll give it five years before he trades up for a newer model..."*

"Hi, Summer!" a voice called to her from a few yards away.

"Hi Mrs. Perrin," she replied.

It was Margie Perrin, co-owner of the restaurant, 11 Maple St., who had recently given Summer a part-time job waiting tables. It was an up market place so Summer had to look the part and be knowledgeable about the menu but the tips tended to be better than most of the other restaurants in Jensen. She also still loved going there for special nights out with her friends and seeing how much they could afford to eat.

Margie stopped and stood next to Summer's table.

"How're your mom and dad?" she asked.

"Oh they're fine, thank you, in fact Mom's due here in a few minutes, I'm getting her to buy me lunch during her break!" laughed Summer.

"Well, tell them I asked about them and send them my love!" Margie replied, laughing as she walked away.

In the sports pages, she read about a soccer match between two teams called Liverpool and Juventus, thirty-nine spectators had died with over 250 injured.

"What's that about? I thought soccer was a sport, not a war!"

"How's my girl?" another female voice cooed along the sidewalk.

"Mom! I'm so glad you're finally here, I'm starving!" Summer replied.

"Well, as it's just you and me now, I have to spoil my only baby left at home, don't I?" Reyna replied, taking the other seat at the table.

"Correct answer!" laughed Summer, offering her mother a menu, "I'm having fried calamari with seafood sauce and then I'm having a cheeseburger because this place makes the best in town."

"Well I guess I'm going to be boring then and have a Cobb Salad!" said Reyna, "Some of us still need to look after our figures!"

Summer laughed because her mom was so beautiful and most men turned to look when they saw her.

"I was reading some of the newspaper before you arrived. Why is it that they only seem to report bad news? Is that what's going on in our world? It's so depressing," said Summer.

"As you grow older, sweetheart, you just become more aware of the terrible things that are happening on our planet," said Reyna, "The only thing you can do is to take a positive stance to life. But why are you feeling down, it can't be all about what's in the news, surely? I guess you must be missing Autumn, now that she's at college? I know I do, I can't stop crying every day!"

"Oh Mom, you've still got me and you know I'm your favorite!"

"I don't have favorites and you know it! But I'm going to lose you for a little while in December when you go to New York, aren't I?" asked Reyna, "Who are you staying with, by the way? I hope you didn't ask Jake."

"No, of course not, but he is going to meet me at the airport and make sure I don't get lost," replied Summer, a little coyly, "I think his days and evenings will probably be taken up with work most of the time but he promised to take me ice skating at the Rockefeller Center, which is one of the big reasons I'm going."

"That's so sweet of him but make sure you don't put upon him too much. Remember, he has his own life and career going on," her mother replied, "Otherwise we'll never see him down here again!"

Hmm, that definitely wouldn't do...

They ordered their lunch and Summer wondered if her mother had something else on her mind that necessitated having lunch with her on a school day.

"So, is there anything else on your mind, Mom? I know you're missing Autumn but we don't usually meet up for lunch during the week, just the two of us."

"Yes... there is. Your dad and I have been talking about the future and we know that you're only nine months away from leaving to go to college yourself. The thing is, it's bad enough with your sister gone but once you leave too, I don't know how we're going to cope," Reyna said, tears beginning to form in her eyes.

"Oh Mom, that's ages away yet and we'll both be coming back for all the holidays, you know that!"

"I do, but your dad had an idea that maybe we should move nearer to the college so we can be close to you. That is, if you decide to go to Florida State too."

"That's the plan, but why would you want to leave Jensen Beach, it's perfect here and you love it. You love your home too and all your friends are here. You can't sell our home, Mom, and go somewhere else! This is where we want to come back to, this is the only home we want!" Summer said, realizing that her own cheeks were streaming with tears now.

"Oh Summer, you don't know what that means to me, I'm not handling the empty nest syndrome too well, I guess. When your sister comes home at Thanksgiving, I'm sure we'll start to deal with it more rationally. I think it just takes getting used to, that's all. But if you want us to stay here, then we're more than happy to do so, but just make sure you leave slowly and come back quickly!" said Reyna.

"We will, Mom, you know you and Dad are our rocks, we couldn't survive without you," Summer replied.

"Ahem… who's having calamari?" said the waiter, having just arrived at their table holding aloft a tray filled with food.

"That would be me, I'm famished!" Summer grinned.

Chapter 33

"What are we?" Perryman asked.

"How do you mean?" replied Sofia.

"I mean, well, I'm gay, you're bi, so what the hell are we?"

They were lying on the carpeted floor of Perryman's guest cottage, listening to music, the two of them sharing a rare bottle of wine, Bryan Adams' "Run To You" playing on the stereo.

"We are what we want us to be. I know it's confusing for me right now and I'm guessing you're having the same issues so God knows what it must be like for other people who know us," Sofia said, smiling at Perryman, "But I've never felt this strength of bond with anyone before, Vaughn, I'd literally kill for you if I had to," she said, not realizing the potential irony in her words.

"But the thing is," Perryman said, "I realize I'm not openly gay and I like that that façade is maintained because it just makes my life a lot easier. But I don't even know if I can be labeled 'homosexual' because I don't have sexual feelings about other men. Maybe I'm more asexual than anything else?"

"I'm having similar feelings, Vaughn. I've had lesbian experiences and I enjoyed them a lot but I've never gone all the way with a man either. Have you ever been with a woman?"

"I tried it once but I just didn't have a clue what I was doing so it kind of put me off, I guess," he replied, "But I need to tell you something. You've been incredible all the time I was recovering in the hospital. Barely a day went by when you didn't come by to see me or bring me stuff that I wanted. I don't know how to say this, Sofia… but I think I've fallen in love with you."

Sofia got up onto her knees, leaned in to him and took his handsome but now scarred face in her hands and said, "Look, you big hunk of gorgeousness, I've been in love with you for months now but just didn't know how to tell you or even if I should tell you. I don't know what's going on with me right now because I've tried reading up on similar situations to this and I can't find anything that compares. You know I prefer girls but I can't stand the idea of being without you so what does that make me? I'm as confused as anyone!"

He smiled, his new teeth once more highlighting his natural boyish charm.

"So what are we?" he asked again.

"We are what we want to be, Vaughn, but as long as I have you, I'm a happy girl!"

Vaughn leaned in to Sofia and for the very first time, and in a hesitant and slightly awkward moment, they kissed…

Chapter 34

Gaylord Talbot was painfully aware of the irony in that most people viewed Perryman as a man's man, a stud even but that he, Talbot, was often assumed to be gay. It was forgivable though, Talbot did enjoy the more cultured things that life offered. He did enjoy cooking and loved being in his kitchen, so much so that at one point he'd even considered ditching law in favor of becoming a chef.

He loved art too and his unique fondness, in Florida anyway, for all things Shakespeare, didn't help to advance his status as a red-blooded male. A redneck, he would never be.

William Shakespeare had always been a conundrum to Talbot, he believed that Shakespeare was either the most advanced thinking man in the 1600s or as many scholars asserted, he was simply a combination of a dozen or more sophisticates writing under one single nom de plume. In his own mind, he thought that The Bard might even have been a woman, disguising her gender because of the fact that four hundred years ago, women were not widely accepted as serious writers. But Shakespeare's words had such a feminine quality to them that he realized that this theory might hold water.

But Talbot definitely wasn't gay. Far from it, in fact. He'd grown up with Perryman and from their early teens, he knew that Perryman was gay, but in the early 1970s, it wasn't something you advertised in America, anywhere in the world, in fact. Jake was one of the only other people in their circle who also knew, not that it had ever been stated, it was just an accepted fact between the three of them.

But Talbot had grown tired of being seen as a latter-day Quentin Crisp, the man who was a friend to everyone, who was always the happy chappie and the bon viveur host. He wasn't exactly a virgin though. He had had several one-off, but short-lived relationships with girls but because he wasn't seen as a typically testosterone-fuelled male, these relationships dwindled into friendships, albeit lasting ones.

But Autumn was different. She wasn't a typical Floridian teen looking for a good time like many of her friends. She and Summer elicited many of the sophisticated qualities that her mother exuded. Reyna had raised these two girls to be extensions of herself, and it showed in their early maturity. Both of them mixed well with their peers at school and also around adults, but it was fairly easy to see that they were different in so many ways from most of the girls in town.

Recently, he'd been at the Cantrell house as Autumn had driven away to begin her four years at university. He'd secretly cried at the thought that she would no longer be around, except for holidays; Spring Break, Summer, Thanksgiving and Christmas. The truth was, Talbot did have a secret, just as Perryman did. He had fallen in love with Autumn. He was aware that she had no clue as to how he felt and he'd managed to hide his secret from everyone who knew him, but it was something that burned deep inside him. He also chided himself for jokingly hurling the hypocritically slanderous 'Uncle Chester' comments at Jake during the Summer.

"Talbot, the hypocrite," he said aloud as he pondered his future at his office desk, "There is nothing either good or bad, but thinking makes it so…"

Oh come on, give it up, Talbot!

His thoughts were interrupted by the telephone ringing.

"Talbot?" the voice asked.

"Reyna, how lovely to hear from you, how are you?" he replied.

"I'm great but I wanted to tell you I just had a call from Krystal Steiner, and apparently Perryman's Woody is ready and she wants to present it to him next week with as many of his friends that can make it," she said, "Can you come?"

"For sure, I wouldn't miss that, he's going to be so stoked!"

Chapter 35

Krystal Steiner wasn't a woman to be messed with. She'd despised her husband for many years now and even though she'd been screwing plenty of much younger men at the tennis club, he was so wrong about Perryman. Vaughn was very special to her and she wouldn't let anything harm him but she didn't trust Emerson. Although incapable of most things, she knew he was capable of organizing a hit on Vaughn.

She strode through their ridiculously gigantic home, not something she'd ever wanted to live in, but her dick of a husband demanded it so that people would think he was a success at something. But it was only the two of them living here, plus the maid most days.

And it was 12,000 square feet, for crying out loud...

She found him in the drawing room, reading another of his tawdry novels, smoking a cigar with a brandy glass on his side table.

"Bit early for that, isn't it? I mean, it's only three in the afternoon! And what have I said about smoking those fucking awful things in the house?" she said, her voice elevating in strength.

"It's my home too," he responded, without looking up from his book.

Not for much longer, it ain't...

"Emerson, we need to have a discussion. I think you need to tell me what you've been up to," she said, limiting the ferocity she felt inside.

"I have no idea what you're talking about, Krystal. As usual, you're delusional in whatever it is that your silly little mind of yours is cooking up," he responded.

"I'm talking about what happened to Vaughn back in July. I want to know if you had anything to do with it," she said, an air of self-control being her main concern right now.

"Are you honestly suggesting that I had something to do with that? That's a ridiculous idea, you're being preposterous now as well as hostile," he replied, not realizing the pent up anger lurking inside his wife.

"Did you not think I'd notice the five grand missing from the safe? Did you think I was too dumb to miss it? Right before Vaughn was attacked, I'd put that money there to pay the landscapers for work they were due to carry out in August but then suddenly, when I went to retrieve it, it had gone."

"You must have spent it on one of your many shopping sprees, my darling, perhaps you just forgot?" he replied, drawing deeply on his Cohiba Esplendido.

"I don't use cash for shopping, Emerson, how stupid do you think I am?" she replied.

"I think you're probably answering your own question, Krystal, I'm assuming it was rhetorical?" he smirked.

"What's fucking rhetorical Emerson, is how much of a boring, ignorant and sexually useless old man you are," she yelled.

"It takes two to tango, darling, you're not exactly God's gift these days," he replied.

"Well, I can give you one heck of a long list of boys I've fucked who'd probably disagree with you, you bastard!" she shouted.

"Of course, my dear, but I suppose a leopard never changes her spots, does she?" the smugness returning to his jowly features, "But don't kid yourself, you're no oil painting these days."

"Why on earth did I ever marry you, Emerson? All you've ever done is to leech on me, spend my money and put me down to everyone we meet," shouted Krystal.

"You married me because no one else would have you, dear," he replied, "You should be happy that I took you on or you'd be a lonely old spinster now."

"But why Vaughn? What did Vaughn ever do to you?" she cried.

"Well, if you hadn't been screwing him right under my nose for the past three years, maybe it wouldn't have happened," he said smugly, then suddenly realizing he'd admitted his guilt.

"Screwing him? Is that what you think, you moron! He's gay, you stupid fuck!!"

"He's wh…what?

"He's gay, you dumbass, how did you not know? Vaughn is like the son you could never give me, you impotent shit!"

"I… I… I never knew! Honestly, you have to believe me, Krystal, I had no idea! I thought he was screwing everyone down at the beach. I'd never have wanted to hurt him if I'd known. I promise you!" he quivered, realizing the terrible mistake he'd made.

"Well, you got your wish, Emerson. What you did won't make me a lonely old spinster but it will make me fucking happy when I divorce your ass!"

She picked up a lead crystal vase and hurled it at her husband. It slammed into the side of his face, causing a deep gash now oozing blood on his monogrammed blazer.

"Please, Krystal, please sweetheart, I didn't mean any harm, I was just jealous, I'm sorry! Please forgive me?"

"Fuck you and fuck your apology, you're going to pay for what you've done!" she yelled, "And d'you know what, Emerson, you won't be seeing a penny of my money once I divorce you! I hope you die in hell, you motherfucker!"

Chapter 36

I was replaying recent events in my head. Although these particular instances were separated by some length of time, it felt as though everything was happening at once.

It was almost a year ago since I first fell for Summer, even though she didn't know it at the time.

Thank the Lord, Jake, she was sixteen...

But then meeting her on Talbot's boat had made me even more conscious that I didn't want to hurt her emotionally and in all honesty, I didn't want to be hurt either. During the Fourth of July celebrations, it had been an amazing holiday weekend but our brief encounter in the kitchen that night had left me feeling extremely vulnerable. And then the attack on Perryman brought a tragic end to the holiday.

Adding in my coffee machine dalliance with Charlotte and my more recent adventure recently with Tara, I was beginning to question who I was and what I wanted.

"Do you come here often?" a disjointed voice whispered in my ear.

Never heard that line before...

I was sitting in a bar on Canal St. in Soho, vaguely taking in a Knicks basketball game where they were going down like the Titanic. *"Time to switch allegiance to a team that wins occasionally,"* I mused.

"I'm sorry, do I know you? Have we met?" I replied, turning around on my bar stool and finding myself nose to ample breast with a tall, slim and dark haired stranger.

She took the available seat next to me and asked the next chat up line in her book of what not to say to strangers in bars.

“What does a girl have to do to get a drink around here?” she continued.

She reminded me a little of Cruella de Vil, the woman in the *101 Dalmatians* movie. She was clearly tall, even without her pumps I guessed she was maybe 5’11” and she wore a white silk shirt, black pencil skirt and had draped a fur coat across the back of the stool.

Another one who doesn’t see the need for bras...

“I’m just taking in the game and drinking a couple of shots and a beer or three. I’m Jake, what can I get you?” I said, offering my hand to her.

She clasped my fingers gently with both hands, her pale and almost translucent skin reminding me even more of the aforementioned Ms. de Vil. Her fingers slowly dragged off my hand leaving my limb motionless in the air.

“Vodka Martini is my vice, thank you,” she replied, and it’s Valeria by the way, Valeria Jaramillo.”

Her hair wasn’t dark, it was jet black. It harshly framed her face, the bangs cut high on her forehead and the remainder of her hair cut in a severe pageboy style, normal at the sides but slashed savagely high into the back of her head. It looked like a wig because it was too perfect. But although she wasn’t beautiful in the accepted sense of the word, unless you counted women who closely resembled Russian assassins in James Bond movies, she was certainly very attractive.

Several drinks and a heavy bar bill later, I was having trouble focusing on anything. The room was not quite whirling around me but I sensed I wasn’t in complete control of all my faculties.

“Let’s go back to my place,” Valeria said, “Maybe we can have some fun!”

I think I’ve mentioned before that I’m quite a compliant sort of fella, I tend to do as instructed, never wishing to upset anyone’s feelings.

The cab drew up outside her apartment building on the Upper West Side. I crawled out and steadfastly held the door open for Valeria or maybe I was holding on to the door to avoid falling over. Why hadn't the drink affected her the way it was affecting me?

Beyond the canopied entrance, a doorman, dressed in a purplish red suit and peaked hat, quickly hurried to the glass doors to welcome us in, saluting us as we entered. By the time we'd called the lift and stepped in through the doors, Valeria was having to hold me up and for some reason, the world was beginning to spin.

"Come on, big boy, let's get you upstairs," she whispered.

Big Boy? Where had I heard that before?

We finally arrived at her floor and she guided me down the corridor to what appeared to be her apartment. As the door opened, I took in the opulence of a very grand and majestic space; at first glance, it was bigger than most houses, maybe three thousand square feet or more from what I could see.

"Sit down, Jake, while I fix some drinks for us," she said, guiding me to an oversized sofa in a group of seating surrounding an open fireplace.

Drinks? Really? I'm already drunk!

I collapsed with some degree of gratitude, hoping I could snuggle down and sleep this off. The sofa was more comfortable than my bed so I was happy to stay the night just as long as I could sleep.

Valeria came back into the room a few minutes later, carrying a tray with two drinks. The difference now was that she was butt naked, her pale body, slim but toned, topped by a chest that I assumed had been surgically altered.

Oh fuck...

She set the tray down on the coffee table and placed one of the glasses in my hand, curling up next to me, smiling at her own inappropriateness. The room was moving at some pace now as I gulped the Vodka Gimlet far too quickly.

"Why don't you take off your jacket, Jake? In fact, why don't you take off everything? I've been thinking all night about what you'd look like naked, big boy!"

And there it is again...

I complied, as is my wont, but on closer examination, Valeria saw that there was a distinct lack of engorgement in my penile companion. I was a little shocked too. She wasn't unattractive but I guess she wasn't my type either. What the fuck was I doing here?

"Don't worry, Jake, I'm pretty sure we can fix this," she said, immediately burying her head in my groin area without invitation.

She had a modicum of success, notwithstanding my blurred vision and general alcoholic malaise. She got up from the sofa and laid across the table, parting her legs in invitation.

You remember what I said about being compliant?

I slithered drunkenly off the sofa and knelt before her, grasping her thighs to avoid falling over. I felt sick now, not just dizzy.

"Come on, Jake, you're not going to last forever and I need a little something from you," she whispered, taking hold of me and gently inserting my not yet fully grown friend into her hungry arena.

So I did my best. I tried to focus on a painting on the wall opposite, just to give me balance. Was I imagining it or was that a fellatio scene?

However, I stroked as best I could, given my lack of fortitude down there but it felt more like a chore than anything exciting. Valeria seemed to be enjoying it though so I didn't want to be a killjoy and pull out now, so to speak.

"I want you to come first!" she moaned.

Hold on then, let me think of someone…

She was screaming now, like she was being murdered! I wasn't even in this movie that she seemed to be reliving. Finally, I was able to summon the energy and the required firmness to climax. Kind of a damp squib, although you'd never know from the way Valeria was thrashing, moaning and yelping.

"That was intense, Jake, now go down on me!" she ordered.

Really? Can't we just snuggle?

Of course, I complied and acted like I was hungry for her, manfully diving into her lady pool to wreak havoc on her labial cloister.

Two hours later, Valeria shuddered the shudder I'd been waiting for. By now, my lips were numb and my tongue ached from overuse. My neck had a chronic ache too and all I wanted to do was sleep. The dizziness had fortunately worn off and as I pulled on my pants and shirt, Valeria seemed to be awakening from an intense moment.

"Are you leaving?" she asked.

"I need to get up in about two hours time for work," I replied.

"Leave me your number!" she whispered, as I bent down to kiss her cheek.

"I'll call you…"

Chapter 37

Emerson Steiner knew that the gig was up. Krystal wasn't stupid at all. Taking the five grand from the safe that he'd given to the bikers to make the hit on Perryman, was foolish on his part. She didn't miss anything, she was much smarter than he. She was also well aware of the hundreds of thousands, no millions of dollars, that he'd 'invested' in doomed business ventures and he realized now that the game was over. He didn't love Krystal, never had really, but a bulging bank account was such an incredibly attractive quality in a woman. Sex had been good initially, if a little mechanical, but even that had stopped once he failed to get to launch mode.

He looked at his naked reflection in the mirror, bloated, overweight, jowls now hanging from what was once an entirely acceptable, if not handsome face. As his body had enlarged, his penis had gone in the opposite direction, now like a timid tortoise's head peeking out from under its shell. He couldn't even see it without looking in the mirror because his gut was so distended these days. He'd had the gym installed in the basement of the property but couldn't remember visiting it since it was first put in. Krystal used it every day though and if he were forced to admit it, she looked pretty sensational for her age, although he'd never tell the bitch. The sad truth was that as she had grown fitter, slimmer and more attractive, he'd become a fat, worthless and wholly unattractive sloth.

He hated her for that. He hated that she blamed him for all his business failures, hated her for the fact that she blamed him for never being able to produce children. Not that he'd ever wanted any; he despised children almost as much as he despised Krystal. If they'd ever managed to have children, they would probably have turned out just like their mother and he didn't need any more Krystals in the house, one was enough.

The truth had hit him this week, after the horrible fight with Krystal the other week that illustrated how meaningless his life had become. Even his friends at the golf club weren't really friends, more acquaintances who hung around him to see if they could siphon some more money out of him. Well, out of Krystal really. None of them had a clue that it wasn't his money they were leeching. In fact, he suddenly realized that he didn't have any real friends at all and he had a wife who was embarrassed by his very existence, let alone the personal hatred she felt for him on a daily basis.

He regretted having signed a prenup agreement when he married Krystal but he'd never envisaged his life as it was now. He knew, of course, that she had all the power and he'd be left penniless, an embarrassment to his so-called friends and his soon to be ex-neighbors. He had enjoyed his time on earth, well, except for maybe the last ten years, but without any money, he couldn't visualize any kind of future for himself.

It was good while it lasted...

In the alcove where his Bang & Olufsen minimalist stereo sat anonymously waiting instruction, Steiner ran his hand down a case of CDs. His fingers stopped at a particular favorite of his, Delibes' Lakmé. Inserting the disc into the machine, he pressed 'play' and increased the volume on the amplifier to the maximum level. The vast entrance hall filled with Delibes' classical masterpiece, rebounding off the domed ceiling, a cacophony of female soprano voices filling the house.

He'd placed the stepladder in the center of the entrance foyer, below the chandelier that dominated the soaring vaulted ceiling. Prior to doing so, he'd rolled out a blue vinyl tarpaulin that he'd found in the garage, that now lay across the width of the floor, the stepladder deliberately centered on it. He'd climbed to the top step of the ladder and fastened the rope to the central pole of the light fitting, checked for firmness in his knot and made a noose at the other end of the rope.

Standing naked on the penultimate rung of the ladder, he slowly and methodically placed the noose around his neck.

"I suppose this is it, Emerson. An end to your pain and everyone else's," he whispered to himself.

For about forty seconds, he just stood there at the top of the ladder, his nudity grotesque, with the rough but sturdy rope tied loosely around his neck.

Time to bow out...

He kicked the ladder away and as it clattered noisily to the ground, he felt the rope tighten as his bloated mass pulled down hard on the chandelier above. He felt immediate pressure on his thyroid cartilage and a screaming sense of hissing and ringing in his ears and brain, caused by his jugular veins being squeezed and partially closed. The compression to his larynx and trachea resulted in his tongue being crudely extended from his gaping mouth and his eyes strained to escape their sockets, like peas popping from their pods.

He was confused now and his vision was partially occluded, as if he was staring into the sun. His face had changed from tanned to an angry purple color as he clawed at the rope, kicking his legs, causing the noose to become tighter and increase the venous pressure. He felt a hardening in his penis, something he'd not felt for many years and his sphincter began to lose muscle control, the floor spared from his involuntary bowel movement by the tarp below.

For the first time in his life, he realized that he'd made a terrible mistake and as he hung helpless, swinging in the silent foyer, kicking his feet and clawing at the noose, not even able to scream, an intense fear took a hold on him. For several minutes, he thrashed violently at the end of the rope while Delibes' Flower Duet exploded from the stereo, drowning out his futile attempts to scream, until a prolonged lack of blood supply to his brain induced cerebral asphyxiation and then finally, coma.

Without anyone noticing, without farewell, fanfare or shedded tear, and with Lakmé's hypnotic tragedy ringing in his ears, Emerson Steiner departed the world as naked as the day he'd arrived.

Chapter 38

I sat in Central Park, having found my favorite bench next to the Imagine Mosaic that had just recently been installed. It was dedicated to the late and great John Lennon, in memory of his life after he had been viciously murdered almost five years ago to the day. He was shot dead just across from this very spot outside the Dakota Apartments Building where John and Yoko had lived, where Yoko still lived. It had been unveiled on October 9th, the day when Lennon would have turned forty-five years old.

As I breathed in the frosty air, I leaned over and opened my briefcase, spying the pastrami sandwich, desperate to be eaten, that sat wedged in one corner of the case. As I unwrapped it and savored it's gloriously and uniquely Jewish taste, I picked out an envelope from my case that had arrived in my morning mail but that I hadn't yet had a chance to open.

A small throng of people sat gathered around a young man playing an acoustic guitar and singing a classic Lennon song on this bitterly cold day. Since the Imagine Mosaic had been unveiled, this little piece of Strawberry Fields had drawn an endless band of performers and visitors alike, all of them hoping to breathe in some of the magic that Lennon left behind in this shrine to the boy from Liverpool. It was almost December and it was New York cold, everyone wrapped up from the chill of the city. I looked over and realized that the singer's hands were blue from the frigidity as his fingers bravely and numbly attempted to find the chords for the song...

Imagine there's no heaven

It's easy if you try...

The song had become synonymous with peace. Although he'd written it fourteen years prior to his death, I couldn't help thinking that

John Lennon had known something more than the rest of us and left this song for us all to ponder, an anthem to peace in the world. Even in the freezing temperatures of this afternoon, as I munched hungrily on the hot pastrami sandwich, the simplicity of his words and their meaning bored into everyone who sat listening in this little piece of heaven…

I hope someday you'll join us

And the world will be as one…

I once again glanced at the envelope I held in my hands and could see that it must have been caught up in the frantic Christmas mail season, as it was postmarked two weeks ago from Jensen Beach. As my gloved hands tried valiantly to open the envelope, I realized it was futile and simply tore it open with my teeth. I prized out the contents and discovered that it was a letter from Talbot and he'd enclosed a number of photos with it.

The letter read:

Dearest Jake,

So sorry you couldn't be here for the big unveiling! I had to take some photos and send them to you just to show you how it went down. I wished I'd had a video camera but this will have to do for now until you get back here again. We rounded up as many people as we could, who would keep the secret and be able to make it on the night of the big event.

The Cantrells were all there, except Autumn, she's at college right now, Tara came (you remember her?), Cheyenne also and I don't think you've met Perryman's new best friend, Officer Sofia Brunson from the SPPD? Krystal Steiner hosted it at her home and of course, as you know, she put up most of the money for the work to be done.

Anyway, we all crouched in the darkness of her garage, the Woody hidden under an enormous blue tarpaulin while Krystal made a call from her house to Perryman's guest cottage, asking if he could come up the driveway and give her a hand with something in the garage. So anyway, he comes up to the garage and the roller door is down in the closed position. He'd assumed it would be open with Krystal inside so he keyed in the code on the side panel and waited for the door to rise. When it did, we all jumped out from the shadows and surprised him. He was stunned into silence, he had no idea what it was all about!

Then Krystal said, "Vaughn, we've been waiting for you to get fully recovered so that we can give you a little something to lift your spirits!"

And with that, she yanked off the tarp that had been hiding the Woody and there it sat, gleaming like it had just rolled off the production line in 1950! You should have seen the look on his face! He was speechless, tears streamed down his face, and then he just fell to his knees not knowing what to say, not even able to comprehend what had happened. I have never seen that boy lost for words in my life, if only I'd had a video camera!

Anyway, take a peek at the photos I've enclosed and they'll give you some idea of the emotions and pure happiness of that fantastic evening.

Come and see your friends soon, Jakey boy!

Your buddy,

Talbot.

PS. Summer asked after you too. But if I'm not mistaken, I think she has the hots for you so be careful, fella!

I stared at the photos. He was right, the Woody was immaculate, and whoever had done the restoration on it was a genius. It really did look like a brand new vehicle and Perryman's face was filled with complete and utter awe in just about every shot. The Sodium Green color which was apparently the original paint shade, was now repainted to a finish probably far better than it had been back in 1950. It was quite stunning.

I wasn't sure how much our little group had raised to go towards the cost of the work but looking at the Woody now, I could see that Krystal Steiner had probably paid for most of it out of her own pocket. She was a class act and had more than a passing fondness for our boy, Perryman. I'd heard during the last week about the strange suicide of Emerson Steiner and I was still stunned by the entire story. Although having met his wife Krystal, it was easy to see that Emerson was punching above his weight, the man was clearly out of his league with the delightful Mrs. Steiner. Still strange though, to make a big production out of his suicide. Seemed like the man was making a statement.

As I continued to look through Talbot's photographs, I could feel myself smiling at the thought of what had gone on that evening and the joy that I would have seen on my friend's face if I'd been able to attend. Vaughn deserved a lift in his life after what had happened to him back in the Summer. And it still incensed me that no one had been brought to justice for the malicious attack on him.

But as I put down the photos and looked over once more at our resident musician next to the memorial, I realized he was playing what would become a particularly important and pertinent song, "Grow Old With Me", the last but sadly unfinished song that Lennon would ever write before his death. It wasn't a song well-known by most of the people in this world but to those that gathered around this lone musician today, the words came freely to them as they sang along with him…

Grow old along with me

The best is yet to be

When our time has come

We will be as one…

I thought hard about Talbot's addendum at the end of his letter. I would need to tread very carefully.

Chapter 39

A thousand miles away, as Jake sat in the bitter cold of New York's Central Park, Talbot sat in his air-conditioned office in Jensen Beach, thankful for the coolness as he relaxed back in his chair, staring out at the glistening ocean beyond his window.

His office was a converted 1920s single story home that was situated on Indian River Drive, a couple of hundred yards from Jensen Beach town. Its owners had removed all of the inner walls and made two offices from the space left with a small reception desk between them and a kitchen and bathroom at the rear of the property. It was painted a bright yellow with white trim and had a small white picket fence surrounding it. Talbot shared the building with another attorney and because the owners had been close friends of Talbot's parents, he paid only a peppercorn rent for this perfect idyllic 'home from home' office.

Talbot mulled over recent events which were more than a little unusual in a place like this. The most crime that went on in any of the local towns was maybe a stolen car or some late night drunkenness after the bars had closed. But Emerson Steiner's death had been a huge shock to the residents in the Sewall's Point neighborhood. There had never been a suicide in the town before and Talbot guessed that, based on the number of families who lived there who relied often on a wife's family wealth, it might not be the last.

The letter he'd received this morning had shocked him. It was one of extraordinary generosity but tinged with utter sadness. He still didn't quite know how to deal with it or even how to deliver the news. Clearly, he'd need to talk to Perryman today but he wasn't sure how the man would receive this latest development.

He picked up the letter from Krystal Steiner and reread it once more.

Dear Mr. Talbot,

As you know, I have always been very happy with the various property transactions that you have dealt with on my behalf. I see you as more than just our family attorney, in fact, I see you as a trusted family friend and confidante.

Emerson's death has come as a complete shock to me, to our entire family. Although he and I have had our differences, and for the past few years have lived what you might call, separate lives, he was my husband and I had never expected him to take his own life. I had planned on divorcing him, yes, but even though I threatened to leave him penniless, it was never something that I would do in reality.

Emerson was a flawed man in many ways but he was more a fool to be taken advantage of than a man who sought to wreak havoc on others. He left a note in my bedroom. In it, he admitted responsibility for having Vaughn attacked and beaten. It was another of his stupid decisions, one designed to hurt me in the most direct method possible. His guilt fairly quickly got the better of him and not seeing any way out of the situation, he decided to take his own life.

I can't stay in Sewall's Point now as the memory of what has happened will never leave. I can't abide the thought that I will be talked about behind my back by all the gossips either; I'll become a sad old laughing stock of a widow.

Therefore, for the foreseeable future, I have decided to move to Europe and start a fresh life for myself. I am extremely fortunate in that money has never been an obstacle in my life so making the transition will be relatively easy and painless for me. For the immediate future, I will spend my summers in London and my winters at Lake Como and I have included those addresses with this letter so that you are able to contact me at any time. There are of course telephones in both homes and the numbers are noted.

In the interim, my family has urged me to sell the Sewall's Point home on River Road as it will no longer be used, for now or in the future. But I have decided against their advice on this occasion and have made a decision which I think will bring some finality to the last few weeks and make reparations to our patient still living in our guest cottage.

Therefore, as my attorney, I ask you to transfer the title of the entire property to Vaughn for one dollar. He may do with it as he wishes, live in it, sell it or give it to charity. He may wonder how he could manage to run such a large estate but I have hopefully taken care of that also. I have deposited $500,000 in an account bearing his name and those funds should be used to upkeep the home and pay for his living expenses for as long as he chooses to stay there.

By the time you read this note, I will already be on a Pan American flight to London, stopping briefly before I continue my journey on to Italy. I must therefore ask you to deliver this news to Vaughn, along with my everlasting love and affection for him.

Yours,

Krystal Steiner.

Talbot was still having trouble absorbing the contents of the letter. It was an extraordinary act of generosity on Krystal's part and it was clear to see how much she adored Perryman. The question for Talbot was whether he should share the letter with Perryman or simply tell him that he had received an unexpected windfall. He wasn't certain how Perryman would handle knowing that Emerson Steiner had been responsible for his injuries.

"The evil that men do lives after them; the good is oft interred with their bones."

He decided to call Jake and get his thoughts on the letter.

Lifting the phone from its cradle, he called Jake's firm and asked to be connected with him.

"Hey Talbot, good to know you still care about me!" said Jake.

"That's your problem Delaney, you're so friggin' needy!" he laughed.

"Brevity is the soul of wit," Jake replied, quickly clutching for a Bard-like response.

"Bravo, Jake, bravo, that was a fine riposte but I really need to talk to you about something that's bothering me."

"Okay… tell me what's on your mind," Jake replied, realizing quickly that his friend was in a serious mood.

"I received a letter today from Krystal Steiner. I won't read it to you as it's quite long so I'll cut to the chase."

"Okay, let me have it…"

"Emerson Steiner took his life out of guilt from the fact that he'd paid to have Perryman beaten up."

"I think I guessed that, although I'm still in shock."

"Krystal cannot live with that fact and has decided to move to Europe."

"Okay…"

"But here's the icing on the cake. She has asked me to transfer title of the River Road property to Perryman and has made $500,000 available to him to upkeep the house and I guess, himself too."

"What!!"

"I know, I thought the same thing when I read the letter," said Talbot.

"Wow Talb, it's all a big shock and I'm stunned by the news but you said you needed my help. What's the problem that I'm not yet seeing?"

"Emerson Steiner left a suicide note admitting guilt. Krystal wrote about it in the letter. My concern is, should I tell Perryman the real reason he's inheriting or do I just say that Krystal wanted to show her generosity for all he'd done for her?"

"There is only one answer, Talbot, and I think you already know what it is. If it was you or I that had been the victim and then been the grateful recipient of a windfall like this, wouldn't we want to know the real reason why? I certainly would."

"You're right, Jake, of course. I just don't want it to set Perryman back psychologically because he's making a fantastic recovery, that's all."

"Make the call, Talbot, and don't forget you're going to be seeing my sorry ass very soon! Later, man!"

Talbot put the phone back in its cradle and thought for a moment. Well, he definitely couldn't tell Perryman the story over the phone, he'd need to meet up with him and tell him face to face. And sooner rather than later.

He picked up the telephone again and dialed Perryman's number on the rotary dialer.

A voice answered and Talbot realized he'd reached Perryman's answering system.

"Perryman here, Vaughn Toulouse to his friends! Leave a message; I'll get right back to ya! Surf's up, dudes!"

Talbot chuckled at his friend's own unique and childlike sense of wit but at the beep, he did as instructed.

"Perryman, it's me, Talbot. I need to come and see you and impart some news I've just received this morning. I'll be at your cottage at eight tonight but don't worry, it's not bad news, my friend, in fact it might be the best news you've ever had…"

Chapter 40

A week later, Summer left the driveway of the Cantrell family home and navigated her way down the winding road of Skyline Drive. Turning left on to Main Street, she passed quickly through the town of Jensen Beach, the town itself not being more than five hundred yards long, comprising two strips of buildings that housed restaurants and art studios in the main.

At the traffic signal, she waited patiently, and gazed out at the water's edge, her mind in thoughtful mode. When the light changed to green, she turned right and slowly made her way along Indian River Drive, wary of the 25mph speed limit that was a veritable source of income in speeding tickets for the town's police force.

After the road became Sewall's Point Road, she waited at the traffic signal before continuing into Sewall's Point, taking a right at Hillcrest Drive and up the hill onto River Road. She located the Steiner home and pulled the Bronco in next to Perryman's Woody. Perryman must have heard the loud guttural noise from the V8 because no sooner had she jumped down from the truck than his cottage door opened and he was scurrying out to meet her, his arms waving wildly.

"Summer! Look at you in your Bronco! Man, you're a sight for these sore old eyes!" he roared.

He wrapped his Popeye-like arms around her, lifting her in the air and spinning her around like a rag doll, planting kiss after kiss on the top of her head.

"Hey Perryman, you're looking good yourself! I hope I'm not interrupting anything?" she said.

"Ain't nothing I wouldn't interrupt to see either of the Cantrell babes!" he responded, "You can have any moment of my time at any hour of the day, because you're officially royalty in Perryman's book!"

He took her by the hand and led her excitedly into the cottage, instructing her to make herself at home.

"As your mama would say, mi casa, su casa!" he chortled, "Now what can I get Princess Summer to drink? I've got Coke, Sprite, Ice Tea, Orangina, you name it girl, whatever you like."

"Sounds perfect, Vaughn, I'll take a Coke, if that's okay?" she replied.

She sat down on Perryman's tired old sofa, the backs of her thighs chafing on the coarse but threadbare material. As with any other day in South Florida, she was dressed for the weather; cut-off jean shorts, thin white t-shirt and flip flops.

The cottage was homely, Perryman having furnished it with things he'd either been given or found discarded at the side of the road. All the furniture had a feeling that it was on its fourth or fifth go around but this was a man who was immaculately clean and tidy, something that didn't necessarily sit comfortably with his outwardly surfer boy persona. But much of life for Perryman thus far, had been a vital but necessary act for him, as she had secretly already guessed.

"So I heard your good news. Why are you still living down here in the guest cottage? Are you going to move into the main house? Do you need a hand? Or are you going to sell it after all?" she asked, her questions coming at him like a machine gun.

"Whoa, princess! One question at a time, you know this simple brain of mine can't answer multiple questions!" he laughed, offering her the tumbler of Coke, brimming with ice.

"Sorry! It's just that it was the biggest story to hit the news around her and I'm so excited for you," she said apologetically, "But how are you now, how do you feel about everything? It must have been a shock but also an amazing windfall?"

"You want the truth?" he said, suddenly a little more somber than he'd been seconds earlier, "I didn't appreciate Emerson having those thugs set upon me, it's taken a long time for me to recover and I'm still achin' but on the other hand, if he thought Krystal was messin' around with other guys, me being one of them, well, then I can kinda understand how he must've been mad about it"

"Yeah, but organizing a hit on you? That's kind of overkill, don't you think? Couldn't he have just filed for divorce like most sane people do?" Summer replied.

"Ain't no one can predict what's in a man's head when he feels threatened, Summer. I guess it was too much for him to take, even though there ain't been nothin' going on!" he said, "The thing is, and I think I can tell you but not many people know this, but I'm kind of a gay man, Summer. Girls don't really interest me so that's what's so crazy about the whole darned thing anyway."

"Err… hate to tell you this, Vaughn, but me and Autumn already knew. Even my mom knows. We girls have a certain way of knowing when a man is into girls or not," she replied.

"Oh, don't get me wrong, I love girls! Just not in the way that most boys do. Heck, I don't even know if I'm gay or whadda they call it now? Asexual?" Perryman's down home southern accent drawing the word out to its fullest extent.

"You're asexual?" she asked, "Do you really think so? What about your relationship with Sofia, how does that work?"

"Gettin' a little personal, princess?" he said, winking at her.

"Oh God, I'm sorry, I didn't mean to overstep the mark, that was dumb of me, I'm so sorry!" she exclaimed, her cheeks reddening when she realized her error.

"No worries, Summer, we ain't got nothing to hide anymores anyway. Be honest? We don't know what we've got, all we know is that we love being with each other but that's as much as I can tell you right now!" he said.

"But putting that to one side," he continued, "What do I owe the pleasure of a visit from my favorite girl today? It's gotta be something important," he said, the word 'important' coming out as *impotent.*

"Oh it's nothing serious," she replied, "I heard that you guys were maybe planning on spending Christmas and New Year here, well not here in the guest cottage, but up at the main house?"

"Your ears must've been burnin' girl, 'cause there are plans afoot, as Talbot would say!" he responded, doubling up at his own joke, "The plan is to move in before Christmas Eve and for the boys to come and stay all the way through til New Year's Day."

"The boys? You mean Jake and Talbot?" she asked.

"I do, Summer, I do mean those scurrilous vagabonds. Ha, there I go again, using Talbot's long words!" he laughed, "But what's your interest, Summer? Do I sense that you might have a little fondness in your heart for a certain Mr. Jake Delaney?" he asked, sensing her sudden discomfort.

"Can I tell you a secret?" she asked, now worried that the cat might be out of the bag, "Since Autumn left for college, I can't even talk to her about it except when she's got change for the dorm phone and even then there's a line of people waiting to use it!"

"You can tell me anything, Summer, your secret's safe with your Uncle Vaughn," he replied, "C'mon, spill the beans."

"Well… I, well you're on the right track. Ever since I met Jake on Talbot's boat, I've been in love with him, but I can't tell him, of course. I mean, what would he think of a dumb seventeen-year-old girl feeling that way about him?" she asked.

"You're not a dumb seventeen-year-old girl, Summer. What you are is a bright, lovely and beautiful young woman who most boys would give their eye teeth to date. Do I think he's too old for you? Maybe. But you know, as we get older, the age difference starts to mean less and it's more about where our hearts take us that's important."

"Thank you for not laughing at me, Vaughn, it feels so good just to be able to talk about it with someone. It's like a big weight has been lifted from my shoulders," she said.

"Let me tell you this, princess, I've seen many a girl fall in love with someone they maybe shouldn't oughta, but most of them girls had looks that didn't match their age. You're different, you look all grown up but your mind is way ahead of your years so believe me when I say I've got your back," he said.

"Thank you, Vaughn, you have no idea what that means to me."

"So what I'm guessin' now is that you want to know what's happenin' during the Christmas festivities at Casa Perryman and I suppose you want to know if you're invited?" he asked, winking at her.

"How did you know?" she said, grinning at her newly discovered confidante.

"Just a wild guess Miss Summer, but I can tell you this, if you're not at the parties, Uncle Vaughn would be très miserable!" he said, "Come on, let's take a walk up to the house and I'll show you around."

Chapter 41

Summer had called me at work and said that she'd unfortunately not been able to raise the money to buy a plane ticket to come to New York in the run-up to Christmas. My feelings switched back and forward on this piece of news. On the one hand, I was more than a little concerned about having a seventeen-year-old girl staying with me and I'm not even sure she'd told her mom about that part of the trip. On the other hand, I was incredibly disappointed that she wouldn't be coming. I'd put my mind in a mature state, telling myself that I would play the gracious host and show her the city and that she'd be comfortable sleeping on the sofa.

But that other niggling problem still remained for me. Here I was, a man looking at the next milestone in life of reaching a quarter century in years, having fallen for a girl who wasn't yet out of high school. She wasn't just beautiful though. If it was only that, I could forgive myself for being blinded purely by her looks. But Summer had something much more than that, she had an intellect and an intelligence that far surpassed her tender age. She was a woman in a girl's body and I needed to remind myself of that. Every day actually, unless I wanted to get arrested.

The other big news was what had been going on at the Steiner house, which by all accounts was apparently now the Perryman house from what Talbot had told me. I hadn't yet managed to speak to Perryman but I assumed he must be elated with his own good fortune, even if he'd almost died achieving it.

And suicide in Sewall's Point? I go away for five minutes and all hell breaks loose…

"Mr. Delaney, Jake?" whispered our new PA, "Do you have time to see Arthur? He's waiting in his office for you."

"No problem, Margaux, I'll be right there," I replied.

Margaux Charrette was not the imagined picture that her name might imply. Margaux was more Auntie Agnes than French provocateur. She barely grazed five feet in height, wore her hair in a gray bun, and the word 'dowdy' would be a compliment to describe her appearance. The thing about Margaux, unlike most of the piranha women who work in the firm, is that she's lovely, quite lovely in fact. She is no vision of beauty but each morning when I see her beaming face, it makes my day. I love Margaux.

"Arthur, you wanted to see me?" I asked, as I stood in front of his desk waiting for him to look up.

"Sit down, Jake," he commanded.

Oh fuck, what have I done? Does he know about Charlotte and the coffee machine?

"We have a problem, Jake," he continued.

He knows, he fucking knows!

"With what, sir, what's wrong?" I asked trying to stem the beads of sweat that had made an unwelcome entrance across my entire body.

"This tort you've been working on, the one against the tobacco company," he said.

It was Sunday, Arthur, it was Charlotte's fault; I was just an innocent bystander!

"The case is not going to court," said Arthur.

I was staggered. This was the biggest case that the firm had ever taken on. It had the possibilities of ending in a bumper payday for the firm, maybe with bonuses for the grunts who'd been doing all the legwork. The downside of the lawsuit is that we had invested so much in it financially and in man-hours, that there was a chance that it could bankrupt us. Personally, I didn't believe that, but there had been office whispers.

"W..wh..why not? What's happened? How did we fail? I can't believe it!" I replied, beads of sweat now trickling down beneath my shirt collar, my chest perspiration already beginning to soak through my shirt.

It's not going to court…" continued Arthur.

Here it comes, the end of Jake Delaney's short-lived career in law…

"It's not going to court," he repeated, "Because the tobacco company settled out of court!" yelled Arthur, "We won, Jake, we goddamned beat the bastards!"

I cannot describe the relief that passed through my entire body when I realized that: one, Arthur had no clue about my coming of age with Charlotte, and two, I still had a job.

"Do you have any idea what this means, Jake?"

I still have a job?

"No sir, but I am supremely happy that all our work has not been in vain," I replied.

"What it means, dear boy, is that you're going to receive a bonus for all the endless hours you put into the project. A pretty nice bonus too."

He reached into one of his desk drawers and extracted an envelope.

"This is for you, Jake, with my deepest gratitude."

"Thank you, sir," I replied, slipping my finger beneath the flap to open it.

"No, no, Jake, not now, put that in your pocket and open it later. I have something else to show you, follow me."

Arthur doesn't need to mix with the hoi polloi when he navigates his way between floors in the building. One of his specific requests when his own office was built, was that he had his own personal and very private elevator installed.

I followed the man into the elevator and waited as we made a rapid descent.

When the doors hissed open, I saw that we were in the parking garage.

"You've got me confused, Arthur, did we come down too many floors?" I asked.

"Follow me boy, this way," he commanded, his octogenarian frame propelling him forward at a speed I'd not seen before in the man.

I had no idea where we were going but continued to follow, barely able to keep up with him. Suddenly, he stopped, put his hand in his pocket to retrieve something and tossed it towards me. I played soccer at school because I was no baseball player but I still managed to catch the thing.

"I'm confused, what's this?" I asked, staring at the keys he'd thrown at me, "Do you need me to drive you someplace?"

"No, they're yours, Jake," he replied, "And so is this now," he continued, pointing at what looked like a brand new Porsche 959 Convertible sitting smoldering in its parking spot.

"Are you serious?" I asked, incredulous to what had just happened.

"Serious as a heart attack, Jake, you earned it, boy!" he laughed, amused at his own joke.

I was, possibly for the first time in my life, speechless. I was at a complete loss for words. My mouth was moving but nothing came out.

"And one more thing, Jake, I heard about your adventure in the kitchen," he said.

O Lord, he knows, I am so fucked...

"Watch out for Charlotte," he continued, "She can be a bit of a cunt."

How does he even know that word?

I looked on, marveling at the man as he spun on his Edward Green heels and made rapid progress back to his elevator. And then I looked back at the black beauty that sat waiting for me.

Pinch me, somebody, I really should wake up now...

I pressed the button on the remote key fob and the car's flashers signaled that it was now unlocked. I climbed in, turned the key and listened to the roar of the engine, this Siren from Stuttgart willing me to taste her wares.

In the excitement of what had just happened, I had completely forgotten about the envelope I'd stuffed in my pocket that Arthur had given me in his office. I retrieved it and tore open the flap. Inside, was a check, but not just any check. This was made payable to one Jake Delaney in the sum of $50,000!

This was going to be a Christmas to remember...

Chapter 42

Sailfish Point is a closely guarded and exclusive enclave on Florida's Treasure Coast. It is almost its own island, a peninsula sitting out in the Atlantic Ocean and reachable only by a single narrow winding road called MacArthur Boulevard, one road in, one road out. To say it's an enclave is a little bit of an understatement. Sailfish Point is home to some of the very wealthiest families in the country, a genuine Billionaires Row in the ocean.

The guards at the gated entrance are armed and deal with unfamiliar visitors as unwelcome irritants. There is a certain military feeling in their manner which is inherently designed to keep out the ne'er-do-wells and interlopers. At the heart of the compound is a magnificent, finely manicured, Jack Nicklaus designed championship golf course, its signature 18th hole finishing on a green just steps from the ocean. If ever there was a paradise lost, this is a veritable paradise found.

Sailfish Point didn't begin life as a playground for the über-wealthy. It was originally owned by two brothers, Bill and Ben McCoy and its name in 1915 was actually The Blue Lagoon of the Coral Strand. The McCoys became rumrunners, almost pirates in reality, but their rum became known for being just about the best you could find, thereby coining the phrase, 'The Real McCoy'.

On MacArthur Boulevard, just before arriving at the entrance to Sailfish Point, a House of Refuge still stands, once a haven for shipwrecked sailors and now home to a museum. In fact, pirates and sunken treasure form much of the history of the Treasure Coast, itself taking its name from the unfortunate Spanish galleons that sank off its treacherous coast, spilling their treasures of gold, silver and jewels to the bottom of the ocean.

Tara Fitzgerald's family home is situated at the very tip of Sailfish Point, a panoramic view from every window in the exotically designed house. The outer tip of the 'island' curves from the east to the west and the Fitzgeralds had designed their home to curve with the land, giving the unique experience of seeing the sun rise in the east wing and the sun setting in the west.

The entire house, which sits high on the end of the peninsula, was designed and built to a set of plans which incorporated curved walls and windows, and spectacular domed ceilings. Sixteen bedrooms, twenty-two bathrooms and three kitchens illustrate the sheer size of the building. It is more akin to a hotel than a family home.

On arrival at the automated gates, the journey up a snaking drive through an avenue of ancient oaks dripping with Spanish Moss, reveals an ethereal white and green glass obelisk rising ominously from the ground as you ascend the driveway and draw near. If Stanley Kubrick had ever built a home that captured his own Space Odyssey, this was it.

"Tara, how did everything go on your trip to New York?" asked Heath Fitzgerald.

Tara was lounging on the vast sundeck that formed a twelve thousand square feet semi-circle at the rear of the house. The pool, which although almost twice the size of an Olympic pool, was an abstract set of rounded pools that combined to make a single indefinable shape, its curving edges linked by footbridges that crossed from pool to pool.

"It was wonderful, Daddy, I had the time of my life as well as hosting your business partners. The boat is so perfect to entertain on and I didn't even have to travel to go home to sleep," said Tara.

"Well, my darling, I thank you for taking care of that for me. I'm afraid that at my time in life, I can't stomach the confines and hubbub of the city so I'm grateful for what you do now in my absence," her father replied, "But I can see from the receipts that arrived on my desk this morning that you were no stranger to the stores on Fifth Avenue."

“Daddy! You know it can’t be all business and no pleasure! There are far too many distractions and temptations in Manhattan, surely you don’t want to deprive me some of life’s pleasures?” she said, a smile forming that showed her intensely white and genetically benefitted teeth.

“I don’t, you know that and I’m only teasing! But tell me, how do you manage to go through $35,000 in one week?”

“Well, there’s a Chanel store there, a Gucci, a Louis Vuitton, a Cartier…”

“I know that, darling girl, but it doesn’t mean you have to financially support all of them!” he chortled, “Anyway, aside from that, I hope you managed to find time to have some fun while you were there?”

“I did,” she said.

“That’s it? That’s all you’re going to tell me?” said Heath.

“I’m sorry, Daddy, I didn’t mean to be coy but yes, I had a lovely time. I had dinner with a very nice man too,” she replied, “He lives in the city although he went to college here in Florida.”

“Does the boy have a name, or should I keep guessing?”

“His name is Jake, Daddy, Jake Delaney, and I don’t know but I’m pretty smitten with him, I guess,” said Tara.

“Jake Delaney, huh?” he replied, his face now showing a little concern for his daughter’s welfare, “Should I have your brother take a closer look at him for you, see what he’s all about?”

“Oh Daddy, don’t be so silly, what on earth would Guy do, run him through the CIA?” she laughed, “Guy is my brother, not my personal secret service agent!”

“Don’t think that there isn’t a line of gold-diggers out there, Tara, who would do anything to marry into this family. You know that my only thought is for your own protection. I don’t want to spoil your fun, but the Fitzgerald empire is almost as big as that of our neighbors, the Walgreens, next door."

"To be honest, I don't even know if he has the same feelings towards me, I haven't known him long and we've really only met on a couple of occasions," she responded, "Although I'm hoping to see him again during the Christmas holidays."

"Well, have him come over for lunch or dinner, let me have a closer look at your new paramour!" said Heath.

"I don't think so, Daddy, not yet anyway. You and Guy would be all over him, picking him apart!" she laughed.

"As you will, my dear, but I think if you become serious, it might be prudent for me to meet him and gauge the character of the boy," he replied, "Meanwhile, I'll leave you in peace to take in some more of this glorious winter sunshine."

As her father strode away, Tara reclined the chair to an almost horizontal position. The tiny triangle of white material that barely covered her pubic area, only aided in showing off her exquisitely toned body that seemed to glimmer even more brightly in the December sun. The turquoise of the Atlantic stretched out before her, an occasional dolphin slowly arcing up from the water to greet its audience. As she laid back, her lips freshly balmed with a cherry salve, she smiled contentedly and pondered the situation.

I don't know if Jake's interest in me is mutual, but Christmas will be a wonderful opportunity to lay my claim to him...

Chapter 43

Not two miles away, in a house that was not quite the movie star house in which Tara lived, "Song To The Siren" played gently on Summer's stereo, its melancholy message sung hauntingly by This Mortal Coil's Elizabeth Fraser. It was only a week until Christmas and Summer was incredibly excited as was the whole Cantrell family to have been invited to Perryman's for a Christmas Eve party in his new abode on the water in Sewall's Point.

"I love that!" said a voice from outside her bedroom door, "What's that song and who's singing?" said Reyna as she peeked into the room.

"I love it too, Mom, it's one of my favorite songs right now. The singer is Elizabeth Fraser. She's English but the song was written by an American, Tim Buckley. I think you know him, right?" Summer replied.

"Oh yes, of course. Now I recognize it. He was such a talented man but died too young. I think he was only twenty-eight when he died from an overdose."

"Oh Mom, now that makes the song even sadder!" said Summer.

"Well, I don't want that so let's change the subject. What are you doing today, anything I can help with?" asked Reyna.

Recently, since Autumn had left for college, Summer had noticed that her mom was spending a lot more of her time attending to Summer's needs. She guessed that her mother was feeling a little unnecessary, needing to be needed. She would have to include her mom in more things and she had an idea.

"Well… you know we're going to Perryman's party on Christmas Eve? I've decided that I can't live my life in Daisy Dukes and t-shirts for the rest of my life so I wanted to get something special for the party. Would you mind helping me?" she asked her mother.

"That's a mama's job! Of course I want to help, I'd love to. We can make a day of it, just you and me shopping for the whole day together and we can get lunch too and of course, I need something to wear…." said Reyna.

"Okay, mama, we are *doing* it!" shrieked Summer, "How about tomorrow?"

"You're on, sweetheart, it's a date! Your Daddy is going to need to fend for himself for the day!" replied Reyna, "I'll leave you be for now and get some of my chores done," closing the door as she left.

Summer turned up the volume on her stereo to listen to the last part of the song…

Swim to me, swim to me, let me enfold you
Oh my heart, oh my heart is waiting to hold you…

"I want Jake to see me looking my very best on Christmas Eve, I want him to realize that I am a woman, and not a little girl. I know he loves me, I just need to light the way, sprinkle some clues in the snow…" she said to herself.

Chapter 44

Perryman's new inherited home was not quite at the level of Tara's but it was still palatial. The first floor housed a drawing room, formal dining room, kitchen, billiards room, gym, multiple guest bedrooms and bathrooms, as well as powder rooms and a vast entrance hall that had been the site of Emerson Steiner's untimely demise. The floor above was one enormous glassed lounge that spanned much of the width of the property, save for the twin master bedroom suites that occupied the two wings facing the water. It wasn't just palatial, it was sumptuous.

I'd driven the Porsche the thousand-mile trip from New York and enjoyed every moment of it. For much of the journey, I had to keep pinching myself that Jake Delaney owned this beauty. Actually, I had jaw ache from grinning so much. I must have looked like The Joker from Batman to everyone I passed on the I-95. I seemed to have come a long way in life and fairly quickly too. My good fortune was not something I had expected but it wasn't something I wanted to let go of either.

When I'd arrived and shown my buddies that I'd had my own little piece of good news, and was given the nod of approval, Perryman graciously made room in the six-car garage for my newly acquired boy toy.

After a chorus of high fives, hugs and boisterous and stupidly immature jokes, the three of us found ourselves seated amongst the many sofas and chairs that graced the upstairs sun lounge. The view from this enormous room was astounding, the sparkling, shimmering water of the St. Lucie Bay spreading out intoxicatingly before us. This was the world of the 'haves' and the 'have nots' and somehow Perryman had found himself on the right side of the coin.

"Well, it's not often that it's just the three of us together, just hanging out and chewing the fat, is it?" I said, "And Perryman, man, did you luck out, fella, this place is sensational!"

"I have to agree with you, Jake, but I'm still showin' the scars," said Perryman, "But you know what? I'm beginning to think that it was worth it although if it had been anyone else other than Krystal, I'm not so sure it would have turned out this way."

"Have you heard from her since she left for Europe?" asked Talbot.

"Actually, yeah, I have," Perryman replied, "She's living out at Lake Como now, wherever the fuck that is! But in all seriousness, she did write me a really sweet letter. I'm not gonna bore you with it but it was really emotional. I cried when I read it. For me, the good thing is that leaving me this house and the cash in the bank was no big deal for her financially, but emotionally, it was the only way she knew how to come to terms with it. She knew about my sexuality but she loved me so much, I know that now, and I'm happy it turned out okay."

"I tend to agree, it's a tragedy that turned into a nice positive," I said, "What about you Talb, what's happening in your life? I feel that we've lost contact recently since we've all had so many things going on."

"Same old, same old…" he replied, "But I'm feeling the need to find a mate!"

"Seriously?" I asked, "Do you really think anyone's gonna want you?"

Perryman broke up in shrieks of laughter as he stretched out on the sofa. "Talbot, everyone thinks you're the faggot in this group, not me!!" he said, unable to control his howls as he fell to the floor in hysterics.

"All the world's a stage, and all the men and women merely players. They have their exits and their entrances. And one man in his time plays many parts…" Talbot responded, just a little pissed that Perryman found the idea of him with a girl so amusing.

"Haha! Romeo, Romeo, wherefore art thou, Romeo? Hahahahaha!!" Perryman yelled, unstoppable now that he'd baited him.

Perryman's been spending way too much time with Talbot…

"You two, just stop! It's not fair anyway; I want to see Talbot with someone just as much as I'm amazed that you're with a woman now, Perryman!" I said, desperate to stop myself from descending into laughter from Perryman's delight at his own ruthless humor, "You've got to be honest, none of us saw that coming!"

"Okay, enough, change of subject," said Perryman, "How about you, Jake, what's happening in your love life?"

"It's all kind of complicated I suppose," I replied.

"Well, spit it out, fella, you know it's not gonna go any further than us three," Perryman said, suddenly aware that I had things in my head that I needed to share.

"Yes," chimed in Talbot, "We are nothing if not your sworn allies, Jake. You seem like you're carrying a heavy burden at the moment. You can confide in us. 'The better part of valor is discretion', I believe."

"It's been a strange year or two for me," I said, "I have had some very odd encounters with some extraordinary women, as I've told you."

"Well, we know about Charlotte, and Valeria and of course, the lovely Tara, but who else is in the frame, Jake?" asked Perryman, "Seems like you've been fucking anything with a pulse, or at least a recent one!"

"I know you're going to laugh if I tell you and then tell me I'm a jerk for even thinking about it so maybe it should remain a secret," I replied, "There's no future in it anyway, so it's a pointless notion to begin with."

At this, I think Perryman had an inkling of what was going on and drew himself close to me, more serious now, the laughter having quickly dissipated.

"Jake. I think I might know what's eating you," he said, "Would I be close if I said that it might have something to do with Summer?"

"Shall I compare thee to a sum…"

"Stop it, Talb, this is serious," said Perryman.

I was with my two best friends but with the realization that Perryman had deduced something from the situation, beads of sweat suddenly began to form on my forehead when I began to believe that he may not be the only one to have worked it out.

"Could be," I said, "I'm not saying definitely, but yes, definitely maybe," I replied.

"So what's the problem?" asked Perryman.

"She's seventeen, Vaughn! That's the fucking problem!" I yelled, surprising myself with my heated reaction to the question.

"Hey man, take a chill pill, it's cool, don't worry," he said, "Right now, yeah, age is an issue but it won't always be that way."

"I think Jake's problem right now," added Talbot, "Is one of perception. He doesn't want to be seen as a cradle snatcher, wouldn't you agree, Jake?"

"You nailed it, Talb, I just can't be seen as this supposedly grown-up New York lawyer falling for a teenage girl," I said, "It just looks so wrong. I look like such a dick."

"But Summer isn't a dumb teenager, Jake," said Perryman, "She's way ahead of her age in terms of her emotions and her thought process."

"I think I know that now, but however mature she is as a girl, no, as a woman almost, I need to keep a lid on things if I'm going to maintain any kind of respect around here," I replied

"I must confess, I have similar feelings too," said Talbot.

Talbot! What the fuck!

"Whaaaa!! You mean you've got the hots for Summer too?!!" shouted Perryman. "Am I the only man she's safe to be around?"

"No, you idiot! Not Summer!" Talbot said.

"Who then?" I asked, aware that Talbot was already becoming embarrassed at something.

"Autumn."

"Autumn?"

"Yes, Autumn, what is this, a fucking echo chamber?" yelled Talbot, displaying an unusually high level of emotion not usually seen in his perpetually calm demeanor.

"Hold on," I said, "You're telling me that you have a thing for Autumn? But how is that possible? She's at college so when have you even had a chance to see her?"

"It's not like that, nothing's happened and I'm not even sure what she thinks of me. She is only nineteen after all," he said, "But I have been in communication with her, we've been exchanging letters and occasionally we speak on the telephone when the dorm phone is not being used by a hundred other girls."

"Jeeeezzz!!" said Perryman.

This was all pretty big news to me. I'd been so caught up in my own little world that I hadn't given a thought to what Talbot had been hiding.

"Well, listen guys, we need to try and keep this under our hats because it's not something either Talbot or I want to be made public. We have the party tomorrow night and I think we should all be on our best behavior. Right?" I said, "Right Perryman?"

"If music be the food of love, play on…"

I knew, I just knew he'd say that...

Chapter 45

The following evening, the weather had decided to smile once again on the little haven of South Florida called Sewall's Point. It was a balmy, cool evening, the kind of night where the windows and doors could be flung open and there was no need for air conditioning. Perryman's new home stood majestically between a labyrinth of Royal Palms, each one enhanced by carefully placed and individually colored uplighters. It looked like a scene from a fairytale. For Perryman, it probably was.

"Who's in charge of the music tonight?" I asked to no one in particular.

"Talbot's got it covered, Jake, he's commandeered that Bang & Olufsen unit downstairs but it pipes music through the entire house so we're cool," replied Perryman. "But I'm finding out things I never knew existed, the longer I'm here."

As if by magic, a Bryan Adams song I knew well from a few months ago began to filter through the speakers mounted within the ceilings of the property…

Oh the way you held my hand

I knew that it was now or never

Those were the best days of my life…

In the driveway, a couple of sets of headlights indicated that some of the guests were beginning to arrive. I headed down the wide and curving stairway to see who was here. Talbot had clearly taken over as host of Perryman's new abode as he welcomed guests into the house, flinging his arms around them with his synonymous animated gestures, hugging them to within an inch of their lives.

I paused midway down the staircase to take a peek at who had already arrived. Reyna and Joe were the first through the doors but no Autumn or Summer. They were probably at the age where they didn't attend en masse as a family now, the girls preferring to arrive fashionably late as teenagers love to do now. Cheyenne followed the Cantrells into the house, her unique Native American style and enigmatic appeal instantly drawing people to her.

Cheyenne? I wonder if she has a last name? Smith, perhaps... or maybe she's like Madonna, or Prince or Bowie, only one name required...

I ambled down the remainder of the stairs and started to emulate Talbot's 'meet and greet' shtick, telling people I'd never met how pleased I was to meet them, when in fact I was really only looking for one guest who'd not yet arrived. I spotted Tara, who looked killer in a form-fitting one piece jumpsuit, her body seemingly sparkling in silver lamé, like a bauble that had fallen from Perryman's twenty-two foot Christmas tree that stood sentry in the entrance hall.

"Jake!" she called, gliding towards me, apparently without the need to move her feet.

"Tara," I said, "How are you? It seems like an age since I last saw you. I love your outfit!"

Actually, the last time I saw you, you weren't wearing that, in fact you weren't wearing much at all ...

"I'm fine, really good," she said, "But I have missed you, I've missed you a lot."

Eeek!

"Well, I'm here now, and so are you, can I buy you a drink?" I said, being suddenly over generous with Perryman's bar tab.

"I'd love that!" she replied, clearly happy to see me, "Can I have a screwdriver?"

Well, later maybe, but you know I'm not the driver, right?

“Come with me, lovely lady, your bar awaits you,” I said, guiding her up the gigantic stairway to the upper lounge where at least thirty or forty people were now gathered, swigging back Perryman’s generous hospitality.

I ordered Tara’s cocktail and a club soda for myself, wary that the night was still young and I wanted to be as sober as possible for as long as possible. We made small talk while Don Henley was belting it out on the stereo…

Well I'm a-runnin' down the road

Try'n to loosen my load

I've got seven women on my mind

Four that want to own me, two that want to stone me

One says she's a friend of mine…

I spotted Perryman over by the gargantuan glass doors of the lounge, which were opened out to the St. Lucie Bay, as he serenaded a gaggle of eager females who couldn’t get enough of him.

No chance there, girls, shit out of luck…

Perryman had changed a little since the goings-on of the last few months. He had always been pretty outgoing but now he was more gregarious in his personality as though a weight had been lifted from him. This evening, and bear in mind that the man is in shape, he was wearing flowing white bell bottom pants with a white silk shirt that was slashed open to his navel, his golden-tanned hairless chest on display for all to see.

Even his footwear had changed. I’m not a prolific authority on men’s shoes, preferring the ones that grace the female form but if I wasn’t mistaken, I think he was wearing a pair of electric blue Gucci loafers, replete with diamonds sewn into the velvet uppers. He was starting to remind me of a cross between Barry Gibb and Liberace. But it suited him and I kind of liked it.

Talbot was spinning a rare mix of music tonight, I think the racks containing the hundreds of CDs next to the B&O system had turned his mind. He was like a disc junkie, his selections veering wildly between Gary Moore and Doug E Fresh to Scritti Politti and Kool & The Gang, but from the way people were doing their mini dance moves while they chatted to one another, it seemed to be working out okay. Although Ashford & Simpson might be pushing it…

Tara had shimmied away from me after we'd exchanged pleasantries and in some ways I was relieved. It's not that Tara isn't incredibly beautiful and generally, she has men hardening as she passes by, if not from her appearance then definitely from her scent. It's just that although I felt a deep affection for her, I realized that she had possibly fallen for me and I didn't share reciprocal feelings. My heart wasn't in it I guess, even though she checked every other box on the list.

"I don't get it," said Talbot as he sidled up to me.

"Explain?" I said.

"It's…, well…, ...I, I just thought that all of the Cantrells were coming but I haven't seen either Autumn or Summer yet."

"What's the time, Talbot?" I asked.

"It's just past nine, why?" he replied.

"Don't you know anything about girls?" I asked.

"You've lost me, what do you mean?"

"I mean, that no self-respecting late-teens girl is going to be showing up at a party with mom and dad cramping their style," I replied, "They want to make an entrance and they preferably want it to be the last one of the evening, my naïve little friend!" I explained, wrapping my arm around his slumped shoulders.

"You're right, Jake, I hadn't really thought about that," he said, "What a klutz I am, why would Autumn ever be interested in me anyway? I must be stupid to think it's anything more than a friendship for her."

"Talbot. Don't you see? It's exactly what she likes about you, just the fact that you are you. You're a rare breed, my friend, you're articulate, knowledgeable, handsome in your own way and as well as being an outrageously fine chef, you have the manners of a prince," I replied, "It's not easy you know, just getting along on looks and charm alone!"

"Stop it," he said, now back to his usual chipper self, "I need to change up the music, get everybody a bit sexed up, I think..." he continued, sauntering off to the B&O.

I watched my gallant little friend disappear and Reyna caught my attention so I went to chat with her for a few minutes.

"And how is our lovely Mr. Delaney," she cooed.

"I've never been better, Reyna," I replied, "Work has been frantic but just lately, it seems to be paying off for me."

"Something is definitely making you happy, Jake, new lady in your life?"

"No, no, not like that, but I am going apartment hunting when I get back to New York, I think I've got to that stage where a shoebox isn't enough to live in!" I replied, "But how are you? How is life with Autumn now at college?"

"Joe copes better than I do, I guess. I miss her like crazy and I'm always aware that next August will see Summer leaving too so I'm going to get pretty lonely," she replied, "Maybe I should take a lover?"

I nearly spat my drink out when she said that...

"Are you serious?"

"Just kidding, Jake, really, only messing with you!" she said, winking at me as she strode away to mingle with the other guests.

As I turned to head towards the bar to grab myself another glass of wine, I noticed a set of headlights heading up the driveway outside. The unmistakable rumble of a Ford V8 told me exactly who was about to make an entrance. I refilled my glass and took a position at the far side of the staircase to watch as the Cantrell girls came through the entrance doors downstairs.

Madonna's 'Get Into The Groove' had just ended on the stereo and the familiar guitar sounds of Prince came screeching lethargically from the speakers…

I knew a girl named Nikki

I guess you could say she was a sex fiend

I met her in a hotel lobby

Masturbating with a magazine…

Oh Lord…

When I'd finished admonishing Talbot with my best evil stare, I looked over and saw Summer and Autumn stepping through the doorway.

I didn't immediately pay much attention to Autumn as my eyes were glued to Summer.

Wow!

This young girl I'd met only eighteen months or so ago, had undergone a dramatic but stunning change from a bashful teenager into a young woman. She was beautiful then but now she somehow had an enhanced confidence in herself, not arrogant, but definitely no longer a shy little girl.

She walked across the entrance foyer towards where Talbot was lining up his CDs. She wore a striking but fabulously simple black dress that hugged her figure and ended around six inches above the knee. Her shoulders were bare as were her tanned legs, her simple black pumps accentuating their length.

Her hair flowed naturally down her back, longer now than I'd remembered and for the first time, I was seeing her with just a hint of make-up. Nothing showy, just a bare highlight here and there but the effect was startling. And there, nestling on her golden chest, was the sea glass I'd given her six months earlier. She wasn't just a picture of beauty and elegance; she was one of God's divine creatures. The old maxim, 'Less Is More' came hurtling back to me.

I was keen to avoid Summer thinking that I'd been keeping an eye out for her arrival, even if that was a lot closer to the truth than I cared to admit. I headed out to the terrace that stretched across the rear of the second floor to catch a breather from what I'd just seen. It was such a perfect night, the air thin and fresh and the sound of the waves washing up ashore on Perryman's beach made me feel like I was in one of those epic James Bond movies. I was shaken by what I'd just seen downstairs and possibly, even a little stirred…

I saw Cheyenne making a beeline for me and raised my glass to her as she neared.

"Hello, the mysterious Mr. Delaney," she purred as she clinked her glass with mine, "Where have you been hiding all evening?"

"Not hiding, Cheyenne, just mingling and doing my best to maintain a sensible alcohol level," I replied, "But you and I have only met on a couple of occasions and although I feel I know you fairly well, I just realized I really don't know anything about you at all."

"Ergo, I must therefore be the mysterious one, Jake," she giggled, clearly having imbibed a little more than I had thus far in the evening.

"So tell me about yourself, I literally know nothing about you and I'm guessing my name has probably been painted black by my excellent but treacherous friend, Talbot," I said.

“Actually, Talbot only speaks in the highest terms about both you and Vaughn,” she replied, “You come with a highly prized and talented reputation.”

“Well, that’s kind of a relief, but come on, spill the beans, tell me all about you.”

“There’s not a great deal to tell, really, my family is as you probably guessed, and as they say in American politically correct parlance, Native American. I’m actually, as you may also have worked out, a member of the Cheyenne tribe in Wyoming, which is where I was born.”

“So how did you get from Wyoming to Florida?” I asked.

“Kind of a long story but what do you know about Indian tribes, Jake?”

“Err, would I look ignorant if I say, not much?”

“No, don’t be silly, of course not! It’s just that there are many myths about our funding and the drunkenness that comes about as a result of that funding. You probably know that casinos are often built on Indian land because it bypasses many of the laws and the red tape involved in trying to build them on the preferred sites.”

“Yes, I think I get that, so what, the tribe gets a little money under the table?” I asked.

“Not a little money, Jake, a lot of money. Half of all the casino profits from my reservation are distributed by the tribe’s governing body to all the members of the tribe, even if they no longer live on the reservation.”

“Wow, so is that a lot of money?”

“Depends on the size of the tribe but yes, every member receives a lump sum at the age of twenty-one and then a ‘salary’ for the rest of their lives. It’s a lot!”

“May I ask what sort of money we’re talking about?”

"Well, in my tribe, I received one million dollars when I was twenty-one and I will receive fifty grand a year for the remainder of my life. It's not chump change."

"Wow, that's unbelievable!" I said, "So you really don't need to work at all. Ever."

"That's true but actually, I choose to work. If I didn't, life would be pretty dull," she replied, "In fact, I work for PanAm out of Miami which is probably why we rarely bump into each other. I tend to travel a lot."

"So," I said, "In just a few short minutes I've gone from knowing nothing about you to knowing almost everything."

"Not quite, Jake, but I do feel we're so much better acquainted now, don't you think?" she said, giving me a view of her naked back as she turned to leave, "Gotta go mingle, Jakey, but maybe I'll catch you later…"

Jakey…

Left alone, and attempting to hide the fact that no one seemed interested in me, I began my predictable behavior of people watching. The throng of girls surrounding Perryman appeared to have grown exponentially in the last hour. I felt like I was watching a latter-day Jesus Christ with his adoring disciples. The guy was certainly garnering a new level of attention now.

Wonder why…

I gazed out across the water, my eyes following the trail of lights glistening on the wooden dock that stretched endlessly from Perryman's house. I looked to the right at the point where the dock ended and where I spied the enormous 125 foot Royal Huisman motor yacht that idled at the end, tied to its moorings. I wondered if Perryman had yet set foot on it or even if he was aware that he now owned the thing.

Doubt it…

"Remember me?" a voice said from behind me, waking me from my reverie.

"Summer!" I said, "You look so beautiful tonight, I didn't know you were here."

"You're such a liar, Jake, I saw you at the top of the stairs, silly!"

"Guilty as charged, your honor, I've been found out!"

"Do I get a hug?" she asked.

"I thought you'd never ask," I replied, throwing my arms around her.

We hugged for just a fraction too long I suppose, because we clearly didn't want to part and it felt awkward when we finally did.

"So what are you doing, sitting out here all alone?" she asked.

"Well I've done the meet and greet thing and I've chatted until my jaw ached so I thought I'd take a quiet rest out here," I replied, "And it really is quite beautiful don't you think?"

"It is, but when I spotted you, you seemed a little lonely which is not what I had expected from you."

"The thing is, I suppose I'm not as outgoing as Perryman over there and of course, Talbot, in his own inimitable way. I guess I just don't have that outgoing ability that they possess."

"Yes you do, Jake, you just don't know it!" she replied, "But I saw you gazing down at the dock there, would you like to go and explore?"

"I'm not sure you'll make it to the end of the boardwalk in those shoes though," I said.

"No problem," she said slipping them off and passing them to me.

We walked towards the entrance of the long wooden plank path that led towards the boat a couple of hundred yards away.

"Here, hold my hand, I don't want you falling into those murky depths," I said, taking hold of her as I guided her along the footway.

We arrived at the end of the dock and I felt dwarfed by the sheer size of the vessel moored there. I had no idea of the value of the yacht but it had to be in excess of a million dollars.

"So tell me what's been happening in your life, Jake? It's been so long since we've seen you down here," she said.

We chatted about all the things that had happened over the previous months, and I told her about my good fortune at work and my plans to upgrade my living situation. Summer told me how hard she had been working at school and at her job in the restaurant. It was surface conversation in many ways as I think both of us felt a deep connection and attraction that remained the elephant in the room but an elephant that still needed to be confined.

"So, did Perryman inherit this also?" she asked, pointing at the enormous Royal Huisman idling next to us.

"He did indeed. Actually, this is where I'm sleeping tonight. I've only ever stayed onboard a yacht once but I'm keen to do it again," I said, remembering the night with Tara, "Besides, I think the house might be a wreck after the party's over and it'll be a great place to escape to."

"Kind of romantic too, to fall asleep listening to the waves lapping against the side of the boat…" she whispered.

Phyllis Nelson's classic, "Move Closer" began to filter through the speakers of the dock…

"Would you like to dance?" Summer asked.

When a song like this is playing, I don't need to be asked twice…"

When we're together, touchin' each other

And our bodies do what we feel…

I held Summer lightly, maintaining a sensible distance but the elephant was definitely trying to escape its shackles. Our eyes met and locked…

This is crazy...

"Beautiful song, Jake," she said, "I really like it, it puts me in another place altogether."

"Ms. Nelson does have that effect," I replied.

"Well, don't you think we should listen to her and do as she tells us?" she asked.

"How do you mean?" I asked as the chorus began as if on a predestined cue…

Move closer

Move your body real close...

She moved into me, laying her face against my chest and I wrapped my arms around her as we swayed with the music, fully aware that I was cradling a seventeen-year-old girl against my body, but a very mature and extremely attractive one at that.

"Merry Christmas, Jake," she whispered.

"Merry Christmas to you too, Summer," I replied, "I hope you get everything you want this year."

I already have...

Chapter 46

The following morning, the clean up began in earnest. Well, not really, more in slow motion to be precise. Talbot was somewhat worse for wear as he valiantly attempted to fill black garbage bags with the debris that lay strewn throughout the house. Perryman made little attempt to follow suit, instead preferring to lord it, wearing a floor-length silk kimono dressing gown and sipping on Bloody Marys. I think he was slowly metamorphosing into Jay Gatsby. But I didn't disapprove either; it was kind of nice to see my friend really enjoying his life.

Sadly, Sofia was on duty at the police station today; she'd drawn the short straw. She looked cute in her uniform though and during the party last night, I'd gotten to know her a lot more. She is an incredibly true person and without telling me in so many words, her love and affection for Perryman was deep and I was grateful for that.

"Are you going to be around for the rest of the week, Jake?" she asked.

"Oh for sure, I don't need to leave until New Year's Day but I do have a thousand-mile journey back so I won't be drinking on New Year's Eve, officer!" I replied, mildly wary of the fact that she was still a policewoman.

"Stop it, Jake, you're teasing me, I know that. So bad!" she said, "But what about today, are you going to be here when I get off work?"

"Not sure yet. Talbot and I have been invited over for Christmas lunch at the Cantrells and I don't know how late it will go but we also want to give you and Perryman time alone on Christmas Day. Don't want to be wheels number three and four!" I laughed.

"Yeah, make sure it's late! But joking apart, you didn't tell me, Jake, is there someone special in your life, do you have a girlfriend? Or a boyfriend maybe?"

"Sadly no, but I'm nothing if not patient. There might be someone but it's a long story. Do you have time?"

"No chance, Jake, I've gotta run, some of us have to work, big boy!"

Hmmm...

"I won't stop you then, go catch the bad guys!"

"I will! And Jake?"

"Yes?"

"Merry Christmas, Perryman has a wonderful choice in friends. Thanks for being there for him," she said, as she closed the door behind her.

I just got a compliment from the very tough but cute Sofia, so Christmas Day was starting well. 'Big boy' too, glad she recognized that straightaway.

At around noon, Talbot and I dumped a sack of presents into the back seat of the Porsche and made our way across town to Jensen Beach. Christmas Day, 1985, was turning out to be outstandingly beautiful. Not an ounce of humidity, clear blue skies and the sunshine warmed our faces as we drove with the Porsche's roof down. The endless and vividly exotic colors from the bougainvilleas that lined the sides of the road seemed to transform every part of the journey into a series of Technicolor moments. As we drove along beside the Indian River, even the dolphins seemed to know it was Christmas, as they launched themselves repeatedly from the shallow waters.

After pulling into the driveway of the Cantrell's home, I could see that Reyna had been busy with external decorations for the house. That was one thing that always stayed with me about people in Florida, they go big on Christmas, there is no expense spared on sparkling lights, animated creatures, inflatable reindeer and snowmen and countless other baubles that I had rarely seen in New York State at Christmas time.

As I parked the car in front of the garage, it suddenly hit me how beautiful Joe and Reyna's home was. The colors they'd painted it were so bright and tropical and although this wasn't a grand palatial home like Perryman's, it oozed warmth and charm and a true feeling of homeliness. It was nothing less than a chocolate box, Hansel and Gretel abode.

The front door was open wide because the weather was sublime but we knocked as we entered, shouting, "Merry Christmas!"

"Welcome Jake, welcome Talbot! And a very merry Christmas to both of you!" said Reyna, beaming that eternally radiant smile, "Come on in and have some Eggnog!"

We hugged Reyna, went to shake hands with Joe but he parried us away, instead embracing the two of us in a bearlike hug.

I could hear the sound of clattering feet up above as a signal that Autumn and Summer had heard the mass of greetings downstairs and the two of them were hugging both of us within seconds. It was like a hug festival. Gotta love it.

"We come with gifts like the two wise men!" said Talbot.

"Aren't there meant to be three?" I asked.

"Beggars can't be choosers, dear boy!" he replied, reverting to a *Proverbs* expression by the great John Heywood in favor of his preferred Shakespearian parlance.

I can't win...

"I thought that we could sit down after lunch and exchange gifts," said Reyna, "These two girls have already had a mountain of presents they've opened."

"Mom!" shouted Autumn and Summer in unison, "Why wait?"

“Because your dad is hungry, so are these boys, and I’m ready to serve!” she responded.

“Oh, Mooooom!” the cry came again from the girls.

“Don’t be brats! Anyway, you boys, I’ve set up outside on the patio because the weather is so nice today, so go on out and make yourselves at home,” Reyna instructed, “Summer, Autumn, can you give me a hand, please?”

Talbot and I followed Joe out to the patio which overlooked the lagoon and to describe what awaited us as sumptuous was somewhat of an understatement. The table, which could accommodate eight people was fully laden with scrumptious foods and decorated for Christmas in a way that only a woman knows how. In the center of the table stood a large oval serving plate with a turkey and a prime rib of beef. Surrounding it and covering the whole length of the table were dishes of roast potatoes, mashed potatoes, corn, green beans, broccoli, glazed carrots, peas, lima beans and something that was really rare in Florida, Yorkshire puddings. I guessed that this must have been something to do with Reyna’s English roots because it wasn’t typically found on an American dining table at Christmas.

“I didn’t contribute much today, fellas, but I did make the gravy for the turkey and a nice little port reduction for the beef but you don’t have to have it if it’s not your thing,” said Joe, taking a seat at the side of the table. This was interesting for me because I had assumed he’d be at the head of the table but his pure sense of gentlemanly thinking was to save that honor for his wife.

Note to self...

“I can’t believe what Reyna’s prepared, Joe, and the reduction you made, well it’s definitely got a home on my plate,” I said.

“You’re very kind Jake, but Reyna does all the hard work. Without her, there’d be no home, just a house. She… what is it you say… oh yes, I know... she just rocks my world!”

"Damn!" said Talbot, "Hold on, I left the champagne in the car, I'll run and get it."

As Talbot sprinted out to the driveway, Joe said to me, "Great party last night, did you have a good time?"

"I had a great time, Joe, but I only knew a handful of people there," I replied, "But Perryman seemed to be enjoying it."

"He did!" Joe replied, "I noticed that too. He's suddenly got his own fan club."

"Funny how that happens!" I said.

"Just before Reyna and I left, I noticed you down at the end of the dock where the motor yacht is moored."

Oh fuck...

"Oh yes, I was down there chatting to Summer," I replied, the tiniest traces of perspiration now gathering once again on my forehead.

"Really? I thought you were dancing?" he said, his eyes suddenly boring into me.

"Oh, yes sir, we were, but it was all above board, I can assure you," I replied, the perspiration now forming complete droplets.

"Jake, stop worrying, son! I'm not going to go get my shotgun!" he laughed, "But listen to me."

"Yessir."

"My daughters are so special to me and I trust you implicitly," he said.

"I understand, sir, I really do," I said.

I need to change my shirt, this one's soaked...

"But I want you to remember, she's only seventeen, Jake."

"I know sir, I'm more than aware of that," I replied.

"So when she's with you, I want you to protect her just like I would."

"Absolutely, I won't let anything happen to her, sir."

"But if anything was to happen to her," he continued, "Trust me that I'd hunt you down and kill you like a dog."

Gulp!

"Joe, please trust me that I will always guard her with my life. I promise."

"I'm just messing with you, Jake!" he roared, laughing so hard he nearly choked.

What is this, 'Mess with Jake Week'?

"But you do know how much my girls mean to me, don't you?"

"Truly, Joe, I'd only ever have their best interests at heart," I replied, the fear now beginning to diminish.

"So who wants champagne?" said Talbot, breezing back out onto the patio, a tray of glasses in one hand, a bottle of Moët in the other.

Perfect timing, Talbot, well done buddy...

The girls joined us and we stood as they took their seats.

"I'd like to make a toast," said Joe, raising his glass, "To great friends, beautiful girls and gratitude to the Florida weather for allowing this lucky family to be eating Christmas lunch in our little piece of paradise!"

"Cheers!" we all said, knocking back a welcome shot of French fizz.

The lunch was truly amazing, Reyna really had surpassed herself. After helping ourselves to large portions of coconut cake and the inevitable chocolate gateau, we eventually retired to the Cantrell's lounge to exchange gifts.

"Oh Joe, you shouldn't have!" exclaimed Reyna, immediately trying on the diamond earrings her husband had given her.

"It's always my pleasure, sweetheart, but they'll never be as pretty as the diamond I married!" said Joe.

Smooth. Extra note to self...

And this was the way it continued for the next hour or so, squeals of joy and "You shouldn't have!" when we all knew it really meant, "I'm so glad you did!" I'd given Joe and Reyna a joint present, probably a bit dull but they seemed to like it.

"A cappuccino machine!" shrilled Reyna, "How did you know?"

Just a wild guess. I guess....

I gave Autumn her present and I actually think she was delighted with it. Really.

"A Polaroid camera!" she squealed, "Just what I've always wanted!" Although she seemed almost a bit too overjoyed and that concerned me…

Talbot was a difficult one to buy for because he was extremely niche in what he truly loved. But I'd come across a cool clock in a flea market back in New York that had been made from a vinyl album with a clock mechanism installed.

"This," said Talbot, "Is a truly thoughtful gift that absolutely plays to my love of music and art and will therefore find a worthy position on my wall! Thanks, Jake!" he said, hugging me.

Why's everyone gone so huggy today?

"Summer, you're the hardest one to buy for but like Talbot, I know you love your Walkman so I thought I could upgrade it for you," I said, handing a couple of packages to her.

"Are you serious?" she said, having torn the wrapping away, "A Sony Discman! Jake, I couldn't have wished for anything better, no one has these yet in Jensen!"

She threw her arms around me and kissed me on the cheek several times and I cast a glance at Joe to see that I wasn't crossing any line but he seemed engrossed in the cappuccino machine.

"There's more," I said, "You need to open the other package too!"

I'd bought a dozen CD albums to go with the Discman and it was as though I'd just given her the gift of life. Her eyes were agape with delight.

"Jake, I know everybody's been saying "you shouldn't have" but you really shouldn't have. This must have cost a fortune. But thank you, thank you so much and now I have a gift for you."

"Summer, I didn't buy you a gift just to expect one back. You need to save your money!"

"I have a job now, so it's okay. And it isn't much but I thought you'd like it," she replied.

She handed me the present and I opened it, actually with a smile on my face with how this girl had thought so hard about the right thing to buy for me.

It was a white t-shirt with these words displayed on the front:

"It's perfect, Summer, it's just perfect," I said, taking her hand and giving it the tiniest of squeezes.

If I never remember anything else, I'll always have the image of her face, beaming with unbridled delight, permanently seared into my memory.

The afternoon quickly became evening and Talbot and I, not wanting to outstay our welcome in case we weren't invited back again, thanked Joe and Reyna for their hospitality and the two girls walked us out to my car.

"Jake, you've gone up in the world! A Porsche?" said Autumn, "Who did you have to kill to get this?"

"Jake couldn't kill if his life depended on it, Autumn, he'd be vegetarian if his meat wasn't killed for him!" laughed Talbot.

"I like it," whispered Summer as she stood up on tiptoes to get closer to my ear. "But I think I liked the rental Camaro better," she said, grinning at me.

"Well, as Talbot said earlier, beggars can't be choosers and as an additional thought from Mr. Heywood, you can't look a gift horse in the mouth," I said, winking at her as I climbed into the car.

"Take me for a drive soon," she shouted as I reversed out of the driveway, "I want to see how fast it'll go!"

"It's a date!" I said, waving as we left the property.

What did I just say?

Chapter 47

"Don't think I didn't see," I said.

"See what?" asked Talbot.

"You know, I'm not blind," I replied.

We were sitting in Perryman's vast sun lounge, for some odd reason drinking Schnapps. I'm guessing it may have been left by the Steiners.

"Still don't know what you're talking about."

"Talb, I saw that little smooch with Autumn when we left the Cantrells!"

"But… Jake… really.., it was nothing, just a friendly peck on the cheek was all!"

"Yeah, if you say so, particularly if Autumn's mouth is on her cheek!" I replied, laughing at the poor man's embarrassment.

Sofia, who'd arrived home from work a couple of hours earlier was clearly enjoying our friendly little exchange, as she sat on the end of the sofa, knocking back a Heineken.

"So Jake's not the only child molester amongst us, then?" she said.

"Hold on, I take exception to that, Officer, I'll have you know that I've been exemplary in my behavior, particularly since my warning from Joe today at lunch," I replied.

"What do you mean?" asked Perryman, "Did he warn you off Summer?"

"Kind of, just told me that he didn't want to go loading both barrels of his little friend," I replied.

"Truth be told, fella, from what I've seen, you've been on your best behavior but Summer does have a thing about you, you know that. In the end, it's always gonna be the girl that has the final say, right Sofia?" he said, winking at his partner, "But at least Talb's on legal ground with Autumn!"

There we go again, Uncle Chester...

I'd had enough of being warned today and let's face it, it was Christmas, peace and goodwill to all men so I decided I needed to catch up on missed sleep from the previous night.

"Alright you boys and girl, I'm done for the day, I'll see you in the a.m." I said, "If you need me, I'll be on Perryman's mobile manse at the end of the dock."

As I made my way to the boat, it hit me that I was definitely getting used to staying on the yacht. It gave me my own personal space and peace. But it also made me even keener to find something much bigger to live in when I got back to New York.

The master bedroom itself, located at the rear of the lower deck, was like a sultan's palace. I didn't really have much need for the rest of the boat, I could literally survive in this suite alone without ever venturing out. It had its own bar and refrigerator and on closer inspection, I discovered an excellent selection of wines. I decided on a particularly inviting and hopefully expensive 1966 Batard-Montrachet Grand Cru, poured myself a generous glass and made my way up the winding staircase to the deck above.

It was a picture-perfect night, and I took a seat on one the ridiculously comfortable loungers on the pool deck. I realized it would be very easy to quickly become used to this lifestyle. I looked up at the sky which tonight wasn't actually black, more of a midnight blue lit brightly by the stars, every one of them clear to see as they looked down at me.

I sipped the Montrachet, becoming acutely aware of the difference between an okay wine and a great wine. I kept sipping, also aware that in a week's time, I'd be drinking something less palatable once I got back to the city.

I heard the faint sound of music and as I looked back at the house, I could see Perryman and Sofia dancing together. Perryman was naked except for what appeared to be a pair of pink silk shorts and Sofia was also naked except for a G-string and a police cap. As I remained in voyeur mode, wishing that I had had binoculars to hand, I could just about make out that they were singing the words of the song to each other, taking turns on each line. I recognized the song as the British singer, Belouis Some's "Imagination"…

Imagination - could make a man of you

Imagination - could make me love you too

Imagination - is all I want from you…

In truth, I was thinking along the lines of a couple of movies I'd seen, *Strange Bedfellows* and *The Odd Couple* but you know what, these two seemed more suited than a cup and saucer.

My gaze returned to the mangroves and sea grapes that protected the water's edge and I became entranced with the moonlight dance of the dragonflies that flitted amongst them. I glanced down at the side of the vessel, a strange slurping sound and a slow ripple coming from the starboard side. I gasped as the enormous whale-like shape of a manatee slowly glided through the black water, its grace and dignity more than making up for its unfortunate ugliness. Often dubbed the sea cow of the ocean, this creature was very much overshadowed by the beauty of its cousin, the dolphin and to be fair, I'd seen better looking cows before. I don't mean to be *porpoisely* rude but a dolphin it certainly ain't. But this was the beauty of Florida, particularly so close to the ocean, whenever you think you've seen everything, there's always something else to surprise you.

I drained my glass, respectfully denying myself a refill and made my way back to my stateroom. I stumbled around, a little dizzy now, but managed to find the light switch to bring darkness to my ocean suite. I was exhausted and I let my clothes drop to the floor and could feel myself falling asleep even before my head hit the pillow.

Chapter 48

Someone was on the boat! I'd heard noises but maybe I was dreaming them? Maybe too many Schnapps and the final half-liter of Montrachet had done it. That must be it because whatever I'd heard, was no longer making a noise. I sank my head back into the goose down pillows and invited slumber to take me back to where I'd been…

Something touched my face… I wasn't dreaming that! Was I? Oh Lord, no more drinking, that's it, New Year's resolution…

"Jake," a voice whispered, "Are you awake?"

"Summer?!!!" I said, "Is that you?"

The room was in darkness but I recognized her voice immediately.

"Yes, it's me, Jake," she said, "I hope you're not angry that I came."

"No, of course not, but what are you doing here, why are you out so late?"

"I crept out of my bedroom window and jumped off the roof but I couldn't take my Bronco because of the noise it makes!"

"So how did you get here?"

"Um… I cycled?"

"You cycled all the way here in the dark, Summer? Do you know how dangerous that is?"

"I'm sorry, Jake, I knew you'd be angry."

"No, no, not angry at all but you have to understand that I made a promise to your parents that I would make sure you were always protected in my company and I'm not doing a very good job right this minute," I replied, "Much as I am flattered that you wanted to come and see me."

"Do you want me to go?" she asked.

"Well, yes, but hold on, what time is it?"

"It's just past midnight," she said.

"Listen, I don't want you to feel you've made the trip for nothing so here's what we're going to do. You go up to the pool deck while I put some clothes on and I'll make us some hot chocolate."

"Do I have to?" she asked, a grin forming on her face as I saw the white of her teeth.

"Go! Now!" I ordered, in as nice a way as I knew how.

Once she'd left, I picked my clothes up from the floor and hurriedly dressed before going to the kitchen to heat some milk. While it was warming up, I went and found Summer, lying on a lounger on the pool deck, wearing nothing much more than skimpy shorts and a cashmere pullover.

"You must be cold," I said, "Would you like me to find you something warmer? I think there are some robes in the guestrooms."

"I'm fine, Jake, really! Stop fussing!" she replied.

I was doing everything in my power to prevent me from stealing glances at her bare legs. I think I was going to need a robe myself shortly…

"Let me go check on that hot chocolate, I'll be right back," I said.

When I arrived back with two steaming mugs of chocolate, Summer had obviously found where the pool's music system was, because Berlin's "You Take My Breath Away" was crooning through the speaker system.

I handed Summer a mug and asked,

"Have you enjoyed your Christmas?"

"This might be the best Christmas I've ever had, Jake, I really am loving every moment of it," she replied, "And… I get to spend the night with you."

I almost choked up a mouthful of hot chocolate when she said that…

"Summer, you are not spending the night here!"

"Well, can't we at least dance?" she asked.

"That would be my pleasure but I am taking you home after we've finished our hot chocolate."

As we slow danced to Berlin, I chided myself for loving the feeling of holding this girl when I should have been driving her home immediately I'd found her in my bedroom. But it was Christmas so I decided to let us both down easy.

Watching every motion, in my foolish lover's game

On this endless ocean, finally lovers know no shame

You take my breath away…

I couldn't help thinking that every song I was hearing now was a reflection of something or someone in my life but in all honesty, I kind of liked it. Maybe that's how it always is when you think you might be in love and suddenly every song on the radio seems to be directed entirely at your own little world.

Summer's arms were around my neck, her face nuzzled into my chest. I realized that I had better not let the situation go on for too long in case her parents discovered her missing and raised the alarm.

"I love you, Jake…" she whispered.

"I love you too, Summer, I love all of your family," I replied, although choosing not to whisper.

"No, Jake, you don't understand, I'm in love with you, don't you see?"

I very gently took her hands from behind my neck and guided her towards one of the sofas that surrounded the pool.

"Summer, listen to me. This is important. Whatever you're feeling right now, is probably something like… I don't know… probably a kind of crush. I've been through similar emotions myself in the past. But it's not love, I promise you, you're far too young to be falling in love, you have so much ahead of you in your life to let crushes or emotions stop you achieving everything you desire," I said.

"But you don't understand, Jake, ever since I first saw you, I fell in love with you!" she said breathlessly, "I'm not a little girl anymore, I may have been a couple of years ago but I'm not now, I promise."

"I didn't mean that, I meant that you're a stunningly beautiful and intelligent girl but I'm so much older than you, Summer, I don't want to lead you on and there's just nothing I can do about any of this right now."

She leaped at me, forcing me back against the sofa, her mouth finding mine, her tongue suddenly buried deep in my mouth. For a split second, I wanted to wrap her up in my arms and take her to my room but thankfully, common sense prevailed and I pushed her away, although possibly a little too harshly.

"You can't do that, Summer! You just can't." I said, not realizing the force of my voice against this now terribly vulnerable and probably frightened girl.

She jumped up from the sofa and ran to the gangplank, hurrying down it and sprinting off back up the dock towards the house. I jumped up from the sofa and followed her, shouting her name, with the sudden realization that I might be waking some of the neighbors but that was all irrelevant now, I had to catch up with her and make her understand.

But by the time I arrived in the driveway, there was no sign of her, no sign of her bike either. I went back to the yacht and retrieved my car keys and after raising the garage door from inside the house, I reversed out and began the journey towards the Cantrell home.

As I followed Indian River Drive towards Jensen Beach, I became acutely aware that I was driving a convertible Porsche in the middle of the night and that I was probably over the limit as far as my blood alcohol level was concerned. So I slowed down to just below the 25mph speed limit and continued my journey, hoping that I would spot Summer on her bike taking the same route. But the lack of street lighting on this particular road told me that I had either passed her without realizing or she'd taken a different route home that I didn't know about.

Having arrived at a completely deserted town center and not seen her on the road, I decided to approach her house from the reverse way round so that I could get to the highest point of Skyline Drive, kill the engine and cruise noiselessly downhill to the Cantrell property. The last thing I wanted to do was to wake Joe and Reyna. I also remembered at the last moment to turn off my lights which made navigation a little more hazardous.

I parked outside the house, my car fortunately hidden by the high hedge that stood between the twin entrances of the driveway. After twenty minutes or so, I saw a dark shadow and realized it was Summer pushing her bike up the hill towards where I was parked. I silently got out of the car and carefully closed the door and walked towards her.

"Go away!" she said, "I can't talk to you, Jake!"

"Summer, please! I never meant to upset you, I promise you," I said, "I'm so sorry, I feel like such an idiot."

She finally came to a standstill in front of me, holding her bike, her cheeks stained with eyeliner which told me that she had been crying.

"It's not your fault, Jake, it's mine. I never meant for this to happen, I never meant to fall in love with you and I'm sorry too. Sorry that I messed everything up!"

"You haven't messed up anything, not at all! If it means anything, Summer, I could easily be in love with you and if we were a few years older than we are now, it would be fine, no one would raise an eyebrow, don't you see?" I said, desperate to calm her and put her at ease with what had happened.

"I know Jake, I get it. Your mind is on Tara, right?" she yelled, as I became wary of the now heated tone about to wake everyone in the house.

"Take this and give it to her!" she screamed, ripping the little sea glass necklace from her neck and throwing it at me.

"Please Summer, don't be like this, it's not fair! I'm trying everything I can to do the right thing here!"

"Then go away and leave me alone!!" she yelled, running into the property and disappearing behind the garage.

I looked down and bent to retrieve the pieces of the necklace that had fallen at my feet. Tears began to form in my own eyes now as I turned towards the car and slumped in the seat.

What the hell did I just do?

Chapter 49

Two or three days passed by since our upset, without me seeing or hearing from Summer and I felt terrible about it. Ever since I'd arrived in Sewall's Point, I'd loved every moment of the holiday and then that night happened and I seemed to have screwed up pretty badly. I decided not to tell either Talbot or Perryman about what had gone on in case word got back to Joe and Reyna, so I continued staying at Perryman's as though nothing had happened.

A strange feeling seemed to envelop me today and along with that came a monsoon type of weather pattern common in South Florida. The clouds weren't just dark, they were black and ominous, even threatening. When the rain finally came, it didn't just pour, it pummeled the earth as though it was angry about something and the lightning flashes that preceded the deafening cracks were bright white and lit the sky like God's own firework display. I'd witnessed major hurricanes before when I was at college and the emotional effects of those systems were mentally destabilizing and I was beginning to feel a similar feeling right now. And I didn't like it.

I'd spent the day just chewing the fat with the boys until Sofia and Cheyenne had arrived, at which point I took my leave and ran through the driving rain to the yacht to be on my own. After I dropped my clothes into a basket in the laundry room, I grabbed a robe and went to the kitchen for sustenance. Sofia, being the incredibly sweet and caring girl that she was, had dropped in some supplies during the day and I was grateful because I was famished.

I fixed myself a plate of cooked Tiger shrimp and seafood dressing and snagged a packet of chips to take to my room. I realized that there was still that half bottle of Montrachet in the wine fridge so I emptied it into a large Bordeaux glass, which was the biggest I could find. I did note that there were a dozen or so more wines in the fridge that I'd never heard of and was still keen to sample before I left for New York.

Turning on the television, I was reminded that in the USA, television content literally dies a death around any holiday season and after flicking through the channels and finding re-run after re-run, I decided to play some music instead.

The nice thing about staying at a place like Perryman's is that there is no limit on the spending that goes on to impress people and although I realized that all the CDs were bought by the Steiners themselves, probably Krystal in reality, the range on offer to their guests was outstanding. The audio system on the boat had some fancy type of pop-out turntable which you loaded with six CDs, pressed the button to close the tray and the unit randomly selected songs from each CD and played them. I was suitably impressed.

Lying back on the bed, (I was getting very comfortable with goose down pillows and a bed that seemed to be about twice the width of a standard King mattress) I stretched out and stared up at the ceiling as the rain battered the boat outside, and the first song came on the stereo…

They pulled in just behind the bridge

He lays her down, he frowns

Gee my life's a funny thing, am I still too young?

He kissed her then and there

She took his ring, took his babies

It took him minutes, took her nowhere

Heaven knows, she'd have taken anything, but

All night

She wants the young American...

I loved this song. I had been fortunate enough to see Bowie perform in New York at Madison Square Garden in 1983 and had become a fan ever since. The man never stopped reinventing himself, delighting an adoring public wherever he went, his music a timeless trail affecting so many people in so many wonderful ways.

I picked up another of the gigantic Tiger shrimp and dipped it in the sauce, biting off half of it and simultaneously stuffing my mouth with chips.

God, when did I become such a slob?

The stereo switched to another song and I listened as Kid Creole and his Coconuts sang "I'm A Wonderful Thing, Baby" followed by Joan Jett belting out "I Love Rock 'n Roll"…

I'd drained the Montrachet and got up to go off in search of another victim in the wine fridge. I decided on a 1971 Penfolds Grange, again a wine I'd not seen before but guessed that it must be pretty decent. After relieving the bottle of half its contents, I adjourned back to the bed to sip its seduction. I wasn't disappointed, this wine was something very special.

As I rearranged the pillows, brushing away the crumbs from the chips I'd been stuffing, I noticed an envelope under one of the pillows. It was addressed to me in a very artistic cursive script. I wondered who it could be from but when I turned the envelope over, I could see that the initials SC were written across the flap. Opening it, I found a single sheet of writing paper inside. I tugged the sheet out and began to read…

Dear Jake,

I'm so sorry for what happened the other night, I wish now that I'd never come to see you and I wouldn't be feeling the way I do right now. I feel so crushed and I feel foolish for acting so childishly towards you. I really do understand now that you were only trying to protect me and make me understand that sometimes the timing of things just isn't right. I do now understand what you said outside my house about age difference and how sometimes it matters terribly and then other times it doesn't matter at all.

The only good thing that has come out of this is that I have finally been able to tell you how much in love with you I am, I've truly fallen for you, Jake, and I don't know what to do about it. I think you feel something for me too although I don't know if it's in the same way and I now realize that even if you did feel the same, you wouldn't be able to show it.

I snuck this note into your room today because I didn't want you to go back to New York and think that I was just a naïve girl with a crush on you. In August, I will be going to college for four years and I don't know how much more I will see of you once I leave. But I want you to think highly of me, I want you to be proud of what I can achieve and of course, I hope that one day you'll love me as much as I love you.

Always loving you, all of the time,

Summer xxx

I lay the piece of paper on my chest and I could feel tears collecting in the corners of my eyes. Tears turned to sobs as I realized I'd broken this young girl's heart and I had no idea how to fix it.

Chapter 50

On my return to New York City, my apartment suddenly felt smaller than it had been before the Christmas break. It could literally fit into one of Perryman's closets. I had to do something about it and I had to do it now.

I'd stayed for the beginning of the New Year's Eve party in Sewall's Point but my heart wasn't really in it so I decided that leaving at 9pm would get me a good part of the way home before I needed to stop for a rest. I'd managed to sleep in late that day so I didn't feel tired at all and I was back in my rabbit hutch by sundown the next day.

The following morning, I reached for a copy of the Yellow Pages that was lying under my desk and turned to the section marked 'Real Estate'. I was looking for a realtor to help me find a new condo to rent and I was specifically looking for a Jewish name because I knew that in New York, the Jewish fraternity in real estate was hungry like the proverbial wolf.

And I soon spotted a name that might be just the right candidate:

Regina Bergmann

Realtor

Sales & Rentals

I called the number listed, spoke to Regina and arranged to meet her the following week once she had put together a list of potential rentals.

The New Year at Newman, Hart, Stratton, Turnbull, Glass & Finnicombe started with a bang. There was no gentle easing back into the working week, it was foot to the floor right from the off. And although I knew that I was lucky to be in the position of driving a brand new Porsche and looking to rent a pretty nice apartment, there was no avoiding the fact that this firm wanted its pound of flesh in exchange. It was only now in this first week of 1987, that I suddenly realized I might not be cut out for this lifestyle but for the moment, I just needed to knuckle down and put in as many hours as the company needed from me.

Later that evening, when most of the big hitters had left for the day, I crept into Arthur's office and stole some of his elegant writing paper he kept for writing private notes to people he liked. I needed to send a note to Summer, firstly to make her feel better about herself and about what had happened but also to satisfy myself that I wasn't the jerk I thought I'd become.

Dearest Summer,

Thank you for your note but it was completely unnecessary because it was me who should have been apologizing. I think a great deal of you and if I'm honest, I have done since I first laid eyes on you but circumstances have not been kind to us I suppose.

I also have enormous respect for your mom and dad so if I were to offend or upset them in any way, it would be as bad for me as upsetting you. Your family has welcomed me into their home as part of your family and I place an enormously high value on their generosity.

I know that soon you'll be leaving for college and that your life will change dramatically, as mine did when I left home to go to college. It's a life-changing moment and you'll be mixing with people older than you from many varied walks of life.

I don't see me being back in Florida for some time because of the added pressure I am getting at work. The good news is that I plan to finally move out of my apartment to live in something much nicer, hopefully in Soho. I hope to be back in Florida for Independence Day and if possible, maybe even during Spring Break but right now, there's no guarantee.

But in the meantime, I want you to call me if you need me, or just need someone to talk to. I'm always here for you.

You're an amazing girl, Summer, and one who is so easy to fall in love with...

My love to you as always,

Jake xxxxx

I dropped the letter into a USPS office on my way home, with the hope that I had somehow managed to right some of the wrong that had happened over Christmas. The truth was, I couldn't get her out of my mind and I hoped that a long break without seeing her would change that. But unfortunately, the nagging voice at the back of my mind was telling me that I was probably more in love with her than she was with me.

Chapter 51

Regina was a character, a real-life New York character. She was like a fizzing dynamo, pent up energy just bursting out of her too tight pantsuit. She spoke at rattlesnake speed and fired of Jewishisms faster than I could translate them. I felt badly in need of a Yiddish Handbook just to keep up with her. Each sentence was punctuated by a wheezing cough, a trail of cigarette butts strewn behind her as she chain-smoked her way across Soho.

"Schmuck!"

"Feh!"

"Kvetsh!"

"Shlemiel!"

"Goy!"

These were just a sample of words that she used disparagingly towards the agents showing us rental apartments. That was until we met with what appeared to be a fellow Yiddisher at our seventh showing of the day.

"*Mentsh*," she muttered.

"I'm sorry, what does that mean, Regina? Is this a no-go too?" I asked.

"No, Jakey, *mentsh* is a good word. This man is decent. Finally, *oy veh*!"

Did you notice she called me Jakey?

We followed Moische Finkelstein into the lobby of the converted apartment building, which according to Moische had been a garment factory back in the day. Now, the building had been redeveloped to create much-needed apartment dwellings for the growing Manhattan workforce.

When Moische opened the door to Apartment #7, I couldn't believe my eyes. The whole floor, all 2,000 square feet of it was one big open room with just four supporting columns and no dividing walls to be seen anywhere. Refinished parquet flooring shone like polished glass, contrasted by the stark white outer walls under the twenty-foot ceilings. I felt like the Tom Hanks character in that movie, *Big*.

"How much?" I asked Moische.

Twenny-five hundred a month," he replied.

"I'll take it!"

Regina roughly grabbed me by the arm and dragged me away from Moische. We stood facing each other by one of the enormous glass windows looking out over Canal St.

"*Klutz*! What are you doing? What, you think you're in a movie or something?" she said, trying to keep her raspy voice as low as she could, "You don't just pay the asking price, you *shlimazel*!"

"I.. I.. I like it, Regina, I want it. The price seems okay to me!" I replied.

"Wait here, *meshugener*, let me deal with Moische..."

After what appeared to be a completely undecipherable conflab between the two of them, Regina returned to me with a look of triumph spreading across her face.

"It's yours, Jakey, you move in next week!"

"How much?"

"Two grand a month. Now in future, trust your *bubbe* and don't go paying retail. You gotta live by the word, 'wholesale'. Kapish?"

Italian too?

"Yes, Regina, kapish'"

"Mazel Tov!" she said, giving me a huge cigarette-aroma enhanced hug like the adoptive grandmother she seemed to have become over the last six hours.

In fact, I did 'kapish' and I'd learned a valuable lesson with Regina that day. The woman was probably pushing eighty, I doubt she'd ever been a looker, even when she was twenty, but I completely adored her. You could spend an hour with Regina and learn more than you could in a week at college. She was brilliant, streetwise and unbelievably charismatic. More importantly, she'd found me my new home in the trendy Soho district of the city and I was more than excited to leave my shoebox and say farewell to my neighbor's pussy. If you see what I mean…

The next weekend saw me gathering up my meager collection of belongings and tired sticks of furniture and moving into Canal St. I'd told my mother my news and she immediately instructed her current flame, a fireman from South Carolina, going by the moniker of Chauncey Beauregard, to help me with the sofa.

Where does she find these people?

Truth be told, Chauncey was a really nice guy, even though he looked like a male stud model from Playgirl magazine. But that's my mom, she loves her accessories and they have to be pretty.

But here I was, I'd really arrived! I had my own Tom Hanks style loft in Soho even if I'd have to drive the Porsche twenty minutes uptown to the office each morning. But hell, someone's got to do it and I wasn't complaining.

Someone pinch me!

Chapter 52

"I got a note from Jake today!" said Summer to her sister.

"What did he say?" asked Autumn.

Summer had finally gotten hold of her sister at college and was eager to tell someone her news. The handwritten note had arrived in the afternoon mail and the relief she felt from reading it was palpable.

"You remember I told you about what happened when I went to see him on Perryman's boat?"

"Yes I do, it didn't turn out too well, right?"

"So I wrote him a note, pretty much apologizing for my juvenile behavior."

"Wow, Summer, that was pretty brave, did he respond positively or negatively?"

"He was so nice, Autumn, I can't tell you how sweet that man is. He even took the blame on his shoulders and said that if the timing and ages were different, we'd probably be together now."

"So… how do you feel? I mean, the timing isn't any different and he's still hung up on his age and yours, so where does that leave you?"

"I'm going to wait for him, of course!"

"But why? You're going to be at college soon and there are boys here who aren't teenagers, boys you'd really like!"

"You don't understand, Autumn, I'm still a virgin and if it's going to be anyone I share that with, it's going to be Jake."

"Well, I get that, I mean, he is really charming, and good looking, probably sensitive too… maybe I should call him!"

"Stop it! Anyway, I know you have this thing going on with Talbot so Jake's off limits to you."

"Yeah, Talbot… I have to tell you that since my first time with Caleb, there hasn't been anyone else."

"So? Are you and Talbot 'seeing' each other or not?"

"Well, hardly seeing but we are calling when I can find an available phone. I like him, sis, I really do. I guess I want to take it slow and see where it goes. And although there are plenty of willing studs in college, I'm seriously not interested."

"I'm proud of you, Autumn! And I love Talbot, he's such a gentleman and he's so different!"

"I'll let you into a secret, when I first met him I just assumed he was gay! But then we find out that Perryman's the gay one of the group so it's kinda confusing. Anyway, we've had some fairly… umm… kinda naughty conversations on the phone and he definitely isn't gay!"

"I think there is a big difference between college boys and properly grown up, well mannered and charming young men, don't you think?" said Summer.

"I do, Summer, I really do. So now that I think I've found my perfect man, don't friggin' blow it with Jake!"

Chapter 53

Although I'd promised Summer that I would try to get down to South Florida for Spring Break, I hadn't been able to come through on it. Work had meant that more of my time was devoted to toiling for the rewards that I was currently enjoying courtesy of Newman, Hart, Stratton, Turnbull, Glass & Finnicombe. But over the next few months, I had been in telephone conversation with Summer and I felt that we had finally put our 'relationship' back onto an even keel. She was excited that I was definitely going to make it down for Independence Day and our midnight chats took on a new flavor.

There was something about her that had changed since Christmas and I mean that in a good way. She had suddenly grown up a lot and for the first time I felt as though I was talking to someone of my own age even though there was still the seven, almost eight year age difference. She was excited when she told me she had been pre-selected for the same college as Autumn and was really looking forward to joining her there in August. It was then that it hit me that this incredible girl would likely go away for her college years and I'd possibly never see her again. I felt an overwhelming sadness at this notion but had to tell myself that it was probably for the best in the long run.

But although I was unable to get to Florida, Florida did manage to come to me. Talbot and Perryman flew up one weekend to see me and I was keen to show them my new life and where I now lived. It was a spectacular weekend, with very little sleep, the three of us eager to cram in as much guy time as possible in the now rare moments that we spent together as a group.

We did everything a tourist would do. We went to the top of the Empire State Building, we toured the Statue of Liberty in a helicopter, we had lunch in Grand Central, dinner in Times Square and we even saw the musical Starlight Express on Broadway.

If we weren't out somewhere in the city, we were playing soccer in my apartment. It was one of those memorable weekends that I wondered if I'd ever see again but one that I wanted to stay in my mind and heart for the rest of my life.

But then at the beginning of June, as I was sitting at my desk at Newman Hart, I received a phone call from someone I hadn't seen since the Christmas Eve party at Perryman's house.

"Remember me?" the voice said.

How could I forget?

"Tara!" I said, "How are you, long time no see?"

"Exactly, which is why I'm calling," she said.

I'm not sure why this was but I had an uncomfortable feeling in my stomach. I couldn't explain why any man would feel that way when Tara called because she was such an outstanding beauty. And rich.

"Enlighten me, then. What's going on?" I asked.

"Well, for the first time in simply ages, I'm going to be in the city at the weekend and I'd really like to see you!" she purred.

"It would be lovely to see you too, Tara, but remembering what happened last time, lovely though it was, I don't think it would be right to revisit that night again," I said.

There was a moment of silence on the other end of the line…

"Jake, you know I think a lot of you and I suppose I often think about you but you must know I'm not going to force you into anything."

"Of course, yes, I know that but I guess I just wanted to be completely transparent with you," I replied, "Anyway, what do you have in mind?"

"I'm arriving on Friday evening and will be staying the weekend at the St. Regis so I was wondering if we could have dinner together? You choose the restaurant?"

"Sure, that sounds great. Let me come up with somewhere you may not have been to in the city but I'll come pick you up at say, 7pm?"

"Wonderful! It's a date, Jake, see you then!"

Oh Lord, did she say 'date'?

"What's up, stud muffin?" said Charlotte Acosta as I hung up the phone.

"Nothing, Charlotte, nothing. Nothing that you can help me with anyway…"

Chapter 54

Saturday night came around and I arrived in a cab at the St. Regis at 6.55pm. A doorman held the door open for me as I walked through the grand entrance and into the decadently impressive lobby. This hotel was beyond opulent; gold, stone, glass and marble unapologetically featuring at every glance and in every step. Even the hotel's mailbox was so ornate it seemed better suited in a glass case in a museum than in a swanky hotel. I chuckled to myself because although it was never a hotel I could come close to affording a weekend stay there, for Tara it was nothing much more than a Holiday Inn. Well, not quite, but you get the picture.

I'd given tonight some serious thought though, and had decided to try and take Tara out of her St. Regis comfort zone and take her somewhere that would hopefully make her realize that whatever thoughts she had for Jake Delaney would finally be put to bed with what I had in store for her. So early Friday, the previous morning, I had made a beeline to the Mail Room at Newman Hart and found our resident muso, Troy Vogel, half asleep at his desk, a stack of letters and manila envelopes yet to be franked and mailed. Troy was one of those guys who knew exactly what was going on in the New York music scene and always had access to tickets that no one else could score. A hundred bucks later, I was in possession of two of the most prized tickets for Saturday night.

As I loitered conspicuously in the St. Regis lobby, having told the desk clerk that I was there to meet Tara Fitzgerald, my head nearly dislocated from my neck when I saw her descending the grandest of grand staircases, her toned and sensual curves barely disguised by a form-fitting little black dress. Her face was flawless with whatever make-up she'd applied seemingly invisible. Her eyes had received some intricate treatment though, with eye shadow applied in three converging strips of color, magenta, rose and gold and lashes that appeared endless. Her lips, swollen and gorgeous, had a faint tone of aquamarine. I had to admit, she looked sensational. Oddly enough, her look wasn't dissimilar to that of Summer when she'd arrived at the Christmas Eve party at Perryman's.

Hmmm...

I greeted her with a polite kiss to both cheeks, savoring her eau de parfum scent, complimented her on her stunning appearance and escorted her out to the taxi line.

"You're being very secretive, Jake, what have you got planned for tonight?" she asked.

"You'll see!" I said, "But I'm just not sure it's going to be your cup of tea."

"I'm pretty flexible, you know, or do you think I'm just a rich girl who only likes the good things in life?"

"Umm... Tara, you're staying at the St. Regis," I replied, "You're not exactly slumming it!"

"I know, I get that, but it's not important to me where I stay. I'd be just as happy in a regular hotel but Daddy insists I stay in these kinds of places," she said, "I may seem like high maintenance, Jake, but really, I'm not at all."

It was interesting hearing Tara say that because I suppose in my heart of hearts, I knew she was a pretty straight up girl even if she was spoiled. But I couldn't really blame that on her because I truly believed she had a very kind heart. She must have to have feelings for me. Either kindness or pity, I guess.

Our cab finally pulled up outside an address on the Bowery in the East Village. I doubted if Tara had ever ventured into this area previously but I was willing to be proved wrong.

"CBGB!" she said excitedly, "I've always wanted to go there!"

"Well, it's not exactly CBGB that we're going to," I said, "We're actually going next door."

CBGB is a music venue that has spawned countless artists and bands since the early 1970s, Blondie, The Ramones, Talking Heads, Patti Smith and Joan Jett to name just a few. It is almost legendary as the birthplace of the New York punk revolution, which is a little ironic because CBGB actually stands for Country, Bluegrass and Blues.

"What's next door?" asked Tara.

"It's part of CGBG actually, it's called the CBGB Record Canteen," I replied.

"Canteen? What, it's a restaurant?"

"No, but it's a much smaller version of the main club next door and tonight, I've got tickets for something I think will be pretty special. Have you heard of Guns N' Roses?"

"Yes, I have and I like them. The singer's called Axel or something and the guitarist… Splash… or Slash?"

"You got it! Axl and Slash. Anyway, tonight, they're playing a short acoustic set which is going to be so different to how you've heard them before with all the big guitar sounds and drums and screaming vocals."

"Fantastic, Jake, what a great call getting tickets for this. My friends are going to be so jealous!"

So taking Tara out of her comfort zone hadn't really worked so far, in fact it was having the opposite effect, I think she liked me even more now. Maybe when she gets inside and smells the place and sees how filthy it is, she might change her mind.

But the show was incredible. I'd heard a lot about Guns N' Roses and realized they were going to be huge so to be able to see them sitting down playing an acoustic set with no more than a hundred other people in the room was amazing. And although they only played six songs in total, it was worth every cent of the C-note I'd given Troy. The band had the audience actually laughing when they played their third song of the night, "Used To Love Her"...

I used to love her, but I had to kill her

I had to put her six feet under

And I can still hear her complain...

Tara was dancing now, really enjoying herself and I could see the utter joy on her face that she was doing something and experiencing something that was not part of her world in any way. And although my plan was to try and put her off me in as gentle a way as possible, I was enjoying the fact that I'd brought some fun to her life. As she danced, I also became acutely aware that she'd forgotten to wear a bra that night.

The set lasted for only around thirty minutes but the band stayed behind and chatted with the audience and signed autographs. Tara was elated and bought a Guns N' Roses t-shirt which Axl duly signed for her. Actually, I think Axl wanted to take her home with him but I quickly guided Tara out of the club before she got herself into trouble. I couldn't see Daddy Fitzgerald being too happy with me if his only daughter ended up as a Guns N' Roses groupie.

"Jake, that was just the best, thank you so much!" she squealed as we pushed through the exit doors and outside onto the cigarette butt littered sidewalk of the Bowery.

"Well, the night is still young so I thought we'd go and find a club somewhere," I said, "And I think I have just the place for us."

I directed our cab driver to Hudson St. and we found ourselves outside a club called Area which had been open for around three or four years. It was sometimes hard to gain admission but Troy had kindly included putting our names on the guest list as part of his hundred buck trade.

We skipped the line and found ourselves walking through a kind of tunnel made from stone with statues lining the sides of the walkway. It reminded me more of a museum entrance than a nightclub. Every few steps there would be a window to one side and beyond the glass would be a live reptile or a performance art piece and in one of the last windows before we entered the club, I'm pretty sure two people were having sex but of course, it was in the name of art.

At the end of the tunnel, we found ourselves in a dark but terribly sexy nightclub, where Tara once again seemed to find herself immediately drawn to its inhabitants; fashion divas, musicians, artists, photographers and wannabes.

"Is that Sting?" she yelled, barely able to make herself heard over the music.

"I think so, and that's Boy George sitting over there at that table in the corner!" I replied, "And I think Andy Warhol used to come here often, right up until his death a few months ago."

Soft Cell was playing on the sound system and Tara immediately started dancing to Marc Almond's version of "Tainted Love". We stayed for two or three hours, both of us enjoying the music but after a while, it became so excessively hot that we needed to escape and get some air. I was soaked through my shirt but Tara didn't seem to have even broken sweat.

What is it about women, don't they sweat?

"Are you hungry?" I asked.

"Famished! Where do you want to go and eat?" asked Tara, "My hotel does great room service, if you'd like that?"

"Sure, but I could kill a steak dinner," I said, "Do you think it's too late for something like that or should we just grab a hamburger from one of those food trucks over there?"

"At the St. Regis, you can have anything you want, any time you want it!" she said, pulling my arm and guiding me towards a taxi that was parked at the curb.

Back at the St. Regis, we took the elevator up to Tara's room, which was actually The Royal Suite and a vast one at that with amazing views of Central Park and Fifth Avenue. As I stood looking out of the window, I suddenly realized how easy it would be to become accustomed to this kind of life.

I used one of the bathrooms to freshen up while Tara ordered our food from the room service menu and fixed some drinks for us. As I sat back on one of the sofas, I greedily drank from the glass of whiskey and Coke that Tara had handed me, savoring the sweet burning sensation as it slipped down my throat.

And after that, I really don't remember much.

All I know is that the room at some point began whirling and spinning and I couldn't focus on anything. I don't remember eating anything and I don't have any idea what happened until I woke up the following morning in Tara's bed. My mind was still foggy and I felt like I'd been hit over the head with a baseball bat. I looked over and saw that Tara was asleep next to me, the sheets low down, revealing her naked body.

What the heck happened last night?

Chapter 55

It was mid-June and I'd just made arrangements with Perryman to go and stay with him and Sofia in Sewall's Point for the Fourth of July celebrations. I'd decided to use a week of my vacation allowance so that I didn't have to rush back to the city as soon as I got to Perryman's. Sofia had moved in with him and they were officially a couple. The odd couple. I'd chatted to Talbot too and he'd told me that his relationship with Autumn was looking more positive than ever now although they still hadn't planned on revealing anything to Reyna and Joe.

As I sat at my desk, it felt strange how everything seemed to be changing. A couple of years ago, the three of us, Talbot, Perryman and myself were just three fresh-faced kids out of college with no real idea where life would take us and now everything seemed to be becoming much more grown up. Both Talbot and Perryman appeared to be fairly heavily involved with Autumn and Sofia respectively and yet here I was, still the same single Jake Delaney. Maybe I was never destined to be partnered with anyone or maybe the timing had never been right. But I didn't want to spend the rest of my life alone and unloved.

I'd thought about what had happened that night with Tara at the St. Regis but I still couldn't remember anything at all. I don't know if we'd had sex and I didn't want to ask Tara because it wouldn't exactly be a compliment to her own sexual prowess if I said that I couldn't remember if we had or hadn't. More of an insult. But if I couldn't remember, then I must have been out for the count and therefore nothing happened. But why did I wake up naked in her bed? And why was my penis so sore?

"You appear to be deep in thought, Jake," said Margaux Charrette, appearing in front of me as I sat glazed over in my chair, "Is there anything I can help you with?"

"Have you ever lost a night of your life and wondered what happened to it?" I asked her.

"I do remember one night back in around 1948, I think. Cocaine was a popular party companion," she said, "And like everyone else, I tried it and for the life of me, I have no idea how I got back home. All I know is that I woke up in my own bed and there was a man lying next to me and he wasn't wearing anything!"

"Margaux! I'm shocked! I had no idea you went to those types of parties!" I said, now suddenly wide awake from my slumber.

"Oh that was nothing, Jake, you should have seen the fun we had with the orgies…" she said, walking away from my desk, aiming a little wink at me as her face took on a new glow that morning.

Margaux Charrette, daytime Mary Poppins, nighttime sex fiend...

Chapter 56

Perhaps foolishly, I had declined Arthur's offer of a free ride down to South Florida on his jet but the truth was, I just loved my car and any chance I got to drive it for any length of time, I grabbed it with both hands. I'd now mastered the thousand-mile journey and found that by leaving my apartment at 4am I could be at Perryman's house by around 6pm, stopping twice for gas and snacks.

I drove into Sewall's Point, the town becoming more familiar each time I arrived there, and quickly found Perryman's driveway snaking upwards from River Road. I turned off the ignition and looked around but couldn't see anyone else on the property. I assumed I must be the first to arrive.

"Just in time, Delaney, we're prepping for a barbecue on the beach. It's gonna be hot but we've got a nice breeze washing in off the water," said Perryman, as he surveyed my arrival from the second-floor balcony, looking more like a Greek god than ever before. A moneyed existence was definitely agreeing with the man.

His white-blond hair had grown even longer now, and I couldn't help thinking as I looked back up at him that he was playing Juliet in a real-life Shakespearian tragedy. Any minute I thought, Sofia's Romeo was going to come running outside, yelling up to him, "Juliet, Juliet! Wherefore art thou, Juliet?"

"I'll be right in, just let me grab my bag. Is it okay to leave the car here or do you want it in the garage?" I asked.

"No, leave it there, there ain't gonna be no rain tonight, that's for sure," he replied.

Inside, I was surprised to find fifteen or sixteen other people already there, including all of the Cantrells. But I was disappointed to see that Summer appeared to be with a boy of around her age. Maybe in the previous six months she'd finally decided to hook up with a boy from school? Maybe this was how it should be. However, I was relieved to see that Tara hadn't been invited or that she was busy. I wasn't sure I could handle the two of them being in the same room together at the same time.

Perryman's home was a perfect party and entertaining house. I could see that a barbecue had been set up down on the beach to the rear of the property and chairs had been scattered haphazardly across the white sand with a couple of dozen tiki bamboo torches placed in the ground, circling the entire seating area. If you could imagine one of those vacation brochure photos where life is just about taking it easy for a couple of weeks, then this was the real-life version.

I slowly made my way through the small crowd, introducing myself to a couple of guests I hadn't met before and giving hugs to those I already knew. Eventually, I met Summer's eyes and she smiled at me in that enchanting and mischievous way I remembered from when I first met her on Talbot's boat in 1985. I smiled back, not so enchanting when you've got a face like mine, and we both took steps towards each other.

"It seems like years since I saw you," I said, scooping her into my arms and hugging her tightly.

"I know, I've really missed you, Jake!" she replied, returning the fondness of my hug.

"I see you've got a boyfriend, are you going to introduce me?"

"He's not my boyfriend, silly! That's John Shea, from school! He's really nice but he's not my type, Jake. I only have one type and you know that."

"So why did you bring him? I'm a bit confused although I have no right to be," I replied.

"Think about it. Mom and Dad are here and they already suspect something between us so I thought that by bringing John it would be good cover for me and they would think that there was nothing going on between you and me," she said.

"I get it now. But Summer, is there anything between us?" I asked.

"Jake, you know there is or are you just playing with me?"

At that moment, Talbot sidled over with Autumn, and interrupted what was becoming an interesting conversation between us.

"Well, if it isn't Talbot, the true Bard of Jensen Beach," I said as my friend embraced me.

"Uneasy is the head that wears the crown," he replied, in true silky smooth Talbotesque fashion.

I hugged Autumn and it occurred to me how much these two sisters had grown up in recent months. Gone was the girlish awkwardness that was previously apparent in both of them, now replaced by the confidence of two very alluring and intelligent young women.

"How's college treating you?" I asked her.

"It's fine, Jake, but what I miss most are the home comforts, I guess. I hate sharing a bathroom with three other girls and I didn't realize until I left home how gross girls can be," she replied, "Last week, just before I left to come home, someone had left a used tampon in the toilet, I wanted to throw up!"

We all laughed hysterically and I added,

"Well, I think you'd probably find it a lot worse if you were sharing with boys. I mean, I remember once when I was at college, one of the guys sharing my apartment got so drunk one night, they couldn't wake him up the next morning. So they spray painted a heart on each buttock. Poor guy spent the next three months trying to get it off!"

"That's what you get when you spend your life amongst the Neanderthals of this world," added Talbot, "Most men don't properly mature until they're around fifty!"

"Shall we adjourn to the beach?" I suggested, "Before anything gets revealed about me?"

Down on the beach, we gathered around the barbecue which in itself wasn't the normal size you'd find in a Florida back yard. This one was more akin to a chef's kitchen that had been relocated outdoors. Perryman had an enviable choice of food cooking away, hamburgers, ribs, sausages, lobster tails, New York Strips, chicken wings, pork kebabs, corn, baked potatoes and that wasn't including what was on the huge table which had every type of salad on offer as well as cold cuts.

The four of us filled a plate each and found a seating arrangement just by the water's edge. It was certainly a warm and humid evening but Perryman was right, the breeze made it perfect for a Summer barbecue. I hadn't eaten all day, apart from some chips and a sandwich I'd picked up on the way down so I was ravenous. I bit hungrily into a hamburger, realizing too late that I'd literally bitten off more than I could chew.

"Hungry, Jake?" asked Summer, giggling at my inability to respond, "Eyes bigger than your belly, piglet?"

"We know what we are, but know not what we may be," Talbot chimed in.

"Go frig yourself, Talbot, you haven't been traveling for the better part of a day without sustenance!" I said to him.

Autumn laughed at my discomfort but that only added fuel to Talbot's educated wit.

"How sharper than a serpent's tooth it is to have a thankless child!" he said with a little too much glee.

"Well, as long as you're all enjoying yourselves at my expense, I think I might go grab me a lobster tail now," I said, getting up from my chair and making a beeline to the barbecue.

Summer got up and followed me, grabbing my arm as I paced across the sand.

"Jake, you know it was only a joke, don't you, we were only teasing."

"Of course I do, don't you realize how long I've known Talbot? I'm only teasing too, I'm not upset!" I laughed, "But if coming away to get more food means that I get to talk to you alone, I'm happy to be the butt of Mr. Gaylord Talbot's jokes!"

"Gaylord?"

"Oops! That's another story for another time!" I replied.

We found a private spot away from the rest of the group and sat down to eat some excellent lobster tails. It hit me now that the discomfort I'd previously found spending time alone with Summer was now replaced by an incredible sense of joy. This girl was really everything a man could dream of, even if I was a lot older than her. Because in terms of mental age, Summer was far beyond me.

"Isn't it beautiful?" she asked, "How lucky are we to be sitting here and enjoying the best that South Florida can offer?"

Someone had gone around lighting the tiki torches and I could smell the sweet scent of citronella drifting through the night air.

"We certainly are," I replied, "And it's funny, but when Perryman first began living here, it still felt like the house belonged to someone else, but it doesn't now."

"I totally agree, he seems to have put his own flavor on it now, but it's not the messy surfer dude style I was expecting, it's more F. Scott Fitzgerald, don't you think?"

“I hadn’t thought about it that way before but at Christmas, I did sense a touch of the Great Gatsby about him. He’s changed a lot but I really like what he’s become,” I replied.

“And talking of Fitzgerald, I heard that you and Tara went out on a date recently,” she said.

“No, no, no, not a date! She just happened to be in the city and wanted to meet up, so I was the indefatigable host!”

“So, nothing happened?” she asked, “At the end of the date?”

“No! Nothing at all!” I replied.

Not that I’m aware of anyway...

Chapter 57

The following morning, I decided to go out to the supermarket on the island and pick up some wine and provisions for the holiday period. I realized that Perryman had no need for me to buy anything but I'd arrived empty handed and my mother had always taught me that a guest should always arrive with goodies when staying with friends.

The store was packed out, everyone and their mother piling groceries into shopping carts like someone had just announced the end of the world.

I decided to buy a few things that Perryman's maid might not have bought, including a selection of French and Spanish cheeses, Camembert, Emmental, Roquefort and Manchego being amongst my favorites. I was amazed to find that this little supermarket sold Foie Gras so I tucked a terrine of it into my cart. I snagged a case of Prosecco too, along with a few bottles of Port while I was in the deli and wine section. I bought six cases of beer as well. I mean, Perryman had to drink something too…

After I'd paid for my swag at the checkout, I loaded my groceries into the back of the Porsche, taking care to put the cheeses and Foie Gras into my cooler, and decided to take a quick tour of the area. I turned left out of the supermarket car park and drove at the 45mph speed limit along the strip of land which was Hutchinson Island. It was one of those rare places on earth where you could look to the left and see the Indian River Lagoon and to the right, the Atlantic Ocean with just a narrow highway separating the two. It always amazed me every time I came here that no one had yet clued in to the fact that this area was so much nicer than its big brother down at Palm Beach. This particular part of the Treasure Coast remained the undiscovered jewel of Florida and in my own heart, I hoped it always stayed that way. But in reality, I knew it wouldn't.

As I neared the 'beach' area of Jensen Beach, I decided to take a left over the Jensen Beach Causeway and take in the views as I drove across to the mainland. It was spectacular and I could see that all the avid boaters in the area had begun the holiday early as the water was littered with sailboats, cruisers, whalers and simple rowing boats with outboard motors attached. They called this area the Sailfish capital of the world but in truth it seemed like it should be called the Sailing capital of the world. Most everyone who lived here, jumped at the chance to get out on the water any time they could.

I floored the gas pedal and grinned as the Porsche fishtailed up the bridge leaving black tire marks in its trail but then slowed as I reached its summit and began the descent to the other side into Jensen Beach town. I loved this time of year, just the locals enjoying their little piece of heaven, no longer disturbed by the seasonal tourist invasion. As I purred through Main Street, I heard the familiar sound of Summer's Bronco. You always heard it before you saw it. She was on the other side of the street, heading towards me and stopped when we were level with each other.

"D'you want to come over for something to eat on the boat tonight?" I shouted above the roar of the V8.

"I'd love to," she said, "What time?"

"Come on over at eight but come down through the side entrance straight to the dock," I yelled, "And don't bring anything, just yourself!"

"See you then!" she said, accelerating away.

You're a lucky man, Jake...

Chapter 58

I'd made shrimp salad to start with and I'd picked up a couple of filets from the market which I planned to prepare with a topping of Foie Gras, asparagus and new potatoes. I'd held back a piece of the Manchego and a baguette to snack on before we began dinner and I'd noticed that the exquisite wine stock had remained untouched since my last visit to the boat.

I was thankful that rain hadn't been in the forecast because I was hoping we could eat outside by the boat's pool. It was already approaching eight o'clock and so I selected some discs to load into the stereo system. I wasn't unhappy at the first random song that stylishly oozed from Bryan Ferry's unique and seriously sexy vocal chords…

Tell her I'll be waiting, in the usual place

With the tired and weary, there's no escape

Slave to love…

I heard footsteps further down on the deck of the vessel and guessed that Summer had arrived. As I turned to look, my heart skipped a beat when I saw her walking towards me. Gone was the teenager in the Daisy Dukes and t-shirt, replaced now by a stunning young woman in a white silk blouse, an elegant fitted skirt showing her amazing and never-ending legs and a refined and simple pair of court shoes, not too high, not too low. Her hair was a wild mane that perfectly framed her flawless face.

"Wow! Look at you!" I said, my words catching slightly in my throat.

"What do you mean, am I too grown up now?" she giggled, knowing that she had put me on the back foot.

"No, not too grown up, just a sight for my sore eyes!" I replied, "You look gorgeous!"

"Oh, stop it! Anyway, I'm hungry, what does a girl have to do to get something to eat around here?"

"Well apparently, not much," I said, "Come on up, I've got some snacks to start you off."

We sat down on one of the sofas by the pool, both of us aware of the circumstances resulting from the last time we'd found ourselves in the same setting.

"Oooh! Manchego! My favorite cheese, how did you know that?"

"Oh, just a wild guess, I suppose…"

The girl was hungry. She'd barely finished her first baguette loaded with the Spanish cheese than she was ripping off a new piece.

How the hell does she keep a figure like that when she eats like this?

"I'd offer you a glass of wine but I'm acutely aware of the age limit in this state," I said.

"Don't be an idiot, Jake, my parents have been letting me have tiny glasses of wine since I was thirteen," she replied, "I'd love one but just a small one because I have to drive home at some point."

I poured her a half glass of Pinot Gris and we clinked our glasses together.

"To us," she said, "And whatever life brings us in the future!"

"To us, Summer," I replied, "But more importantly, to one of the loveliest people I have ever had the pleasure to meet. Thank you for being my friend."

After a few minutes chatting about our day, I departed to check on the evening's dinner while Summer perused the music on offer. As I was tossing the asparagus in herbed butter and black pepper, I recognized a familiar song…

I'll protect you from the hooded claw

Keep the vampires from your door...

Frankie Goes To Hollywood's "The Power Of Love". It was the first song I remembered, the first time I ever saw Summer way back when in Maple Street. I wondered if she'd remembered or whether it was just a coincidence…

The hours drifted by and I can only describe the evening as being one of the most beautiful nights of my life. We both enjoyed the meal I'd prepared, and even without an overindulgence of alcohol, I felt myself walking on air. She was so easy to be with, she was so relaxed and so was I. When we danced that night, it was so easy to forget that there was such an age difference because we seemed to have passed that hurdle and a new beginning dawned…

Chapter 59

It was a perfect and glorious midsummer night, the sky remarkably clear in its blackness, the stars appearing larger and brighter than I'd ever remembered seeing before. It was late in the evening and with midnight approaching, the next morning was already beckoning. I'd escorted Summer out to the driveway to see her safely into her car when she asked an unexpected question.

"Can we go for a drive, Jake?" she asked.

I was a little surprised I suppose but I also knew in my own selfish heart that I didn't want the evening to end.

"Of course we can," I replied, "Where would you like me to take you?"

"The beach!"

"Sure, I'd like that. Which one did you have in mind, we've plenty to choose from."

"My favorite one," she answered, "Bathtub Reef."

"Well, what are we waiting for, let's go!"

"Just one thing though…" she added.

"What is it?" I asked.

"Can I drive?"

I looked into her excited eyes and realized there was no refusing this girl.

"Of course," I replied, handing her the keys, "But take it easy!"

As we climbed into the Porsche and fastened our seat belts, Summer started the engine and I pushed the button to put the convertible top down.

“Are you ready to be driven by a teenager?” she asked, laughing at the sudden panic on my face, “Don’t worry, I’m a good driver, my papa taught me!”

We headed out and found ourselves crossing the causeway onto Hutchinson Island on SE Ocean Boulevard, the incandescent street lights highlighting the shape of the sweeping, graceful bridge that connected the two pieces of land. I glanced across at this extraordinary and bewitching girl driving my car, her face a picture of complete joy and elation as she smiled back at me. Her long wavy hair was running wild in the wind, whipping back and forth as she accelerated across the bridge. I glanced down, not wanting to linger but couldn’t help but marvel at her legs that contrasted entrancingly and seductively with the black leather of the Porsche’s seat.

After a few minutes, we arrived at Bathtub Reef and got out of the car, leaving our shoes behind in the footwells. She took my hand as we walked up toward the beach area and we found a perfect spot to sit and watch the ocean. I spread a towel on the sand, grateful that I’d previously stowed it in the trunk of the car.

We sat silently, listening to the lapping waves that bathed the sand below us, the ocean’s soothing breeze wafting over us, cooling our warming bodies. After ten minutes or so, she whispered something in my ear.

“I want you to make love to me, Jake.”

I turned to look at her.

“I can’t, Summer.”

“Why not?” she asked, disappointment clearly registering on her delicate features, “It’ll be okay, Jake, I promise.”

“No, I just can’t, Summer, it would be so wrong.”

“But I love you Jake, doesn’t that change anything, doesn’t that count?”

“I have this inevitable feeling that I might love you too, but I have to respect you, I need to respect your family too. I don’t want them to think I’m some crazy cradle snatcher. Can’t we just enjoy this moment together without doing something we might regret?”

“But I’ll be eighteen tomorrow...” she whispered.

“That hadn’t escaped my attention. And neither have you,” I said, “In fact, it’s already past midnight…”

“Do you think I’m being too forward?”

“No, no, really you’re not. But you know, this is a big deal, I mean…it’s your first time…it’s got to be perfect…and with the right person…do you see what I mean?” I said to this delicate and innocent ingénue sitting beside me, “It’s such a special thing for every girl and I couldn’t bear for you to ever be hurt. I suppose what I’m trying to say is that I don’t want you to lose something that you may not yet be ready to let go.”

“Jake, I haven’t stopped thinking about you since I was sixteen. I made a decision a long time ago that it had to be you and only you and I’m truly ready now. I’ve yearned for you for so long now, I want you and only you.’

“Are you sure, Summer, are you completely sure this is what you want?” I asked.

“Yes, Jake, surer than I’ve ever been about anything.”

I reached over to her, delicately cradling her face in my hands and eased her gently towards me. She responded and moved with me, turning herself towards me, my face coming closer to hers as our hearts began to beat faster. I grazed her lips with mine and our eyes, not further than inches away from each other, searched each other’s, not knowing what to do next.

“Jake,” she said, “Take off my top...”

I did as she asked me, unbuttoning her shirt and easing it from her shoulders. She sat before me in a minimal but elegantly simple bra that just about hid her modesty.

As I marveled at this winsome, yet alluring beauty before me, she slowly stood and as I looked up at her, she said,

"Take off my skirt," "Please, Jake…"

I slipped my hands behind her and undid the single button and pulled down the zip. Her skirt fell to the ground, revealing a body, the like of which I'd never seen before, even in college. Her bra glowed white under the moonlight and her panties sheer that they were, did little to hide what lay beneath.

"You're intoxicating, Summer, you have me under a spell and I don't want to break it."

She knelt in the sand and took my face in her hands and I could smell her scent, lush with traces of cedar, jasmine and juniper. She pulled me close and touched my lips with hers, fragrant and full. My mouth opened slightly as I invited her to taste me. Her tongue slowly but gently found my mouth and my own tongue touched hers, velvet and moist, darting playfully across my teeth.

We began to kiss, not wishing to force anything, but very quickly our combined passion began to take over. We couldn't get enough of each other's mouths; it was now frenzied, we couldn't hold anything back.

"Can I undress *you* now?" she asked.

"Are you sure?"

"I am," she said, "I've never been more so."

She tentatively began to remove my shirt and as the garment fell to the sand, she ran her hands down my chest, lingering at my navel.

"Do you have any idea how long I've imagined this? I've been waiting and dreaming about this moment for so long now."

"I had no idea, Summer, but trust me when I say that I feel incredibly privileged to be here with you right now."

I stood and she rose up with me. I was still mesmerized by her body; it was a thousand times more than I had ever dared to dream. And guiltily, I had to admit I'd dreamed many times…

She ran her hands around my waist and stopped at my belt buckle where she tugged at it slightly before I felt the release of the belt. Unbuttoning my jeans, she put her fingers on my zip but I reached down and held her hand.

"It's not too late to stop," I whispered, "I don't want you to ever feel as though you'd made a mistake."

"I'm more nervous than you can possibly imagine but I don't want this to stop, I want it to last forever!"

She smiled at me, that innocent smile that has stayed in my head now for almost two years. I let go of her hand and she carefully unzipped me and slowly pulled my jeans to the ground.

I stepped out of them fully aware that my arousal was now clearly evident through my boxers.

"I don't think I've ever felt so embarrassed about myself," I said.

"Would it help if I did this?" she asked.

She reached behind her back and let slip the clasp of her bra, gently letting it fall away. Her breasts were nothing less than perfect. Her pertness and ripeness held me transfixed as I struggled to accept the incredible perfection of God's making that stood here before me. My arousal grew even more when I reached towards her and cupped beneath her breasts, ran my fingers around the areolas and across her now fully responsive nipples.

She gently guided my hand downwards and smiled at me again…

"Take them off, as slowly as you can…"

I knelt to the ground, my mouth level with her abdomen. Without realizing what I was doing, I leaned into her, tasting her aroma, like an addict who couldn't drink enough of a drug into his body. My nose nuzzled against her softness, only the sheer material of her remaining clothing between me and the moist darkness of her femininity.

"Are you sure?" I asked, now begging in my mind for the answer to be positive.

"I'm so, so sure…" she said, breathlessly now.

I took the material between my fingers and delicately pulled it down to reveal her silkiness lying virginal before my captivated eyes.

"Kiss me Jake, please, please kiss me there!" she implored, as her hands cupped the back of my head.

I put my own hands behind her and pulled her dampness to my willing mouth. My tongue explored her, probing deeply into her, tasting everything she possessed. She moaned as my tongue found her, time and time again. She collapsed to the ground, her hands pulling my face to hers, her tongue quickly invading my mouth and finding my own.

We stayed there, kneeling on the ground, clutching each other as though we were frightened that if we let go, we'd lose everything.

After a minute or two, she slowly released me and asked,

"I know it's a weird thing to ask, but did you bring anything with you tonight?"

"You mean, did I wonder if something like this might happen?" I asked.

"Yes, I'm not on the pill, I'm really sorry," she replied.

"Don't worry," I said, "I think I have one in my wallet," I said.

I reached over and retrieved it and she hesitantly took it from me.

"I need to learn sometime," she said, retrieving the packet from within.

"I guess… well,… if you're okay with that?"

"I'm okay, Jake, I've never been more so," she said.

She slid her hands down the back of my shorts and lightly clasped my cheeks, her nails sinking briefly into my skin. Her hands slid my boxers down my thighs and she began to move her fingers around my hips until she came to my own full arousal. Her hands moved onto it with an almost natural action and held me as I felt my blood pump between her hands.

"Oh God, Jake, I don't want this night to ever end!" she said.

"Please, Summer, just for a moment, are you absolutely certain you want to do this? I think you can see what state I'm in right now but I'll stop everything now if you want."

"I've waited so long, Jake, too long, I want you to be the one, I want you to always be the one. My first love, my first time," she replied.

"Do you want me to show you how to do that?" I asked, indicating the packet she held in her hand.

"Yes," she said.

I tore the top from the packet and offered her the contents.

"It can only go on one way and once you place it, just unroll it to the end," I said, realizing then that I'd never given instructions before.

She took me in her hand and began to caress me, my response growing quickly again with every touch. As she unrolled the latex, I wasn't sure how long I could hold on…

She looked back up at me and I was drawn instinctively to her mouth, her lips inviting me to taste her again. I pulled her to me and as I kissed her, I felt her breasts pushing against my chest. My kiss left her lips and moved to her neck, gently nibbling at her taut skin before my tongue explored her shoulders and moved down to her breasts. I licked, kissed and teased and saw tiny goosebumps appear on her skin, highlighted in stark relief by the white light from the moon.

"Jake, I can't hold on, I need you, need you now..." she moaned.

I put my hands around her waist and gently lowered her to the ground. She lay like a precious jewel in the sand, something honed by the ocean and brought to me tonight in a lapping wave, her body lit pale and her soft dark cleft accenting the area between her long, slender and athletic legs.

As I moved above her and between her, she parted for me, taking me in her hand and guiding me to her.

"Take it off, Jake, I want to feel you, just you, nothing else…"

"It's too dangerous, Summer, you know that," I said.

I don't care, this is my first time and I want to feel and remember everything about it… I want to always have the feeling of you inside me… I never ever want to lose it!"

I slipped the condom off and her hand once again reached for me and drew me to her. I felt her welcoming swollenness on my tip and paused as long as I could…

"Please Jake, now, do it now…" she whispered.

"I will, but we have to do this very slowly, really carefully. I don't want to hurt you, I'm going to be as gentle as I can."

I pushed into her as carefully as possible, feeling every inch of her as she took me in.

She gasped, a tiny moan emitting from her, a tear beginning to form in one corner of her eye.

I stopped for a moment…

"Does it hurt, please tell me if you're in pain?" I asked.

"Oh Jake, I can feel you, I can feel you inside me," she replied, "Don't stop, please don't stop…"

"Just move with me Summer, we'll go softly, gently and slowly…together," I said, aware of this precious moment for a girl with whom I now realized I'd fallen in love.

I kissed her, longingly, tenderly, holding her as we remained locked to each other. As the seconds turned into minutes, our bodies undulated together, seemingly lost within each other but physically tied to one another. I could feel the humidity of the air intensify, gathering now as warm moisture between us, our bodies now bathed in perspiration, our minds intoxicated by the feel of our skin against each other. My gaze remained transfixed on her blue, blue eyes, magnetized by her, desperate never to lose this intensely perfect moment. Her lips slightly parted as she took short and intense breaths, a feeling inside beginning to build at a quicker pace now. My mouth hovered within an inch of hers and we could feel each other's hot breath. I didn't want this fleeting and magical moment to ever end...

I was in heaven, her warmth, her wetness, her body arching in ecstasy as I rhythmically pushed inside her and slowly withdrew before doing it again, over and over…

We moved together in perfect unison, a rhythm that neither of us wanted to lose, until… suddenly, our bodies froze and we both felt a simultaneous surge, an electrical moment that feverishly ran through both of us, our mouths locking together in a frantic search for each other's hot and desperate tongues. I'd never felt such an emotion before, I was floating outside of my body in an almost ethereal, other world experience.

The feeling lasted for what felt like hours but was really only seconds before I finally collapsed, exhausted, onto the cool sand, bringing Summer with me, wrapped in my arms, loving her draped across my body, loving the exquisite perfection of her back, her bottom, her thighs…

After a few moments, she lifted herself up and sat astride me, her hands on my chest, delicately touching my own nipples with her thumbs. She was smiling radiantly; she had a freshness in her face and a 'joie de vivre', that told me that everything was finally right in her world. I silently applauded myself for having not messed up with Summer because it was definitely a moment that I could easily have blown.

I'm a man after all...

I was still stunned by this beauty, this teenage goddess who had shared something so beautiful with me, something that neither she nor I would ever forget.

"Jake?"

"What's wrong?"

"Nothing," she replied.

"Then what is it?" I asked.

"Can we do it again?" she asked, an impish grin spreading across her impeccable features, "Is it possible or do you need some more time?"

I thought you'd never ask...

Chapter 60

The next three weeks were a whirlwind. I saw Summer every available moment I could. I paid for airline tickets so that she could come and stay with me in my apartment during the week while I was working and she would spend time exploring the city during the day. And in the evenings, we would find new restaurants to sample and we'd walk everywhere in the city, strolling the streets hand in hand and savoring the gift of New York's moonlit Summer nights.

On many occasions after having dinner, we would lie down on the grass in Central Park, gazing up at the sky and try to identify the stars that seemed to be smiling back at us. Summer reveled in her freedom to explore Manhattan while I toiled frustratingly in my office, desperate for the clock to tick down to going home time so I could be with her once again and repeat a perfect Groundhog Day re-run of the evening before.

At weekends, we would travel back to South Florida together, like two kids excited at the thought of spending even more time in each other's arms but more and more wary of the scrutiny being placed on us by her parents. Nothing was ever said but sometimes the silence betrayed the unspoken words. I knew that Joe and Reyna weren't happy with the amount of time she's been spending with me in Manhattan but they also knew she was eighteen now and she was making her own decisions.

When I was in Florida, I stayed either at Talbot's or at Perryman's and Summer and I would sneak out late at night to repeat what we'd done in the early hours of her birthday, like a pair of nocturnal teenagers for whom sleep had become an unnecessary intrusion to life. At my urging, she finally went to her doctor who prescribed birth control pills because she didn't like me using the dreaded prophylactics. But during the time we were able to spend together, and the countless times we made love with each other, both of us were all too aware of an impending moment that would break the spell for us when she would leave for college to begin her six week Summer term before her freshman year began in earnest.

Neither of us ever really wanted to broach the subject, choosing to banish it to the back of our minds as though the day would never arrive. We had become so comfortable with each other that it was like we were living only for the here and now in what would be her last days of real freedom before four years of college life began. Something told me that her parents were pretty keen for college life to start as soon as possible because I think they felt that Summer had become too distracted and needed to concentrate more on the future.

But eventually, the dreaded day finally arrived. The 26th day of July saw all of us gathered at the Cantrell house, watching as Joe loaded the last of Summer's bags into her Bronco. I stood and watched with Perryman, Talbot, and Autumn as Reyna fought back the tears that were welling in her eyes and Joe tried manfully to maintain his own composure by making himself as busy as possible. Talbot was all too aware of my own emotions and put his arm around my shoulder as I tried in vain to suffocate the emotions that were roiling inside of me.

I had offered to drive Summer up to her campus in the Bronco but Joe was adamant that he needed to do it to show her the route so that when she came back for the holidays, she'd know exactly how to get home. I couldn't argue with him about it because this was his job as Summer's dad to make sure his little girl was safe, now and in the future. I even offered to ride in the back to keep them company but then it dawned on me that this was a very special and unique father-daughter moment, an event where I was surplus to requirement but one that I completely understood.

Summer embraced each of us as we realized that the inevitable moment was upon us. Before she gave her mom a final hug, she came to me and threw her arms around me in the tightest grasp I'd ever felt from her. She stood on tiptoe and whispered into my ear,

"I love you, Jake Delaney, I'll be seeing you soon."

The tears streamed down my cheeks. I could no longer hold back the emotions that were bursting out of me but she was so incredibly strong. She smiled that smile that I'd seen for the very first time on Maple St. and got into the Bronco next to her dad, giving just a little wave to us as Joe maneuvered the truck out onto the road.

We stood there on the driveway as the Bronco growled its way down Skyline Drive, all of us waving until the car and Summer, were finally out of sight, just a trail of exhaust fumes left floating towards the sky. And then she was gone.

Chapter 61

I was shooting hoops in my apartment a week later, trying to make sense of what had happened during the last four weeks, in fact the last couple of years in all honesty. Perryman had generously arranged for a basket to be installed in the spare space at the end of the loft and it had become a nightly routine of mine to practice basketball, something that I'd never been too good at when I was a teenager. I quickly realized what an amazing sport it was and also what an incredible workout it could be. I also needed as many distractions as I could get, so I was grateful for any extracurricular activity.

It was the beginning of August and I felt suddenly very lonely. The time Summer and I had spent together had been so intense without a single wasted moment and we couldn't get enough of each other. I'd lost count of how many times we'd made love but we were insatiable, inexhaustible and relentless. Every moment of passion was like the first time, like a honeymoon that would never end. But now it was as though the car was being driven at 100mph and suddenly the handbrake had been engaged and I'd come to a full stop.

I had few friends in the city but even with the people I did know fairly well, in reality I had little desire to go and hang out. Florida already seemed a thousand years ago and I was feeling the first hint of a depression around me. And in truth, I'm not a depressive kind of man but then again, I hadn't ever fallen in love before. The kid with the crush was now me.

I'd tried calling Summer at college but it had been impossible to speak to her as the dorm phone seemed to be constantly in use. And for some reason, she hadn't called me but I guessed that college life was taking its toll on her in her first few weeks there and as soon as she was settled, I knew she'd be in contact again. I should have realized how much your freshman year takes out of you because I'd been there myself but for a man who had fallen head over heels in love, the rational and logistical lawyerly part of me seemed to have taken a vacation. I just couldn't stop thinking about her. I'd go to sleep thinking about her, wake up thinking about her and the entire day would pass with only her in my thoughts.

I tried to analyze what had happened. I'd spent almost two years trying to mentally repel her when in my own mind, I knew that she was the one. I'd spent that time secretly adoring her but satisfying myself that the timing just hadn't been right and that perhaps one day it might be. But during this time, it also became clear to me how much stronger the entire female race is compared to men. They seem so much better equipped to cope with disappointment, broken hearts, emotional turmoil and relationships in general. Men think they are the stronger sex but in reality, we are weak, fragile and flawed in comparison.

It was odd, because as the time passed and I still didn't hear from her, despite writing several letters to her at college, my sense of loneliness just kept increasing. I thought about driving up to FSU and surprising her but realized that could be a big mistake. In fleeting moments, it occurred to me that maybe she had achieved what she wanted with me and had got me out of her system and that her new surroundings were giving her a different view on life.

But I even felt a disconnect with my old friends in South Florida. Maybe I'd spent too much time with Summer and not enough with them? Talbot had become distant with me and at times, I felt he was dodging my calls although I'm sure it was my imagination. I had assumed that his life was now directed to what his own needs were, his main focus being Autumn. Even Perryman seemed to be putting on a veneer although he was still friendly enough. Both of them claimed not to have heard from Summer though so maybe I wasn't the only one left in the dark. I didn't want to call her parents because I didn't know how aware they were of my feelings for their daughter, so all in all, I existed for some weeks in a capsule where communication with my previous home away from home was practically zero.

In fact, as the weeks passed and then became months, I felt for the first time that whatever thoughts I had had for Summer, were probably now confined to a beautiful moment of what I wanted to be an endless Summer. I guessed that once she had arrived at college, the excitement of her new life took over and she was inundated with offers of dates from the thousands of similarly-aged boys already there. It was nothing new really, every freshman hits an initial high once they leave home for the first time as they taste independence and begin a new life away from their family. I castigated myself for being the naïve one now. Naïve to think that a girl like this wouldn't be immediately in demand and that a man whose next milestone would be thirty, would quickly lose his attraction, replaced systematically by younger versions.

I wrote one final letter to her but realized it would probably go unanswered as had the previous notes I'd sent, although I never understood the reasons why. But then August became September and September became October… I never stopped hoping that the phone would ring or that I'd find a note from her in my mailbox. But the sad truth is, I never heard from Summer again.

Chapter 62

As the fall set in, I threw myself into my work. I realized that whatever I had been thinking for the future was now just a dream, a silly fantasy in reality. I was beginning to think hard about whether I wanted to stay on the east coast or maybe make a total change and move to the west coast. I didn't even know if I wanted to continue being a lawyer.

But I needed something new in my life now, I needed change. I couldn't bear the thought of working in Manhattan for the next thirty or so years because if I really thought about it, I may have been born a city boy, but I truly yearned for something else. I also knew I'd never find it in Florida because already, the memories were becoming sad ones.

I flicked through the channels on my television, hoping to find something vaguely interesting to watch. I'd just eaten pizza and my diet as a whole was turning to shit. I was getting flabby, I even had a paunch.

I switched off the TV and turned on my stereo instead. I'd bought a similar, although less expensive multi-disc system to the one on Perryman's boat and I loved that you never knew what song would come out or in which order.

The first song that came on as I lay back on my couch was the sad ode to lost love by John Waite. I loved this song when I first heard it a year or so ago but had never thought then how much it would mean to me a year later.

I ain't missing you at all

Since you've been gone, away...

Yes, I was drowning in my sorrows and yes, every song reminded me of what had happened in my life. But right now, I just didn't care, I wanted to wallow in self-pity and I needed to be that selfish man.

As the song ended, my telephone rang which to be truthful was still a rare thing and actually now, a welcome intrusion. I'm not one to give out my home number to many people so it either had to be someone I knew or a scammer trying to get money from me.

"Hello?" I said, but the line remained silent. I said hello again and a few seconds later, I heard a familiar voice.

"Hi Jake, long time, no see," she said.

"Tara? Is that you?"

"It is, how are you, Jake?"

"I'm fine… I guess. Well, I'm okay anyway, but you don't sound like yourself. Is everything okay?"

"Not really."

"What's wrong, Tara, why do you sound so low? This is not like you," I said.

"Can we talk?" she asked.

"Of course, tell me what's wrong," I said, not sure at all of what could be making her sound so low.

"I mean, can we meet and talk."

"Sure. Are you in town? If you are, I could meet up with you tonight if that helps?"

"I am. I'm at the St. Regis but could we meet somewhere for coffee?" she asked.

"Sure, I could use a change of scenery anyway. Do you want to meet near your hotel? There's a café I know that's on the corner of 55th and Madison called Café Society, do you know it?"

“Yes, I know it, it’s just along from my hotel. So can we meet at say 7pm tonight?”

“Absolutely, I’ll see you there and it will be really lovely to see you Tara, I feel like I need a friend right now.”

“It will be lovely to see you too, Jake, I feel much the same as you in that regard. See you soon. Bye.”

She clicked off but she definitely wasn’t the Tara I had come to know and love, something was definitely not quite right with her. Well, I guessed I’d find out soon enough.

Chapter 63

I decided to leave the Porsche in its parking bay and I took a cab uptown. It was pointless driving as I'd never find a space to park and whenever I got into my car, all I wanted to do was drive fast with the roof down. I felt so restricted in the city, so done with New York and everything in it. As I sat in the back of the taxi, I realized that Summer should have ended by now but it was still trespassing in the Autumn months and as the season refused to die, something inside me was pushing me to change everything in my life.

The taxi pulled up outside Café Society and I paid the cab driver and looked through the plate glass window to see if Tara had already arrived. She hadn't, so I went inside and snagged a table at the back where it was a little quieter. I ordered a cappuccino for myself and a couple of pain aux raisins and asked the waiter to bring a soy latte for Tara which I knew was her favorite.

As I sat there, resuming my daily ritual of people watching, I felt that I was the loneliest man in the city today. It seemed that the chatter was endless amongst the clientele here and that they were each bursting to relate to their coffee companions how incredible their lives were and all I could do was to think about what I'd lost. But I knew that I couldn't rely on something changing my life, I needed to make the change myself, under my own steam.

At that moment, just as I was sinking lower into the depths of my soul, I could see the door open in the distance and immediately recognized Tara's unique hair as she turned and spotted me at the rear of the café. But as she emerged from the crowd and made her way towards me, I couldn't help but notice that rather than sporting her usually unbelievable figure, she seemed to have put on a little weight since I'd last seen her.

"Hi Jake, aren't you a sight for sore eyes?" she said, flinging her arms around me and kissing me on the cheek.

"Well, you are too, you're looking incredibly radiant, Tara," I replied, avoiding the fact that her weight gain seemed to be the elephant in this particular room.

"Sit down," I said, "I ordered you your favorite and if you've never tried one of these pain aux raisins, you haven't lived!"

"I think I'll pass on the pastry, Jake, but thank you for the latte," she responded.

Oh! So she **is** *aware of her weight gain...*

"What's wrong, Tara, you sounded so down on the phone earlier on, has something awful happened?" I asked.

"It depends how you look at it I suppose. It might be a really terrible thing or it may be the best thing in the world to happen."

"Tell me, you know you can always trust me," I said, more than a little inquisitive on what had her in such a tailspin.

"You're very kind to not mention the obvious though, and I really appreciate that."

"What do you mean, obvious?" I asked.

"Come on, Jake! Look at me! I look like a barrel!" she said, mocking her newly rotund tummy.

"Well, I had noticed that you weren't as hourglass as usual but you look incredibly well anyway and still terribly sexy!"

"I'm pregnant, Jake! Can't you see?" she exclaimed.

"Wow!" I said, "I had no idea!"

"Of course you did, you were just being polite as you always are," she replied, a forgiving smile playing across her features.

"Umm... well... I hate to ask... but, ummm, well, who's the lucky father to be?"

She stared at me for a few moments and in that space of time that seemed like hours, a sickening feeling began to move inside my stomach. A realization that I tried to shut out, couldn't even start to process.

"It's yours, Jake. You're the Daddy. I'm sorry," she said, tears beginning to stream from her eyes, "I'm so, so sorry, Jake."

"Me? How? When? That isn't possible, Tara. Surely there's some mistake!"

My mind was backtracking on recent months and I struggled to put any logic into what Tara was saying.

"I wish for your sake that I could say there has been some mistake, Jake, but I can't. You're the only man I've slept with in the past year."

"Tara, I really didn't know that but… on the boat, that was ages ago so it couldn't have been me," I replied, panic now soaring through my entire body.

"I have a confession to make," she said, "You remember six or seven weeks ago? At the St. Regis when you stayed over? I plied you with too many drinks because I wanted you so badly and we had sex. I feel awful, Jake, it's just not how I normally act, and it's completely out of character."

The room was beginning to spin again, much like it had done in the St. Regis that night a couple of months back, but this time I was able to get myself back under control.

"I'm in shock, Tara, I just don't know what to say, how to respond. You're going to need to give me a moment here to rationalize everything you've just told me."

"Don't worry, Jake, it isn't your problem. Unless you want it to be?"

"What do you mean? Are you going to have the baby? Are you thinking about terminating?" I asked, already aware that I was walking on very dangerous ground suggesting this to a pregnant woman.

"I can't and I wouldn't have an abortion. Not just because my Catholic faith wouldn't allow it but because if this is the only chance I ever get to have a child, I'm going to go through with it, father or no father," she replied, "And my parents are being really supportive about it."

I was well aware who Tara's father was, I'd heard all the stories about him. An extremely wealthy and hugely powerful individual, he controlled everything in his kingdom although I don't think he had such a hold on Tara. She was without doubt his favorite child and whatever Tara wanted, I imagined Tara would probably get. But I was still getting over the shock of Tara's news and right now, I didn't know what to say. Do I just deny all responsibility like a complete asshole or do I offer to be a present and supportive parent?

"I know what's going through your mind," she said, "I've had so much longer to process this than you, so don't panic. I'm not asking you for anything at all, I just wanted to let you know as early as possible so it could sink in and you could think about it."

I was amazed at how calm she was, given the circumstances but as she had said, she'd lived with it for some time now, already processed it and made her decision. But what I admired was how she really wasn't applying any pressure to me at all. She was simply giving me the opportunity to make my own choice.

"I'm in a daze right now but I'm not running away. If we've made a child together, I promise you, I won't shirk my responsibility. But can you give me time to think about everything? Does that sound terrible?"

"No it doesn't, Jake, it doesn't sound terrible at all. Listen. I'm going to leave you now and I'll call you in a day or two or you can call me. I'll be back in Sailfish Point by the day after tomorrow but take all the time you need. I want you to make the right decision, the right one for you, for me and for our child."

Our child...

She stood up and leaned in to kiss me on the cheek and whispered, "You could love me Jake, I know you could."

And with that, she was gone, slipping seamlessly into the café crowd while I continued to sit motionless in my chair, my world more upside down now than even an hour ago.

Chapter 64

Later that evening, I sat in my apartment and found myself thinking deeply, trying to evaluate the cards that life had recently dealt me. On the one hand, I was a youngish, single bachelor, living what was now considered to be a pretty nice existence. A vast apartment in Soho, albeit rented, a new Porsche parked outside, albeit leased and no real shortage of money. I wasn't even lacking occasional mild attention from the female race. But I felt extraordinarily melancholy and more sadly, I felt incredibly lonely. On the other hand, the girl of my dreams had literally vanished into thin air and I still didn't know why, my friends now had new adventures of their own to follow and I was six months away from being a father.

And it wasn't as though Tara was a bad choice as a mate for life, she was outstandingly beautiful, seriously sexy and for a girl who'd been handed everything in life on a silver platter, she was remarkably humble. And she was an incredibly nice person, as well as being the only woman who seemed to be truly in love with me. I had a choice I suppose. Either I opted to continue my bachelor existence and be a long distance father to a child I would rarely see, or I could do the right thing and pledge myself to Tara and our child. Maybe even get married?

A brief search in the kitchen cabinets revealed a half-full bottle of Jack Daniels and after filling a large tumbler with ice, I poured a generous serving into the glass and lay back once again on the sofa. I was now almost twenty-six years old and my plan had always been to establish myself and get married and have children by the time I was thirty but in all honesty, I was beginning to establish myself in a city I didn't really want to be in and there weren't hordes of potential brides beating down my door. I mean, Tara was unbelievably gorgeous, wasn't she? How many men would swap places with me right now just to be with her? The answer is around 100% of every man who laid eyes on her. So what if I wasn't in love with her? It would be so easy to fall in love over time, even she said that I could do that. What was not to love? And, she absolutely adored me.

But she wasn't Summer. No one would ever be Summer. But I guess for whatever reason, I'd missed out on my true love and it was time to get a reality check and move on with my life without her. I picked up the phone and dialed.

"Tara, it's me…."

Chapter 65

The following weekend saw me driving up the long and winding driveway to Tara's family estate, my stomach tied in knots about what I faced when I arrived at her parents' home. I hadn't yet met her mom and dad or her siblings and I had no idea what to expect or what kind of welcome I'd receive when I arrived. I had deliberately avoided telling Talbot and Perryman that I would be in town this weekend because I just didn't feel like explaining the dramatic change that was about to unfold in my life. Everything was too overwhelmingly complicated.

Thankfully, when I rang the doorbell, it was Tara who came to the door and she did look radiant, exotically bewildering even with the first real signs of a full baby bump on show.

"Jake! There you are! I've been so excited for you to come down and meet everyone, they're all so thrilled to be finally meeting you, my love," she said as she wrapped her arms around me and gently pulled me into her home.

"I'm not sure I feel exactly the same way, Tara, my anticipation is more one of dread on how they may be thinking about me. But you look gorgeous by the way, pregnancy is really suiting you. I can't believe how well you look and how sexy you still are," I replied, willing myself to admit that I had made the right decision.

She led me by the hand into the formal drawing room where of course, her father stood erect by the seldom-used fireplace, a crystal tumbler of something expensive in his hand.

"So you must be the mysterious Jake Delaney that we've all heard so much about?" he offered, with more of a look of disdain than one of elation.

“Yes sir, that would be me and I must assume that you are Tara’s father, Mr. Fitzgerald,” I replied, guardedly looking around at the other people gathered in the vast room.

“I am indeed, but you can call me Heath. Let me introduce you to everyone, this is my wife, Carmen, my sons Guy and Stefan and my youngest daughter, Daisy.”

I went through all of the awkward motions of saying hello to everyone and remembered to give Tara’s mother a small present that I’d brought with me which she gracefully accepted and put to one side.

Why don’t we all go through to the dining room and have lunch? I think Grayson is ready for us now,” Carmen said, leading the way into yet another cavernous room in the home.

“Let me take Jake and he can sit next to me so I can grill him over lunch!” said Daisy, grabbing my hand and tugging me off to the dining room.

“No problem, Daisy, but can you make sure it’s just lightly grilled and not charbroiled?” I replied.

I looked back at Tara and could see that she was grinning at the thought of the merciless inquisition I was about to undergo at the hands of her teenage sister.

I’d been impressed on Tara’s yacht at the slickness of the staff who had served us dinner that first night but this was at another level altogether. Apart from Grayson, who appeared to be either the butler, head waiter or maitre d’ of the home, I counted eight other wait staff who literally attended to your every need. Damn, they almost fed you!

I guess I could get used to this. After a while...

So far, the day was going pretty well. The chilly reception I had envisaged was not what I had encountered. Truth be told, and given the circumstances, I was being given quite a warm welcome.

“So Jake,” said Heath.

Here it comes...

"Tell us a little about yourself, what you do, where you're from, what your plans are in life."

So no foreplay then?

"Sure. Well, I'm from New York, born and bred, I went to college here in Florida and I currently work in Manhattan as a lawyer. My plan though is to escape the city as soon as I've got a decent amount of experience and hopefully open my own small, boutique law office," I responded.

"Boutique? How very quaint. Not exactly going to put you on the road to a life of riches though, is it?" he said, all sensitivity now abandoned.

"No sir, but..."

"Leave the boy alone, Heath! There's no need to be rude and abrupt. You've only just met him, for goodness sake!" said Carmen, gallantly coming to my rescue.

"It's okay, Mrs. Fitzgerald, your husband is right, it won't make me rich. But I don't want rich, I just want happy," I interrupted.

"I'm not sure how far that ambition will take you in life but as they say, Jake, horses for courses," Heath replied, already tucking into the first course.

The conversation over lunch was light, informal and in the main, pretty cordial. But this family wasn't any ordinary family. The Fitzgerald name was well-known across the nation, not just in South Florida. The family business owned multiple companies in so many diverse industries that I was literally blown away that Heath controlled a multibillion-dollar empire from his home office on Sailfish Point. He clearly wasn't a particularly nice man and had been raised to love himself far more than he loved others, but fuck, was he rich!

I could do worse...

Daisy turned out to be my ally. Once we'd sat down at the table, I immediately warmed to her. She was seventeen, although she seemed younger, but impishly likable and seemed to be overflowing with sweetness. I didn't quite understand this because she didn't get it from her father and her mom was not exactly Mrs. Charisma. But Tara was pretty damned lovely and although Guy seemed to be giving me the tough guy treatment, Stefan, who was quite a bit younger seemed to be more like Daisy, good-humored and friendly, a smile always beaming from his not unpalatable face. You could see that he and Tara were siblings and I wondered if there was more than one marriage that created all four children.

"Tell me, Jake, when are you and Tara getting married?" came a question out of the blue from Daisy.

"Well technically, I haven't yet proposed!" I whispered in her ear, "I was planning something but I just can't let you in on it yet."

"Why not?" she asked, "I'm really good at keeping secrets!"

"But I've only just met you, you might be a spy for your dad!"

"I'm not!" she squealed, "I think you and I are going to be the best of friends!"

"I like you, Daisy, you're not one to hide your feelings, are you? I think you'll make a wonderful sister-in-law," I replied, grateful to have someone in the family who was on my side, "But as soon as I've asked Tara, and if she says yes, you'll be the first to know. Deal?"

"Deal! And if you need any help while you're here, just let me know. Venturing into the Fitzgerald arena isn't always a bowl of cherries as I think you may already have realized," she replied.

"Yep. I think I know what you mean, Daisy, so I'll tread carefully!"

For the first time in what felt like ages, although in reality it was only a couple of months or so, I began to feel my old self returning, the loss of Summer now just a piece of my life history and it seemed as though a brighter future beckoned.

Chapter 66

I'd been invited to stay for the weekend and although it wasn't deemed appropriate to allow me to sleep in Tara's room, the guest bedroom I'd been assigned was quite outstanding. Panoramic views of the Atlantic Ocean occupied one entire wall of the room and if I'd thought that Tara's St. Regis suite was beyond luxury, my foray into the Fitzgerald compound was proof that there was no limit for the 'haves' in this world.

The bed, which was far bigger than the giant California Kings I'd seen, was mounted on a raised central dais that rotated to give the occupant a view across the water or alternatively, the option to watch a huge wall-inset television on the opposite side of the room. One corner of the suite was taken up with an enormous bar, with seating for eight and every type of drink that you could imagine was on display. Beyond the raised bed area, was a lounge that provided a U-shaped seating area, easily accommodating three large leather sofas and a crystal and onyx coffee table. The lighting was controlled from a panel on the wall but also by a remote control next to the bed and on the coffee table. With multiple light sources, it was simple to choose a preferred lighting setup for whatever your mood. A giant, 120-inch ceiling fan which was nautical in its design in using faux sails as blades, wafted a continuous but comfortable movement of air throughout the entire suite.

I'd made arrangements with Tara to meet her on the most eastern tip of the property at 9pm, once dinner was over. I'd guessed she already knew why but I was still determined to make this moment as romantic as possible, given the circumstances.

The evening temperatures were beginning to fall now and as I waited for her to arrive, the Atlantic's gentle breeze was a welcome relief to help cool me down as I prepared to ask a question that would change my life forever. I'd read a novel once about a man who loses the girl he truly loved but in the end, managed to find happiness with another woman. I was sure it happened all the time but for me, the wound was still raw even though I had someone else in my life who truly seemed to love me and who was carrying our child.

She arrived at exactly 9pm and she looked radiant, a beauty of the night. I'd asked one of the staff to bring some champagne and glasses to the table that had been set up on this eastern tip, for what I hoped would be the best decision of my life.

"Now you're getting thoroughly romantic on me!" she cooed, "Champagne, a cool Autumn evening and the most handsome man in the world!"

"Well, I'll settle on the first two, not sure about the latter though," I replied.

"You're so modest but then I think that's what I love most about you, you always seem to underestimate yourself," she said.

"Well, I'll take that as the highest form of compliment but tonight, it's all about you."

"What do you mean?" she asked.

"Sit down, Tara, you're pregnant and we need to make sure you stay well and aren't under any strain."

She sat down and I knelt before her, taking a knee as I'd seen in the movies. I pulled the box from my inside pocket and reached for her hand.

"Tara, you make me very happy, the happiest I've been for a while now and I think we're good for each other. I think we could build a wonderful life together if you'll have me. Tara, would you do me the greatest honor and marry me?"

Her face was a picture, I'd never seen such glee in her before. Tears came quickly but the smile never left.

"Of course, Jake, of course I will! I can't think of anything I'd rather do than to be your wife and spend the rest of my life with you, with our child and hopefully so many more to come!"

And so that was that. Jake Delaney was about to go from single carefree bachelor to husband and father in one fell swoop. And my life was about to change in so many ways. Please read on…

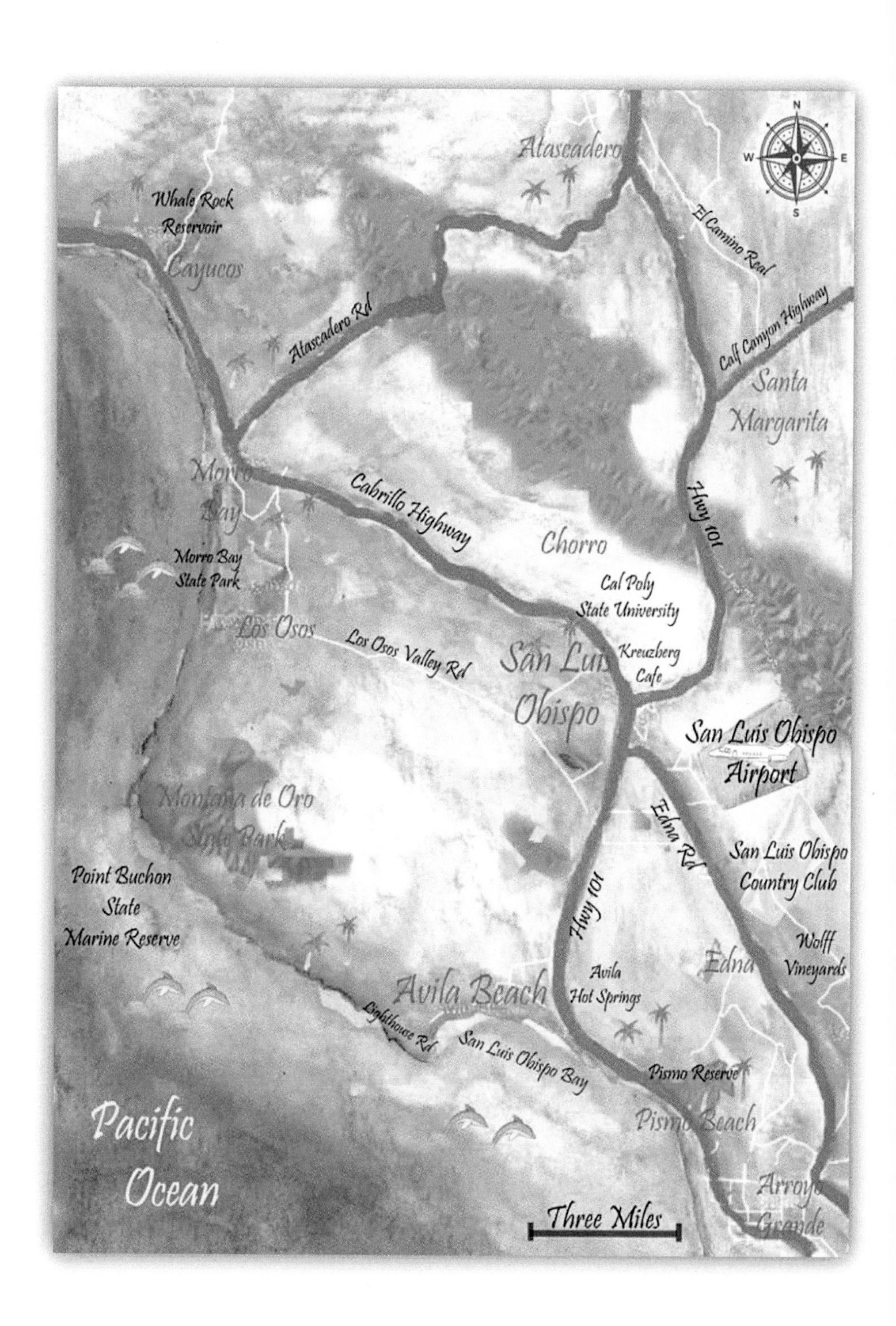

N
W
E
S
Atascadero
Whale Rock
Reservoir
Cayucos
El Camino Real
Atascadero Rd
Calf Canyon Highway
Santa
Margarita
Morro
Bay
Cabrillo Highway
Hwy 101
Chorro
Morro Bay
State Park
Cal Poly
State University
Los Osos
Los Osos Valley Rd
San Luis
Obispo
Kreuzberg
Cafe
San Luis Obispo
Airport
Montana de Oro
State Park
Edna Rd
San Luis Obispo
Country Club
Point Buchon
State
Marine Reserve
Hwy 101
Wolff
Vineyards
Edna
Avila Beach
Avila
Hot Springs
Lighthouse Rd
San Luis Obispo Bay
Pismo Reserve
Pismo Beach
Pacific
Ocean
Three Miles
Arroyo
Grande

Chapter 67

Part Two

September, 2010

I live in California now. It wasn't a place I would necessarily have chosen but for want of a better excuse, circumstances dictated that this is where I should land, to enable me to run away from the all the people I had hurt, including the only girl I ever truly loved. New York and Florida are now just fond but distant memories for me.

When I discovered that Tara had become pregnant back in 1987, it was impossible for me to stay on the east coast, knowing that Summer would be so close and with the realization of the mistake I had made. I say mistake, because I loved Summer, loved her from the moment I first saw her, all those years ago back on Maple Street in a little town I'll always remember with such abject fondness. I'd just made a mistake in falling for someone so young. But life has its tragedies and also its celebrations. Tara had given me two amazing children, my incredible son Tom, and my darling daughter, Lily.

In all honesty, I never discovered the truth about whether Tara had become pregnant deliberately or if it had just been a simple mistake. I'd like to think it was the latter but the thought has always remained in my mind that she had made a conscious decision that we should be together, no matter what needed to be done to achieve it. Fortunately, Tara shared few of her father's autocratic characteristics but her desire to have what she wanted, no matter what the cost, was one of those that she did inherit from him.

I've never told Tom that he was actually unplanned, never told him that right up to the time of his birth, I resented that he even existed. But once he entered the world and I held him in my arms, my whole body shook that this little thing, with all twenty toes and fingers, was part of me and I've worshipped him ever since. When my beautiful daughter came along a couple of years later, I became a man, but a man who was complete. The tragedy of Lily's birth was that as she entered into this world, my wife Tara, departed. We lost Tara's life as she gave life to Lily.

For the last twenty-something years, I have tried my best to be mother and father to my kids. I don't know if I have succeeded, I don't know if they missed out on their mom not being around to see them grow up. I only know that any man would be proud to be the father of these two wonderful children. They are my world, they make me get up in the morning and when I go to sleep at night, they give me the strength and reason to wake up again and live another day. In short, they are my salvation.

I did come close when my son was born, to fall for the cliché of those dads who pass their names to their sons, ridiculously adding the word Junior. But Tara had grown up reading everything Mark Twain wrote and she truly adored the Tom Sawyer character, and so Tom he became. When my darling daughter Lily followed a couple of years later, she got her name for a more simple reason. I just like lilies.

Although I was always very fond of Tara, I was never really in love with her. I mean, head over heels in love. She was an incredible girl and she was blessed with all the best things that Mother Nature could bestow on her but if I was really being honest, she wasn't the one with whom I was destined to spend the rest of my life.

Her father, Heath Fitzgerald, made sure that I did the right thing and he paid all the costs to have us secreted away to the west coast where we would be hidden from the family's social embarrassment. He didn't like me from the very beginning but then again, he didn't much like anyone, except himself. The feeling remains very much mutual. The only member of Tara's family with whom I have remained constantly in touch, is Daisy, Tara's younger sister. She has been a bright light for me and has come and stayed many times at the house. The kids adore her too so we always look forward to her visits.

Since Tara's death, I have never been in love or romantically linked with another woman. That may sound like a man who is still mourning the loss of his wife but that's not entirely the case. The truth is that I believed it was my lack of care and judgment when I was younger that caused so many people harm and I didn't want to allow it to affect anyone else again. I had detached emotionally from women, I suppose. I hadn't become anti-women, far from it, I adore women. Most people here seem to assume that I'm some kind of 'player' and I'm happy for that illusion to prevail. I think that like an agnostic who has no belief in or need of a god, I don't have a need for sex or relationships. I've become sexually agnostic, almost asexual I suppose.

But, if it sounds like I drew some kind of short straw, it would be an incorrect assumption. Tara and I found ourselves living in sumptuous luxury, occupying a stunning home that overlooks the Pacific Ocean in San Luis Obispo Bay, around 180 miles north of Los Angeles and 220 miles south of San Francisco. For almost half my life, I have been proud and pleased to call it home. It was a gift from Heath Fitzgerald although it takes most of my salary to upkeep it. I didn't receive or ask for anything else from him or the Fitzgerald family, although he made sure that our children would never want for anything in the future, having set up trust funds for each of them.

It has been an incredible place to raise my kids and to watch them grow into young adults. They are both now at college, Tom at Pepperdine, just down the coast in Malibu and my bright little baby, Lily, closer to home at UC Santa Barbara, around ninety miles south of here. Tom wants to be a professional soccer player just like his dad wanted to be, although he's also taking an engineering degree. Lily is studying Fashion and Design whilst also playing on the UCSB Women's Golf Team. I secretly enjoy the fact that both of my children chose to be student-athletes at college and not take the easy option of just hanging out between classes. If it's done nothing else, it has kept them focused as well as keeping them incredibly fit. I love it when they come home though, they bring life to the house and joy to my life.

For my own part, while my kids are away, I run a very small law firm in the town of San Luis Obispo but it's enough to make a decent salary and I enjoy the company of the people who work there with me. I have a wonderful support system of friends and colleagues who have helped me through the dark times and given me the fortitude to carry on and make me realize that it's not all about me. These are the people who share my world, the people I love and who love me back in spades. In many ways, I really don't deserve them but again, I'm so happy to have them in my life.

Chapter 68

My office is situated in the heart of San Luis Obispo, which for locals is referred to as 'SLO' because it's such a mouthful to say all the time. In some ways, it reminds me very much of those Treasure Coast towns of Jensen, Stuart and Sewall's Point but it's slightly larger in size.

It is, quite simply, the cutest town I've ever known. It was built around the Mission that was first constructed in 1772 in honor of St. Louis, Bishop of Toulouse, France, a 14th-century Franciscan monk. The Mission itself is typical of the exquisite Spanish architecture that pervades California, simple design employing chalk white walls, arched windows and doorways and terracotta barrel-tiled roofs, the latter the first to be used in California to protect the Mission from invaders' fireball arrows.

San Luis Obispo is easy to navigate, the street layout following the typical east-west, north-south crosshatch pattern. The street names are a mixture of traditional Spanish names like Chorro, Osos, Morro and Higuera along with many of the familiar American ones, Broad, Marsh, Beach and High Street.

The weather here is sublime. Humidity is a rare thing and rain even rarer. Mostly, the region is blessed year round with pretty much perfect weather. So when I'm walking through town, browsing stores or even just grabbing a cappuccino and pastry on the sidewalk, I watch other people enjoying their own day and realize why this is such a happy place to be. There's nothing to be unhappy about. Notwithstanding the fact that San Luis Obispo has a thriving student population from its state university, Cal Poly, these students are bright, joyous and positive kids and they add to the flavor of our town rather than detract from it as is often found in other U.S. college towns.

San Luis Obispo does not have as wealthy a population as for example, its cousin Santa Barbara further south, but there doesn't appear to be any shortage of money here either. It feels financially stable and healthy. In fact, the health of the local population seems to reflect that, with no real evidence of the obesity seen in many other parts of the United States. It is typical of the wealthier areas of California where fitness, diet, lifestyle and eco-awareness take center stage in middle-class society. In many ways, it should be a template for living.

My office can be found on the corner of Garden St. just near the intersection of Pismo. The premises aren't big at all and in fact the layout often reminds me of Talbot's office back in Jensen Beach. I have my own office at the rear, our reception and phones are taken care of by our receptionist, Teresita Chan and there is one other office that is occupied by our office manager and paralegal, Edie Camarillo. She also happens to be one of my closest friends and someone who has given me incredible emotional support through some very dark times.

Edie is one of those people whom you cannot dislike. Her character is hard as concrete but also incredibly soft at the same time. If she needs to metaphorically slap you to open your eyes, she'll physically and mentally embrace you with love and affection afterward. She's not a tall woman but she's athletically built and everything she does is done at a brisk pace. She's not even what you would call beautiful but she is intensely charismatic and ultimately desirable. A fairly severe and blonde pageboy hairstyle frames a sharp, almost hollow face with hooded eyes that magnetize your attention. Everything about her feels hard, sinewy and permanently flexed but there's no doubt that she's an extremely attractive lady. As well as being my colleague, she's also one of my dearest friends. She has been my rock and if she weren't happily married with three kids… well, you know.

"Good morning, Teresita, how are you today?" I asked as I stepped through the entrance door to our office.

“Every day is a good day, Señor Delaney!” she responded, her olive-skinned face revealing an ever-present smile that literally flashed from the whitest teeth I’ve ever seen in my life.

“Did you have a nice weekend?” I asked.

“Bueno, Señor, magnifico! It was my son’s fifth birthday and we had a wonderful celebration.”

Teresita is Mexican and she’s married to a Chinaman from San Francisco. They’re not as odd a couple as Perryman and Sofia but they are certainly interesting and entertaining. Sammy Chan is a part-time private investigator having served in the SFPD for fifteen years and then retiring from the force on medical grounds. He’d been investigating a chop shop that had been successfully stealing high-end automobiles in the Bay Area of the city and he’d lost out in a chase that ended in a narrow alley, resulting in Sammy’s squad car colliding with a dumpster. When he’d got out to examine the damage, he was shot and almost killed by one of the city’s many homeless people with a gun that had been dumped in that same alley. It was a terrible ordeal that saw the homeless man running away from the scene and left Sammy fighting for his life.

Fortunately, Sammy went on to make a reasonably good recovery after a month spent in the hospital but the emotional trauma remained and he was no longer able to effectively pursue his career as a detective. During his time in the hospital, he met and fell in love with Teresita who at the time was working as a relief receptionist at San Francisco General Hospital. The feeling was mutual and a romance blossomed that resulted in them relocating for a more peaceful life in San Luis Obispo where they continue an unyielding love affair and adoringly raise their only child, Esteban.

“Any calls for me this morning or is it a quiet day so far?” I asked, heading directly for the coffee machine that has become the epicenter of our office.

"Nada," she replied, "I think the whole town is still asleep! But Edie asked me to let her know when you arrived. I think she wants to talk to you about something."

"Thank you, Teresita," I said, taking my coffee mug and heading towards Edie's office.

"Morning Edie," I said, as I opened the door and entered her lair.

"Hi Jake, I wanted to talk to you about a couple of cases we have that need your attention," she said.

That's the thing about Edie, she's all business, doesn't waste time on niceties, gets right to it.

"Sure, what's happening?" I asked.

"Well, the one that's most pressing at the moment is that divorce case for the Kirklands. I had a call from Burl this morning at 8am and he's still convinced that Leola is fucking someone," she replied.

"Nicely put. Have we ever had Sammy take a look at it for us?"

Sammy Chan occasionally works for us when we need some private detective work done and he's excellent at what he does but chooses only to work part-time because he prefers to spend his time at home raising Esteban.

"Not yet, but I think Burl wants us to put him on it. He's convinced there's someone else involved."

"Yes, but really and truly, under California divorce law without a signed prenup, it's always going to be an even split on their assets so he's wasting his time. The marriage is over; he should just deal with it, work out the details with Leola and move on. It doesn't make any sense investing four or five grand in Sammy's time just to find out something he doesn't need to know that will continue to hurt him after the divorce."

"Not sure he sees it that way, Jake, I think his pride is still hurt. Anyway, he's authorized the budget so I just wanted to make sure you were on board to get Sammy started on it?"

"Of course, put him on it, give him a week or two and whatever he gets in that time, let's see it and meet with Burl."

Once Edie had acknowledged my thoughts and her eyes went back to what she had been reading before I arrived, I realized that the meeting was officially over, Edie-style.

Walking back into my own office, I could see a pile of mail on my desk and was inquisitive about one item in particular, a package from Apple. I'd decided that I needed to modernize my lifestyle and it seemed as though the world and its wife owned an iPhone these days, so I'd gone online and filled Apple's coffers with a few more bucks.

Once I'd opened the package and retrieved the iPhone, I stared at it for a minute or so, not really knowing what I should do next. It was beautifully made and the design was outstanding but for heaven's sake, I didn't even know how to switch the damned thing on!

I fumbled around with it and found the cleverly hidden power switch and somehow made the phone light up, a bright white Apple logo emerging in the center of the black screen. But then things got tricky once it began the initialization process and I quickly realized that registering the phone was beyond my knowledge or understanding. Technology now seemed to be aimed firmly at teenage customers who seemed to have an innate ability to deal quickly and easily with every new device that hits the market.

I decided that help was needed and I'd phone Lily this afternoon to see if she could guide me through the process of registering the thing. But there was a part of me that was smiling inside that in this new technology-driven world, I had made what might have been one small step for mankind but which was one giant leap for Jake Delaney.

Chapter 69

I didn't just like the Maserati, I absolutely adored it. When we first arrived in California, Tara presented me with the Maserati, a car that was delivered to our driveway wrapped in a bow. And although my wife knew that I would forever be her friend, partner and husband, she fully understood that the Quattroporte would always be my sultry and exotic Italian mistress from Modena. Most people mistakenly assumed that I must be ludicrously wealthy and although it had cost Tara something north of $60,000 in 1987, which would probably be around $180,000 in today's market, I think it remains a true bargain with a current value of around $16,000 for a bonafide supercar.

My buddies and I meet on Wednesday evenings at a boutique hotel and restaurant in the heart of San Luis Obispo, called The Granada Hotel & Bistro. It's not the same as the days of Talbot and Perryman down in South Florida but these guys are great friends and I am proud to be part of the group. They were amongst the people who rescued me when life was taking a downward turn for me when Tara died.

The thing I love most about this eatery is that it has a fabulous patio up on the second floor complete with fireplace and cozy dining sofa sets under patio burners. When you arrive in the early evening, the light that spreads across the deck and out onto the tree-lined street below is spectacular and once the sun has set, there is an endless supply of blankets to keep you warm for the remainder of the night. In fact, if I were romantically involved, it would be a perfect date destination.

"Jake Delaney! I do believe it might be time to finally welcome you to the twenty-first century!" exclaimed my friend, Preston Pryor, "For a man who owns a car that spends more time in the shop than on the road, I fear that he is finally now the proud owner of an iPhone! Apple's shares must have spiked today!" he continued, laughing at his joke and as usual, at my expense.

He wasn't wrong of course, I was famous in my small circle for the fact that I was utterly tech-phobic and actually, although Lily had successfully guided me through the process of setting up the iPhone when I'd got home, I still had no clue how to use the thing. I suppose I didn't really see the point. Usually, if I wanted to call someone, I just picked up the phone in my home or at my office. And what was texting all about? I could say more in a call quicker than I could tap out a typo-laden text message. And I had the internet on my computer, not a Mac of course but my faithful desktop. And I knew how to send emails although I never really understood how that worked. What else did I need?

"Next thing you know, he'll be tweeting, posting mug shots on Instagram and connecting with all his old buddies on Facebook," Preston continued.

Tweeting? Instagram? Facebook?

"I have no idea what you're talking about Preston, as usual I might add. As long as I can make a phone call on it, that will suit me fine. But thanks for your interest." I quipped.

We were seated at our usual table on Wednesday nights, up on the outdoor patio that overlooked Morro Street in the heart of downtown. Tonight, I was grateful for the gas burners and firepit to take the chill off this late fall evening. It never got that cold in San Luis Obispo or out at my house in Avila Beach, and we certainly never saw the winter temperatures that I'd experienced in New York City. But it was never as beautiful as the winters in Jensen where the thermometer rarely witnessed the needle falling much below 65F.

Preston Pryor and Frankie Cohen were my two closet friends in California. Preston owns an old established garage in the town that buys, sells and restores vintage European automobiles. There is always a gaggle of passersby stopping to admire the mostly British sports cars that are parked outside in the sunshine. Preston deals mainly in Triumphs, Astons, Austin Healeys, Jaguars and MGs and many of them go through an exhausting renovation process to bring them back to their former glory before offering them for sale to the public. He views my old Maserati with some contempt, albeit sympathetic, because he knows how much I fork out to keep her on the road.

Frankie is another story. Frankie doesn't sell cars, he steals them. That is to say, he used to steal them because he is now an officially reformed criminal. I'd met Frankie when Preston had asked me to defend his friend in a case where Frankie had stolen a super rare Ferrari Daytona and had finally been caught by the police. The two of them had grown up together, even attending the same college at Cal Poly, here in San Luis Obispo. I managed to negotiate a deal for Frankie with the D.A. with just a short period of probation as punishment. But it was Frankie's promise to go straight that made me believe he had finally decided that the car theft game was something from which he should probably retire. That and the threat of six years in jail. But I never did find out if Frankie had ever supplied any cars to Preston over the years. I choose to believe that he didn't.

Hmmm...

"Joking apart, Jake, I'm really pleased that you've made the effort to catch up on technology. These things are going to control our whole lives in the future and I can only see them becoming even more popular than they are already," said Preston.

"Really? You think that these are going to catch on and people will actually run their lives on them?" I asked, "I can't quite believe that, Pres, I mean, what can they do that we can't already do? Seriously, I know I'm not technically adept like you are but there has to be a limit on what they'll be able to offer except for texts and emails and things. I mean, the internet is not exactly lightning fast on this thing anyway."

"Trust me, Jakey, the future is right there in your hand. I've been buying Apple stock every month for the past couple of years," he replied, "There's an explosion of fantastic tech companies in Silicon Valley, now that that the dotcom disaster has been forgotten about. The truth is, I just don't have enough money to invest in all the companies I'd like to buy into, but you'll see, Apple and the likes of Google and

Facebook will become the wealthiest companies in the world. And although Apple is the only one actually manufacturing a series of real products, the design and quality are like something that's never been seen before. It's only going to get better. Mark my words."

"Yeah, yeah, sure, I'll take your word for it," I said, "But what's an app? I keep hearing this word all the time particularly amongst the students here in town and I feel a little undereducated."

"App just means 'application', Jake," chimed in Frankie, the two of them now ganging up in their quest to educate me, "You know, like when you use Microsoft Word to write a letter or Excel to make a spreadsheet, you're using applications, or apps. On your phone though, there are thousands of them being developed right now in garages and spare bedrooms all across the country to tell you what the weather's gonna be like or enabling you to follow your favorite sports team. They say that soon you'll even be able to do all your banking on it and rent a car and book your vacations and flights. Preston's right, the whole market is getting ready to literally explode to a whole new level."

"I don't know about that but I'll bow to your combined infinite wisdom and take it under advisement," I replied.

"Ever the lawyer, Jake, maybe you should take a chance one day, spread your wings and come out from under your own shadow!" said Preston.

He was right of course, I was hesitant about everything but this new technology that they were talking about that I apparently now held in my own hands was certainly interesting. I'd need to investigate further but not with these two, I needed a close confidante to help me for what I had in mind.

"So, what are we having?" asked Frankie, "I'm guessing the usual?"

We'd been coming to The Granada every week now for years, but rarely did we stray from our usual menu choices. We were not particularly adventurous as a threesome when it came to culinary exploration so the wait staff generally knew what we were going to order even before we'd opened our mouths.

Samantha, one of our longest standing and possibly most patient waitresses here, was already writing in her pad as Frankie began to spout the weekly food and drink order.

"Preston'll have the Hanger Steak, I'll have my Bacon & Onion Jam Burger and Jake will have his usual Rack of Lamb," he said.

"Actually, no," I said. "I've decided to change things up tonight because I've realized I'm getting predictable and dull. Sam, can I have a dozen Pacific Gold Oysters and a plate of Ahi Tartare, please?"

"Shit! What's happened to you?" asked Frankie.

"He's a sophisticated man, Frankie," said Sam with a wink to me, "No problem, Jake, good to see you trying something different, the rest of the menu's wasted on these boys!"

"Okay, okay, well, if Jake's going off the straight and narrow, I guess we'd better follow! What do you say, Frankie? You wanna join in?" asked Preston.

"You knock yourself out, Pres, I'm having my burger."

"Okay then, Sam, can I try the Goat Cheese & Beetroot Terrine with an Arugula Salad?"

"Wow, guys, I'm impressed. Except for you, Frankie!"

"Alright, alright, give me the Smoked Salmon & Kale and a bucket of tagliatelle then!" he quickly responded, keen not to be the only one who wasn't trying something new.

"And no beers tonight, Sam, can we have a bottle of champagne, please? We're celebrating my soon to be announced induction to the modern world!" I said, as our waitress looked quizzically at her weekly group of aging men who seemed to be taking pills of some sort tonight.

"Don't fret, Sammie, we'll be back to the usual next week," said Frankie, "It's not every day that Jake tastes technology!"

“Don’t be so sure, Frankie,” I said, “You are looking at the new and very much improved Jake Delaney tonight, version 2.1!”

Chapter 70

Later that evening, I sat down on the sofa in my lounge with a glass of wine, a case of which I'd recently bought at a local vineyard. The Tolosa Winery was the subject of a recent visit for Lily and I, and during the tasting which had lasted for a couple of hours, I'd fallen fairly heavily for two of their wines as had my daughter. The winery didn't offer a huge selection as it was still relatively new but what they did have was outrageously good and not even particularly expensive.

On our return home that day, Lily and I had savored a truly exceptional Edna Valley Chardonnay. It was unusual for Lily to really enjoy any wine as she mostly didn't care much for alcohol. While many of her peers at college couldn't wait to leave home and get to college with the notion of independence, freedom and the alcohol availability that came with it, neither of my kids had ever felt the need to get wasted on a nightly basis. They were unbelievably sensible people.

Dad of the year...

My patio doors open out on to a view of the San Luis Obispo Bay which is punctuated by a piece of coastland that juts out into the Pacific Ocean to the north, a spectacular headland that can be best appreciated on a walk along the Peco Coast Trail. An evening's stroll on this piece of God's paradise affords a spectacular setting sun which on a cloudless night, literally bathes you in gold. California is an enormous state but even after more than twenty years living here, I feel I really haven't even begun to discover it because it has so much innate natural beauty of which most Americans remain completely unaware.

The house was quiet tonight, as it often was now that the kids were both at college and I yearned to see them again. Even though the distance from Avila Beach to either of their respective universities was no more than three hours drive, it sometimes felt like they were on the other side of the planet. I needed some noise in my too tranquil home and having retrieved a leather case from next to the couch, I fished through my badly organized collection of CDs, hoping to discover something that would give me a little cheer this evening. It wasn't that I felt sad but when you devote your life to your children and they're suddenly taken away from you as part of your daily existence and routine, a loneliness easily builds to the point where any noise, any distraction makes a difference.

I dug deep amongst the discs, none of them housed in their original plastic cases and many suffering traumatic scratching over the years, but eventually I pulled three CDs from the box. On further examination, I couldn't help but smile when I identified one that Summer had made for me so many years ago, a compilation of her favorite songs. It had a sticker on it that read, *'For Jake, my first, my last, my everything!'* I smiled, realizing that it sounded like a Barry White song.

I inserted the disc into the CD player and waited to be reminded of what she'd compiled just for me during our brief but magical period together. One of America's most underrated artist's soulful tone poured soothingly across the Bose speaker system and I immediately recognized the unforgettable song from the irresistible Terence Trent D'Arby and with it, his memorable and tender lyric…

Let her down easy, her heart is on a dime

Let her down easy, and she'll grow up in time...

I felt my eyes quickly becoming moist and soon a tear or two began to emerge and begin their slow and sorrowful journey down my cheeks. The pain still remained. I began to sob, alone in my privileged world but safe in the knowledge that no one would ever hear or see me cry. I thought back to 1986 and the events that had unfurled. Had I been a coward? Had my own immaturity taken over when I should have been more of a man? Had I chosen the easy way out?

Looking back now, I realized that I should have been brave enough to find out why Summer had decided to cut me out of her life and how easily I had given in to Tara and taken a route less encumbered. Or maybe for some reason, her parents had intervened and insisted that she cut me out of her life. But whatever had happened in the ensuing decades, I realized at that moment on that sofa that I had never gotten over losing Summer and sadly, I knew I never would. My tears kept coming, my sobs too hard to contain and my sadness remained buried in a hollow deep down inside of me.

Chapter 71

A week later, I had a meeting scheduled with Sammy Chan to find out what he'd discovered about Leola Kirkland and her daily and nocturnal activities. He'd happily taken Burl Kirkland's money to track Leola's movements to find out exactly what she was doing, who she was seeing, where she spent her time each day and night. And it seemed that Burl was going to get the bang for his buck but maybe not in the way he'd first imagined.

"She's some chick, your Leola," said Sammy, reclining back on the old but extremely cozy Chesterfield sofa in my office. I would often arrive back from lunch to find my enormous staff of two, munching their sandwiches on it. It had one of those 'come to me' comfort levels.

"Sammy, I should point out that she's not *my* Leola," I replied, "She is merely the object of one man's fascination and that isn't me. God forbid."

"Well, she may be that, but old Burl might get a bit of a shock in that it's not only him who's fascinated by her."

"So, you did get results, then? Come on, lay it all out for me," I said.

"Okay. The easy thing about this particular job is that Leola doesn't seem to care too much about who sees what she gets up to. She is not what you would call a guarded woman, Jake."

"Yeah, I think I already got that impression from the one meeting I had with her."

"So, following her was easy, I don't think she even looks in her rear view mirror. And the woman can spend. She's a member at just about every club around here, including SLO Country Club over out where you live. And the restaurant bills must be huge because she only eats at the nicest places."

"But nothing to be seen that Burl would want to know about?" I asked.

"No, nothing in public but it's a whole different ball game when she thinks she's not being watched. And the thing about Leola is that she doesn't have a habit of pulling the drapes in her home or closing the shutters so it makes easy filming for me. Let me show you, I already put a DVD in your machine so you could see for yourself."

He clicked on the TV and a paused video frame came to life. What happened next was definitely not what I had expected. A naked Leola entered a bedroom and lay down on the bed, followed by another woman who was also naked.

"She's gay?" I asked, shocked by what I was seeing.

"Hold on, it gets better," said Sammy.

As I continued to watch the scene unfold, another female entered, this one maybe ten years younger from the look of her body, which due to Sammy's impressive surveillance skills and superlative equipment, was easy to see on the video image.

"Crikey, Sammy, she's into lesbian threesomes! Not sure how Burl is going to react to this."

"Hold on," he said.

Around two minutes later, a twenty-something man entered the frame and joined the three women on the bed. Even at this distance, I could see that the man was hung like the proverbial donkey. I had to admit that I was impressed. Well, intimidated really. The thing that purported to be a penis stood out from him like a rapier sword, a weapon certain to cause vaginal distress.

"Okay, I think I've seen enough, Sammy, I can imagine what happens for the rest of the tape."

"Oh, you have no idea, Jake, but you don't need to see it," he replied, winking at me when he realized how uncomfortable I looked watching the video.

"The only shame is that we don't know who any of these other participants are. How do we go about putting names to faces?" I asked.

"Already done, compadre, that was actually the simple part," Sammy replied, obviously wanting me to ask how he'd managed to find out.

"Come on, spill the beans, I know you want to!" I said.

"Well, you know what Facebook is, right?" he asked.

"Vaguely. It was started as some peer to peer thing in college by a tech nerd who couldn't get a girlfriend, as far as I know. But I've never used it so that's about all I do know."

"Okay, let me explain. If you sign up to Facebook, you can either remain private or go completely public with your details, and that includes your identity, birthday, friends, favorite movies, passions etc. Well, Leola ain't no shrinking violet. She puts it all out there and those three in the video with her? Well, they're all Facebook friends of hers because I was able to identify all three of them from her 'friends list' which she chooses to allow visible in the public domain and be seen by anyone who's interested."

"Wow, Sammy, that's incredible! You basically hooked into her life from a laptop? Not sure how Burl's going to handle this new information but you certainly earned your fee," I said, never failing to be amazed by the new techniques Sammy used to gain intel on his subjects.

"You're welcome, Jake, call me if you need anything else," he said, making a beeline for the door, clearly eager to get back to his son who was at home with the sitter.

"I will, and thanks, Sammy," I said, closing the door behind him and returning to my desk, having ejected the DVD from the player. As far as Burl Kirkland was concerned, I didn't know if his ticker would cope with seeing what was on Sammy's disc but unfortunately, I was obligated to show it to him. That's where the law sometimes works against better judgment but then again, I don't write the law, I just adhere to it.

But intriguingly for me, what Sammy had shown me this morning or rather the techniques he'd employed, had me thinking about my own personal situation. It was probably a long shot but it was still worth a try.

Chapter 72

After lunch, I wandered into Edie's office.

"I know you want something," she said, without looking up.

Am I that easy to read?

"Why do you say that? Couldn't I just be dropping by to shoot the breeze with you?"

"No."

"Why not? You're one of my best friends and isn't that what friends do? Just chew the cud?"

"No."

"What about a pay rise?"

"No."

"Alright then, I'll come clean, I want some help with something but I don't want anyone else to know anything about it," I said.

"Oooh, now you've got my attention, Jakey, I'm intrigued."

There's that old favorite again, 'Jakey'...

"Tell me what's on your mind," she continued, "Ever since you got that iPhone, something has changed in your demeanor. Come on, what's going on, big man?"

"Well… what do you know about this thing called 'social media' or whatever the term is?" I asked.

"Okay, I'm definitely interested now. Jake Delaney, the man who still has a typewriter, is interested in the modern world. I can help but clearly you have an agenda of some sort. Why don't you spill the beans and let me help you find out whatever it is you're looking for?"

"If you have a moment, can you explain to me what these social media things are? I just feel like the world is passing me by in the land of technology and I'm a pretty modern guy really but I just never saw the need to use these… what are they now? Oh yeah, apps."

She looked at me with her killer stare and she knew that I wasn't telling her the whole story but she relented and sighed.

"You're a fucker, Jake Delaney. But I guess you'll tell me when you want to so let's just take you through the basics. Come on, grab a chair and let me show you," she said, pulling up a web page on her screen.

We sat there for about an hour as she showed me what the basic principles were of what appeared to be the three main social media websites, Twitter, Instagram and Facebook. Twitter felt like a daily chat and gossip show, Instagram I didn't quite get at all but Facebook seemed to be relatively easy to follow and it also seemed like the best app for my own inquiry.

"So look, I've now signed you up with User IDs and passwords for all three sites so although I wouldn't normally advise this, write them down, keep them safe, and try and memorize them. Comprende?"

"Yes ma'am, and thank you!" I replied, "Actually, when I get home tonight, I'm going to have a closer look and work it all out. But you're right, Edie, I do have something on my mind but honestly, I just can't tell you anything about it at the moment. But don't worry, it's nothing to concern yourself with. Probably won't go anywhere anyway."

"I do love you, Jake Delaney, you know that, right?" she said, "If you need me, you know I'm always here for you."

"I know, Edie, and I love you too but just for the moment, I need to keep this to myself to find out if there's anything to be had in my thinking or whether I'm chasing a lost cause. I promise, you'll be the first to know when I'm ready to share."

Chapter 73

It was mid-March and my kids were finally home for Spring Break. It was a week I really looked forward to when the house suddenly became alive again with the sounds of youth and vitality and I reveled in it.

It was a glorious spring morning, not a cloud marring a perfect azul sky. We were sitting at the family table in the kitchen, munching on warm croissants and sipping steaming hot chocolate, a guilty pleasure we shared as a family whenever we had the opportunity.

"I'm kind've impressed, Dad," said Lily.

Lily was the image of her mother. If you saw her, you'd be hard pushed to tell that I was her father. She possessed the same hair as Tara, long, thick and straight and appearing as if it had been spun from gold. Her cat-like eyes were identical to Tara's too and although she didn't share the same femme fatale womanly shape as her mom, her slim and athletic form coupled with her statuesque height of around 5'9", meant that just about every boy at college stole a second glance at her when she passed by. But the lovely thing about Lily is that she remains blissfully unaware of the attention she draws and of the salivation of her male compatriots at school.

But her question had caught my attention.

"Why's that, sweetheart? What did I do to make you so impressed?" I asked, biting into a second croissant, the melting butter dripping unembarrassingly down the side of my mouth.

"You've gone all twenty-first century on us, Dad! You've finally got social media accounts and you're attached to your iPhone like a baby with a bottle!" she replied.

"Yeah, I've gotta admit, Dad, you kinda surprised us with all that," chimed in Tom, "Does this mean you've ditched the typewriter too?" he continued, with a smirk on his face as he tucked into the pile of pastries in front of him.

"Yeah, yeah, yeah, go on, mock your old man, have at it!" I replied, actually enjoying the teasing from my kids on this beautiful morning, "And no, the Remington's going nowhere. I can still use it when there's no power."

I suppose Tom is a lot like I was at his age, certainly in appearance if not in persona. He stands 6'2" tall, a muscular and lean athlete with a thick shock of dark and wavy hair. His skin tone is a perfect mixture between his mother's and mine and although he isn't the typical California kid, he is a handsome young man who is never short of female attention. He'd inherited his mother's eyes which were almost a green-gold color, making his visage uniquely striking. You can probably tell that I adore, admire and worship my kids.

"But seriously, Dad, you're on Facebook," Lily said, "That's kind of a big step forward for you, right? I'm not mocking you, I'm just surprised. I also saw that some of my college girlfriends made Facebook friend requests to you!"

Now I was embarrassed and I knew they could both see it as my cheeks reddened quickly and a small sweat patch began to form on my forehead.

"I accepted their requests just to be friendly, Lily! How would it look if I denied them, they'd think your dad was an old curmudgeon," I replied, desperately trying to hide my embarrassment that I was now friends with a bunch of twenty-something college girls.

"Don't worry about it, Pops, you're a bit of a stud in those girls' eyes, the silver fox who's never romantically involved, a man of mystery. You've got that George Clooney aura about you, so just enjoy some attention for a change, even if you are considered a bit of a DILF" said Tom, idly texting one of the stream of his female admirers, while dishing out advice to his father without even looking up.

“DILF?” I said, “What the heck is that?”

“You know what a MILF is, right?” replied Tom, “Well, DILF is the dad’s version.”

“I’m not so sure about that, Tom, but I appreciate the compliment, if that’s what it was,” I replied.

“But seriously, Dad, you’re a great looking guy, for your age anyway, so why haven’t you ever hooked up since Mom passed? I mean, you’re not a monk and you must have plenty of women gagging for you?” added Lily.

“I know you guys never really knew your mom but she was a truly amazing and lovely woman. I wished you could have known her because she was so proud as a mom and she was a wonderful wife. But it’s strange I suppose, when someone is taken from you so suddenly and so early and with the sudden awareness that I was on my own in raising two children, you make adjustments to life without even realizing you’ve made them,” I replied.

“In what way, Dad, how do you mean?” Lily asked.

“Well, as a single parent running a fledgling business, raising two very small children becomes your whole focus outside of work. It wasn’t that it felt like a burden because there was nothing more I wanted from life except to see you two grow and flourish but during that time, I guess it just left so little time to think about a future romance. And if I’m really putting my cards on the table now, I couldn’t ever be sure how you and Tom would react to a replacement for Mom.”

“Come on Dad! You’re forty-nine and you’ve still got it. You can’t worry about what we would think! We love you man, just want you to be happy,” said Tom.

Tom's response really surprised me. Secretly, I had always felt that Lily would like me to meet someone special but to see Tom show this kind of thought and feeling was new to me but something I really welcomed.

"But that doesn't mean you need to go on one of those dating apps, Dad, you've got way more to offer a woman than wasting your time on those sites," said Lily, "Why don't you start going to some of the parties and functions at the country club? That would be a nice gentle introduction to meeting women and there are some gorgeous ones I've seen there during the holidays."

"Oh, this is great, dating advice from my kids!" I laughed, "But you're right, both of you, I have become a hermit and I need to get out there in the world, show 'em who Jake Delaney is!"

"Calm down Dad, one step at a time, big fella," said Tom, "… does anyone want this last croissant?"

Chapter 74

I felt like a stalker. It didn't seem right to be trying to find Summer but suddenly, with the thought that I might somehow be able to contact her again, not a single moment went by without her being on my mind. But I was a novice at this whole tech search business and so far, my inquiries had been for naught. I couldn't find Summer Cantrell anywhere, at least not the one I was looking for.

Although Edie had set me up with IDs and passwords for the various accounts, I had still to learn the fundamentals on how they worked and the new language that each site seemed to use. Fortunately, Lily had spent the afternoon with me showing me how to approach them and Facebook seemed to be the website that was easiest to understand and possibly aimed more at my generation than hers. But I still didn't really understand the interaction and what I should be doing. She'd shown me the concept of building a 'Friends' list which I understood but I didn't quite know what to do with it although at least I was now visible to others who knew me.

I hadn't told Lily who I really wanted to search for because I wasn't sure if she would understand or even if there was anything in it so once she'd gone out for the evening, I searched for Summer and couldn't believe how many Summer Cantrells there were out there, all over the world in fact. But I was being dumb. Summer would surely have got married, changed her name, changed her state, maybe even changed countries by now. Who was I kidding? I was so new to this whole thing and I was really just pissing in the wind. I just didn't have the knowledge to go much further than to search by her given name. But I felt this burning need now to find her, to ask her what had happened all those years ago and I suppose, just to find out how she was and if she was happy. To tell her… to tell her I was still in love with her.

Chapter 75

"My kids think I should start dating," I said.

The sky was blue, sapphire blue. The Pacific beyond my home was calm, twinkling in the morning sunlight, wishing me a gentle good morning. The air was warm with a slight chill that was washing in off the ocean. All in all, it was just another Southern Californian day. The SLO natives are in many ways oblivious to their perfect climate but as an outsider, even after more than two decades living here, I am fully aware of how lucky I am and I pinch myself most every day.

It was rare that I would be out in the front yard tending to the garden but somehow on this exquisite day, it just seemed like a nice thing to do. The bougainvillea was erupting, a spangle of glorious color seeping over the fence, a shrub that never knew when to stop growing. As I conquered the mechanism of the clippers and idly clipped away, I imagined myself as an American Monty Don, nurturing and encouraging my Californian 'English' garden.

"I think they may be right, Jake," said Martha, my neighbor who lives next door, as she watched my haphazard horticultural efforts, "Because you make a shitty gardener."

"And good morning to you, Martha, how lovely to see you too," I said.

Martha is a recent divorcee, albeit an extremely happy one. She's forty-six, a couple of years younger than me and a not unattractive woman. Like many of the SoCal divorcees, she maintains a fabulous middle-age body along with a fairly fabulous lifestyle. She had been married for twenty-four years to a highly respected local surgeon, Richard Donovan, but his delectation for post-teenage nursing staff finally became too much for Martha to ignore and she chose to get rid of him instead of killing him. Richard, or cocksucker, as Martha prefers to call him, was repentant but admitted that he couldn't change his ways. The outcome was that she got the house, half the cash and a substantial alimony payment with an undefined time limit, as well as all the cars in the six space garage. Martha Donovan was one happy bunny.

"Anyway, what prompted the suggestion? Are they feeling sorry for their old dad?" she asked.

"Do I look like the kind of man to be pitied?" I asked, "Surely I'm not past it yet, Martha!"

"No, I didn't mean it like that, Jake, stop being so defensive, you miserable fucker," she responded.

When Martha uses this type of language with me, I should explain that she means it in the nicest way. It's just that she has a potty mouth and it's her way of being personal and loving. It's funny though, Edie is also a lot like that when she talks to me. Must be my pheromones. Whatever.

"I know, Martha, it's fine, I'm used to it now," I replied, "But I think they've maybe suddenly realized that now they're not at home all the time, that I sometimes might get lonely. And to be honest, in some ways they're right but at the same time, I do enjoy my own company most of the time. Just not all of the time, I guess."

"Well, I'm already back in the dating game and it's all fine but I haven't met anyone yet who's set off the fireworks," she replied, "But I am enjoying myself so I don't much care if the right man isn't out there at the moment."

"I haven't even started down that track yet but I think Tom and Lily are right, I should get out more and mix with new people. They said I should start at the club, what do you think?"

"SLO Country Club?" she asked.

"Yeah, Lily says it's full of available women although I've got to admit, that somewhat scares me!"

“Don’t be a fucking pussy, I can’t believe what a sad twat you are sometimes,” she responded with her usual compassion, “But here’s a thought, there’s a fundraiser with an auction on Saturday night over there, why don’t we go together, make things a lot easier for both of us looking for potential bedmates? We can bid on shit too.”

“Not sure we’re on the same thought track but actually, an evening over there with you would actually be fun so if you’re brave enough, well I am too. I think…”

Chapter 76

The event was better attended than I could ever have imagined. As I pulled up outside the club entrance in my old Maserati, a valet immediately opened my door and handed me a receipt for the car. As he drove away to the parking lot, clearly uneducated in the use of a clutch and a stick-shift, I politely put my hand on Martha's back and guided her towards the dining room where the main event was being held. I have to confess that Martha did look fabulous, an elegant Avila Beach socialite in a figure-hugging, white full-length dress with a plunging neckline down to her waist, so I felt a certain pride at being her chaperone tonight.

My heart began to pound a little when I realized just how many people were crowded into the dining room, a cacophony of animated conversation coupled with an unlimited supply of champagne glasses being snagged from passing waiters' trays, seconds after having been replenished. I could feel my pulse quickening and prayed that my claustrophobia wouldn't kick in, as it often did at galas like this one.

Breathe, Jake, breathe…

But to my surprise, I had friends here. Even as Martha immediately drifted away to greet her own friends, I could already see that there were many people in the room that I knew through work and also socially. I'd even spotted Leola Kirkland near the gaming table and it was clear that she didn't intend hiding any of her surgically enhanced assets. From the looks on the faces of the group of male admirers surrounding her, I imagined that her stock had risen exponentially this evening and it could turn into a veritable bear market before the night was out.

"Look what the cat dragged in," said a voice behind me, "Who would've thought we'd see *you* here, Jake Delaney?"

"Edie! Hello love!" I replied, kissing her cheek as I greeted her.

"You okay? I know you don't like full on gatherings like these," she said.

"I'm just about coping but I'm glad you're here," I replied.

Edie was one of my close friends who understood my claustrophobic condition and my adversity to gatherings in restricted environments and she generally dealt with it as though it was she who had the problem and not me.

"Come on, let's go out onto the patio, get you some air. I'm feeling a little closed in myself anyway."

See?

We made a beeline for the patio doors which opened out onto a vast patio area where there were more tables set up for those guests wanting to eat or drink and chat al fresco.

"Phew! That feels better already," I said, "Sorry to drag you away from the fun."

"It ain't fun in there, Jake, it's like a cattle show, I'm just glad of some company that I know and love. Alan's enjoying himself though, poor love doesn't get out much!" she replied, "But listen, how are you getting along with your new venture into the technological world these days?"

At this point, Preston had spotted us sitting outside and made his way over to join us.

"He's a slow learner, Edie, you know you can lead a horse to water but you can't make it drink!" he said.

"Screw you, Pres, I'm getting the hang of it, slowly and surely. I've already got fourteen friends on Facebook now," I replied.

"Oh, that should do it then, Jake, you're good to go. Haha! Fourteen? You need fourteen hundred my friend or your circle of conversation and debate is going to be somewhat limited, don't you think?"

"I hadn't thought about it that way but I guess you're right. What should I do to increase my list?" I asked.

Edie stepped in at this point in order to ward off Preston.

"You can start by letting Facebook examine all your phone and email contacts and then it will suggest them as friends. Once you gather a bunch of people, then friends of those friends might make requests to you but it's not a race, it's a slow build, so don't worry."

"I suppose so but how do you go about finding people from your past who have maybe changed names, moved state or may have even died?" I asked both of them.

"Sammy Chan!" they both responded in unison, laughing at their likeminded thinking.

"Sammy? Oh, because he's a detective?" I asked.

"Well yeah but not just that, Sammy has access to all sorts of police information systems that none of us could ever get into, LexisNexis, stuff like that," said Edie, "Give him a call and tell him about whoever it is you're trying to find, whatever her name is."

"I didn't say it was a 'her', did I?" I said.

"Didn't have to, Jakey, call it a woman's intuition," she replied, winking at me as she gathered her purse to go off in search of her husband.

Preston leaned in toward me, a rare look of concern on his face and now with a much more subdued tone.

"What's going on buddy, anything you want to share with me or anything I can help you with?" he asked.

"Right now Pres, probably not, I don't think so anyway. This is something I just need to keep to myself for the time being and I may be chasing rainbows anyway. But thanks for the offer, I really do appreciate it."

"Well, if you need me, I'm here for you, you know that because you'd do the same for me in a heartbeat," he said, "So, if there's nothing to be done on that right now, I think it may be time to grab a couple of Mint Juleps and take a peek at that little blackjack table inside."

After half an hour of watching the 'gambling' at the table, I decided to leave Preston to it, (it wasn't real gambling but they'd set up the betting to be part of the auction later on, so the more chips you won, you more you could increase your bids. Yeah, I didn't understand it either).

I caught up with Martha who was herself gathering admirers during the evening and I asked her to dance. Fortunately for me, the music immediately changed from lively to real slow so she leaned into me and wrapped her arms around me. She did smell lovely and as we danced, I could feel most parts of her body moving against mine, and well, the lady was in shape.

"It's a good job I don't have a thing for you, Jake, because this night could end awkwardly," she whispered into my ear, "I'd fuck you right here on this dance floor. But you are a lovely neighbor even if you're not my type."

"Oh, I was thinking just the same thing Martha, it just wouldn't work at all, would it? Good job I'm gay, I suppose!"

"Oh fuck off, Jakey, there's nothing about you that's even bordering on gay, you just haven't found the right woman yet."

"You may be right, Martha, but it's not a race, is it?"

"Not at all, just as long as you get your dick sucked at some point!'

"Were you born crude or did you take lessons?" I asked.

"I've no idea what you're talking about, Jake, but if I don't get laid tonight, I might have to knock on your door later on…"

Chapter 77

When I arrived at the office on the following Monday morning, I had asked Teresita to let Sammy know I needed to talk to him about something and to have him call me whenever he wasn't busy. Neither of the Chans had attended the charity ball but they didn't really miss much and I guess it really wasn't their idea of a good night out. But it was definitely good for me to get out and mingle and I really did enjoy meeting new people and catching up with old friends but I was glad to get home in the early hours and then spend a relaxing Sunday with Tom and Lily. Spring Break was over too quickly as usual and by Sunday evening, I knew I would be sobbing when I saw their taillights disappearing as they both headed south again to get back to college.

But on this Monday morning, it was good to be back in the office amongst friends who also happened to be colleagues. My business wasn't really about making paycheck for me, more a way of giving me a comfort zone of sorts, and I suppose I was doing my bit for America in keeping people employed.

My desk phone rang…

"Sammy's on line two for you, Jake," yelled Teresita from the front desk, "You free to take it?"

"I've got it, Teresita, thank you."

I picked up the phone and heard Sammy's interesting blend of American and Chinese accents coupled with a bastardized Native American/Latino greeting.

"Hola, kemosabe, what's 'appenin'?" he asked.

"Sammy, just the man," I said, "I think I could use your talents with something personal," I replied.

"Name it, you got it, Jake," he said.

“I want to try and find someone from my distant past. I’ve tried searching social media websites but alas, to no avail. But I really don’t want other people knowing who I’m trying to find so can I trust you to be utterly confidential?”

“Of course, you know I wouldn’t breathe a word, not even to Teresita,” Sammy replied, “But what have you got for me to go on?”

“Well, that’s the bad news, I don’t have much. It’s a woman and I have her name, age, birth date and birthplace but that’s about all I’ve got. Do you think it might be enough?”

“I can definitely work with that but if she was single when you first knew her, then she may have married, might have a different last name now. But that shouldn’t be an issue with the systems I use. Give me what you’ve got.”

“Okay, her name is Summer Cantrell, she would be around forty-one now I think and she was born in Jensen Beach, Florida on July 3rd. Does that give you enough to make inquiries?” I asked.

“Oh, for sure, I think I can find her with just that. But Jake, did you want to tell me why you’re trying to find her? What’s so important about this Summer Cantrell?”

“Sammy, if it’s okay with you, I’d prefer to just keep it to myself for the minute, but most of all I’d like just to see if she is still alive and if she is, what’s she’s doing. Are we cool?”

“You bet, Jake, mom’s the word, partner! Leave it with me and I’ll get back to you when I have something,” he said.

After ending the call, I knew that if anyone could come up with any information on Summer, then Sammy was the man for the job. I also believed he wouldn’t tell a soul so I felt confident that I wouldn’t be disrupting anything in her life or in mine.

There was a knock on the door and Edie walked in and dropped onto my couch, a cup of coffee in her hand.

“I loved seeing you out on Saturday night,” she said, “So what happened when you got back home with Martha? Are you banging the neighbor or have you forgotten what your dick’s for by now?” she said, laughing at her unique line of questioning.

“Yeah, good morning to you, sweet talker. No, I’m not banging the neighbor as you so crudely put it and yes, I do believe I still know what it’s for. I may be rusty but I’m not dead yet,” I replied.

“Well, I do worry, Jakey, you’re beginning to be known as the Monk of Avila Beach these days, why don’t you just get some practice in for whatever you’ve got planned in that little brain of yours? Just a couple of one night stands, fuck ‘em and leave ‘em type dates,” she replied, subtlety never one of her strong points.

“Putting your disgusting language to one side for the moment, I can assure you that I don’t need practice, everything is in good working order. You know what they say, it’s like riding a bike,” I responded.

“Yeah, but you just need to ride a few more bikes, some really filthy ones, some that don’t get cleaned too often and need a good greasing,” she said.

“I’ve got work to do,” I said, “You can go now but thank you for your concern and advice.”

“I haven’t even started Jake, and you know you *are* going to tell me what you’re up to, big man, Edie needs to know and Edie doesn’t like waiting!” she said, getting up from the couch and turning to leave.

“Don’t forget, you tell me first,” she continued, “Kapish?” she demanded, reminding me of a lovely realtor who’d helped me years ago.

“Kapish, Edie, kapish…”

Chapter 78

The week was an unremarkable one. Just another beautiful spring day in San Luis Obispo where nothing much really happened and the biggest news of the day was the forecast of a desperately needed spell of rain later in the month.

That is until we heard some disturbing news on Thursday morning. I had FedEx'd all of the information Sammy had recorded on Leola Kirkland to Burl at his home address. I really didn't relish the idea of sitting in my office with him, going over the photographic and videographic evidence that Sammy had supplied, so I suppose I chickened out by sending it to him so he could peruse in his own time and on his own dime.

But the news was that Burl was in the Intensive Care Unit at the hospital and Leola was in a holding cell at the police station. I made my way over to Sierra Vista Regional Medical Center to see what had happened and to find out if Burl's injuries were life-threatening. I didn't need to go, didn't even want to go but the man was paying our firm a large amount in non-discounted fees so I felt an obligation.

When I arrived at the hospital and located Burl's room, he was awake, in fact, he seemed pretty effervescent, almost in high spirits. This was particularly interesting bearing in mind that Sammy Chan had called me in the car and told me that Burl had suffered two stab wounds at his home, courtesy of his wife, Leola.

"You seem to have made a miraculous recovery, Burl, what happened?" I asked.

"Oh, don't let my outward appearance fool you, Jake, I'm hurting like a motherfucker. Leola certainly knows how to bring a man to his knees, right?" said Burl, winking at me.

"I don't get it, what happened? How are you not in a body bag right now? And Leola did this? Really?"

"I got lucky, I guess. The first stab just missed my liver and the second one stuck in my hip bone. But Jake, you need to get down to the police station and get her out. Now!" he said.

"I need to do what? Burl, your wife tried to friggin' kill you, why do you want her out, for Christ's sake?" I asked, incredulous to the man's request.

"Don't you see, Jake? The woman's in love with me! To risk going away for life, it has to be love, right?"

"But what about all the evidence that Sammy shot for you? Doesn't that change everything?" I asked.

"I told Leola about it and that's what got the woman all fired up. She was so pissed that I'd been spying on her and on all the things she'd been getting up to when I wasn't around. But fuck it, Jake, did you see the action on those DVDs? Who wouldn't want some of that? I don't wanna divorce her, I want to spend the rest of my life with the woman!" he responded, his face lighting up, the happiest I'd seen him in months.

"It's your choice and your money, Burl, but I hope you're making the right decision. This would be your chance to be free of her," I said.

"I don't want free of her, I want her back home. Go get her out, Jake, I ain't pressing charges!" he said, letting me know that that was his final word.

It's a thin line between love and hate...

Chapter 79

I felt like I hadn't really earned my fee with Burl Kirkwood but the man was too rich to count all the money he had anyway, so what the hell. And overall, the case had brought some welcome revenue into the firm and Sammy got a nice check out of it. But I'd also learned from Sammy's investigative talents that almost anyone is findable, no one can stay invisible in the twenty-first century. I was hopeful that he might get back to me soon with some news on Summer although every time I thought about it, my stomach turned at the thought that he might not find anything at all.

The evening's sunset was glorious. As I sat back on the sofa, mindful of my good fortune to be looking out at a magical and mystical Pacific Ocean, I once again pondered what I would do, what I would say if I did manage to locate Summer. I mean, how does it work? *"Hi Summer, how have you been?"* I guessed not and I really couldn't be sure that if I did find her that she'd even want to have anything to do with me. There had been a lot of water under the bridge in the past twenty-something years and if she was still alive, she was doubtless leading a new life and was probably immensely happy in it. What could an old man from her past possibly bring to her life apart from memories of another era?

I'd been expecting Sammy to come to the house at 7.30 and right on time, the doorbell sounded.

"Hola, Jake, how goes it, man?" said the ever-chipper little man as he brushed past me and walked into the lounge.

"I'm good, Sammy, drink?"

"Sure, but make it something weak, I have a full evening of driving tonight, keeping an eye on a fella who thinks he doesn't have to stick to the rules while wearing an ankle monitor!" he said, pulling his laptop out of his briefcase, "Give me a double hit of Jack, thanks."

"Back in a sec," I said, making my way towards the kitchen and marveling at his ability to seemingly bypass the alcoholic effects of neat bourbon.

By the time, I'd fixed his drink and made my way back to the lounge, Sammy was up and running and clearly had news for me.

"I think we struck lucky, Jake, I think I've found your girl and she's alive and well," he said, a smug look of pride etched across his cherubim Asian face.

It was the moment that I'd simultaneously been dreading and yearning for the last few weeks. I had no idea if what I was doing was a good thing or even the right thing.

"She's in Tennessee. Married, two kids, name now is Summer Larsen. Husband is James Larsen, an orthodontist and they have a boy and a girl, Casey and Poppy," he stated matter-of-factly and then continuing on, "Summer works part-time at home, making her own jewelry. And she's good at what she does by the way, I looked at her website, it's artistically really interesting and she has a unique style."

I was stunned. Shell-shocked into silence. My mouth was dry, my tongue felt like a rasp and a shimmer of perspiration began to form on my forehead. I had to sit down before I collapsed.

"She's alive… Summer's alive…" I said, trying to fight a rushing feeling that had appeared inside my head from nowhere.

"Oh, she's definitely alive and she's doing well. She's hot too, Jake, that girl is some guapa mama," said Sammy.

"What? You've seen her?" I asked, "Where, where did you see her?"

"Not in the flesh, obviously, but there are plenty of photos of her online," he replied.

"Where? How?" I asked again.

I must have sounded like I'd not yet entered the world of current technology to Sammy because he just stared at me incredulously.

"Where?" he said, still bemused by my tech ignorance, "Fucking social media. Jake! C'mon, wake up big fella! She's all over Facebook, Twitter, loads on Instagram and she uses Pinterest a lot too. All of these websites are fantastic for promoting her business.

"Her business…" I muttered, hearing but not hearing.

"Haven't you been listening to anything I've been saying, Jake. What's wrong, man, you look like you've seen a ghost. Hold on, let me get you a drink," he said, heading towards the kitchen.

I got up from the couch, still bewildered and amazed at what Sammy had uncovered, and wandered out onto the verandah. Gripping on tight to the iron railing, I began to compose myself and felt my breathing and heart rate begin to return to normal as the sun began its final descent below the horizon. Below me, the path that wound along the cliff edge, bounded by a post & rail fence to stop cell phone junkies tumbling to their deaths, was alive this evening with walkers and vacationers taking in and admiring the prodigious views and scenery that this part of California offered.

"She really meant something to you, then?" said Sammy, finding me outside and handing me a glass of Jack Daniels, "This isn't some wonder-what-she's-doing-now kind of thing, is it? You're still in love, aren't you, big man?"

"I think I am, Sammy, I guess I must be. Summer was one of those rare people who you can never forget. But please, you can't say anything to anyone about this for the moment, not even to Teresita," I said, "Can you do that for me?"

"My lips are sealed, my friend. I can see you're struggling with all of this new information so I'll leave you in peace. But if there's anything else you need, let me know. And there's no charge for this, I'm pro bono for you, you know that, right?" he asked.

"Thanks Sammy, I appreciate it, I really do. I don't know what I'm going to do with all this, I guess I need some time to process it but to say you've made my day is a minor understatement. You've just made the last twenty years for me," I said, hugging the little man with everything I had.

"De nada, Jake, any time for you. Listen, I'll see myself out, I've got an ankle monitor to follow but call me if you need anything else. Anything at all."

As I watched him go back to the lounge and collect his laptop, I pondered what my next step would be and the burning question of whether I should make contact with Summer or just be content that she was alive and seemingly leading a blissful and happy life. But I think I already knew the answer.

Chapter 80

The following morning, I rose early, shaved, showered and dressed and with my laptop stowed on the passenger seat, I steered the Maserati out through the gates of my home and followed the road as it wound through the town of Avila Beach. My destination on this bright and sunny Saturday morning was my favorite café in San Luis Obispo, Kreuzberg Coffee Company on Higuera Street. I'd put the top down on the car because it was one of those perfect convertible weather days and luckily, I found a parking meter just a few yards from Kreuzberg.

It's an odd place, Kreuzberg. It caters in the main to students who want to use the café's free internet connection to study for the price of a latte but also to people like me who like to bathe in the youth of its clientele whilst also sampling the menu's delicious pastry offerings and multifarious and memorable variants of coffee. I'd also recently managed to work out how to log on to the Wi-Fi which was a minor miracle in itself. It's not that I don't have internet at home but coming to a place like Kreuzberg and searching the internet away from my home seemed more adroit to me, even if I was doing it in a public place. I can't really explain it but I just felt less guilt about what I was doing by coming away from the family home. Go figure.

From what I'd heard, Kreuzberg had been founded by two Cal Poly students a couple of years ago. It was a no-brainer really in an upscale college town like San Luis Obispo. They'd simply followed the basic rules of life, men would always hanker after their next car, women would value an appointment at the hair salon before food on the table and we'd never as a nation, ever tire of handing over five bucks for a cup of coffee.

I found an unoccupied alcove with a couple of old mismatching leather armchairs and a battered coffee table and set up my laptop and logged on to the café's Wi-Fi. I'm not sure what the building had originally been used as but I guessed maybe a retail store of some kind. The fairly large interior had a vaguely European hipster feel about it with furniture apparently found at yard sales. I think it's called shabby chic, but more shabby than chic. But to the left and to the right of the building are two glassed-in pocket windows that serve as private cocoons for those of us not wishing to hang out with the groovy people.

They make a particular offering in the mornings that I would almost kill for. It's a simple pastry called a Morning Bun but the taste, lightness and texture is unlike any other I've ever experienced. Their almond croissants come a close second too.

As I munched eagerly on the bun, I opened my laptop to my Facebook page and typed in the name, 'Summer Larsen'. A multitude of women and girls appeared in the results section but I immediately identified her. She really hadn't changed at all. It was like looking back into the 1980s again and seeing her for the very first time.

I clicked on the link and opened her home page and just stared at her photo as she looked back at me. My body shivered, I felt a tingling sensation that I hadn't felt since that very first evening in November, 1984. I couldn't take my eyes off her. I felt like a thief, a technological stalker as I pried into her life. I knew that you had the option to make your Facebook profile private if you wanted to or alternatively, make it available to be seen by the whole world, but thankfully, for me anyway, she'd chosen the latter.

Pictures of her two children were in her uploaded photos section; Casey and Poppy, quite beautiful siblings who shared their mother's blonde hair and blue eyes. Although, having also seen a photo of her husband, James, it was clear that the children's looks could equally be due to his obvious Scandinavian ancestry. James was indeed a good looking man. Sammy was right, the family lived in Nashville, Tennessee on the outskirts of the city. More photos revealed a pretty craftsman style home that was meticulously maintained. It wasn't flamboyant or ostentatious but instead had the feel of a warm, happy and inviting home. Two Weimaraners completed the Larsen family.

Pangs of guilt ran through me as I spied on Summer and everything in her life. But I couldn't stop myself, I was like an addict who told himself, *"just one more won't hurt..."* I couldn't see how old the kids were as they'd both cleverly and smartly, made their profiles private. But looking at them, I guessed that the daughter was the older of the two although I couldn't be sure as girls often look older than boys at that age, something I knew from past experience.

My neck was beginning to hurt from crouching over my laptop so I returned to the counter and ordered another cappuccino from a bored looking barista called Lola. I felt as though she was either looking through me or past me which is often the nature of young people's attitude towards me now. I'm considered ridiculously old at forty-nine and as far as her generation is concerned, I might as well be invisible or dead. Preferably the latter. She told me to collect my order from 'over there', wherever that was. I thanked her politely and removed myself from her vision.

After collecting my caffeinated concoction, replete with a chocolate heart stenciled on top, from a somewhat more hospitable and friendly pony-tailed young man called Baz, I slipped back into my hidey-hole and resumed my search from where I'd left off. I clicked on Summer's website for her home-based business and was amazed at the detail and quality of her products. She was a true artist and her jewelry designs were like none that I'd ever seen before. The photography was excellent and the layout and navigation easy to follow too. It seemed that she had a large and growing following of very loyal customers, according to the comments displayed in the feedback section.

Everything that I looked at on her website and on her Facebook page told me that this was one very happy woman who had made it in life and was surrounded by love and deep affection from her many friends and her family. This was a girl who didn't need interference and reminders of her youth from an old man whose heart had been broken over two decades ago.

But try as I might to forget this fact, I still felt the need to somehow contact her, to find out more about her and I suppose, finally close a chapter of my life that had remained unexplained. But as I continued to pore over the details of her life, it suddenly hit me how I could contact her without the need for her feeling obliged to respond. I packed up my laptop, gathered the rest of my things, gave an unacknowledged wave to the lovely Lola and headed back to my car, a sudden need to retrieve something that I'd kept at my home from many years ago.

Chapter 81

Back at the house, I had quickly climbed the stairs to my bedroom to try and locate what I was certain I'd kept in my 'memory box', a gallimaufry of bits and pieces I'd collected and stored over the years. There is no reason why we as a race, accumulate and drag things with us wherever we go, things that in most instances, we'll never look at again but we still do it. When I moved to California, I took very little with me except for my clothes although to be fair, I didn't have much anyway. Tara, however, had a lot.

I rummaged through the box, pulling out all sorts of items that I'd forgotten about, old photo albums, varsity pins and college letter bars as well as my soccer kit from Stetson. Why on earth would I keep a soccer kit? There were cassette tapes and CDs and even a couple of old 8-track cartridges. When was I ever going to find something to play those on again? I found a note from Summer too, with a lock of hair inside the envelope. I stopped my search and reread it once again and it brought back more memories, more raw emotions.

But I kept digging through the box and finally, right at the bottom, I found what I'd been looking for. A small velvet pocket with a tiny drawstring sat in my hand, daring me to open it and take a peek inside. As I gently pulled the little bag open and turned it upside down to empty its contents, there sitting in my hand now was a broken memento from 1985. The sea glass necklace that I'd given Summer on her seventeenth birthday brought back memories of that sad evening when she'd hurled it at me and it had hit the ground causing the sea glass to come away from its mount. Two pieces no longer together. Like Summer and I.

I'd never really understood why I hadn't had the necklace repaired and returned to her at the time, maybe we'd both just forgotten about it once we'd returned together from that incredible evening on the beach at Bathtub Reef. Maybe the necklace suddenly seemed unimportant in the scheme of things but right now, it was the only piece of her that I had left.

I raced downstairs to my home office and grabbed a piece of paper and a pen and began to write…

Dear Mrs. Larsen,

I wonder if you might be able to help me. I have enclosed a broken necklace, something I'd given to a girl many years ago but that had sadly been broken one night. It would mean a lot to me if you were able to restore it to its original condition so that one day I might return it to the only girl I ever truly loved.

Yours, in anticipation,

Jake Delaney

I found a padded envelope in my desk drawer and copied the address from Summer's website which I assumed to be her home address. I put the note and the velvet pouch inside and sealed it. I'd need to send it FedEx with a Signature Service so I could be sure it found its way to her but having made the decision to contact her in this way, I felt a sudden sense of fulfillment and happiness.

I checked my watch and realized that most of Saturday had vanished and that I was due to meet Preston and Frankie on the practice area at SLO Country Club to try and teach them some of the basics of how to hit a golf ball. But before that, I needed to get the package down to FedEx before the last pickup.

Chapter 82

In many ways, Preston and Frankie would make a good golf team. Preston's slice was as bad as Frankie's hook. But unfortunately in golf, two wrongs never make a right. I've never been a great golfer but I've always managed to be a half decent one, never having the worry of embarrassing myself in front of accomplished players. Someone once told me that if you're good at soccer then you'll likely be good at golf too and to be fair, all the soccer players I'd met in my life were mostly very good amateur golfers, some of them good enough to play professionally. Unfortunately for these two miscreants, they'd never played soccer and would always remain hopeless comedic distractions on any golf course.

"So, did you fuck her?" said Frankie, dispensing with any form of etiquette or niceties and getting straight down to business.

"Who?" I asked.

"Your neighbor, the chick you brought to the fundraiser. She was all over you like a cheap suit!" he replied, thwacking yet another ball to the left of the range.

"Oh… Martha, you mean. No, there's nothing going on with her and actually, I don't think I'm her type, not exactly her cup of cocoa. But I'm not interested anyway, she's my neighbor and I like it that way. But she's a lot of fun," I said.

"I'd do her. Give me her number, I'll call her up, show her a good time," he continued.

Frankie is a short, stocky man, tousled black curls and a barrel chest. His hands are like plates of meat and although he's on the short side, you wouldn't want to get into a bar fight with him. He kind of reminds me of a smaller Incredible Hulk or at least he reminds me a little of the actor who plays him, Lou Ferrigno. The way he gripped a golf club made you feel he wanted to strangle it to death rather than use it to launch a golf ball.

Preston on the other hand, was quite the opposite of Frankie. He towered over both of us, a lanky and slim 6'5" of undeveloped muscle. I think he fancied himself as a lord of the manor kind of character, even down to the fact that here on the driving range, he was wearing a Panama hat instead of the requisite golf cap worn by everyone else. He favored tweed suits and often donned a waistcoat from his collection of colorful silk purchases and like the gent he was, a handkerchief was always tucked into his top breast pocket. His shoes were ordered from Charles Church in London and instead of wearing golf shoes today like the rest of us mortals, he was sporting what he described as vintage calfskin and linen shoes which looked like they'd been made in the 1930s and which apparently, according to Preston, they really had been. In short, his secondhand Charles Church Shanghais had cost somewhere north of a thousand bucks which would buy you half a dozen pairs of extremely decent golf shoes.

"I think what our dear Frankie is alluding to in his usual charming tone is that we were both hoping that you were getting a little action just south of your zipper, my boy," pronounced Preston, launching yet another ball far to the right and close to the Members lunch patio.

"Nah, he just needs to get laid once in a while, that's all. I'm only thinking about his genital health," said Frankie.

"I think you mean general health," replied Preston.

"I know what I meant, wiseass!"

"Just leave it alone and worry about how badly you play golf," I interjected, "I don't need your help in my love life but you do need my help with your swing."

"But Jake, you're going to be fifty this year and there's not a single woman on your horizon. Don't you get bored in your own company all the time? Wouldn't you like to occasionally taste the pudenda of the feminine gender? Get a little ticklish with the clitoris? Become a finer diner of the vagina…"

"Stop it! You're as bad as Frankie but I have to tell you guys, I really don't need your help. As a young man, I was never short of the occasional admirer and I know I'm much older now but I think I still know how to treat a lady and when that lady turns up, I'll know what to do, trust me," I said, "Now Frankie, keep your left arm straight, Preston stand a little closer to the ball and bend your knees a little more."

Amazingly, they both hit almost straight shots and the look of joy on each of their faces told me that they would hopefully be temporarily forgetting about my love life, or the obvious lack of one.

"That's amazing, Jake! I can master this game after all!" said Preston.

Well, probably not, but as long as you stay off my back, I'm more than happy...

Chapter 83

With your long blonde hair and your eyes of blue

The only thing I ever got from you was sorrow...

David Bowie's rendition of The McCoys' 1965 song bounced off the speakers in the Maserati as I pulled up in a parking spot behind my office building. But I wasn't feeling sorrowful at all this morning, I actually felt a modicum of real joy for the first time in years.

Having said good morning to Teresita and Edie, I sat down at my desk and called up the FedEx website on my PC. After entering the tracking number, I could see that my envelope was safely in transit to Summer's address and the estimated delivery date was in two days time, Wednesday.

I was on tenterhooks I suppose because I wanted to see how she would react when she opened the envelope. Would it be with a feeling of horror or one of subdued joy? I just couldn't be sure because so much water had gone under the proverbial bridge and we were two different people back then in the 80s. And what did I really expect or want? Was I being ridiculously romantic in thinking that she still harbored some morsel of love for me or was I just acting like a naïve teenager?

I picked up a set of darts from my desk and began to throw them at the dartboard I'd installed on the far wall. I'd begun playing the game in an 'English' pub back in New York and I'd got hooked. It's not a massively popular sport in the U.S. but ever since I'd begun playing, I'd been addicted to it.

I buzzed Edie's phone and asked her if she had a few minutes to spare to chat with me.

She came in as I was eyeing a triple twenty. That's darts-speak.

You're never gonna beat me, you know that, right?" she said.

"Yep."

"You think snagging some extra practice here and there is gonna help?"

"Nope."

Edie is one of those irritating people who takes up a sport, if you can call darts a sport, and becomes immediately proficient at it. Kind of like those natural golfers who pick up a club for the first time and they instantly have a perfect swing. Pisses me off.

"So what's up, Delaney?" she said, flopping down on the Chesterfield, "There's a tiny little spring in your step today and a giant glint in your eye that I haven't seen since… well, it's been a while."

"Okay, you're right but it's maybe something or nothing. Do you want the long version or the short one?" I asked.

"Short," she replied. Edie never wasted words.

Many years ago, when I was in my early twenties…"

"Oh for fuck's sake, Jake, I said the short version for Chrissakes, you're gonna send me to sleep!" she interrupted.

"Stay with me, Edie, this really is the short one and it won't take too long to explain."

"Go on then, but I've got lunch in an hour."

"Okay, I fell for a sixteen-year-old girl almost eight years my junior back in the mid-eighties, and when she turned eighteen, we finally made love. I'd fallen head over heels in love with her, we couldn't get enough of each other and I think she felt the same about me, even though I knew she was about to leave to begin college. But then, a few weeks later, she left for college, and I never heard from her again. All my letters went unanswered and cell phones didn't exist back then," I said.

“Met someone else, nothing new there, Jakey,” Edie responded with the sensitivity of a stormtrooper, “Did you think you were the only pretty boy around?”

“Maybe and no, I’m not that naïve. But I was pretty devastated, I thought we would marry someday and raise a family, I really did.”

“Such a schmuck.”

“And that’s when I found out that Tara was pregnant and I was apparently the father.”

“So you were fucking two girls at the same time?” she asked, “You’re such a cunt, Jake.”

“No, it wasn’t like that, I’ve no idea how I came to be the father of Tara’s baby, our baby, my Tom!”

“Give me strength…”

“I know it sounds bad, Edie, but you had to be there. I actually have no recollection of the moment that ended up producing Tom. But, I think I did the right thing by staying with Tara even if it did end up tragically for her…”

“You mean you were out of options and Tara looked like a good bet?”

“No! It wasn’t like that! Not at all! I really was in love with Summer but she’d just vanished off the face of the earth.”

Oh, okay, *Summer,* the girl finally has a name!” said Edie, “So forget all that and tell me what’s made you so happy this morning. Cut to the chase,” she said, clearly tiring of my story of lost love.

So I recounted the story of how the necklace had been broken one night during a silly spat between myself and Summer and how I had just sent it to her on the weekend, courtesy of Sammy’s detective skills.

“So, what do you think?” I asked her.

“What do I think? You mean, about a fifty-year-old man chasing his fantasy wet dream?”

"Forty-nine."

"Whatever."

"It matters."

"No it doesn't. What matters is that you may be about to completely destroy someone's marriage, wreck a family, traumatize two children and for what? Because Jake Delaney couldn't get over being dumped and he's still got a hard-on for an underage fantasy girl?"

Her words may have been harsh but that's what I like about Edie. She gives it to you straight, but her stripped bare summary was beginning to bring a real moment of truth to the here and now.

"I see what you're saying but it wasn't like that. I really did fall in love. Did I made a mistake sending the necklace to her? Was that a schoolboy thing to have done? I've made a fool of myself, haven't I?"

"No Jake, you haven't, sweetheart," she responded, her tone much softer now, "What you did was to fall in love with someone and it ended with unanswered questions, questions you still need answers to. Something major obviously went down at the time and she couldn't bring herself to tell you. If you want my true opinion rather than my hardass Edie opinion, I think it's kinda lovely that you still feel this way and the method you've chosen to make contact with her again, well, it's crazy romantic. If it was me, I'd be smitten and I'd roll over for you. But that ain't gonna happen while my husband's still got a pulse so you're safe. But, don't get your hopes up. You get that, right?"

"I do. Thanks Edie, I appreciate that, and you're right. I do need answers, if nothing else. I need to close the story or begin a new chapter."

"Okay, that's all the time you're getting from me today, schedule another appointment next time and make sure you have wine to hand, and preferably food too," she said, ending the meeting as she closed the door behind her.

Edie was right. Whatever I still felt or thought I felt was in my own mind and probably not in Summer's thoughts at all. I chastised myself for sending the necklace to her. Yes, it might have been a romantic thing to do but she was unavailable so who was I kidding?

Chapter 84

Summer Larsen, for all intents and purposes, lived an idyllic lifestyle. She loved her home and her neighborhood, as well as the friends her family shared in their tiny little Tennessee town. Her husband, James, was a successful orthodontist and she had two children that in her mind's eye, were about as perfect as you could wish for. She adored Poppy, possibly and guiltily more so than Casey but she never shared that thought, you can't have favorites. But she knew it wasn't really true. However, she just put it down to the fact that Poppy was her firstborn and so she maintained her thought as a secret one. And she adored Casey anyway, probably too much that she sometimes smothered him with love.

It was only halfway through spring but already the weather was beginning to change, slowly becoming more humid by the day. It was sunny though and the endless blue skies gave her a good feeling inside. She was a Florida girl and she couldn't stomach winter weather for too long. She often thought of her life back in Florida and how much she missed the ocean. She missed the beach and the laidback lifestyle too but as her mom used to say, you make your bed and you lie in it. And it was a pretty good bed she'd made. But she missed her parents and wondered when she'd see Autumn again, if ever. But right now, she was missing her two dumbass Weimaraners because for the countless time in their young lives, they'd run off again and before the day was out, she'd end up dragging them back from a neighbor's house again. Dumb mutts.

There was always music playing in Summer's home, she couldn't live without it, it just made her feel alive. Today, she had the radio on and Far East Movement's "Like a G6" was playing…

Now I'm feeling so fly like a G6

Like a G6, Like a G6

Sippin on, sippin on sizz, Ima ma-make it fizz

Girl I keep it gangsta, Popping bottles at the crib

This is how we live, every single night

Take that bottle to the head, and let me see you fly

Hell Yeah

Drink it up, drink-drink it up,

But Summer couldn't identify with today's music. The language was so foreign to her, even the artistes' names were strange. Ludacris, Iyaz, Lil Wayne, Pitbull…

"I must be getting old," she said, "Had to happen sometime, I guess."

She yearned for her teenage years, when the British Invasion was going on for the second time in the 1980s. She realized that she rarely heard a record from across the pond these days. It was all Beyoncé, Taylor Swift, Kesha and Katy Perry. Where had all the great male artistes gone, where were the bands now, why was everything so plastically produced on talent shows? Yeah, she was definitely getting old at forty-one.

She was in the front yard, clipping back some of the bougainvilleas like her mother used to do in Florida, when she heard the familiar sound of the FedEx truck pulling up in her driveway.

"Hey Tanner!" she called out to the driver.

Tanner McGuire was her regular delivery guy. He was surfer boy gorgeous, his biceps bulged from beneath his ugly brown FedEx shirt and he was permanently tanned and never without a grin on his face. He reminded her a little of Perryman back in Jensen Beach but Tanner was definitely straight and trying to make it as a country singer here in Tennessee. Almost every night when he could find a stage to perform on in a Nashville bar or a club, Tanner would be there pouring out his heart in a stream of self-penned love songs.

"Hey Summer, I've got a bunch of deliveries here for you," he replied.

"I hope it's some of the supplies I've been waiting on, I'm running low at the moment. Can't make new jewelry if I don't have the raw materials," she said.

Tanner jumped down from the truck and handed her a pile of three parcels and a padded envelope.

"Thanks Tanner, you're my hero!" she said, realizing how good his legs were as he jumped back into the truck. Where did that thought come from? Was she turning into a cougar now?

"Now don't let me stop you, get on and make something beautiful like you!" he replied, easing the truck out of her drive and back onto the road.

"Yep, that's me, cougar mom," she said to herself.

In her kitchen, Summer had begun making tea as she eyed the pile of parcels that sat on her kitchen table. Just like her mom, she too enjoyed watching the tea percolating in the glass teapot. She missed her mom.

"Now what do we have here?" she asked herself.

The first package contained a selection of raw and unpolished inexpensive jewels and crystals as well as a multitude of tiny shells. She would enjoy making something with these little gems. The second package was a vast selection of mounts, which included earring posts and clasps, silver chains for necklaces and pendants and ring mounts, some in silver, some in rose gold. There were also various leather bands for making bangles and natural bracelets. In the final box, she discovered the LED lighted magnifying mirror stand that would replace the one that had finally died on her.

"Now what's this?" she mumbled, as she picked up the padded envelope, "Mailed from San Luis Obispo, what did I order from California?"

She tore open the envelope and emptied its contents onto the kitchen table. A note and a small velvet bag sat staring back at her. She opened the bag and slipped the contents into her hand and was so taken aback with what she saw that she had to sit down quickly on one of the kitchen chairs. A feeling of nausea enveloped her. Summer never perspired but in this moment, in this kitchen and holding what she had in her hand, a heatwave spread across her face and she felt her forehead instantly begin to moisten with perspiration.

"My sea glass necklace… oh God," she exclaimed to an empty kitchen.

She grabbed the piece of paper that had accompanied it and began to read. Her heart was pounding, her body was weak and her stomach lurched as she read the words Jake had written.

"How did you find me? Why would you do this?" she blurted, her eyes instantly filling with tears, now beginning to stream down her still youthfully pretty face.

Memories of her first sight of him, her instant love for him and her longing to be with him came flooding back to her like enormous crashing waves on a storm-filled day. She had thought that the last two decades would have made her forget the man she fell in love with so many years ago but in an instant, she realized that she would never, ever get him out of her system. However happy she was and whatever life she had built for herself with her family, Jake would never leave her heart.

"Oh Jake… fuck, fuck, fuck! Why now?"

Chapter 85

By Friday, I had learned that the package had made its way to Summer's home and that if I was honest with myself, I realized that there was little chance that she would make contact. I felt that if I had meant anything to her, then she would have called or texted or emailed. Something anyway. At least I knew that she was okay and happy, even if it was without me in her life. I'd given it what I thought was my best shot and she'd probably decided for her own obvious reasons that any future contact with me would be strictly avoided. It was understandable. And although it would never heal my own heart, there was something inside me that was beginning to accept that I was finally making closure and that maybe, just maybe, it was time to move on and find a partner. At least my kids would approve, which was something.

Saturday night, I'd been invited to dinner at Martha's home. I didn't know who was going and hoped it wasn't just me and Martha but at least I didn't have to drive so drinking wouldn't be an issue. The one thing I had hoped was that Martha wasn't arranging the dinner to set me up with one of her friends. I was more than aware of the existence of the ABCDE, the Avila Beach Club for Desirable Ex-wives and I didn't particularly want to venture into that tent.

I'd spent Saturday morning at the gym, hoping that it would take my mind off a certain woman in Tennessee and then in the afternoon, I went to Whole Foods to stock up the pantry. As I wandered up and down the aisles, I realized that I would never get over my awkward sensitivity of that moment when other shoppers looked into my shopping trolley and everything in it suggested that I was cooking for one. Often I would buy more of something just to fashion an illusion that I was a happily married modern man just out shopping while his wife was busy doing something more important at home. But I also knew that unless I had a stack of 'meal for one' cartons in my haul, most people wouldn't even notice, or even care. I just didn't want to be pitied, was all.

My iPhone chirped.

"Hi Preston, what's up?" I said.

"Where are you, fella?" he asked.

"I'm in Whole Foods, what do you need?" I replied.

"It's not what I need, Jakey, it's what you need. Get your ass over to the showroom, pronto."

And with that short directive, he was gone.

Oh well, nothing ventured...

Preston's old fashioned 'showroom' of classic cars was not far from Whole Foods in the middle of town and in less than twenty minutes, having paid for my groceries, I found myself parked opposite his place of business and walking into '*Pryor Motors, European Automobiles of Distinction*'.

The building itself is one of the town's original structures first erected in the late 1920s and it still had that vintage air about the place. The classic English vintage feel had been further enhanced by Preston's addition over the years of a handful of glass-domed gas pumps scattered throughout the building. There were hundreds of British and European hubcaps and car marque badges adorning the walls and polished radiator grills and bumpers pinned up like hunting trophies for the delectation of the automobile enthusiast rather than the lover of bloodsports. As I walked across the concrete floor, I noticed for the first time that every piece of the wooden structure was painted in British Racing Green so it felt as though you were stepping back in time to what a 1950s English car showroom must have been like.

I found Preston in his office which still had the decades-old aroma of cigars and oil and the furniture matched the era too. Preston was as usual, leaning back in his old leather and oak office chair, feet up on the gnarled desk, in animated conversation with either a fellow enthusiast or more likely, a willing and financially able punter. 'Punter' was a term that Preston always used for his customers, a word that he'd gradually adopted from some of his suppliers in London. It means 'customer' but not in a particularly respectful way, more a victim of prey.

I sat down opposite, in what I guessed was the punter's chair and waited as he continued his monologue. He cupped a hand over the mouthpiece in a conversation gap and said, "Put the kettle on, make us some tea and I'll be with you in a mo," and went back to the conversation.

I did as instructed and once the tea had steeped to the dark brown color that Preston preferred, I took the two mugs back to his office and sat down again just as he was hanging up.

"Jakey! Have I got something for you! You are so going to thank me for this," he said, more animated than I was used to seeing him.

"Don't tell me, you've got me a replacement for my Maserati which will give me more trouble than my own car gives me right now?" I said.

"I think you're being a bit hasty, but you're on the right track. But it is something special, just arrived from England this morning. I bought it sight unseen but from someone I've bought from for more than twenty years," he said, clearly excited about whatever he'd snagged from across the Pond.

"Come on, she's out back, I've had the boys give her the once over to make sure she's exactly what I thought she was in the photos."

And with that, he was bounding out of the office leaving me in his trail.

As I said, nothing ventured...

I caught up with him in the quadrangle at the rear of the showroom and spotted a car standing in the center of it with a sateen cover draped across, hiding its identity.

"Are you ready for this?" said Preston.

"Sure, show me what you've got, but I'm not buying," I replied.

He whipped off the cover and revealed underneath the most beautiful automobile I'd ever laid eyes on.

"Wow!" I said, realizing that my instant excitement over a car was satisfying and thereby proving one of my three rules of life that I'd mentioned earlier, "What is it?"

"What you see here, young man, is a 1963 right-hand-drive E-Type Jaguar in mint condition," he stated.

I noted that he pronounced the word Jaguar as Jag-you-are as per the original English pronunciation as opposed to our own version, Jag-wah.

"Actually, it's more than mint but I'll get to that in a minute," he continued.

I couldn't take my eyes off it. It was the sexiest thing on four wheels I'd ever seen. But it wasn't just sexy, it was pure elegance. The paint was the pale blue color of a duck egg and the interior leather was a light tan. As I walked around the car, my eyes took in the gleaming chromed spoked wheels, the mahogany steering wheel punctuated by the shiny steel screws that encompassed it, and a manual wooden knob stick shift indicated that this car was meant for fun. The sheer beauty of this car's design was something to behold and the front and rear ends were capped by the most elegant and slimmest of chromed bumpers, designed to avoid detracting from the car's perfect lines. The top had been folded down and was wrapped with a matching tan leather tonneau cover. I'm not a man who generally lusts over cars but she was simply breathtaking.

"She's the most beautiful thing I've ever seen!" I gasped, struggling for a superlative that did justice to the Jaguar.

"You're not wrong there because in fact, this model has recently been officially declared by car enthusiasts and experts from all over the world, as the most beautiful car ever designed. And she's got your name written all over it," Preston replied.

"I don't know about that, Pres, I'm fairly sure that British cars of this era have a pretty bad reputation for always being in the shop. I'd be no better off than I am with the Maserati," I said.

"Fortunately for you, that's where you're wrong, Jake," he said, "This is no ordinary E-Type, this is what we in the trade call a RestoMod."

"RestoMod?"

"Yep. What you see is a carefully restored body and an interior that is now better finished than the day it left the factory in Coventry, England almost fifty years ago. However, all of the things underneath that used to let this baby down have been replaced with the finest modern Jaguar running gear. That includes a custom made lightweight aluminum chassis, a brand new Jaguar V8 motor, modern disc brakes, hydraulic suspension and a six-speed manual transmission from Jaguar Racing. This car will be as reliable as a brand new Ford. More so, in fact."

"Really?" I said, "How much is it?"

"If I told you I wasn't making a dime for myself except for the cost of my boys' time here today, would you believe me?"

"I've known you a long time, so probably not," I replied.

"Well, it's the truth. I'll take your car in as a trade and let you drive this away if you write me a check for eighty-five grand," he said casually, "And that is a bargain as well as an investment, Jake."

I let out a lungful of air, "Can I drive it first?"

"You won't need to but sure, get in, buckle up!"

Chapter 86

Later that afternoon, as I guided the Jaguar into my driveway, I was aware that my jaw was aching from the grin that this beauty had put on my face for the entire time I'd spent with her. It was like a first date.

Martha was out in her front yard and spotted me as she watered her hydrangeas.

"Oh Jakey! I like it! That is so sexy. I'm gonna have to put my fuck-me pumps on!" she yelled as she continued with her illegal watering, "Don't forget, dinner is at 7.30, you'd better not be late."

I waved politely and waited embarrassingly for the garage door to open before parking my recently acquired girlfriend in her new home. Preston had been right. I'd held on to the Maserati for too long just because it was a gift from Tara and I had always felt pangs of guilt when mulling over the idea of selling it every time I got a new invoice from the repair shop. The Jaguar was every bit as stunning to drive as Preston had promised. It felt like I was driving a rare piece of English history but one that was not fraught with mechanical failure. Although I'm not short of money, I'm not rich either but handing over that check to Preston was one of the easiest and guiltless things I've ever done in my life. I felt a new sense of freedom.

Once I'd managed to pry myself away from the car, I started to get ready to go to Martha's. After showering I began selecting an outfit for the evening. Now, I don't do this often but I caught myself checking out my physique in the full-length bedroom mirror as I passed by, still naked from my shower.

"Not bad, old man. Not bad at all."

I had to admit that for a man soon to celebrate his half century on this earth, I still looked okay, mostly due to regular visits to the gym and healthy eating and fortunately, I still had most of my hair, just a little grayer than it used to be. And thankfully, my dick still worked, even if I hadn't used it in a long time. When I thought about poor Frankie, who's Erectile Dysfunction had been so debilitating that he'd been forced to have a penile implant installed, I was grateful for small mercies. I'd never relished the idea of pushing a concealed button in my nut sack to get an erection although Frankie claimed it worked better than ever now. Rather him than me, though.

But try as I might, as I stood there examining my almost fifty-year-old body, someone two thousand miles away was still on my mind and I knew I couldn't shake it. Oh well.

I'm not a serial shopper and my closet isn't awash with clothes. Many years ago, my mother had taught me the rules of when and what to buy. She always said that it was better to buy one single item that you'd love and cherish always, rather than two or three items just because they were on sale. The price, as far as she was concerned, was immaterial. Save up for it if you can't afford it and then be proud of what you're wearing and know that it will always look exceptional. And she was right.

I selected my favorite pair of black Versace pants and contrasted them with a light blue Armani shirt. A pair of midnight blue suede Bruno Magli slip-ons completed the look.

It was still early so before I went round to Martha's, I sat down in front of the computer in my home office to check my email and Facebook messages. There weren't any, which didn't surprise me but I just had the thought that maybe, just maybe she would have sent a one-line note or something. What was interesting though, was that since the fundraiser ball, I'd had numerous Facebook 'friend requests' which was heartening. I now had more than a hundred people in my circle which made me feel pretty good even if the truth was that there was only one friend I needed to make me feel completely whole.

I closed the computer down and with a bottle of Rombauer in my hand, bravely ventured outside and rang Martha's doorbell.

Chapter 87

It was another Saturday night at 2805 Georgia Avenue, in Green Hills, Nashville. Summer was snuggled at one end of the sofa watching a re-run of Seinfeld while her husband, James was picking a fantasy football team on his iPad. It wasn't that she didn't like this way of life but sometimes she wished they did something a little more exciting occasionally. Her husband was a good man, he worked hard to provide for the family, was a pretty great husband in most ways and did a good job helping to raise the kids, although he had a temper sometimes. But she did feel a little lonely recently. Since the kids had gone away to college, her life had changed dramatically and she paid more attention to the calendar for when they would be home for breaks or school holidays.

"How's your week been, Sum?" said James, without looking up from his iPad.

"Oh, pretty good, much the same as any other week but I did finally get the materials I'd been waiting for. At least I can get back to work now," she replied, "How about you?"

"After a while, one set of teeth looks like any other but I can't complain. We have a nice life so I'm grateful," he said, "So, you're going to be making lots more of your trinkets then?"

"They're not trinkets, Jimmy, I make custom designed jewelry. I know it's not expensive and doesn't make huge profits but people like what I do and I like doing it," she responded, a little miffed that he seemed to be belittling her thriving and somewhat successful home-based business.

"That's good then… so what do you fancy for dinner tonight? I was thinking that we could pick up some Chinese food from Mao's. Unless you wanted to cook?"

The last thing she wanted to do was to cook on a Saturday night and she despaired at the thought of eating monosodium glutamate laden Chinese food.

"How about sushi?" she said.

"Ugh! Raw fish! No thanks," he replied.

"There's a great new Vegan restaurant downtown, why don't we go there?" she suggested.

"I need meat, not fodder, Summer, and I love Chinese, you know that."

"How about Thai?" she asked, realizing she was playing a losing game.

"No, too spicy for me. Don't worry, I'll call in an order at Mao's."

Mao's Chinese Restaurant was on speed dial on his phone so in less than ten seconds, he was placing an order.

"Yeah, Larsen on Georgia, can you deliver? You can? Great. We'll have the usual and I'll pay cash when it arrives. Thanks, Hong," he said, hanging up.

I guess we're having Chinese then...

As James returned to his team selection, she began to think about the necklace and the note that had arrived in the mail on Wednesday. She was still shaken by it and didn't know what to do about it or even if she should respond. It was like being hurtled back through a time warp tunnel to another life. A life that she loved and missed but that belonged to another time.

"I miss Poppy and Casey, it seems they're gone for so long between holidays," she said.

"Well, they should be, Sum, they're meant to be learning and getting degrees!" he responded, having gone back to deciding on a quarterback for his fantasy team, "You'll have to let go at some point."

"I don't want to let go, Jimmy, I never want to let go. I just wish I could see them more often, and with them so far away in Arizona, it feels like they're in a different country sometimes."

"It's good for them to be independent, Sum - before Poppy went to college I was beginning to feel that she'd never grow up and Casey was fast becoming a mommy's boy. You know that. And Jeez, I can't wait until they start bringing some money in," he said, his eyes still glued to his iPad screen.

Summer decided to let his last comment go without a response, she didn't want an argument on a Saturday evening. Instead, she focused back on the Seinfeld episode playing on the television…

Soup Nazi: *Hey, what is this? You're kissing in my line? Nobody kisses in my line!*

Sheila: *I can kiss anywhere I want to.*

Soup Nazi: *You just cost yourself a soup!*

Sheila: *How dare you? Come on, Jerry, we're leaving.*

Jerry: *Do I know you?*

Elaine: *So, essentially, you chose soup over a woman?*

Jerry: *It was a bisque.*

Summer laughed, she could watch these re-runs forever.

"What's funny?" asked James.

"Oh, nothing, Jimmy, nothing at all…"

Chapter 88

Martha had gone all in for tonight's dinner but to be honest, she wasn't short of a few bucks. Formal waiter service, three cooks in her kitchen and a sommelier to select wine for each course. Kind of overboard but I wasn't complaining.

"Jake darling, come and meet the girls," she drawled, an indication that she'd already opened a bottle or three earlier in the evening.

'The girls' were a group of women of varying ages, that I suspected belonged to the ABCDE because as yet, I hadn't spotted another male guest. Eyeing the table that was set for eight, and with a quick count up in the room, I realized that I was the only male dining companion this evening which made me more than a tad uncomfortable.

"Stop worrying, Jake, they're not gonna eat you… they'll play with you first anyway," whispered Martha as she snatched another martini from the cocktail waiter's tray.

I tried to hide my embarrassment of the fact that I was the only man in the room and did my best to mingle. But happily for me, the truth was that this group of ladies was incredibly lovely, they were very complimentary towards me and overall, just a lot of fun. They were actually making me feel really chilled and comfortable. Whether it was because they were now free of their marriages or just enjoying independence and their own wealth, I didn't know, but none of them sounded like they were desperate to get hitched again. All in all, they were an unbelievably refreshing group and after an hour or so, I was truly grateful that Martha had invited me.

Martha had also selected an iTunes playlist which was straight out of my younger life and memories flooded back as I began to recall some of the songs that were playing quietly in the background. In fact, the music coupled with the multicourse menu being served tonight, reminded me of my first evening with Tara, when we'd dined on her yacht in Manhattan. I was assuming that tonight wouldn't end in the same way though.

At my end of the table, I was sitting closest to three ladies who had all divorced in the past year or so, Charity, Heidi and Ginger. I wouldn't describe them as typically beautiful but each had a definite allure about them. They weren't what I would call obviously pretty girls but there was no doubting their individual attractive features and overall sexiness, and these ladies were far more interesting than just how they looked.

Heidi had been watching me as I chatted to Charity. I wasn't imagining it, I could actually see her in my peripheral vision. I was guessing she was formulating a loaded question but I felt so relaxed now that I didn't mind what anyone asked.

"Have you really been leading a monk's life for the last twenty years?" she asked, "I've heard that story but I don't believe it for one minute."

"Well, I hate to disappoint but the story is true. My wife died shortly after giving birth to our second child and for one reason or another, romance, dating and marriage never found its way to me after her death," I replied, "But it's okay, I'm not a hopeless case or a tortured soul. I'm surviving."

"I don't believe you, Jake," she replied, "That just isn't possible in any man."

"Why not?" I asked.

"Because men need sex, men need looking after and men can't raise children on their own, most men can barely even cook," she replied, "And now you're trying to convince me that you are the one man on earth who negates that theory?"

I sensed that Heidi had been through a lot in her previous marriage and couldn't help thinking that her talons were out to put some scars on me but I needed to make friends, not antagonize so I tried a different approach to the group of women closer to me at the table and went all in.

"Ladies, you are all survivors of failed marriages. But can I ask you something?" I said to all three of them, "What is it that you actually want in a man, in a husband or partner?"

"You mean one particular thing or just a general description, Jake?" asked Ginger, who was sitting next to me.

"Well, it could be the one thing that is the most important aspect of a man or it could be a bunch of things that are mandatory for a relationship. Sometimes, it's easier to say what you don't want but let's ignore that for the moment," I replied.

I realized that my question had attracted the attention of the rest of the table and a hush came over the room as all eyes were now on me. A mild sweat began to appear on my forehead.

So much for feeling relaxed...

"I can give you one," said Martha, "No fucking Republicans!"

"I was hoping for something more about their personality traits rather than their political views, Martha, but why not, let's put that in as our first requirement. Must be a Democrat..."

Another voice from Martha's end of the table made a suggestion,

"No baggage! I can't deal with other people's issues being brought into my relationship," said Carla, "The marriage would be doomed before it even began."

Charity chimed in now, "I want my partner to treat me, see me, accept me as an equal. I don't want to be seen as someone who is inferior. I've had all that already and I'm over it," she said.

"It would be nice to meet someone who is spontaneous," said Heidi, "That would be cool."

"How do you mean, what's your version of someone being spontaneous?" I asked her.

"You know, someone who doesn't plan everything to the nth degree. Like waking at midnight and saying we should drive to the airport and catch a plane to Paris. Maybe not that indulgent but maybe drive to a cabin in Tahoe or something, but without any kind of plan involved at all."

"I like it," I said, "That goes on the list."

"How about someone who doesn't judge me all the time, that would be a breath of fresh air," said Liz, who'd been pretty quiet for most of the evening.

"You mean, you'd like to be able to say things freely, not scared to voice your opinion?" I asked, "Shouldn't that be a given too?"

"Exactly, someone who might actually listen to what I have to say and maybe even appreciate it," replied Liz, now much more animated.

"Someone I could be open with," came a quiet whisper from Ginger, "And who could be open with me."

Ginger was a spectacular lady; a potpourri of colors that made me feel almost gray and invisible. Her dark skin, which I assumed was from African rather than West Indian origins, was a perfect silky canvas for all the color that embellished her. Her hair was not really ginger, more of a fiery red and her makeup was I suppose, pleasantly flamboyant; purples, violets and raspberry colors. I had never seen an African-American with blue eyes, well, not the color of hers anyway which were more the color of cornflower than anything else. Her dress style was definitely rooted back in the 60s and 70s, every color of the rainbow showing off her assets under her form-hugging catsuit. She was without doubt, a remarkable woman, to look at and to listen to.

"I don't think you'd have a problem being open with anyone, Ginger, surely?" I said.

"You'd be surprised, Jake, you'd really be surprised," she replied, her hand now laying on top of mine and her fingernails drawing up across my knuckles like a cat when it's happy and purring.

"So what else? Anyone, just be open and honest about what you want," I said, addressing the entire table while gently removing Ginger's hand from mine, "What about things like manners, courtesy and kindness?"

"Shouldn't that be a given too? Isn't that what we all expect before anything else?" said Suzanne, who'd been quiet up to this moment, "You know what I'd like? Someone who has faith in my ability, someone who would be willing to take my own career seriously."

Martha had told me about Suzanne. She had started a business from home which dealt with homeopathic healing and natural meditative therapy for people who were suffering any kind of stressful issues or imbalance in their lives. Martha had said it was called Reiki or something like that. But her husband had laughed at it even though Suzanne had now opened her sixth location, the latest one in Santa Barbara. Needless to say, the husband was no longer in the picture and Suzanne was a much happier lady.

"What about honesty and trust?" I asked.

"Again, that shouldn't even be a requirement, Jake, we expect that as a standard to work from," said Martha, pouring a generous glass of Montrachet, without waiting for the wine waiter to attend to her thirst.

I'm done with men who can't be challenged," said Heidi, "What's so bad about debating something without it having to end in a row? Whenever I spoke up about anything that interested me with my last husband, he could never understand why I needed to have an opinion."

"Fair point," I said.

"Someone who would love me, warts and all, for all my failings and slip-ups," offered Charity, "Why do we have to be perfect all the time?"

"I just want someone who'll make me laugh," said Ginger, "I don't think it's too much to ask for, right?"

"Absolutely," I said, "Did you hear the one about the bear hunter?"

"No!! I don't mean just telling jokes, I mean someone who has a natural sense of humor, who sees things in life that just make them giggle," she replied, "I'm sure you're like that, Jakey."

Jakey, hmmm...

"So," I said, "Let me summarize. What you want is a kind, open, courteous, spontaneous, non-judgmental, humorous, appreciative, honest, trustworthy Democrat without baggage who can debate issues and who listens to you and takes you seriously? Oh, and he should love you no matter what. Have I got everything or did I omit something?" I asked.

"Yeah, you're right, Jake. That man doesn't exist. Think I might try women next," said Martha, draining yet another glass of two hundred dollar wine.

"Anyway, Jake, enough about what we want as women, what do you want in a girl, assuming you're still straight?" asked Carla, "I kind of pity the good men in life now as it seems that sometimes they feel the need to apologize for being male with all the douche bags in this world!"

"Honestly? I haven't really ever given it too much thought. I fell in love once, many years ago and at the time I guess I thought I'd found the perfect girl but then that relationship evaporated," I replied.

"You mean Tara, your wife," said Carla, "I'm sorry, I didn't mean to make this a sad discussion, you must have felt so much pain for so long."

"No, no, it's really okay and in fact, it wasn't Tara I was referring to, even though I loved her very much. This was someone else entirely," I replied, "But truth be told, I guess all we really want is to be loved, right? To be loved unconditionally by someone who'll forgive our little foibles, overlook our failings and embrace our sensitivities. I think we all want that, but it's not always so easy to find that perfect compatible partner in life, although I haven't been looking recently."

"I don't think you'd need to look too hard, Jake, there are six other women in this room who'd back me up on that," said Martha, "Would anyone care for a glass of Port with the cheese?"

The evening continued as a jovial and interesting debate on life and its mysteries and was, as far as Martha was concerned, a resounding success. I'd actually really enjoyed myself; I'd gone from the point of really not wanting to go at all, to the other end of the scale of not wanting it to end. But midnight came and I decided that I shouldn't overstay my welcome and said goodnight to everyone.

As I opened the door in the foyer to leave, Martha caught up to me, clearly drunk but amazingly still quite lucid.

"Don't underestimate yourself, Jake, you're a catch for so many wonderful ladies," she said, "You need to get back on the bus before you get old. Thank you for coming, neighbor, you were my star this evening."

I bent and kissed her cheek and gave her a warm and affectionate hug.

"No, thank *you*, Martha, you've woken me up and I appreciate it. This was a really lovely and educational dinner party," I replied with a smile on my face.

"See you in the morning," she said.

"That you will," I replied, stepping through the doorway and immediately taking in the incredible aromas from the night air, an unmistakable west coast mixture of juniper, musk sage and California spicebush blending intensely with the moist salty sea air breezing in from the Pacific.

You're a lucky man, Jake...

Chapter 89

Back at home, I rushed to my office once again to check on any response from Summer but sadly, there was nothing in my inbox. Although I did see that there were a number of new friend requests on my Facebook page, three of which came from some of tonight's dinner guests.

Is that how it works now? You meet someone, they like you, then friend you with the possibility of romance in the future? Seems like Facebook might be more of a dating site than I'd originally thought...

I gratefully accepted all three from this evening, knowing that I might be seen to be leading them on but what could I do? If I ignored them, it would just look plain rude.

I picked up my iPhone and armed with a glass of Margaux snatched from the kitchen, I sat down in one of the oversized armchairs in the lounge. I'd left a log fire burning this evening because although the days were balmy, the evenings had a chill to them and as I'd grown older, I realized for some reason that I was beginning to feel the cold. I guess it must be my east coast blood.

I sent a text to each of my kids, as I had begun to do more frequently since I'd bought the iPhone. It was a great way of letting them know I was thinking of them and also for me to know that they were both okay. All it needed was a one-line reply to make me feel happy and sure enough, within thirty seconds of my texting, I had a reply from each of them. Both were at parties but also the designated drivers so I was more than happy that they wouldn't be drinking. I love my kids, they take after their mom.

I also sent a late night text to Preston to thank him for the Jaguar. He responded, telling me that he already had a customer for the Maserati. Wow! It seemed as though I'd buried another memory but for the first time in so many years, I actually felt good about it and I think Tara would have felt the same way.

I sat contentedly in that armchair, sinking low into it and became transfixed by the flames of the fire as I stared at it through my wine goblet. I hadn't felt so chilled for a long time, even though I hadn't had any kind of response from Summer. But who was I kidding? As Martha said, it was time to get back on the bus.

I called up an app on my iPhone, something called Pandora which was a music application that you could use to select a style or type of music you prefer to listen to. It also gave you the option of choosing a particular era so I typed in '1980s' and a playlist appeared with so many recognizable and memorable songs from my youth. Tom had set up my surround sound system to take a Bluetooth connection from my iPhone so I didn't even need to turn on the stereo. I hit 'play' and the room was immediately filled with music from another life.

The unforgettable and spine-tingling voice of Yazoo's Alison Moyet came hurtling from the speakers…

All I needed was the love you gave

All I needed for another day

And all I ever knew

Only you…

Moyet's voice reminded me of the recent female British import to the USA who had an equally powerful voice and range, the wonderful Adele. If ever these two English chanteuses decided to perform together, I'd pay good money to go and see them. They literally give me goosebumps to hear the soul and emotion they put into their work.

Listening to the rawness and simplicity of this song, it was like being taken back in time to a world I'd loved, to friends I'd adored and to a place I'd never return. But tonight was a wakeup call. I had to stop with the sadness and start looking forward. I would be fifty soon and suddenly, I was determined to stop life passing me by.

The song ended too quickly and "Every Breath You Take" by The Police began its instantly identifiable opening bars just as my doorbell rang. I couldn't think who could be calling in at that time of night and I begrudgingly got up from my chair and opened the door.

"I heard music and wondered if you were up for a nightcap?" said Ginger, as she stood luminescent on my front porch.

Be careful what you wish for...

"Ginger!" I blurted, "I thought the party had ended?"

"Maybe the party hasn't even started yet, Jake," she said, "Can I come in or should I stay out here?"

"No, no... please... come on in," I replied, still ruffled at a post-midnight visit from this Californian Amazon but embarrassed that I'd left her standing on the porch, "Can I get you a drink?"

"Sure, if you have more of what you have in your hand," indicating my still half full glass of Margaux, "I'd love one!"

"Please, go on through to the lounge and make yourself comfortable," I said, "I'll be right back with some wine."

When I returned with my topped off glass and a fresh glass for Ginger, I saw that she had already made herself comfortable, half sitting, half lying on the chaise longue by the fireplace.

"I'm loving what you're listening to," she said, "This is my go-to era."

"I'm glad you approve, did you want to choose something else?" I asked, handing her my iPhone.

"Sure, love to... let me see..." she said, obviously well acquainted with the Pandora app.

"I'm finding it hard to get a handle on today's music. It all feels a little temporary to me whereas the songs that came out of my teens and twenties seem as though they'll never fade," I said, wary that she didn't seem to be hearing me.

"You like Mr. Bowie?" she asked, still not looking up.

"Very much," I said, "Pretty much everything he puts out."

"Yep, one white boy who bridged the soul divide," she replied, "Think I've got something for you here…"

David Sanborn's sax intro to "Young Americans" came oozing through the room, the song filling the room with its unique Philly sound and backing vocals.

"I only just realized that Luther Vandross did backing vocals on this album," I said, trying to sound like an intelligent muso but probably failing dismally, "And Ava Cherry too, she was outstanding on backing vocals. In fact, you remind me a lot of her."

"Yeah, I get that a lot," she said, "Probably because I'm black."

"Noooo! I didn't mean it like that, but you have a similar look and you're both beautiful and… oh God, I'm digging a hole for myself, aren't I?"

"I'm just fucking with you, Jake, don't worry!" she said, standing up and moving towards where I was sitting.

"I'm sorry but since I met you earlier tonight, I haven't been able to get your similarity to Ava Cherry out of my head, it's uncanny."

"When I said I get that a lot, I meant it. But let's forget about that for a moment…"

Ginger probably stood at around an inch short of six feet and she was lithe, her body almost snakelike in her catsuit. There wasn't an ounce of fat on her and her skin appeared to be as taut as someone half her age. She was a natural athlete/model without even trying. Thankfully, she'd discarded her heels because she seemed to tower over me when she was wearing them. However, her choice of shoes, a pair of dark red matte leather Christian Louboutin pumps, was not lost on me.

So I like shoes, what can I say?

Her slender feet now revealed pale pink nail polish on her toes and as I gazed at them, she bent down and kissed me ever so tenderly on the lips.

"I…I…"

"Don't fret, Jake, I won't eat you. Not yet anyway…" she murmured.

"Umm, this is not what I had in mind for a nightcap," I said, aware of an immediate stirring in my pants.

"Don't tell me, you've never had a black chick before?" she said, giggling at my discomfort.

"Well, that's actually true but it wasn't what I was thinking. I just haven't been in the making-out game for a very long time," I replied.

"It looks like you're still functioning okay," she said, grazing her fingers across the obvious protrusion in my pants, "Wouldn't you like to test drive it and make sure you're fully functioning before you get back into the dating world?"

"This feels so weird, Ginger, I've only just met you, I barely know you," I said, "Is this something you do often because I'm just a beginner here."

She sat astride me, carefully avoiding my stiffening embarrassment, and cupped my face with her elegant fingers.

"Jake, don't you realize that there is a real dearth of men like you in the world? Jesus, that discussion you began at the dinner table tonight was making me moist just listening to you. I've never met a man who seems so in touch with his feminine side!"

"Oh, I don't know about that but I'm interested in what women want, what makes them happy, I guess."

"You're not gay, are you? That would really fuck with my mind," she said, "But looking at what's going on down there suggests to me that you're a regular red-blooded male."

"No… no, I'm not gay, I just don't think about sex very often, if at all I suppose, but I've never had any gay tendencies, I promise!"

She leaned forward and very gently bit my bottom lip before easing her tongue into my mouth to connect with my own tongue. There was nothing urgent about the kiss, it was like it was happening in ultra slow motion. I breathed the scent from her cheeks as my hands found her shoulders, warm to my touch.

"Are you okay," she whispered, "Not too much for you?"

"It's more than okay, it's really lovely, thank you," I replied.

She kissed me again, this time deeper, her tongue extending far into my mouth and searching every part of me. I'd never kissed anyone with a tongue like this that seemed to have a mind of its own.

She slowly pulled away from the kiss and straightened, still sitting astride me.

"I know it's been a long time, Jake, but it's time you dipped your toe in the water, don't you think?"

As she said this, she slowly pulled down the top half of her catsuit, revealing incredibly pert, north facing breasts. They were on the smallish side but pretty much perfect in every way with the darkest nipples that had likely never experienced breastfeeding.

"You're allowed to touch, if you like," she said, "Even taste if you feel like it."

"You're incredibly beautiful, Ginger, and so sexy too," I said, at a momentary loss to adequately describe the vision before me.

"So are you, big fella, you just need a little awakening, I think," she replied, pulling my hands to her breasts as she leaned in to kiss me deeply once more.

I couldn't deny that everything that was igniting in my body was a welcome moment of ecstasy for me but I was unable to shake the image of the woman I really wanted to be kissing at that moment. I felt stupidly unfaithful in my own ridiculous mind.

I tenderly took her face in my hands and eased her lips from mine, a look of surprise registering on her bewitchingly attractive features.

"You don't like it?" she asked, "Was I too forward?"

"No, honestly, I do like it, I like it very much but would I offend you if I told you that I only have thoughts for someone else right now?"

"I'd only be offended if you didn't tell me, Jake, but I understand, really I do," she replied, kissing me lightly on the lips as she said it.

"In another time, I would be honored to make love with you but right now, I just can't. I'm so sorry," I said.

"Don't worry, I won't take offense even if you are the first man who said no to me!" she said, pulling her catsuit top back up and re-zipping it, "Listen, why don't we just curl up on the sofa and listen to rest of that album? And maybe tell me why you have a thing for Ava Cherry…"

"I'd like that," I said, "I'd really like that."

And that's what we did, we snuggled into each other, listening to the soulful Mr. Bowie, eventually falling asleep in each other's arms.

When I awoke several hours later, she was gone but I felt something had changed in me. I felt like I was being reborn.

Chapter 90

I spent Sunday at home, doing things that I'd been putting off for ages. I had a spring in my step which was a new feeling and I was doing abnormal things like clearing out the attic and de-cluttering the garage, chores that I'd never usually volunteer for but I was doing them now in earnest. I wasn't sure if my sudden energy surge was because of what Ginger had done to me last night or just the fact that I had begun to make changes in my life but whatever the reason, I felt good. Even though there had been no contact from Summer, I felt that maybe a new chapter in my life was being allowed to begin.

I'd called ahead on Monday morning to let Teresita know that I would be in later than usual. I'd felt the need to drive the Jaguar for a prolonged distance and so I drove out from my home town of Avila Beach and headed south down the 101 until I reached Price Canyon Road and from there I headed inland towards Edna Valley. The wide-open countryside and hundreds of thousands of acres of vineyards are about the best scenery you could hope to find when driving a 1960s E-Type with the top down. It is also a little warmer further inland which makes the experience even more wonderful.

As I steered the Jaguar through the winding roads of the valley, I marveled at the beauty of the car's elegant lines that flowed before me, resplendent in the baby blue color that seemed to reflect the cloudless sky today. My mind wandered as I passed each vineyard, their endless rows of grapes ripening in the morning sun. I'd often imagined myself as a vintner, a master of his own grapes and supplier of the wine on the family table but then I realized that to do so, you needed to be talented, hard-working and smart, none of which applied to me. But it did feel on the surface that it must be extraordinary to own and run your own winery.

I stopped at a favorite of mine, Wolff Vineyard, to sample their latest offerings and hopefully load a case into the Jaguar's passenger seat. It has often occurred to me that when people talk about Californian wine, the assumption is that the areas north of here towards San Francisco and beyond in Sonoma, Russian River and Napa are the only ones that exist. But in truth, just in our own county of San Luis Obispo, we have dozens of outstanding vineyards on our doorstep.

Wolff Vineyard occupies what I think is one of the most enviable locations in Edna Valley. The views are endless and breathtaking and the atmosphere is charming and friendly, much of that due to the fact that the business remains owned and operated by its namesake.

As I entered the tasting room, I immediately felt at home and quickly realized why I had such a desire to own my own vineyard. What I secretly wanted though, was this place.

"Ah, Mr. Delaney, so good to see you again, my friend!" said Jean-Pierre Wolff, the co-owner of the winery, "Elke will be so pleased to know you're here!"

"Good morning, JP, how can I keep away?" I asked, "Is it too early to sample?"

"It's never too early, Mr. Delaney, come right over, I have something I think you'll appreciate," he said, refusing to use my first name, ever the gentleman during the fifteen years I've known him.

Jean-Pierre and his wife Elke bought the MacGregor Vineyard back in the late 1990s and renamed it. They also brought to it their own ideas which included and artisan winery. The majority of the 125-acre estate is given over to their award-winning Chardonnay and Pinot Noir grapes but they also produce a small quantity of Teroldego, Syrah, Petite Sirah and Riesling. Their two sons, Clint and Mark also work in the family business which for me is an added bonus, as there is a true sense of warmth about the place, and a feeling of pride of ownership.

"Try this," said Jean-Pierre, "It's a 2010 Chardonnay which I believe is one of the best we've ever produced."

JP was never in the habit of giving me just a tasting amount, the ample glass was half full so I needed to be careful how much I drank this morning. The perfectly chilled Chardonnay was sublimely palatable, rich buttery undertones with a sweet hint of almond.

Jake Delaney, wine connoisseur...

“It’s fabulous, JP, I’m already sold!”

“Wonderful!” he said, clearly proud of his baby, “It’s a beautiful morning, why don’t you take the glass outside and enjoy it on the patio? I’ll bring you something else once you’re finished with the Chardonnay.”

“Thank you JP, I’m already looking forward to it,” I said, as I made my way out to the delightful terrace that afforded a panoramic vista across the entire Wolff estate.

I sat down at one of the tables haphazardly arranged across the patio and drank in the morning sunshine, marveling at the view before me. If God had made heaven, then I was looking at it.

I checked my iPhone to see if I had any messages and realized sadly that I had become one of those annoying people I’d previously mocked who couldn’t be without their electronic handcuffs.

“Ah, Jake! Jean-Pierre told me that I’d find you out here, it’s so lovely to see you again!”

JP’s lovely wife Elke wrapped her arms around me like a long lost son, her embrace one that I’d never tire of feeling.

“Elke, you look lovely as usual so life must be treating you well! Either that or your wine is keeping you young,” I said, returning the hug.

“You’re such a master flatterer, Jake, but I’ll take it!” she replied, “Wait here, Jean-Pierre has asked me to have you taste our new Pinot, it’s pretty spectacular, even if I say so myself,” she added, scurrying off to seek out a bottle of the Wolff 2010 Pinot Noir.

I spent the next thirty or forty minutes sipping on the Chardonnay and then later, the Pinot. I'd never felt so relaxed as I did sitting on the Wolffs' patio with not really a care in the world. I didn't even have to be anywhere; if I wanted I could stay here all day which was becoming a more and more interesting proposition.

And then a swish sound came from my phone…

I didn't rush to check what it was but it was likely an email from a client or from the office. The morning was too grand to spoil it with work-related issues.

But as I drained the last of the Pinot Noir, my conscience and curiosity got the better of me and I decided to check the phone. It was an email but not from a colleague or client, it was from Summer. I was quite simply shocked to the point where my stomach flipped and I felt butterflies. I had written off the chances of Summer responding to me I suppose and I'd cleared my mind to go forward in my life instead of procrastinating. I almost dared not open it for fear of disappointment but eventually I did and I read the note she'd written…

Dear Jake,

I received the necklace from you a few days ago. I haven't seen that in so many years, I didn't even know you still had it. I've repaired it and it's as good as new so I'll send it back to you tomorrow and there won't be a charge as I was the one who broke it. I suppose I'm still stunned that you found me after all these years but I'm so pleased to know that you seem to be living the life you always wanted on the west coast.

I feel at a loss for words really. Part of me wants to know what's been happening in your life, the last I heard about you was that you had married Tara. She was really nice, do you have children? I have two, a boy and a girl, Poppy and Casey, both at college now. I've been happily married now for over twenty years, I met my husband James at college, just as he was graduating. Guess I always liked older men!

Anyway, I won't bore you with my life but I just wanted to let you know the necklace is fixed and also I suppose, to find out if everything turned out well for you in your new life.

Summer x

PS. I'll send the necklace back to the return address on the package.

I didn't know what to make of the note. It felt like it had been written by a virtual stranger in some respects and I also had no clue as to how I should reply. It was a short email and almost matter of fact in its tone. I kept rereading it, trying to see if there was anything to read between the lines or whether there was something she wanted to say but was hiding it. She did at least seem to invite me to write back and tell her about my own children so that was something. And she'd put a kiss at the end. But that probably meant nothing. What I really wanted to know was why she had disappeared without a word? Why did she break my heart? What had I done that was so bad that she needed to eliminate me from her life? Or did she simply meet someone else?

But I knew that if I wanted answers to these questions, it would be a delicate path to tread if I didn't want to risk her disappearing again. I had no idea what the future held, I didn't even understand how my own mind was working but this little twenty line email was precious to me. It might even be a new beginning.

Chapter 91

Summer had spent some time trying to write the email that she'd sent Jake. Too many times she had finished writing and then deleted it all and started again. She was still in shock to hear from him after all these years and part of her was desperate to find out more about what had happened to him in the interim. But she didn't want to rock the boat at home either; she knew that it would be dangerous to tell Jake what had happened that made her disappear all those years ago. It would have to remain her secret for now. So her email was fairly perfunctory in its content and she guessed that she may not hear back from him.

She picked up her iPhone and selected a David Bowie album called *Lodger* and hit play from where she'd last been listening the previous evening. "Look Back In Anger" filled her kitchen with music…

And what did she really want from him? The 1980s were so long ago now and both of them had probably changed so much. She sat at her kitchen table waiting for the tea to brew, much like her mom had done all those years ago. Had she become her mom now? No, she hadn't, she knew that, because her dad worshipped her mom and her marriage with James was not quite the same. Yes, everyone viewed hers as the perfect middle-class family, loving successful husband, bright and good looking children and a chocolate box home in a Tennessee suburb. They even had the obligatory pair of dogs although most of the time she wished James hadn't bought them as she spent so much of her time retrieving them when they'd run away.

"Boys Keep Swinging" followed on and she loved this song, it always made her physically smile when she heard it.

But no one saw the dark side of James, the times when he lost his temper and the only person he vented on was her. He didn't beat her so it showed though, he was very careful about that. He only delivered punches to her stomach and to her back so that her face remained unflawed. As far as anyone else knew, James was the model husband. And it didn't happen often, not like some of her friends who often bore the scars of a drunken Saturday night from their husbands.

But how had she gotten to this position in her life? She had always desperately wanted to be like her own mom, an independent, intelligent and beautiful mother and wife but somehow she had messed up somewhere along the line. Getting married so young hadn't helped. She hadn't even finished college before she was wedded to James and raising Poppy. And she knew she'd never really been in love with him when he asked her to be his wife but he seemed so nice and knew what he wanted from life and she was flattered to have been asked to marry him. In fact, she knew that in her entire life, she had only ever fallen completely in love once and that man was now two thousand miles away.

"Repetition" came on next and as soon as she began to listen, she could almost identify with what Bowie was imparting in the lyrics...

Johnny is a man

And he's bigger than you

But his overheads are high

And he looks straight through when you ask him how the kids are...

Often she'd thought about leaving James but she realized that it would be so hard to raise two children on the money she made from her jewelry design business. And he wasn't really a bad man most of the time. He had a terrible temper sometimes but it didn't show out too often and she'd learned over the years to avoid pushing the buttons that made him angry. But since the children had both gone away to college, life had changed in so many ways. She missed them of course but now she was finding that she and James were spending more and more time together and the longer this had gone on, the more she realized that they had so little in common with each other.

And the food is on the table

But the food is cold

(Don't hit her)

"Can't you even cook?"

"What's the good of me working when you can't damn cook?"

She picked up the teapot and poured herself a cup of tea, adding a small amount of milk to the brew. The ceiling fan in the kitchen continued wafting cool air down on her and as she sipped her tea and felt the warmth of the cup in her hands, she wondered what might have been. She also wondered if she should have been friendlier in her email to Jake. But what would have been the point? Jake was probably a happily married man with a couple of kids leading the perfect life out there on the west coast. As her mom would say, "You make your bed and you lie in it."

And she still missed her mother so much. And as this thought hit her once again, the tears ran uncontrollably down her cheeks.

Well Johnny is a man

And he's bigger than her

I guess the bruises won't show

If she wears long sleeves

But the space in her eyes shows through...

Chapter 92

I'd driven home from Wolff Vineyard with my two cases of wine safely loaded into the passenger seat of the Jaguar and during the entire journey had thought about nothing else except how to respond to Summer's note.

"Damn it!" I said under my breath as I spotted Martha in the front yard tending to her flowers and plants. I really didn't want to get involved in a long conversation with her right now when all I could think about was Summer.

"Hey Stud!" she yelled as I pulled into my driveway, my finger already pushing the button on the remote to raise the garage door.

"Hi Martha, thanks so much for a lovely evening on Saturday," I responded courteously.

"Was my pleasure, Jakey. I heard you had a little late night spice, baby, a little Ginger Spice!"

"Oh, just a nightcap," I replied, willing the garage door to move faster.

"Well I know you didn't fuck her but why not? What the hell's wrong with you, Jake?" she laughed as I guided the E-Type into the garage and hit the close button.

After I'd stowed the Chardonnay and Pinot in the wine rack, I went to my office at the back of the house and slumped into my chair, thinking hard on how I wanted to reply to Summer. It hit me then that I was over-thinking everything and that I should just be myself, like an old friend catching up with someone from the past. If I started grilling her on what had gone on back then or became overbearing in any way, she'd run a mile. So that's exactly what I did…

Dear Summer,

It was so nice to hear from you today. When I received your email, I was tasting a new wine in a vineyard near to where I live and I'd love to have shared a glass with you.

Too schmaltzy? No, it's fine…

It doesn't seem possible that the last time I saw you, you were just going off to college and now you have two children doing the same thing! I'm in a very similar situation, my two (also a boy and a girl, Tom and Lily) are around a hundred or so miles north of where I live but I miss them badly when they're gone.

I never remarried once Tara was gone. Her death left me an emotional wreck I suppose and for whatever reason, I never got back on the love train.

Love train? Really? Oh well…

But I have a good life out here and I love the climate, it seems to suit me very well. I have a very small business, a law firm obviously, as I'd be hopeless at anything else! But I have two or three people that work with me and they're like family. I have some close friends too, a couple of guys, Preston and Frankie, although they're quite different to Talbot and Perryman! In fact, when we moved out to California, I pretty much lost contact with those two and it still makes me sad that everything changed so quickly and so dramatically.

Don't ask the obvious question, Jake, baby steps…

When I discovered that Tara was unexpectedly pregnant with my child, I obviously did the right thing and asked her to marry me but I think I was a bit of an embarrassment to her father and that's how we found ourselves out here. And I suppose that most of the time, it all worked out pretty well in our marriage, the usual ups and downs like everyone else. Tara got pregnant for the second time, again strangely unplanned, and sadly she died during childbirth because of complications. So I lost my wife and gained a daughter, all in the same day.

I'm sorry, that all sounds a bit depressing but it shouldn't. I see myself as being a pretty lucky guy really so I have no complaints. But I still have fantastic memories of life back on the east coast in the 1980s and I cherish those times, sometimes wish I could turn back the clock, I guess.

Well, enough about me, tell me more about your life. It sounds like you landed on your feet and you have an amazing life! How are your mom and dad? How is Autumn, did she get married also? Do you hear from anyone back then? Talbot? Perryman and Sofia? How did those two work out? I'd love to hear your news when you have a free moment but in the meantime, I'm so glad to know you're okay and that life worked out well for you.

No you're not…

Oh, and the necklace? Please, I want you to keep it. It is yours anyway! I just wanted to make sure it found its rightful owner once more.

Hope to hear from you soon!

All my love,

Jake. xxx

I reread the email a couple of times and once I'd decided that I was happy with it, I hit 'Send' and hoped for the best. This could go one of three ways. She could close me down altogether, she could remain cool in her response or she might open up and tell me what did happen all those years ago. I truly hoped it was the latter.

Chapter 93

"What's cooking, Sum?" said James, as he closed the internal door to the garage, "I've had the shittiest of days, sometimes I wish I never had to look into another mouth and lecture people on how to avoid gum disease, pisses me off sometimes, they're so friggin' ignorant."

"I'm making your favorite tonight, Jimmy, southern fried chicken just like mama used to make," said Summer, quickly closing down her laptop as her husband came towards her.

"What was that you were doing?" he asked, "You're not hiding anything from me are you?"

"No, just catching up with an old friend, no one you know," she said, "Anyway, can I get you a drink baby, how about a beer?"

"That'll work, it's hotter than a snake pit out there this evening," he replied, "So, who's your old friend, what's her name?"

She'd read Jake's email earlier in the day and wanted to respond while it was still fresh in her mind. He definitely seemed to have landed on his feet and she felt a small amount of envy, but in a really good way. But it was so sad to hear about Tara, really awful.

"Uh, err… it's just someone from the old Florida days… just a girl I used to know… Jackie, yes, Jackie, really nice girl… just telling me what she's been up to for the last twenty years," she stammered, not expecting James to take such an interest.

"Well, that's good baby, don't want you hooking up with old boyfriends, do we?" said James, picking up the laptop, "What have you been writing?"

"Oh, nothing, sweetheart," she said, taking the laptop back from him, "Just girl's stuff… now, let's get you that beer."

He let her take the computer, wandered into the den and picked up the TV remote to switch on the pre-game show for the evening's football. The pundits, mostly ex-footballers, were already excited about the game coming up and James quickly immersed himself in the event.

"FSU are playing tonight, the old enemy, Alabama. But I can see our Seminoles rolling that Crimson Tide right over! Man, I'm so psyched about this one," he said, slumping heavily into his armchair, "Let's get that fried chicken going, I could eat a horse in here, Summer. And make sure the fixings are just how I like them."

She breathed a sigh of relief that James hadn't pursued the idea of looking at her laptop and that thankfully, he had other things on his mind.

Jackie? Where did that come from? Jake would be laughing at that!

But even so, she'd still done nothing wrong, nothing at all but she was already feeling so much guilt inside. Thank God she had a password on her computer, she didn't relish the idea of a fight with James tonight.

Outside, the oil in the fryer was ready for the chicken and she carefully placed all the prepared pieces into the pot. James was already deeply involved with the pre-game buildup on the television so she went back into the kitchen and sat down to continue writing a reply to Jake. She figured she had maybe twenty minutes before the chicken was ready and there was no chance of James emerging from the den for the next four or five hours so she began writing…

Dearest Jake,

I'm so sorry to hear about Tara, I had no idea what had happened. She seemed like such a lovely person too. But I'm so pleased to hear that you have two wonderful children, which must make you so happy!

As for me, well I'm pretty happy I guess, I'm living the dream in many ways. I really enjoy my little business that I have going on at home and James is a good husband to me most of the time. Sometimes I wished that I'd explored further afield, maybe done a little more in life but I can't really complain. Most of all I miss my kids, more every day in fact. But they have their own lives to lead, I just wish they weren't so far away in Arizona. I plan on taking a trip out to see them soon... maybe we could meet up and talk about the old days. I don't think Arizona State University is very far from you?

There's a lot you obviously haven't heard since you went away and some of it will make you sad, I'm afraid. My parents are no longer around. They were tragically killed in a car wreck while they were on a trip to come see Autumn and I at college. Neither of us ever really recovered from that. We grew up as blessed children in the most loving home you could imagine and our childhood was a dream in most people's eyes. For that, I'm grateful but I miss them both so much.

Perryman and Sofia married and adopted four children, all from Vietnam. They are the sweetest family and believe it or not, they all still live in the same house in Sewall's Point. And the biggest news that you never heard about is that Autumn and Talbot got married! They have one child, a daughter they called Ella and you won't believe this, they moved to England! I think that Talbot feels closer to his idol, William Shakespeare! I've only seen them three times when they've come back here but one day I'd like to go see where they live in England.

I too wish that sometimes I could turn back time and see how things might have worked out. For now, Jake, I can't tell you what happened with us because it's too painful to revisit. Maybe one day I can, but not at the moment. In the end, everything worked out for the best and I think that maybe we were just never meant to be together. You always said you were too old for me anyway so I think you were right all along!

But thank you so much for the necklace, it's such a thrill to have it back and I'll wear it often. You're a very kind and thoughtful man. Send me a photo one day, I'd like to see how you've changed, whether you've become one of those silver foxes! I've attached a recent photo of me, my clothes haven't changed, still flip flops, t-shirt and Daisy Dukes but I look a lot older now!

Bye for now,

Summer xxxx

She checked the email for typos and having read it through once more, attached a jpg of herself from a couple of months back and sent it to Jake. Once she'd sent it, she had the sudden realization that she may have been too candid about herself and tried to see whether there was anything between the lines that Jake might interpret.

"Summer! What's a man got to do to get fed around here?" shouted James from the den, "We've only got fifteen minutes before the game begins!"

I can't wait, Jimmy, I really can't wait...

Chapter 94

The news about her parents shocked me to the core. I couldn't believe what had happened and I was incredibly sad that for all these years, I'd known nothing about it. I felt terrible for her, she must have suffered so much. The only thing that made it easier to digest this news was to hear that Perryman and Sofia were a genuinely happy family and that Talbot had finally got his girl, in Autumn. I made a mental note to myself to try and catch up with them on Facebook if they too used social media. Thinking about them again made me miss them immensely.

Reading between the lines though, I sensed there were problems in Summer's marriage, I don't think it was all happy families in her household so I would need to be a little tactful and tread carefully. There was a fragility to her that I remembered from so long ago. Not the same fragility of carefree youth but something else entirely, even though she still seemed to be that same teenage girl I'd fallen in love with so many moons before. And the photo she sent me… well, she really hadn't aged a bit, she was still the same Florida girl in my eyes.

Over the next five or six weeks, we exchanged daily emails with each other and as the weeks and months passed, we gradually began to get to know one other again. It became a daily routine that for some reason, we both seemed to settle in easily to doing. I'd get up in the morning and have breakfast and sit and write an email in my kitchen before I went to work. She would reply later in the morning and once I came home, I'd send her another email telling her about my day and she would do the same back to me. It was incredibly nice and felt so natural and easy. Like two old friends just shooting the breeze.

From the first couple of emails where we'd both been more than a little guarded, we'd grown to relax in our 'conversations' as we exposed our feelings more openly as each day came and went. We exchanged photographs online of our families and painted mental pictures of where we lived and we'd tell each other stories from our lives, although we never approached the subject of why she had just disappeared from my life once she'd gone to college. It was obviously painful for her to talk about and I wasn't going to push her, I enjoyed having her back in my life too much to risk that.

But at the same time, both of us were nervous too; after all, we hadn't even seen each other in more than two decades. I suppose that because of current technology and social media, at the very least we knew what each other looked like now. I think I'd grown a lot older in looks even though I had kept reasonably fit and healthy, but Summer hadn't seemed to age at all. She was still the same girl I remembered from years ago. In some ways, she was even more beautiful now than when I last saw her.

We didn't know if each other had changed in our outlooks or personalities; emotions that Twitter, Instagram and Facebook were unable to adequately deliver, or even if we would click as two adults who were leading two very separate and differing existences.

I decided that someone needed to make the first move towards some type of 'live' conversation, even though picking up a telephone and calling would have been so much easier. But for whatever reason, there was a fear attached to a real conversation for both of us even though that fear remained unstated, so I decided that I should try another approach.

I texted her for the very first time…

J It's been a long time, Summer.

S I know!

J This is a strange thing to be conversing with you after so many years. I'm nervous, I guess.

I'm shaking, Jake!

I've never, ever experienced a situation like this.

I think we both (hopefully) feel the same way about each other but of course, there's nothing that can be done about it. You realize that, don't you?

I do, there's nothing we can ever do about it. It would hurt too many.

Anyway, we could meet up and not like each other...

Do you think so?

No... I don't think so at all!

I'm not sure it's an entirely physical attraction for me though. There's something else that attracts me more. I've actually never felt it before.

I chose you, Jake. We shared a unique experience. Nobody else could ever know or understand what we shared.

No one knows, no one ever will and I treasure that you chose me. I truly do, Summer.

You took care of me in that small time.

That piece of time forever stands still for me - which is beautiful.

Summer, can I ask you something?... When we made love for the first time, was it okay, was I gentle?

You know you were gentle, you were always gentle.

I want that to be so. I hope it wasn't painful!

It was! In fact there was a time once in your apartment. We had made love quite a few times by then. And I said "ooh it doesn't hurt anymore!" You laughed in surprise and said "it's not supposed to!"

That's funny!

I mean it. You were good with me. The next day it poured with rain and 'The Power Of Love' by Frankie played on the way home. I'll never forget it. That song means so much to me, even now.

That's incredible!

Don't underestimate what you meant to a young girl.

Do you remember sleeping in Talbot's house once when he was away?

I remember everything. I never slept a wink next to you. Too nervous I guess.

Seriously?

I would lay awake all night. Sometimes watching you. Wanting you to wake up.

You snored!

Oh dear!

I wanted you to wake up because I missed you, Jake!

That's so lovely.

I was. ☺

Haha! My last memory of us was after we'd been to see a band at Madison Square Garden and you stayed the whole holiday weekend. I think it was R.E.M.?

Yes, it was... What do you remember?

...you probably thought I was easy,

not exactly the girl next door.

I didn't think that!

S I remember that somehow it was always my turn to make tea in the morning…

J That's surely not true. I didn't even drink tea until I met you!

S Blame that on my mom, she has English roots!

J I didn't know that. Wow!

S Seriously, you must have thought me a bit over enthusiastic.

Not the girl to take home to mom.

J I couldn't see the attraction, Summer.

In your eyes for me, I mean.

From your standpoint. I was too old for you, you were too good for me.

I should have got you pregnant and married you! ☺

Summer didn't respond to my poor attempt at humor. In fact, there was a long gap the text conversation. For a moment, I thought I must have upset her but I decided not to push it. Sometimes I say things that are meant to be funny but apparently, it's only me who's amused.

Jake Delaney, comedian…

I poured a glass of wine and began to prepare dinner. At least I could make myself useful and I was famished. But as I finished my meal and poured a second glass of Pinot, I was starting to realize that I'd possibly said the wrong thing about getting her pregnant and marrying her. So much for the Delaney humor.

About an hour passed before I heard the iPhone ping again…

S I used to fantasize about having your babies. Can't believe I just said that!

J Why? What was so special about me or was it just that I was the first?

S I don't know. Possibly both. But it wasn't a conscious decision. It just was. Couldn't be helped. That's what I felt. Infatuation? Love? Who knows?

J But if you'd married me and then met James, you probably would've dumped me for the younger, more virile man anyway.

S Well here I am still talking to you. Go figure.

J Hmmm...

S I don't know what it is about you...

J Hey! I've got an idea, I could move to Nashville. Always liked that town... Used to know a lovely girl there...

S She's still lovely, rumor has it...

J You're funny! You bring out some good things in me. Since our recent communication began, and I don't know exactly what it is we have, it has been extraordinary considering we've never actually spoken to each other since the 1980s. I just want to tell you how much I appreciate you being in my life, whatever level that takes, and that I totally and utterly adore you. I'm sorry that it didn't happen for us all those years ago but I love that you are in my life now. I hope you like having me in yours.

S I do, Jake. Scared as I am, I do love being back in your world. I don't know how to say this... But...

J What is it, Summer?

S I'm still in love with you...

J Oh Summer! That's so beautiful to hear but I've always been in love with you, always will be.

I was shocked and stunned at the last couple of lines of text that we'd hastily written. I couldn't be sure that she had somehow let her true emotions show accidentally or whether she just needed to tell me how she really felt. But we couldn't press the reset button now, we couldn't unsay what we'd both said. We'd just bared our souls to each other and I liked it.

Chapter 95

Wednesday night meant one thing. It was my weekly catch-up with Preston and Frankie and as the Summer was now truly upon us, the three of us were enjoying a long al fresco dinner at the Granada Bistro, a late setting sun and no real need for the gas heaters on this perfect June evening. But tonight we had one extra in the group as Edie had decided to take up my invitation to join us.

"Edie, it's great to have you join the boys' night," said Frankie, "What's the occasion?"

Edie had just arrived and was putting her Prada leather jacket on the back of her chair. She has an imperious air about her, it's just the way she carries herself and I knew that my two cohorts were a little scared of her. In the nicest possible way, of course.

"Just want to make sure you fuckers aren't bullying my boy," she replied, "Jake's got things going on right now that don't need messing up by a couple of complete fucking oafs."

Targets engaged...

As she sat down, it wasn't lost on me that both Frankie's and Preston's eyes were glued to the fact that Edie wasn't wearing a bra underneath her gossamer blouse. Her nipples reigned supreme.

"Say what you mean, Edie, don't sugarcoat it, sweetheart!" said Preston, realizing even before the words came out of his mouth that he'd made a tragic mistake.

"*Sweetheart? Sweetheart?* Are you fucking kidding me?" she said, "And haven't you ever seen tits before? What are you, fucking schoolboys?"

Missiles launched...

"No, no… I didn't mean it like that, honestly!" he replied, backpedaling, desperately trying to still the waters, "And I wasn't staring, I promise you!"

"I'll let that go but one more like it, you're gonna be eating that fucking grin, Preston dipshit Pryor."

Mission abandoned...

I intervened before she spilled blood.

"Shall we order?" I said, gently putting my hand over Edie's.

A new waiter appeared a couple of minutes later, a young Cal Poly student by the name of Gregory, who was using the Summer holiday months to earn money for tuition fees. He seemed a nice kid but he'd picked the wrong table to wait on tonight.

"What can I get you, folks?" he asked, "Maybe some aperitifs to begin with?"

Edie took control and said, "Sure, can you bring us a bottle of Rombauer… Gregory?" she said, glancing at the nameplate on his waistcoat, "And two glasses, please. These two other idiots will be drinking beer. Maybe bring a pitcher?"

"Have you had a chance to look at the menu or would you like some more time?" asked Gregory.

"No, it's fine, I'll order for all of us. Bring us three dozen oysters and if the lobster's on special tonight, bring us four of those and a bucket of tagliatelle for fat boy over there," pointing at Frankie.

Frankie's jaw hung open in bewilderment, a rare occurrence.

"Certainly, ma'am, coming right up," he replied, whisking quickly away, a look of astonishment now registering on both Frankie and Preston's faces.

"So," she continued, "Who knows what?"

"Enlighten us," said Preston, "About what?"

"Don't be a twat, Pres, you know what I'm talking about. Jake's new long distance cyber love. What has he told you so far?"

"Probably not as much as he's told you but we know he's in fairly serious contact with someone from his past," replied Frankie, keen not to piss Edie off again.

"Okay, let me tell you what's happened so far," I said, "It all began in 1984…"

"Short version, Jakey," said Edie, "Even I can't bear to hear all that lovey-dovey schmaltzy shit again."

"I stand admonished," I said, "Well, the long and the short of it is that back then, I fell in love with someone I shouldn't have fallen in love with…"

"Ha! Sounds like that old Buzzcocks punk rock song!" said Preston.

"Yeah… whatever," I replied, knowing that was coming, "But anyway, for a bunch of reasons, it didn't work out and I lost contact with her, ended up with Tara and you know what happened after that."

"But," I continued, "In the last couple of months or so, I've reconnected with her, mostly down to the joys of current technology. We are in daily, almost hourly contact and well… I suppose part of me is hoping that something might actually come of it. It's early days I guess but for both of us, it's clear to see that the fire still burns. Unfortunately, however, she's married."

"Nicely summarized," said Edie, as Gregory poured a generous couple of glasses of my favorite Chardonnay and set a pitcher of beer before Frankie and Preston.

"So what's the plan?" asked Frankie, "I mean, are you going to meet up, get a motel room or something?"

"So fucking sordid, you ignorant grunt," said Edie, giving Frankie a look that would make even me tremble.

"It's not like that, Frankie, just not that simple," I said, "She's married, got kids, part of the fabric of the community, yadda yadda."

"Yes, dear boy," said Preston, "But is the lovely lady happy? Does she still feel the same way now as when you first met? If she does, then there's only going to be one outcome, no matter her current situation."

"You're not selling banged up motors now, Preston, this is somewhat more fragile and delicate than moving on a pile of unwanted metal," sparked Edie, always at my defense.

"I stand corrected, ma'am," he replied sheepishly.

Our food arrived and Gregory and one of his co-workers expertly set each dish before us and quickly swept silently away again.

"You're both right," I said, "But it's not as though she lives just around the corner, she's in Tennessee which at a guess, is a couple of thousand miles away. Right now, all I do is live each day as it comes and enjoy every moment I can from it. Do I desperately want to see her? Yes, of course, but she's in a tricky situation and I don't want to push it."

"Well, at least you can communicate easily enough," said Frankie, "Just takes a push of a button to make a phone call."

"Well… that's just it, Frankie," I replied, "So far in the last couple of months, we haven't even got to that stage. We haven't actually spoken."

"Jeez! So it really is baby steps, Jake!"

"It really is …"

Fortunately, for the remainder of the evening, Edie was gentler on my two friends and we ended up having a really fun time together. The ribbing came thick and fast and Edie showed her true sense of humor which the boys really loved. When I think about it now, I could see how I had changed for the better since getting back in contact with Summer. I was enjoying life so much more and I didn't want it to stop. But I wanted more from her and I hoped she felt the same way.

After the check had been settled, I made the excuse that I needed to use the bathroom but instead went into the interior of the restaurant where I found Gregory. I palmed a pair of hundred dollar bills into his hand which he stared at with astonishment.

"I've been in your shoes before and I know how tough it can be," I said, "This is just me saying thank you for putting up with my friends tonight."

"Wow! Thank you sir!" he said, barely able to conceal his delight.

"You're welcome, Gregory," I replied, "And it's Jake, just Jake. See you again soon, I hope."

I caught up with Edie and linked my arm through hers, enjoying the softness of the Prada leather.

"What was that all about? You were acting all conspiratorial in there with Gregory, what's up?"

"Nothing, Edie, really nothing at all. Just paying it forward…"

Chapter 96

We had been texting now for some time but a couple of weeks later, I awoke to a stream of text messages from Summer. I'd put my phone on mute while I slept so I wasn't aware that she'd been messaging me. But something had kept her awake much of the night and her dreams were coming more and more quickly and vividly now…

2:47am

Ⓢ Just dreamed about you. Normally I would wake up and feel sad, but today I had to double check because you ARE in my life. I'm so glad you're in my life.

3:29am

Ⓢ I guess my feelings for you still go very deep. In case I get hit by a bus tomorrow...I really do love you Jake. Always have. x

4:53am

Ⓢ Sorry, I was still half asleep when I wrote that. Seemed like the right thing to do at the time.

6:08am

Ⓙ Good Morning!

Ⓙ I love that you wrote that so don't be sorry, it's beautiful that you feel that way. I love you too, Summer, as I have done since you were 16 years old. I like loving you. ☺

Ⓢ Dream was very simple. My sister and I had found the perfect house to live in New York. It was available at an affordable rent. (I was single, no kids etc) and the bit that woke me up was that in the dream I was trying work out how close/far away it was to your apartment. This is a pretty typical dream about you. I've dreamed three times about visiting you (none of them real). This is the first time I've woken up and the reality hit me today that you do actually exist in my life; you are real.

J I am! It's lovely that you even have dreams about me

S ...I dream a lot.

But I do worry where all this will lead. I assume we'll just start messaging less and less after a while.

J What is your main fear? Be very honest.

S Jeopardizing my relationship with my husband and kids.

J I don't think that will happen. You still love James and your children will always love you as you love them.

I don't really figure into that equation.

Have you ever cheated? Has James ever cheated?

S Never ever ever. I've had offers.

I just worry that I'd have a lot of explaining to do I guess.

J I've never done this before, this kind of cyber love affair.

S Are we having a love affair? Am I being unfaithful? Is it right?

J I feel like it is. We 'talk' a great deal and we do love each other but are we being unfaithful? I don't think so, not in the true sense of the word.

Spiritually unfaithful maybe.

S I don't know how to put this, and really I shouldn't. I really feel guilty saying this but James is getting the best sex ever since I've been talking to you.

J I'll send an invoice.

S I think I've paid in advance. ☺

J If we were both single right now, do you think we would be together?

S Right at this second after all these conversations, then yes.

J Me too.

S If I was single I would definitely choose to be with you.

J Summer... I would love to make love with you again.

S Bit difficult. Unless you're planning on doing it remotely. Lol!

J I could try.

S Take your time. I'm not going anywhere xx

J Oh Lord!

S And...?

J I don't have a condom

S Well...I trust you...

J I'm so horny right now. But only because it's you.

S Good. ☺

J Do you think you could be in love with me?

Or someone from long ago?

S I think I've always been love with you, then and now. Night night xxx

Chapter 97

"Who's Summer"

"What?"

"Who's Summer?" Lily asked again.

My kids were finally home for the Summer holidays and I realized that Lily must have seen a text displayed on my phone's screen, from someone she'd never heard about before.

"Oh, that Summer. Just someone I knew many years ago who I reconnected with on Facebook. No one you would know," I replied.

"Is she nice?"

"Yes, she's very nice."

"Where does she live?"

"Oh, miles away, Tennessee I think…"

"Is she available?"

"No! Very much unavailable!"

"Not even to my silver fox dad?"

"No, not even to him," I replied, "But you know what? It's nice to know you've got my back."

"Oh Daddy, you know I just want you to be happy!"

"I know, sweetheart, but I am happy, really I am. Even better now that you and Tom are both home. The house suddenly feels alive again."

"But you need a lady in your life," she said, "You can't die alone!"

"Well, first of all, I'm not dying, second, I'm working on it so don't fret," I said, "Shall we have breakfast?"

Tom and Lily are infectious characters, they both have a wonderful sense of playfulness about them and if ever a dad felt truly loved, well it was this one.

During breakfast, the three of us decided to spend the day on the beach which oddly, is rare for us to do. The beach is on our doorstep but for whatever reasons, we don't go there often enough. But today was perfect, we even came back with mild sunburn, all of us ravenous for dinner. I prepared a simple meal as the kids were both starving so spaghetti Bolognese was quickly served with copious chunks of garlic bread.

After dinner, they were so full from the spaghetti that they begged off dessert and wine and decamped to their bedrooms. But even though I was left downstairs drinking a glass of Rioja on my lonesome, I didn't feel alone at all. Just the fact that they were in the house was enough for me. I was going to enjoy this Summer more than any other.

I began to think about what Summer was doing two thousand miles away and, wary of the fact that there was a three hour time difference and that it was already 10pm in Tennessee, I texted her to see if she was still awake and was delighted to find that she was…

J Do you even remember the sound of my voice?

S Completely. I remember so much about you.

J So tell me what you secretly think about.

S ...washing the sand from the beach off my body in the shower, crumpled rich cotton sheets on an unmade bed, hearing my name whispered in my ear in the dark, a gentle nip on the back of my neck... these are my thoughts of you.

J Oh my! If it's any consolation, you mirror my thoughts entirely. It sounds like you're in a naughty frame of mind right now!

S ... certainly feeling you at the base of my spine and possibly the inside of my thigh...

Caramba!

Remember - you started this! Be careful what you wish for…

Would love to cook you a wonderful meal, share a bottle of wine… gently nip the back of your neck... then make love to you...

Is this a tease?

No!

Leading me on?

Dark night, soft, rich crumpled sheets, a whisper in your ear and a nip on the back of your neck...

I know, I know....

You might not feel the same attraction now. I'm much older ☹

Maybe it's best I remain a fantasy

If you prefer.

...but then I don't get dinner cooked for me ☹

What about breakfast?

Afterward.

I'd love to explore you. Every inch.

I thought you could be breakfast too ☺

I could be.

You fuck me with your mind most days, Jake. I shake at the thought of you.

I'm sorry. I'd like to try other ways too. But I don't want to upset you.

I was fine, and then that line about reconnecting with my body... sent a ripple right up my spine...

I'm flattered.

Tell me more...

Really? You want me to?

Yes... I think I do. I can't believe this!

I'd begin by teasing your mouth,

Yes...

I wouldn't kiss you.

Oh!

I'd softly nibble your earlobes.

Find that spot on your neck and kiss you lightly.

Heaven!

Come back to your mouth which would be slightly open.

Gagging.

And really slowly, push into your mouth and find your tongue.

We'd kiss and caress and play for a while...

Melting.

Eventually I would move my head down to that space between your breasts.

No cleavage ☹

...but I wouldn't be able to last long before my mouth was so hungry for you, I might have to bite down on them.

S God I'm dying!!!!

J I'd move up your spine to your neck. And I'd bite you, but not hard.

S I'd arch...

J I'd open your legs slightly. And then I'd massage your back with oils...

S Seriously melting!

J Then I'd turn you over. Our kissing would be hot now. Feverish...

J ...but then, I wouldn't be able to stop myself.

S Don't... Please...

J I would move down to that special place.

S I'm aching...

J And hover... And drink in your aroma. And feel your heat.

But eventually, I would run my tongue across your lips...

S Oh God!!!!

J But it wouldn't be long before...

S I love that!!

J Before I gently eased my tongue inside you.

S Oh God, Jake....

J And found your swolleness...

And circled and circled it.

And I'd stay in there until I could feel you climax in my mouth. And then I'd drink you. And do it again.

And I 'd move to your face.

Kiss you deeply.

And tell you how much I love you...

S You have no idea what you're doing to me...

J Does it sound nice?

S You are sooooo sexy! I'm a mess!

J Are you OK? Are you wet?

S I was even before you wrote that!

J I'm more than happy. ☺ No touching, OK?

S I'm struggling not to!

J Is there anything that you would like me to do?

S Can't say...really...I can't...

J You can, it's just us...

S Tummy just flipped.

J Do you need a cigarette?

S No, a mop...

Summer's texts stopped at that point. I could only imagine what she was doing but I hoped she was enjoying the moment. Five or six minutes passed before she texted me once more...

S God, what sort of power do you have over me! ...I've never done that before.... It's a deep feeling, and not just sexual.

J How do you feel?

S Out of breath!

J I'm so pleased! ☺ Do you realize we just made love in the ether? The first time in 25 years? It's not sordid, it's incredibly beautiful!

S I had no intention of ever doing what I just did...

J It doesn't matter. I hope you're not embarrassed.

S Well, there's nothing like living a little...think I might need a drink.

J Should I let you go now?

S Yes. And don't do it again!

J Seriously?

S It's my second 'first time' of doing something for the first time with you. ☺

J I hope it's not the last.

S ...and you didn't even have to cook me anything. Cheap date!

J I'm terrible, I know. I apologize unreservedly. Let me chop some vegetables...

S It's almost like you have a formula to follow, to seduce...

J I don't mean to, really I don't. Are you ok?

S Gloriously ok. Feel wonderful.

J Btw, I'm not a seducer. I hope I'm a romantic.

S I'm sorry, my cynical head says you're writing to every other woman under the sun...and if you were then it's cool because you're entitled to. It's no big deal. ☹

J It is a big deal! I can tell you that you are the only woman I am conversing with like this. Believe it or not, I'm just not that kind of man. I'm slightly shocked at myself if that helps.

S But I'm smiling too. And you feel oddly warm. I feel oddly warm.

J I love that!

S Really, really, really think I'm blushing!

J Wow!

S Have a nice evening, Jake.

J Take care, wish I could cuddle you. xx

S Nite xx

I was still shocked at what had just happened between us. It didn't feel possible that we could reconnect so intensely without hearing each other, or seeing each other. I didn't know if I should feel dirty or if I had made Summer feel that way. All of this was so new to me. As far as I was concerned, you met someone, you dated and then it was just a matter of time before you hopefully became physical but this whole cyber sex thing was so new to me and something that I could never have predicted myself being a part of in any way at all.

I knew Summer would never have voluntarily done anything like this and my concern was that I had somehow inadvertently crossed the line and pushed our relationship into an uncomfortable territory that would frighten her. And it was never my intention.

I needed to text her again, check on her, make sure I hadn't ruined everything…

J Are you OK?

S I am. You?

J I was worried that what happened just now may have upset you, that's all.

S What's to be upset about? I just made love with a wonderful man in a whole new way!

J I've just re-read the text again, and it was pretty amazing!

S It's better than housework...

J Haha! But I'd love to actually physically reconnect with you

S Look, I'm not going to be your dirty little messaging tart! The gin will wear off soon enough anyway... ☺

J No!! I'm so sorry! I didn't mean it like that.

S Tell me more about reconnecting with every inch of my body again.

J I will. Soon. You should go, maybe we can talk later.

S I'm still trying to get over what you said about endeavoring to reconnect with every inch of my body... took me totally by surprise, I have to admit!

J I'd begin at the base of your spine...

S Yes.... ...slowly...

Later that night, Summer texted Jake again. It was late, she knew, but she needed to 'talk'...

S So ...shall we go for a record of keeping this one suitable?

J Why start now?

S Good point. ☺

J It was fun tonight, unintentional, but I really enjoyed it.

S To be honest, I have no idea how it happened.

J I feel such a connection with you. I haven't felt like this for many, many years. I hope you feel the same way.

S Ha!!... been feeling it since I was sixteen years old....

J I do wish I could see you right now, though...

S Well some things might always have to stay in your imagination, Jake Delaney!

J I suppose...

S But we need to tone it down a lot!!! Change the subject matter. Think vacuums and cheese!

J I'm torn between an upright or a cylinder... Brie or Camembert...

S I think even that's too much for me to cope with!

J Are you embarrassed about, or regretting what happened earlier?

S I'm still very surprised, but clearly it was something I needed to do. Feel better now. Everything's calm. Everything's all so real.

J Ok, I'm pleased then. I should leave you be for now.

Sleep tight xx

S You too, Jake xx

Chapter 98

The following morning saw Summer in a state of flux. It was difficult enough to believe that her love for Jake had been rekindled over the last few months but even harder to understand what had made her do what she'd done last night during their text messaging. But far from feeling dirty or disgusting, she felt a new elation that she had never felt before. But she also felt so incredibly guilty. She had never cheated on her husband, if this was indeed cheating and she wasn't sure if she could do it again. But whatever she felt, she knew one thing. She had enjoyed what she'd done more than anything since she'd first made love with Jake that night many years ago on a beach back in Florida.

"What's for breakfast, Mom?" came a voice from the stairs.

"Whatever you want, Poppy, it's a holiday so your wish is my command!" Summer replied, "I can do pancakes, waffles, eggs and bacon or how about one of your favorites, Eggs Benedict?"

"Oh Mama, I've dreamed this whole semester about your Eggs B, yes please! But can you do it with smoked salmon and avocado?" said Poppy, as she slipped silently into the kitchen.

Poppy was an eye-catching girl, not least because of her blonde, almost white hair that cascaded down her back. But her eyes were what really held your gaze, the deepest liquid brown, almost the color of hot chocolate. And when she looked at you, you were smitten and it was impossible to look away. She had the same athletic physique that Summer had always had, still had in fact, and she was tall like her father but she was the image of her mother, so much so that they could have been sisters. She wasn't a flirtatious girl though and even now it was hard to believe what a beautiful figure lay beneath the old and frayed plaid pajamas she was now wearing as she sat sleepy-eyed at the kitchen table.

"Come here, my precious girl, give your mom a hug!" said Summer, reaching out for her daughter and wrapping her tightly in her arms.

As she nuzzled in to her daughter's head and kissed her hair and cuddled her for the first time in what seemed years although it was only a couple of months, Summer was reminded that Poppy always smelled like cut flowers. She seemed to be one of those people where there was nothing bad inside her, only fragrance and innocence. She wanted to believe that her daughter was just an exact copy of herself but she knew that Poppy was so much better than her in every way, particularly with the current guilt that still hung over her from the previous night.

"Where's your brother, sweetheart?"

"You know Casey, he's still sleeping, He won't be up for ages," replied Poppy.

"No I'm not, I'm up," came a voice from the hallway, "You know I can't sleep if I know Mom's making breakfast."

Her son loped into the kitchen, and because of his size, managed to wrap his arms around both of them.

"What's cooking, Mom? I could eat a horse!" he said.

"A horse I can't do, but bacon I can, eggs over easy?" Summer replied.

"Like I've never been away! But I'm really hungry, can you make it now?" he pleaded.

This was always the case with her son; he was permanently hungry, always needing food. But he was a fit and strong young man, not a boy anymore. He stood six foot four, towering over her and even over his father. He didn't take much time over his appearance, his dirty blond hair a constant state of mussiness and his clothes generally dragged from whatever he deemed the cleanest or nearest pile on his bedroom floor. But it was easy to see the Nordic features in his chiseled face and in his sky blue eyes. He was one of those boys who couldn't look unattractive if he tried and to be honest, he didn't ever try but still the girls chased him relentlessly. He was also one of the sweetest mannered people Summer had ever known.

"Okay, coming right up, set the table and it'll be ready in ten minutes," she said, as Casey collapsed onto the couch in the den and Poppy went searching for knives and forks in the cutlery drawer.

"Where's Dad?" Casey yelled, as he surfed the channels on their giant television.

"He went fishing early this morning with Ted and Alex at the lake," Summer replied, "I don't think he'll be back until mid-afternoon."

"Well, the man's missing out, his loss!" he laughed.

"Well, he spends all week looking into people's mouths so he needs his play time, just like all of us," she replied.

"What do you do for your play time, Mom?" said Poppy, as she arranged the settings on the kitchen table.

"Oh, I have my moments, sweetie…"

Chapter 99

"You were up late, Dad."

Tom had just emerged from his room even though it was already eleven in the morning and I watched from the lounge as he managed to successfully navigate his journey down the stairs before heading directly to the coffee machine in the kitchen.

"I still think you're too young to be drinking coffee," I said, cleverly avoiding his probing.

"Young? When did the government impose an age limit?" he replied, adding three spoonfuls of sugar and a generous serving of cream.

"No, of course there's no age restriction on when you're allowed to start drinking coffee but I've always thought that coffee was the drug of older people, that's all," I replied.

"Like cell phones are the drug of youth?" he said, sarcastically, "Anyway, back to my original question, what were you doing up so late last night. I came down to get a glass of milk from the kitchen and you were definitely on your phone in your bedroom because I could see the light from its screen. And it was almost midnight."

Oops, guilty as charged...

"If you must know, I was texting an old friend back east," I said, hoping I didn't need to discuss it further with him.

"An old friend?" he said, slumping down on one end of the sofa before giving in and lying down full-length, his coffee mug perched on his bare chest.

"You might want to put a shirt on, you'll burn yourself if you spill that," I said.

"Quit with the stalling, Pops, who were you texting because you certainly weren't talking!" he said, becoming frustrated with my deflections.

"Hold on there, do I ask you who you're texting all day long?" I asked, feeling like I was being scolded like a naughty child for using my phone.

"No, but that's a way of life for me, I'm young, it's my right, my prerogative," he replied, "So come on, spill the beans, who was it?"

"Okay, okay! It's just someone I knew many, many years ago, before I met your mom. We recently reconnected and we're just catching up on the old days," I said, thankful that it was finally out in the open with both of my kids, "And you don't know her so don't concern yourself with it."

"So it's a chick?"

"It's a woman, Tom, she's forty-one years old!"

"Is she hot?"

"Tom! Stop!"

"I'm serious, Dad, is she a potential stepmom, is she a looker, a babe, a milf?"

"Enough!" I said, desperate for a change of subject but knowing he wouldn't give up, "Look, I'll be completely straight with you, she is 'hot', to use your vernacular but she is definitely not stepmom material, Tom, because unfortunately she's married."

"So what? People split all the time. If you're in love with each other, you should be together," he replied, nonchalantly.

"I told you to cut down on the weed, Tom, you're talking nonsensically this morning!"

"I'm serious, Dad, if she's in love with her husband, then I get it, there's no future. But if she's not or she's just more in love with you, then you should get together. What's stopping you?"

"It's just not that simple, Tom, much as I admire your way of looking at things. I guess the truth is that I don't actually know the answer to your questions right now. I have no idea where our relationship is heading, or even if it is a relationship at all. Actually, I'm not sure what it is right now, to be honest with you," I replied, amazed at how my son had managed to easily pry the truth from me.

"Has she got kids?" he asked.

"Yes, and of course, that's another problem," I replied.

"How old are they?"

"They're both at college, a boy and a girl."

"Is the daughter hot?"

"Oh behave yourself, Tom, you're not short of admirers so you don't need any more!"

"No, I'm only kidding but if they're college age, then that's not an issue, is it? They're kind of old enough to understand that people change so you shouldn't consider them a barrier to yours or her happiness."

"I guess not…" I replied.

"How old are you?" he asked.

"Fifty this year," I replied, "What's your point?"

"You're kinda two thirds through your life. You spent the first third having fun as a single man and you spent the second third alone, raising kids. Do you want the final third to be wasted?"

"Wow! When you put it like that, well, I guess you've got a point but I didn't know my demise was pegged at seventy-five!" I replied, always incredulous at what Tom deemed to be rational thought.

"Dad, don't misunderstand me or get upset…"

"I'm not, I promise."

"But Lily filled me in on Summer late last night so I already knew and I guess I've been thinking about your situation," he said.

My situation...

"Okay..." not knowing where Tom was going with this.

"The thing is, we never really knew Mom, we've never really had a mom I suppose and you're the only parent we've ever known, the only one we've ever loved, and we just want you to be happy, that's all," he said, once again amazing me with his maturity.

"Tom, that means so much to me to hear you say that but you and Lily have always been my whole world and I've never thought about making room for anyone else to be in it with us. And your mom was an amazing woman, she would have idolized you two. But you're right; I do need someone, especially as you and Lily are often not around as much now..."

"But is Summer the one, Dad?" he asked.

"Oh yes, Tom, she's definitely the one but like an old Lloyd Cole song from my youth used to say, I don't think I'm ready to be heartbroken. Not again."

Chapter 100

It was in the early hours of the morning when I decided to try and explain in a letter, well email actually, how much of an enormous effect Summer had had on me since we reconnected. I had hoped it wasn't too fluffy in its message but I needed to write something down to express my feelings that wasn't simply another two-way text, something she might keep forever if it meant anything to her. I sent it as late as possible with the realization that she was a couple of hours ahead of me but her phone must have beeped when she received the email…

S Now that's the kind of email I would like to keep and treasure forever!

J You're awake again!

S I am! ☺☺

J I'm sorry, I had to write that note. Did you read it?

We speak such a similar language, don't you think?

S Read it? I couldn't stop reading it, over and over again!

J You know that if you were available, I'd marry you in a heartbeat?

S Thank you but I don't think you and I need a piece of paper...

The whole thing is so unexpected, yet not...I've reached the stage where I'm just accepting whatever this is as divine intervention or something! I mean, just how would you explain to your best friend what is going on without it sounding smutty?

J No, but if you wanted to...

S Awwwww!! I don't think I would ever re-marry. What has happened recently has been worth more to me than that though. xx

But wow!!

I'm just taking that in....

J Do you realize you've probably spent more time talking to me than you have with your husband over the last few months?

S He's around, I'm just very good at messaging....

J I thought about calling you but my actual voice would probably be a disappointment!

S Imagine how romantic it must have been in the old days with letter writing?

J This would have taken three years!

S That's better than 23!!!!

J There's a good chance I'll be in Tennessee later this year. We could meet...

S I'm nervous just thinking about it.

J A hotel room, crisp crumpled white sheets, a nip on your neck, The Power of Love playing...

S Ooooh, that takes it all to another new level....a very real, probably riddled in guilt level.....

J Could you cheat?

S I think we should just settle for a cup of tea maybe, with a pint of gin chaser...

J Haha!

S And then...I'd probably say a series of really crass things,

lose the moment and you'd think, why did you even bother?

I think we would kiss too long to talk and say anything crass.

I don't think I'd be able to go through with it....too loyal, too scared....I'd panic!

Btw, it's kind of difficult to concentrate on work now...

OK, then let's change the subject and be serious for a moment. Try not to get upset at this question... Have you ever had an STD?

No!! But my thinking was...meet up..have sex...omg! what if you have an STD. ..pass it to husband. ..whole fucking world explodes!

Calm down!

A black baby would be easier to explain!

Hahahaha!!

But seriously, I think a lot about a lot of things...

Sometimes I scare myself.

About what exactly?

The moment afterward. The going home. The knowing in my head of what took place. The guilt.

I truly understand.

I've not been in that situation but I understand.

Me either!!!!!!!!

Ever!!@@

I've had thoughts too...

But it's ok because it's just a thought...

Thoughts are ok.

I guess.

J I've had visions of booking a beautiful hotel room, of you coming to the room...

Of making love with each other ...

And going for dinner...

Of coming back and making love again...

Of curling up with you and sleeping...

Of waking up and finding you still there and kissing you awake...

Of lying in bed watching a Sunday morning tv show...

I've had these thoughts...

S That's all truly beautiful but if it's just sex, then it's just an itch. If it's more, then you're looking at moving house, divorce papers, dogs and children, visiting arrangements... now that should scare you off!!

Crash!!!

J But you're not in love with me anyway...

S What's the time now?

J 11.06

S Maybe now...

J ☺ Good to know. But really? Do you only want sex?

S If it's all that's available to us, if at all, it would be nice, don't you think?

Can't believe I'm saying this...we haven't met for how long!!!

J Could you cheat on your husband? I'm not saying you should, I'm just asking if you could.

S I don't think I can, in the moment...but I still can't help but be curious to see you.. .just to see...what it is between us...

Nuts isn't it?

J It is, definitely.

I feel like we're having an affair at the moment. Do you?

S Don't say those words!

J Why?

S Because that makes it real.

I can pretend that it's something else. Not an affair.

J Without physicality, it isn't real. It feels real though

How do you feel now? Do you miss me when I'm asleep? Do you get excited to reconnect? Do you feel things inside, does your heart beat faster? Sorry, question overload!

S I think I've gone through and am going through every feasible emotion since we reconnected. Sometimes I'm in control, sometimes it's such a pull. I still come back to: “I just don't know what it is about you, Jake”.

S So instead of battling with it, I’m not even trying to explore the thought of, “Well, what if you truly do love him, Summer, what if you really do want to see out your days with him - you started with him, so.....” and then I think well, maybe it's just something like a habit, under my skin, I don’t know...

J I have had incredibly similar thoughts and it scares the hell out of me if it's any consolation. I've never been down this road before.

S I have to go, Jake! Sorry! Talk again tomorrow xxx

J Mañana por la mañana! xx

Chapter 101

James arrived home late that night. The fish weren't biting and he'd drowned his sorrows in a sports bar with his two buddies. He was hungry now and tired and pissed with what his life had become. His wife seemed preoccupied these days and his kids didn't want to spend time with him. Hell, even the dogs kept running off.

He came into the house through the door from the garage and saw that Summer was texting or doing something with her phone. Again.

"Don't you ever put that thing away, Summer?"

"Oh I'm sorry, I didn't hear you come in, did you have a good day with the boys?"

"Hopeless. Caught nothing, it was humid and miserable so we ended up at Flanagan's for a couple of beers. I'm hungry though, what's for dinner?" he said.

"I thought you were going to be back sooner than now so I haven't actually prepared anything but I can fix something for you, it's not a problem. Casey and Poppy are already out for the evening so they won't be eating," she replied, standing up and reaching for the fridge.

"I didn't realize that my meals revolved around our kids," he said snidely, "Maybe you can pin up a meal plan so I know when to be around."

"Please, don't be like that, Jimmy, I just thought you would have eaten at Flanagan's, that's all. I can fix something really quickly, what do you feel like?"

"I feel like another beer, if that's okay with you? If it's okay with the kids that is? Jeez, what has my life become?" he grunted, snatching a bottle of Bud from the open fridge door.

“I prepared some beef patties this morning, I could make you a cheeseburger with fries?” she asked, wary that her husband had already had too much to drink.

“I could have ordered that at the bar! Don’t we have any real food? What the fuck do I go to work for five days a week?”

“Look Jimmy, I’m really sorry. The kids only just arrived home for the Summer holidays and I was just enjoying them being here. Just tell me what you want to eat and I’ll take care of it,” she said, eager to calm her husband down before he exploded again.

“It’s okay baby, burger and fries will be just fine. I’m sorry, I didn’t mean to light up on you,” he said, putting his arms around her and kissing the top of her head, “I’m gonna watch TV while you cook. Okay?”

Summer breathed a sigh of relief when she realized that James was calming down.

“Sure, no problem, I’ll only be fifteen minutes, go sit down and I’ll bring it in when it’s ready.”

She reached into the refrigerator and pulled out some lettuce, tomatoes and onions and began slicing them on the chopping board. She switched on the fryer for the fries and put two beef patties in a skillet ready to cook once the fries were almost ready. She could hear the television now, another sports program of some sort. She didn’t much care for any sports really, she sometimes watched with James but rarely did she take in what was happening on the screen, her mind often far away somewhere else.

She began to recall what he’d just said, mindful of the fact that he didn’t like his French fries overdone.

“What has my life become?” he’d shouted.

Well, what the hell has my life become? I could have been with Jake, I could have been happy!

She lit the gas under the skillet and began to prepare the burger bun, mindful also that James only liked it prepared in a certain way; mayo on the base bun, then lettuce, beef patty, onions, tomato, pickles, beef patty, ketchup and finally the top part of the bun. If she didn't make it in that exact order, he'd throw a fit and she couldn't cope with that right now. She wanted harmony in the house now that the kids were home.

"How's that burger doing, honey? I'm famished!" he yelled from the den.

"Just coming, two minutes," she replied, "Can I get you another beer?"

"Sure," he yelled back, clearly happy now that he was back in front of his beloved television set.

She took a fresh bottle of Bud into the den and once back in the kitchen, she poured herself a glass of Chardonnay, her go-to crutch when she felt shaky.

As she sipped her wine, she fired off a quick text to Jake, asking him not to text tonight as it wasn't a good time. In truth, what she really wanted to do was to talk to him but for some reason, she couldn't get to that point. She didn't even know why! She felt she knew Jake as well as she'd known him all those years ago. Conversing with him, even if only by text, seemed so easy, so natural. Even what had happened the other night, what the world was calling cyber sex or sexting these days, felt so right even if it was so wrong. But he was so nice. He complimented her, said beautiful words, listened to her, cared about her… loved her.

"Oh God!" she said out loud as she realized the fries were overcooked and burnt.

She hurriedly reached down to the freezer drawer to fetch a new batch and having emptied the fryer basket contents into the trash, she dumped the new ones into the machine.

A ping came from her iPhone with a message from Jake telling her not to worry and that he'd be back in touch the next day. She loved how he was always considerate and crucially aware that she lived a separate life from his and that their relationship was still very much a secret one.

But she didn't see it coming… only the incredible pain. The intense agony as the first punch connected with her kidney on the right side of her body. The second punch was even worse as he jabbed her hard in her stomach, all the air knocked out of her as she doubled up, writhing with the pain. The final blow to her left side was the one that found her gasping for air, rolled up into a fetal position on the tiled floor.

"That fucking phone! What is your problem, Summer? You got a boyfriend or something? Why can't you even make a man's dinner when he needs it, you useless cunt!" said James, kicking her in the stomach before yanking another beer from the fridge.

"I'm sorry, Jimmy, please don't hurt me, please!" she begged, desperate that he didn't destroy her phone.

He picked up the plate with the burger on it and hurled it down on the floor next to her head, the dish shattering on impact and splinters of it gouging into her face.

"I'm going out, find me some food I can actually eat instead of this shit. Clear this mess up, you're driving me fucking crazy," he yelled down at her, spittle spraying across her face.

"I'm sorry, Jimmy, I'm really sorry," she replied, thankful that the assault was finally over and that he hadn't touched her face.

I can't live like this…

Chapter 102

In her bathroom, Summer examined the new bruises she'd received from her husband's latest unwarranted attack. Thankfully, he hadn't struck her face; she didn't want the kids to know what their father was capable of doing when they weren't around. She would never understand what made him want to hurt her so much but she also realized that she was one of many women like her in the same boat. You didn't have to look too far to see it all around you.

She really believed that underneath his temper, that James was a good and decent man but that sometimes she just wound him up the wrong way without even knowing it. She never meant to, she had always loved him and forgiven him. But maybe all of this new anger was her fault, maybe she was the one causing the pain in her new secret life. She knew now that there was only one thing she could do to stop his abuse.

She had to tell Jake something she knew he wouldn't want to hear, something she didn't want to say…

S I can't do it, Jake. I just can't, I'm sorry.

J Really?? What happened?

Do you want to break off our contact?

S Yes… I have to. I'm really sorry.

J I can't believe this, Summer! But if you truly don't want to hear from me, I really would understand. I wouldn't want to cause you any complication at all. I just feel a very deep connection, that's all. And I can't even explain it which makes it all the more frustrating. I think I probably have deeper feelings for you than I realized and now I get that they might not be reciprocal. But I know I'm in love with you. How ridiculous is that?

S Maybe you're in love with the idea of me? Remember, I carried a torch for you for soooo long. The last few weeks have been immense for me. You will always be significant in what has made me who I am. I don't know how to put this but even by text I'm still incredibly turned on by you.....never saw that coming.

J You shouldn't have carried a torch for me, I'm probably not what you really wanted, just an idea of what you needed.

S I was young!!

J I know that! But I'm a very different person to the man you knew. I think I'm a better person. Least I hope I am. I think you'd like me a lot more. I'm so incredibly flattered that you might be turned on by me, of course, but I'm much, much deeper than that, honestly! One day, I hope we might discover and enjoy each other, more than we ever have before. If you want to... But truly, if our conversations are affecting your life in any negative kind of way, I will disappear. I was hoping we might talk on the phone at the end of the week but again, I don't want to place you in a position of vulnerability.

S What you've described above is friendship - I can do friendship.

J I feel more than friendship towards you. Don't you feel the same? How is it just friendship if you're still turned on by me?

S Good point but I think I've got that bit about you out of my system now.

This was not what Summer wanted to write, she knew that she was saying it just to take away the pressure she felt and to stop the violence that seemed to be coming more frequently from her husband. But she had to break it off with Jake before it went too far…

J So we're done?

S We can only ever be friends. I'm married, kids, ...it's the only way it can be.

J Oh Summer, I've really enjoyed this recent connection though, and I'm sad that it won't continue but I send you my deepest love, forever, always. I hope you'll always think of me in a positive light, you'll always be a shining light for me.

S You are in SUCH a positive light!! Lousy timing. That's all.

J I know, I know. Goodbye Summer, you'll always be loved, particularly by me.

S Thank you Jake. I'm sorry. ☹

Chapter 103

I was thoroughly depressed by what Summer had texted tonight. I really thought that we'd been making inroads to rekindling our love but I guessed that she'd had time to think about what was happening and couldn't cope with it while she was married to someone else. And I got it, I really did but knowing the truth didn't make it any easier. I was in love with her. I really needed to see her. Even talk to her. But I also didn't want to frighten her and scare her away. In truth, I didn't know what I was doing. I needed Edie's thoughts on it.

The following morning at work, I peeked around Edie's office door and saw that she was under siege in paperwork at her desk. Her office reflected her personality in so many ways. It was neat, immaculate, perfectly decorated in shades of grays and light blues that made it an elegant but comfortable place to relax in.

"Got a minute for an old friend?" I asked.

She looked up, the thunderous look on her face changing instantly to a grin.

"Which old friend?" she asked, "Assuming it's not you, Jake Delaney because you don't always qualify."

I sidled in and collapsed in the chair across from her desk, letting out a sigh as I sat down.

"Bad weekend?"

"No," I said, "The kids are home and it's all good, couldn't be better. The house feels like a home again."

"So what's got you down, the look on your face isn't one of pure joy and excitement," she said, "I've seen happier men going to jail."

"It's Summer," I replied.

"I know, beautiful weather."

"Not that Summer, *my* Summer!"

"How did I already know that?"

"It was all going so well over the last couple of months, really well, in fact. But it seems to have all come crashing down this weekend, well late last night to be accurate."

"What happened, did she finally see you for the hopeless sack of shit you really are? Or have you just been irritating her?"

"So cruel," I said, "There's not an ounce of sympathy in your entire body, is there?"

"I've got plenty of sympathy, Jake but come on, you're moping around like a lovestruck teenager. It gets old, that's all. Lighten up."

"I get that, but it's kind of hard conducting a long distance relationship without even speaking to her. And last night she texted me to tell me she can't do it any longer, wants to break it off before it's even really started," I replied.

"Maybe she has issues at home that you're just not seeing or even caring about. Maybe you think that there's only your feelings and your needs to consider. The woman's married with kids for fuck's sake. What did you expect, that she drops everything and lays on her back ready and waiting for the great Jake Delaney? It doesn't work like that, fella."

"You know I'm not expecting that, Edie, you're just being cruel now."

"Not cruel, just fucking realistic. You just don't like hearing the truth when someone tells it to you," she replied.

"Edie, come on, lighten up yourself, I'm just looking for some pointers here! Anyway, you sound like Jack Nicholson in that movie… *"You can't handle the truth!""*

“Oh God, Jake, you’re so annoying,” she said, closing the manila folder that was open in front of her and putting it to one side, “Tell me what happened, what’s the latest development and quit trying to be funny with tired old movie lines.”

“Okay, well I guess it’s a bit embarrassing,” I said, “But over the last eight or nine weeks, our text messaging has become, how would you say, more comfortable.”

“You’re sexting, aren’t you?”

“In a manner of speaking, yes, but not in a crude way…”

“So. Fucking. Disgusting.”

“No! Hear me out, Edie, it just somehow developed into it a couple of nights ago, it wasn’t planned, not something either of us meant to happen!”

“I’m teasing, you fuckwit! I’m just jealous, that’s all. I’ve never sexted in my life so I don’t know how it all works. What do you do, both say ‘Go’ and then start rummaging in your pants, have a fumble and listen to each other coming down the phone? Sounds so fucking romantic, Jake, I can’t think why she’d want to stop doing that. Must give it a try with Alan.”

God, she frustrated me…

“If you’re just going to mock me then I’ll get opinions elsewhere, I won’t waste your time,” I said.

“Whose opinions? A-hole Preston and Fatboy Frankie? Yeah, that should work fucking perfectly.”

“Maybe I’ll talk to Martha or Ginger…”

“Stop being a tool, Jake, just tell me what’s been going down and I’ll give you a true opinion, the only one you’ll need.”

“Well, okay… over the weekend, a couple of texts got pretty intimate and I think we both felt we’d elevated the relationship to a new level…”

“Elevated the relationship? What is this, a fucking poetry class? Stop trying to make it innocent and flowery, Jake, and just give it to me straight. Jesus, it’s like watching paint dry with you sometimes!”

“Glad I caught you on a good day, would hate to see you when you’re pissed with someone,” I replied.

“I’m not pissed at you, Jake, I just want you to cut to the chase,” she replied, clearly frustrated with me, “The problem is, you’ve held a torch for the girl for so long now that you’re scared for anyone to misinterpret it as being anything other than the biggest love affair of all time. I’m sorry to be hard, okay? Just give it to me straight.”

“I get it, really I do, and you’re right. Okay, well Friday and Saturday were the first times we’d got into a sexual nature in any of our text messaging. To be honest, it was pretty amazing and I think she felt the same way. The whole weekend, I was kind of walking on air I suppose and then suddenly, Sunday night I get a text from her telling me she can’t do it anymore, wants to break it off.”

“Maybe she finally achieved a world-class orgasm and she doesn’t need you anymore. She’s spent and you’re surplus to requirements, your meat was too much for her diet.”

“Edie!”

“What?”

“You’re just so crude. Anyway, she’s vegetarian, if you must know.”

“Yeah, but does she know you’re a *vag*etarian?”

“Oh, for fuck’s sake, I can’t win, can I?”

“Just kidding, big boy. Here’s how I see it. This from a female standpoint, even though I’ve never met Summer and have no idea what sort of girl she is.”

“She’s lovely…”

“Yeah, whatever.”

"Sorry, I interrupted, pray continue," I said.

"Pray continue? What the fuck have you been doing, Jake, reading Shakespeare all friggin' weekend?"

"I'm sorry, go on…"

"Jeez!" she said, now clearly exasperated with me, "Think about it. Here's a happily married girl with a perfect family in some cute town in Tennessee, got the husband, got the kids, got the dogs, all that good stuff. Nice picture?"

"Yeah, I guess so…"

"And then the love of her life creeps back into the frame and starts messing with her, painting a canvas of roses and butterflies…"

"I didn't creep back in," I said.

"No, you stalked her before you did that. Anyway, there she is, living the American dream, loving her life and suddenly you turn her whole world upside down. Maybe she doesn't get the kind of attention at home that loverboy Jake is giving her, maybe she's flattered and overwhelmed by your odes of love and irresistible personality…"

"There is that…"

"And then she gets intimate on a keyboard with you and has the biggest feeling of regret she's ever known. She's effectively cheating on her husband and she's overwhelmed with feelings of guilt. She can't deal with it, has to shut it down, go back to her life and forget about you."

"Well, when you put it that way, I suppose it makes sense," I reply.

"It's exactly what happened, Jake, she's feeling the thunderous weight of remorse and infidelity about what happened, it's so fucking normal and obvious."

"So what do I do? I'm still besotted with her!"

"You can't do anything. You can't say anything or text her or call her. You just have to wait and if there's anything between the two of you, if you have any kind of future to be had, then she'll work it out. But give her time and don't chase after her like a lost puppy."

"When you put it like that, it really does make sense. So, just wait? Not even a one-line text to see if she's okay?"

"Nothing, Jake, stay cool. It'll either work out or you'll need to move onto Martha or Ginger or someone…"

"Hmmm…"

"By the way, don't tell your asshole friends, but I really enjoyed the other evening at dinner. I mean, they really are a couple of douche bags but I kind of like them," she said.

"They liked you too but I think they're scared of you!"

"They should be, I like it that way," she replied, reaching for the discarded manila folder, "Now go on, fuck off and let me get on with some work."

Meeting adjourned…

Chapter 104

Four days had passed without any word from Summer and I assumed that it really was over between us and after my conversation with Edie, I had begun to truly understand, even though it hurt so much to believe it. So given the situation and the fact that we didn't have a family vacation planned for the Summer, I decided to take my kids to Catalina for a couple of days just to take my mind off things and really enjoy spending some quality time with them.

As a family, we rarely went on vacation together except for the occasional ski trip to Whistler and once, years ago skiing overseas at Val-d'Isere in France. Lily and Tom are both excellent skiers, having learned at a very young age. It wasn't an effort for them, it just came naturally, as easy as walking. Unfortunately for me, I came late to the party and my attempts at skiing were often thwarted by my realization of my own limitations and also by my perceived center of gravity or lack of it. But this year's trip was closer to home and fortunately didn't involve me tugging on a pair of ski boots.

Catalina, or Santa Catalina Island, to give it its official title, lies south-west of our home, around twenty-two miles off the Los Angeles coastline. It's a well-known tourist destination for many Californians and it's easy to get to with frequent ferries making the crossing to the island on a daily basis. It's around twenty miles in length and maybe eight miles wide and consists pretty much of two towns, Avalon in the south, and Two Harbors to the north. In reality, Avalon is the island's city and Two Harbors is more of a village, the latter made famous due to the mysterious disappearance one night of Natalie Wood while vacationing aboard a yacht with her husband, Robert Wagner and close friend Christopher Walken. Ownership of the island has changed hands many times over the years, with a string of businessmen intent on making it a tourism hotspot and the only one who actually made a success of it without going broke, was a certain Mr. William Wrigley from the company that gave us Wrigley Spearmint Gum.

I had a stroke of luck in being able to make reservations at the island's premier hotel, Mt. Ada on Wrigley Road in Avalon, although the stroke of luck did include payment of almost three grand for three nights stay. But we made the most of our time while we were there, doing the usual touristy things; glass-bottom boat excursions, snorkeling, zip lining as well as visits to the Wrigley Memorial & Botanic Gardens and the breathtakingly beautiful Catalina Island Casino, a circular art deco style building dating back to the 1920s.

I'm not someone who is particularly tight with money but Catalina Island, given that it has a captive audience and that everything on it has to be imported from the mainland, is incredibly expensive so I tend to stock up on goodies for the rooms so that we don't always pay top tier prices for food and drink. It was while shopping for the aforementioned goodies in Avalon's lone supermarket, Vons Express Grocery Store on Metropole Avenue, when I received a text from Summer…

> S Hi. Sorry, I know I shouldn't be here...but what has exactly happened over the past three months? Struggling to process it... All so quick.

I couldn't believe what I was seeing. Edie was right, I did need to give her time to process things. Maybe there was hope, maybe it wasn't over yet. I quickly typed a reply to her…

> J When I saw your message just now, my heart literally started thumping. The last line I wrote to you on Sunday was so hard to write but I didn't want to continue causing you any distress even if it meant I was going to be heartbroken to break off this contact. I don't know what it is with you and I but there is some kind of magnetism between us that for me, has just grown stronger.

> S Was just all so sudden. Out of nowhere. Everything.
>
> Why now???

J I know and I don't know. I do know that I don't want to stop talking but I don't know how you feel. I got the feeling you were over me. Tell me what you feel. Be open with me.

Wish I could hug you!

S Boundaries, boundaries, boundaries - I take full responsibility for the recent overstep. I'm not comfortable with that.

J I'll never mention your body again.

S This is where I am... the last few weeks have been intense and our conversations have been invaluable in helping me put to rest all unresolved thoughts from my younger years. That may not mean anything to you, but it has mattered greatly to me – and I feel better, resolved and relieved and grateful. It may have been selfish of me but it has been so healing for me too. As a result I can let go of my past with love and fondness.

S So as much as there is this amazing connection with each other, it can and only ever will be as friends. That's just the way it is. I love our conversations though, I love banter and I know I flirt in a light-hearted way. I do care for you deeply. But if you feel that there's no point for you in us staying in contact, because you want more than a platonic friendship, then we must stop. I'd rather this now than it complicate your feelings (now I sound like you). I want you to be happy.

S ...but I don't think I've said anything that either of us doesn't already know?

S You probably need coffee...

S But I'm not saying goodbye unless you feel you have to, you are virtually human after all xx

I hadn't expected a monologue but at least she was being honest, I guessed…

J Did you get out of the wrong side of bed this morning? Virtually human?

S That was a joke! That was a nicely constructed message, clear and to the point... just trying to be assertive. ☺

J I'm just lying down for a few minutes, need to recover from the slapping I just had. Always beware of conversations that start 'Hi'.

S It wasn't a slap! And I knew 'Hi' was a bad start. ..

J Terrible. So bruised...

S Like I said, it was all so suddenly... huge. I was trying to make sense of it. Nothing's easy by text. I'm sorry.

I so didn't want to bruise you.

J You're a bit of a conundrum. But I absolutely understand everything you said. I'm not stupid. But answer me this, do you feel an excitement when you hear from me or has that now been cured?

S I love talking to you. I said that.

J That wasn't the question and by the way, you are a master (or mistress) of avoiding answering.

S I came up with the wrong answer?

J I asked if you felt an excitement

S It's a trick question.

J Haha! It wasn't, I promise!

S It was a trick question. If I said yes then you would answer that we cannot stay as friends. So I'll pick no. There, there's an answer.

Ⓙ It wasn't a trick question. But if the answer is genuinely no, then that's fine. I just wondered was all, only because I have a certain excitement when you send me a message.

Ⓙ But, back to the original question. Do you feel a rush of excitement when you hear from me? No caveats required.

Ⓢ I do but there is a bad connection on this battery. What did you say, a cravat?

Ⓙ Caveat!

Ⓢ Caviar?

Ⓙ Caveat!!

Ⓢ Cadillac?

Ⓙ Stop it! I give up. Kind of ironic (now there's a song), when we first met, you were so straight out honest with everything and I was the one who gave slippery responses...

Ⓙ Also, as a non-titillating piece of information, do you realize that you were my only virgin lover? I only just realized that last week.

Ⓢ I knew that.

Ⓙ Did I tell you or did you assume?

Ⓢ I was joking. I had no idea. Just assumed that you can't get that lucky in life.

Ⓙ From whose standpoint?

Ⓢ Yours. ☺

Ⓙ Of course. Should never have told you I love you. Too intense. Wasn't meant to be.

Ⓢ I didn't believe you...

Ⓙ I think it will always be true

S You've only just fallen in love with me.

J Untrue actually...

S Nope, nope, nope, not listening, la la la... I can't hear this. I'm just in the process of getting my head straight!

I should have gone to the gym but instead I went to the gin...must learn that they are spelled differently.

J That was reasonably funny, made me smile! ☺

S But seriously, I'm proud of you, Jake. I'm proud that it was you that time when I was eighteen. Nobody can ever take that away.

J That makes me eternally happy.

S I made such a mistake back then, not realizing what we could have had together. You have no idea the regrets I have inside me. One day, maybe I'll tell you...

J No, look what you have! If you'd stayed with me, you'd be bored with me by now. And I'm old and ugly. And hyper sensitive.

S Yeah, crying all the time. And btw, you're not ugly.

J Thank you... but you have to understand that even though there is absolutely zero chance of something between us in the future, I have imagined making love to you again. It's terribly normal to feel that way, even if it is only my own private fantasy. My secret.

S Well I think it fair to say we're equal on that one now....

J I assume you don't tell anyone about our conversations?

S Absolutely not.

J Okay... Better let you work.

S It's been absolutely lovely chatting to you. Pleasure to banter while I work actually.

That's nice!

Summer was making some additional pieces for her jewelry collection and she texted some photos of a new creation she'd been working on…

Oh God, I love it!

It's been calming

Therapeutic…

Like the ocean

You helped me create it.

I am honored

Nite x

Nite, Summer xxx

Chapter 105

"You really caught the sun, Dad! Your head is like a lobster!"

Lily was referring to the fact that I'd been less than liberal with the high factor sunscreen lotion whilst on Catalina and I was suffering from the effects both physically with the heat-throb I felt from my head and also from the way I looked like a carbuncle about to burst.

She plopped down onto the sofa next to me, swished her legs up underneath her, cuddled in and began to ask me about Summer.

"What was Summer like, Dad?"

"Oh, that's a long story to describe her and the effect she had on me and of course, it happened a long, long time ago. But in answer to your question, I guess she was a lot like you in the way she was very much a free spirit, a child of the ocean and someone who wanted nothing fancy and just absorbed all of the natural things that surrounded her. I gave her a little sea glass necklace once, just some old piece of worn glass that a friend of mine had found on the beach and I'd had mounted on a chain for her. You should have seen her face, you'd have thought I'd given her the Queen's Crown Jewels!"

"What did she look like? Did she look like me too?"

"Same kind of physique, blessed with good genes but also an athletic type of person, just like you. One of the benefits of living in a climate near the ocean. I wonder if either of you would have been as fit and athletic if you'd been born to a cold climate staying indoors for most of the winter!"

She ignored her father's last remark and continued on.

"What was her hair like, her face? Was she tall?"

"Wow! So many questions, Lily!"

"I'm just curious, Dad, I want to know more about this mysterious woman who according to Tom, keeps you up at night," she said, looking up at me with a grin etched on her sweet but precocious face.

"She had long sun-streaked blonde hair and she had one of the prettiest faces I'd ever laid eyes on, except for yours of course! She had golden skin, another benefit of being raised in a seaside town in Florida. She also had the whitest and most perfect teeth I'd ever seen, so perfect that they almost didn't look real. She wasn't particularly tall, I'm guessing around 5'4" but what was most attractive about her was her innocence and absolute joie de vivre, her passion for life and I suppose, rightly or wrongly, her love for me."

"Wow! She sounds like a keeper! What happened? Why didn't you get together, get married? Did you just fall for Mom and everything else went by the wayside?"

"Not exactly… it wasn't really my doing. But she went to college and for reasons still unknown, I suppose she just forgot about me. Often happens at that age which is why I hope you don't meet someone too early in your life and fall madly in love without experiencing what the world has to offer you."

"I won't, Dad, I promise. But has she changed since back then? Have you seen any current photos of her? Maybe she got fat and cut her hair short? Maybe her teeth went bad!"

I laughed when Lily said this, she loved to tease people but she did it in such a beautiful and delicate way that she could never upset anybody.

"Actually, I have seen recent photos and she really hasn't changed much at all, she's still the same girl I remember from the 80s. But of course, as you grow older, I think that you see things differently and maybe she has changed a lot but in my eyes, she's still exactly the same girl I fell in love with all those years ago."

That's so beautiful, Daddy! Now, what are you making for dinner? I'm soooo hungry!"

Chapter 106

Two thousand miles away, Summer was desperate to have a similar conversation that Jake had just been having with Lily but she also knew that it wasn't something she could yet discuss with Poppy. That would have to wait, maybe never happen at all.

As she stood in her bedroom, pondering what life might have been like had she taken a different turn, James's arms reached around her from behind and he gently enveloped her in the tenderest embrace.

"I'm sorry," he said, "You know I never mean to hurt you, sweetheart, just sometimes I get frustrated about life."

She turned around, his arms still wrapped around her, and she nuzzled into her husband's chest.

"I know, Jimmy, but you can't do what you did, you know that. One day, you might go too far and you'll regret it. I'm not a punching bag for when things go wrong for you, I'm your wife and I care for you. Don't you think I get frustrated too?"

"I know that, I do, I really do. My temper gets the better of me sometimes and when I see you on your phone and ignoring me, the rage gets in my head. I'll do everything I can to control it, I promise. And I'm sorry, I'm so sorry if I hurt you."

"I'd appreciate that, Jimmy, I want to be happy, I don't want to live in fear of you," she said, all the time thinking what it might be like to be in Jake's arms right now.

"What do you say we go out for dinner, just the two of us? We could go to The Drunky Monkey, I think they've got a band playing tonight."

She hated The Drunky Monkey; it was a dive downtown where the plastic table covers were always in need of cleaning even after they'd been cleaned. The waiters and waitresses were less than hygienic in their appearance too. But it was better than staying home watching the television again.

"Sure, I'd like that, let me get changed and we can go in the next ten minutes," she replied, dreading an evening of small talk and a band that was sure to irritate.

Later that evening, as they sat down at a table close to the stage, Summer ran a finger across the red and white plastic covering the table and realized that her previous thoughts on the restaurant's cleanliness weren't far off target. The building was dark and the candles that flickered on each of the tables did nothing to hide the smell of mold that permeated throughout the restaurant. Plasma screens wrapped around the bar area with various live sports showing on each of them. As Summer wondered why she was in a place like this, a slightly overweight, bleached blonde waitress came to the table with her order book in hand.

"What can I get you folks?" she asked, ignoring Summer and looking at James who was perusing the menu.

"Hi Debbie, good to see you again," he said, looking up from the menu.

"Jimmy! I didn't realize it was you! How are you? Haven't seen you in a few weeks," she replied, still ignoring the fact that Summer was also sitting at the table.

"Hi Debbie, I'm Summer, nice to meet you."

James looked frazzled when he realized his wife had been ignored and Summer didn't seem best pleased with Debbie's familiarity with her husband.

"This is my wife, I don't think you've met?"

"No, we haven't," added Summer, "Hi *Debbie*, I'll take the potted shrimp to begin with and a glass of Kendall Jackson Chardonnay. A large one, thank you."

“I’ll take the shrimp too and a Schlitz, thanks Debbie,” added James, as Debbie wrote it down.

“I’ll be right back, folks,” she said, quickly spinning on her heels to get away from the table and the obvious atmosphere that seemed to be quickly developing.

“Who’s your friend?” asked Summer.

“Oh, no one, just someone I met here a couple months back and she’s a patient at the office.”

“Right, just a friend. She seemed more than that but whatever. What are you going to have as an entrée?”

“Don’t be a bitch, Summer, it doesn’t suit you,” said James, “I think I’ll go for the ribeye and baked potato with all the fixings. Man, I’m starved.”

Summer let the ‘bitch’ remark go, she didn’t need another fight tonight. If he liked Debbie, he was welcome to her and right now, as she was thinking of Jake, Debbie was welcome to Jimmy. It suddenly dawned on her in the shithole restaurant he’d dragged her to tonight, that she didn’t love her husband anymore. Maybe she never truly had but tonight was the night when the truth had finally hit her like an express train. She only loved one man.

I’ll have the Cobb Salad, I don’t have much of an appetite,” she said.

“Never mind, you’re gonna love this band, I know some of the guys and they’re genuine Bluegrass, hillbillies with attitude!” he said, oblivious to her feelings.

Great. Can’t friggin’ wait...

Chapter 107

The following day, I found myself at my usual haunt. The Kreuzberg Café must be thinking I was homeless with the amount of time I'd been spending there recently but I didn't care, I was addicted to their wares. I'd once again tried my invisible man trick with the ever-enchanting Lola and was not surprised when it worked again, the girl seemingly oblivious to my existence. Hey ho.

As I munched into my Morning Bun and slurped the frothy head from my cappuccino, I realized how lucky I was to be where I'd found myself in life. I had two incredible children, a beautiful home in a sun-kissed corner of California and I was back talking with a girl I had always been in love with. Life was pretty damned good.

Summer had definitely been feeling a new emotion. From what I could tell, she'd never felt it before in her life. I still didn't know what was happening between us, it felt like a rollercoaster most of the time and although my own feelings were now finally fairly level, I could see that she was thrashing wildy around with hers, struggling to come to terms with recent events and how they were affecting her. It was a perfect time to send her a text and find out how she was feeling and she responded almost immediately…

J How are you? Missing me? ☺

S I am. It's not a good feeling. Woke up with it. Thought it would be gone by now. It's not. Don't like it.

J Why's it not a good feeling?

S Because it's a missing feeling.

Which means I must like you.

J Better than disliking me.

Are you writing me a Dear John letter?

S I was pondering it.

But that won't work.

J Why?

S Because.

J Because what?

S Because maybe you're right and I have spent more time with you than anyone else recently... and I'm kind of getting used to it. But then again it's such fun and lovely and exciting and positive....

It's all cool.

Just woke up and missed you, that's all. Actually missed you.

J Do you wake up every morning and miss me?

S I haven't done until today.

J I wake every morning thinking about you.

S I've woken up thinking about you...but not missing you. It's different.

J I see.

S It's not good really.

It's stepping over a line.

I didn't want to.

I'm sorry.

I'll deal with it.

J I'm sorry. Can I be crass for a moment?

S Yeah, why not?

J Every time I talk to you, I suddenly experience a sexual feeling which has never, ever happened to me before, well not since my teenage years!

S So what do you think that means?

J To be honest, I'm clueless but it's clear to see that there is something between us, more on the emotional level than in any sexual aspect.

You make me feel so good.

Do you have similar physical effects?

S Completely!

Right now I'm burning and buzzing and I have to put my hand on my heart area. It's like electricity is coming from me.

J Wow!

S It's not entirely sexual energy, but that is also one part of it. It's a good feeling. But only since I'm talking with you. I didn't wake up like this.

J Same for me... Try orgasming and it should take the feeling down a notch! ☺

S Lol! Normally that is what I would have to do. I'll be crass now, this sounds so, so, so lame, I hate saying this, and it's really hard for me to say, but normally when thinking about you I do get aroused, yes wet (I really, really hate saying this) and that to me is sexual energy and I have to do something about it, end it. But right now, I feel all over energy, which I don't feel compelled to dispell ...it's within me,it's like a bath. It's like being plugged into something buzzing...is the only way I can describe it. This is not how I planned for this chat to go btw...

J It's ok!

S Jeez! Nothing like an afternoon chat over tea!

J Now I need tea!

S But I really really missed you today. Couldn't wait to get home to talk to you.

J That's so lovely!

S I'm glad you're feeling good. ☺

J I am when I'm talking to you

S Ok well... no Dear John letter then.

I've now got stuff to do for everyone else.

J But I don't ever want that letter, Summer.

S ☺ I'll see you later xxxx

An then I'm simply handing everything over to the Universe.

J Me too! Bye xxx

S Bye x

Chapter 108

That evening, Preston and Frankie invited themselves over for a barbecue at my house. Actually, that's not really being fair; they wanted to see Tom and Lily as they hadn't seen them in months. Neither Preston nor Frankie is married and both of them have managed to get through life without producing or being responsible for children. They have been married before but that's another story for another time. So knowing they were both going to be around, I'd decided to invite Martha over and she'd brought her sister along who was staying with her for the week.

Frankie and Preston were chatting to Tom and Lily in the back yard, peppering them for answers about college, sports and significant others, my two kids remaining stoic in the avalanche of sometimes personal questions.

"You're just like your mom," said Frankie to Lily, "Good job you didn't inherit your dad's looks."

"My dad is a good looking man, Mr. Cohen!" she replied, "And he looks younger and younger every time I come home."

"Call me Frankie, I can't cope with the mister stuff," he said, "And Tom, wow, what a good looking boy you've turned out to be, again, no thanks to your dad!"

"Poor Dad!" said Tom, "His ears must be burning because he's coming over."

"Any boyfriends or girlfriends around, or are you both concentrating on college for now," asked Preston, "I guess neither of you is short of willing admirers?"

"Study, sport, study, sport…" replied Lily, "Boys just get in the way!"

“Yeah, I can’t think about a permanent girlfriend right now,” said Tom, “I like to be free and do my own thing, just don’t have time for romantic responsibility.”

“Keep it that way for as long as you can, Tom, I’ve been down that road a few times and it always ends in tragedy,” replied Preston.

“I can only assume that you’re tainting my kids’ minds with your salacious innuendo so give them a break, Frankie!” I said, standing between the two men and Lily and Tom and then addressing my son and daughter, “If you’ve had enough of them already, you don’t have to continue being polite to them, go and hang out with Ben and Katie if you like.”

I’d made certain that neither of my children would have to put up with my friends for the entire afternoon so they’d invited a couple of school friends over to eat with us. They quickly chose to separate from the group and reconnect with Ben and Katie who lived just a few hundred yards from our home, leaving me with Frankie and Preston.

“So you’re Jake’s infamous cohorts,” said Martha as she sidled up to the three of us while we began talking about the recent Lakers game.

“Guilty as charged!” they said in unison.

“We are the rudders of Jake’s life, without us, he’d be floundering in dangerous waters,” said Preston.

“Yeah, right,” she replied, “I don’t think Jake needs your input on anything in his life.

“Well I got him the perfect car,” said Preston, “I can’t be all bad.”

“I’ll give you that but don’t start advising him on his love life, for fuck’s sake, you’re both a couple of losers in that department from what I’ve heard.”

Nothing like saying what you think, Martha...

“I’m Frankie, I don’t think we’ve met?” said my barrel-chested friend, clearly enamored with Martha’s direct approach.

“I’ve heard all about you, you’re the ex-car thief, aren’t you? Although you’re cute for a shortie, can’t deny it. I’m Martha by the way.”

I think it was the first time I’d actually seen Frankie blush. He wasn’t a womanizer in any way but I sensed an attraction between him and Martha which was not what I’d planned, although stranger things do happen.

“I’ve heard a lot about you too, not all of it bad either and you’re much better looking than Jake had us think,” he said, pulling one of his tired old chat up lines from the depths of his brain.

“Well, I can’t say the same about you, but… you’re still kinda cute in an odd way, I just can’t put my finger on why.”

Martha’s sister, Lena, had been watching the exchange in horrified silence, although in all honesty, it wasn’t anything out of the ordinary for Martha to savage men she’d only just met. It’s just the way she is. Go figure.

“Lena, this is my friend, Preston Pryor,” I said, realizing that she hadn’t been introduced to anyone.

“It’s a pleasure to meet you, Preston,” she said, offering her hand to him.

“The pleasure is all mine,” he replied, taking her hand and planting a delicate kiss on her outstretched fingers.

“Wow! What a gentleman!” she gushed, this time her turn to blush.

“When in the company of a stunningly pretty woman, I can only stand and bask in your reflected beauty,” he replied.

“Fuck me, Preston!” said Martha, “I think I’m gonna vomit. Come on Frankie, buy me a drink, I can’t stand this.”

“Would you care to sample some of Jake’s delicious barbecue, Lena?” asked Preston, “It would be my absolute pleasure to escort you to the grille.”

"I'd like that, Preston, I'd like that very much."

So, without malice aforethought, I'd managed to unsuspectingly and quite surprisingly, match up my two best friends with my neighbor and her sister.

I should start a dating agency, I'm that good...

But as I was now standing alone without anyone to chat to and although I was with my family and friends who meant the world to me, I was missing Summer. The more I messaged Summer, the more I wanted to keep up our cyber conversation. It was getting harder each day not to think about her in every waking moment. I was also aware of the risk of sending her a message in the early evening when her husband could be home but I assumed she was taking as many precautions as possible to avoid any confrontation with him.

Everyone at the barbecue seemed to be enjoying themselves and I didn't think I'd be missed for ten or fifteen minutes so I went back into the house and sat down at my office desk, closing the door behind me. I began a new text to her and was amazed when she replied almost immediately…

J Even if there isn't a future for us together, I never want to lose you again.

S Hello you! There's always a future for us, I just don't ever know what guise it will be in. And that means a lot to me.

J Hello! ☺ I'm so glad you're there! I've snuck away from my own barbecue because I was missing you.

S I'm so glad you're there too, hopefully you're free to talk for a minute or two. It's strange, I haven't had you in my life physically for years, yet I have a relationship of sorts with you. ..make sense?

Tell me....you pressed for this the other night...what is the difference between loving someone and being in love with them?

J Being in love is much, much deeper.

You can love someone without being in love with them but not vice versa. For example, my friend Edie's in love with her husband with every breath. That's being in love.

S I see... and how would I know if I was in love?

Do you think you might be in love with me?

J I am.

S I don't believe you. Too easy.

J Maybe I'm just an interesting fascination.

S It's so big to be in love with you, Jake. It's like a cliff. If I step off...there's no coming back. I've only just managed to find the steps from the beach to get back up here ...

J I'm a very different type of person now. Beautifully said btw...

S I don't think you're different. I think I always saw the real you within. There are many times I can recall of how kind you were back then, when you didn't have to be...we were all trying to be cool (well I was) and you could have been cruel to me but you weren't ever! ...you always had heart.

S ... And you were very mature with my feelings. Very rude with my body! It's a good balance in retrospect.

J I thought very deeply of you at that time and have never forgotten you. Recently, I have bared more to you than to anyone and I suppose I love it when you do the same but I think you remain, perhaps understandably, a little coy. I respected you as a young girl too. I could've been an asshole.

S I've got so much to tell you about me...about why I'm coy...reasons to do with me... it's all stuff I'm realizing now..as a person, ...it's like I'm putting my hands on the lid of me, as if I'm a jar, there is so much stuff that has been repressed just waiting to get out....it's scary. I assume everyone thinks like this as they get older...so I grip tight on the lid of the jar. ..but I find myself slowly loosening it...

J I'm glad, it makes me happy. ☺

S Mom said you were a good man with heaps of charisma. I'm telling you, she liked and trusted you enough with her favorite child!

J What a lady!

S Yes! She was beautiful and strong yet as soft as a feather.

She cared too much, she couldn't help it.

She probably had the hots for you too.

J I don't even have a response to that!

S Maybe we're just healing each other?

J Do you need healing?

S Know what...why are we analyzing this?? Shall we just meet up and see if we want to kiss?

J Time to change subject.

S But I just had the answer!!!

J You know we would!

S I don't care anymore. It's too much to think about.

It will be like tossing a coin....

J I do love you.

S But you're not in love with me.

J Yes I am but it's ok for it to be one way - I can deal with it

S So you can love two people at once?

J I'm not sure... But our problem, if we were together, is that we'd never get anything done!

S You'd get bored after a while.

J We wouldn't stop talking!

S Oh, that would be lovely!!

J I talk a lot, my kids get sick of me talking sometimes I think!

S You didn't use to talk a lot.

J Strong silent type back then.

S If you must know… I think of you whilst walking the dogs and I'm turned on. I keep saying I don't know what it is about you.

J Well, it makes me warm that you feel like that.

S It makes me warmer.

J I like that too.

S I shouldn't be feeling like this....we keep having this conversation don't we?

J Can you imagine, making love with someone, not seeing them for a quarter of a century, and then making love again like no time had passed? That could be you and me...

S Here's the thing and don't be shocked. Women don't want penetration all the time, we don't even want sex all the time - I find it a pressure to 'have to perform' to be honest. But with you it's just an instant engagement. I can't explain it...coupled with all our conversations and your sweet, sweet compliments. ..you make me feel wonderful. And then I think of your surely kissable mouth...I'm gone man, solid gone (note: insert line from 'The Jungle Book').

J Haha! Oh Summer, I could talk all night with you but It's late where you are. I'd better let you sleep .

S OK. Nite nite then xx

J Love you xxx

S See you tomorrow?

J Definitely.

S God I am so hot for you!!!!!

J Really?

S I am, Jake. Had to say it. I'm going now. Xx

J Oh Lord, I'd better go too, they'll wonder what's happened to me!

Later that night, after I'd gone to bed, I lay awake for almost three hours thinking about our conversation earlier this evening and knew that I couldn't wait until the morning to talk to her again so I decided to send her a note while she slept. I realized her phone would be switched off so there was no danger that my text would wake her…

1:18am

J Hopefully, you're sound asleep. But while you sleep, and this may be facile of me to say, but I love your humor, I love your beauty inside and out, I love the fact that we joke and kid each other and share the same passion for so many things in music, art and life and I love that you still find me attractive at 49 years old. I feel so flattered and proud. I love that I make you feel warm inside, I love that you think of snuggling on a sofa together or lying on crumpled sheets and me making you tea in the morning and cooking for you but what I love more than anything, no matter how far in the future it might be, is that one day it might be Jake & Summer again. I do love you, I can't get you out of my mind. I'm sorry.

5:09am

S I loved that! You really are a wonderful old romantic. It's what I hope I deserve too… I hope!

6:24am

S ...and I'm most definitely at the edge of the cliff looking up at the blue skies ahead...

Chapter 109

Summer lay in bed, listening to the birds' early morning chorus. The bedroom windows were open wide and she could almost taste the air outside. She often wondered how the birds understood each other or even if it was a conversation they were having. Each bird seemed to repeat the same message over and over again. But it didn't matter, they made her happy, she just loved nature and all it had to offer.

James was still sleeping, his head buried deep in the pillow, gently snoring. That was one thing she did appreciate about her husband, his snoring was never so loud that it woke her up or kept her awake.

I wonder if Jake snores? I don't remember him snoring very much and I often used to just watch him sleeping...

She realized that Jake was permanently on her mind these days. What had begun as a mild interest for her in his recent past had turned into a love affair from two thousand miles away. What was it about him? What was this hold he had on her? But maybe it was just the attention he gave her or the fact that he was interested in what she felt or what she had to say. He was so radically different to James in just about every way. And he was still as sexy as she remembered way back then. He just turned her on and they hadn't even spoken in almost a quarter of a century!

Casey and Poppy had come home late last night and she knew it would be hours before they were awake. And James was dead to the world right now, his repetitive snore almost metronomic in its easy rhythm. She slowly slid her hand down her stomach and gently cupped herself, amazed that she was already damp just thinking about Jake. Goosebumps suddenly appeared across her entire nakedness and her nipples had become almost painfully erect. She closed her eyes, her hand still clamped around her warm sex and began to imagine that Jake was with her even as her husband slumbered inches away. She pictured Jake's naked body as he kissed her neck and nibbled delicately on her ear lobe and she felt him move his hand to her chest as he cupped her breast. His mouth moved to her nipple and he played with it, teasing it with his teeth and then sucking hard on her. She imagined her back arching up to meet his body as his tongue pushed deeper into her mouth and kissed her as though they might never kiss again.

She glanced over at James, still asleep, and realized that she was breathing hard as her fingers had found the hottest place in her body and that she was rubbing herself intensely, almost harshly.

She continued to imagine Jake on top of her now, his hand beneath her back, pulling her up towards him and she felt his hardness brush against her tummy. His hand found her wetness between her thighs and the goosebumps seemed to multiply across her skin. He deftly parted her, making her writhe, found the spot with his fingertips and as he gently toyed with it, he slid inside her. His mouth was hot as she felt his breath above her and his rhythmical and gentle thrusts made her body shiver. She gripped his buttocks and pulled him as far inside as he could go, sweat now appearing on her chest. She felt herself becoming tighter inside and the stimulus was intensifying as she knew both of them were ready to…

"Mom?"

"Yes, sweetie?" she gasped breathlessly, as she realized that Poppy was about to walk through the door of her bedroom.

"What are you doing?" said Poppy as she plopped down onto the bed beside her mom.

"Oh nothing, baby, just listening to the birds singing and reminiscing about old times. Nothing special."

"Oh! I thought I heard you talking to someone. When's breakfast?"

"Soon, precious girl, let me get up and shower and I'll come down and start things going in the kitchen."

"Thank you, mama, I'm starved!"

Once Poppy had left the room and gone downstairs to put some coffee on, Summer suddenly felt the need to send a text to Jake. It was getting crazier between them, like a schoolboy and schoolgirl crush but something that was happening in their forties and not in their teens. She began to quickly compose a text, knowing that Jake wouldn't yet be awake…

Sun 7:35am

S I've just been doing something terribly naughty but I can't tell you what it was. Just know that you were there with me when I was doing it! But here's the interesting thing.. James needs sex, a lot. Our marriage has nearly come apart in the past when I haven't been giving it so freely - he can't help it, he's sex driven, often I'm so, so, so not (he has never forced me though, he's not like that) but I need turning on mentally. He's also aware that I'm bored of all the macho sports stuff. ..but that's where he thrives. ...he can't thrive in my world of music and poetry and art... and he knows I resent how much time he's been absent whilst I've been raising the kids....but for me it might be too late..the kids are grown now, I've done my bit and I'm not sure if James and I will be good company for each other when they both leave home. He knows I want to be free, but I guess I still have responsibilities to my family - I'm also a dreamer ..he's a good man underneath, and is always there if needed... and here I am in love with another man at the same time... I feel like such a bitch. None of this is what you want to hear really, I ought to be telling a girlfriend I suppose. I also know that all of my stronger friends have hinted at feeling exactly the same way about their marriages and all have contemplated leaving...but they don't have a beautiful, compassionate, attentive Jake in their lives...and also, you turn me on, what's it all about?

And to make it worse I think I'm falling in love with you more and more. I don't want to fall in love with you...but I'm slipping so so badly towards you Jake. I'm sorry.

So I guess...this all leads to...an affair. Something that we'd never imagine either of us would ever do in our lives.

Sun 9:41am

J So much to respond to but in truth, I don't really need to respond because we're both aware of what's been going on for the last few months. No, I had never been looking for a new love, an affair if you will, not since Tara died, and I think I understand what you're saying about post-children compatibility. Many women have told me that if they never had to have sex again, they would be very happy ladies. But I think more about sharing thoughts with you, about listening to music together, about walking on the beach and holding your hand, about snuggling on the sofa with a glass of wine, about watching you sleeping and kissing you awake, about simple dinners on a restaurant patio, about holding you in my arms and never letting go. I don't know where we're going or what the future holds but I know I am experiencing something I don't think I've ever felt before. I love it so much and I'm equally scared if that's any consolation. We're having an affair already, Summer, even if it is something of a 21st-century version of one. In the long term, I don't want to shuffle off this mortal coil and have my final thought that I never got to end my days with my one true love, someone who I now know loves me in equal amounts.

Sun 10:18am

S Jake, I've learned so much about you. I'll be honest, originally I did think I wasn't good enough for you, not go-getting enough and not a city type; I thought you must be quite hard. But when I learned from Autumn years ago that you married Tara when she got pregnant, I knew that you had a much softer side and a wonderful heart. Now you've revealed all that to me. I love you, Jake Delaney and it's so high up here on this cliff so catch me if I fall!

Chapter 110

"I approve of your friends, Jake, especially that little Frankie," said Martha from across the bougainvillea hedge that separated our homes.

We should stop meeting like this...

"Well, I'm glad you had a good time yesterday, everyone seemed to get on, didn't they?" I replied.

"Yeah, and the man's got stamina, he's like an Evinrude outboard motor when he gets up to speed."

"Oh Martha! Really? Tell me the image in my head is not what happened after the barbecue. Please!"

"Jake, what is it with you, why are you such a prude? Of course that is exactly what happened later on at my house. It would be impolite not to take advantage of whatever he's got going on in his pants. Did you know he can keep a full erection for hours and hours without the help of any blue pill? We fucked forever; I'm amazed you didn't hear us."

Yeah, but he does have some invisible help, Martha, you just don't know about it yet...

"Anyway, I'm curious," she continued, "What's with all the texting you're doing lately? You seem permanently glued to your friggin' phone. What's going on, Jakey, what are you hiding from Martha?"

"Nothing, I guess the technology these days just has me hooked. Sometimes I feel like a teenager but you're right, I need to stop with the texting and just use the phone like normal people do," I said, "But thanks for pointing it out, I've just realized how rude it must look to everyone else. Fancy a cappuccino?"

"Sure, I'm coming over..."

Martha was right about the texting, it was time-consuming and insular, and often downright rude when people were around me. It was time to talk on the phone to Summer about what the future held. I realized that on so many occasions, the tone in some of our texts hadn't hit the spot at all, in fact on occasions, entirely the wrong message had been delivered. The time for texting was over, the time for talking was here.

Chapter 111

A couple more weeks drifted by and I was enjoying having Tom and Lily around although I was more than aware that the Summer holiday was coming to an end and they would be leaving to start back at college soon. But with my growing relationship with Summer, I felt life was slowly turning around, but very much for the better. I'd managed to send her a birthday gift without it causing too much attention in her home, just a new iPhone that she could use just between the two of us and I'd preloaded it with some of her favorite music from the 80s. She was overjoyed with it and although it wasn't a particularly romantic present, there was little else I could send, given her circumstances.

And during this time, we'd finally begun to talk on the phone which seemed like an amazing advance but it meant that we could feel each other's emotions more easily and truly gauge how each other felt, without having to guess the tone implied in a text message.

At first, when I volunteered to be the one to make the first call, we were both nervous, like teenagers I guess, but after just a few conversations, we felt immediately comfortable with each other. And just hearing her voice for the first time in so many years sent goosebumps all over my body and I knew that for both of us, our love had never died, hadn't been diminished even in the slightest. We were as we always had been, very much in love.

My iPhone chirped and I could see from the caller ID that Summer was calling me.

"Hi Jake," she said, her voice sounding much less bubbly than she normally sounded.

"What's wrong, sweetheart?" I replied, wary that something must be very amiss.

It was that 'hi' word again...

"It's James, he saw a goodnight text from you last night."

"Oh God, Summer, I'm so sorry, I knew I shouldn't have sent it."

She'd told me that James had become more and more curious about the amount of time she spent texting and one of the rules was that we shouldn't text in the evenings unless it was important.

"He got really angry, the worst I've ever seen him," she said, now crying on the other end of the phone line.

"Please tell me he didn't get violent," I said, fearing the worst now.

"It was horrible, Jake, this time he didn't even try to hide his beating, he punched me everywhere he could, he kicked me around like a rag doll."

The anger was coursing through my veins now, I could only think about the violence I would unleash on her redneck husband if I was there and the thought of someone making me that angry made me even angrier.

"Summer, you can't stay, you can't keep absorbing his temper and his fists. This is terrible, I wish I was with you right now," I said, frustrated that I was powerless to do anything for her.

"I know, I know Jake, I can't take this any longer but I don't know what to do."

She was sobbing uncontrollably and there was only one thing to do and I hoped she would agree with me.

"Summer. I need you to listen to me, sweetheart. You can't stay there, neither can Poppy or Casey. It's time, Summer, it's time to leave."

"But Jake, I have nowhere to go! What would I do?" she blurted, still sobbing, still breaking my heart.

"Yes you do, you have me! I want you to be with me, I want Poppy and Casey to come too!"

"Don't be crazy, Jake, you have no idea what you'd be taking on!"

"I do, and I want to, don't you see?"

"Are you serious, Jake? Do you really mean that? Why would you take on a burden like us?"

"You're not a burden, baby, it's what I've been dreaming about for a long time now. I just want us to be together again and I want to meet your children and they would love my two, I know they would. Please come."

"Oh Jake, you know I would give anything to be with you but I don't know how to even go about leaving James. He watches me closely now and so do his friends, I'm under a microscope here."

"Just go the airport and get on a plane, I'll be waiting for you, for all of you!" I said, my heart thumping with the realization that a distant dream might become a reality very soon.

"I can't do that, it's all too much. I would need to talk to my kids first, tell them what's been happening although I think Poppy already has an inkling of what James is like when no one's looking. They're due back to college next week and I can't just leave them here, they're my babies. And I have all my stuff, I'd never be able to haul everything to the airport…"

"Your stuff is not important right now, Summer, we can replace that. The only important thing is the safety of you and your children. You have to get out of there, I'll be waiting for you. Please!" I begged.

"I want to be with you, Jake, I just need to find a way to do it. If I can placate him over the next week or so while the kids are still here before they set off back to Arizona, then I'll find a way. I can't rush this because if he finds out what I'm planning to do, he'll kill me. I mean that, I think he'd literally kill me."

"I understand, but I just wish I could help in some way. It would be so easy for me to book airplane tickets for you, you know that. But I realize you need to do this in your own way, at your own pace. I get it. I just want you here with me, that's all."

"I feel the same way, Jake, and we'll make this happen but in the meantime, we ought to go a bit radio silent, don't you think? I don't want to give him anything that will antagonize him again. I just need to escape without being beaten again, I can't take it anymore."

The thought of her husband taking out his anger on Summer was killing me but I tried to subdue the emotions I was feeling so that I remained a rock for her.

"You're right, it's a good idea, so I won't make contact with you during the next week or so but if you need me, let me know. If you want me to fly out there, I'll do it at the drop of a hat. I can't wait to finally see you again, Summer. I love you."

"I love you too, Jake, more than I can tell you right now but I will tell you when I'm in your arms again. I'll tell you everything. See you soon."

"See you soon, baby, be careful, please be careful," I said.

"I will, bye Jake, I love you."

As the phone line went dead, I found myself caught in a maelstrom of so many different emotions, anger, love, panic, fear, elation… and the worst one of all was how powerless I felt right then.

Chapter 112

It was already eighty degrees and horribly humid when Summer finished loading the Bronco at six o'clock that morning. Fortunately, James had gone out shooting with his buddies a couple of hours earlier which made her escape so much easier. She'd left the letter she'd written to him on the kitchen countertop and closed the front door of her marital home for the very last time. The bruises that she still felt would be the last ones he'd give her, mentally or physically.

She was silently grateful that Poppy had agreed to come with her on the journey although she hadn't told her yet where she was heading or why. There would be plenty of time during the two-thousand-mile journey to explain things in detail to her. But once James knew Summer had left him, it didn't take much to realize that Poppy would be his next target and she couldn't ever let that happen. Casey was bigger and stronger than James and she knew he'd be fine; James wouldn't even dare to vent his aggression on their son.

The plan was to head west on I-40 and drop Poppy off to begin her final year at college in Arizona and then head north-west to Avila Beach where she would finally meet Jake for the first time in more than two decades. She couldn't stop the electricity buzzing through her entire body every time she thought of the moment when they would hold each other again. It was almost too much to think about that this was now going to be a reality.

As the aging Bronco ate up the miles and they crossed the Tennessee state line into Mississippi, Summer and Poppy could have been two sisters making a long-awaited road trip together and they spent much of the time singing with the radio turned up high. As far as Summer could make out, her daughter had no qualms about never returning to Tennessee and it was this comfort that made it so much easier on her. They talked endlessly whenever they grew tired of singing and Summer tried to explain in detail who Jake was and what he meant to her and what the future might hold.

At first, Poppy was shocked at what her mother had been telling her but as the story unfolded, she began to understand and dearly wanted to meet this Jake Delaney. She was horrified to discover what her mother had been experiencing at the hands of James and she shared Summer's fear that he would vent his anger on her next.

But three days of driving and two nights in interstate motels gave them all the time Summer needed to reassure her daughter that everything was going to be okay. During the trip, Poppy was already aware that theirs was a relationship like no other, but as the days went by, mother and daughter bonded even more than either of them could have ever imagined possible.

Chapter 113

James Larsen was sick of the way his life had turned out. He was pissed that his kids always sided with their mother and didn't show him any kind of love at all. He also had a wife whose mind seemed to have been somewhere else instead of in the bedroom for the last five or six months. She was forever buried in her phone although he had no idea what had been causing her fascination with it. The other night at The Drunky Monkey had been another disaster and he wished that Debbie hadn't been working that night. Hell, Summer wasn't stupid, she knew straight away that he was fucking Debbie, not that she'd been any good, it had been like fucking a fat white corpse most times. Probably a good job that Summer didn't suspect any of the other women he'd been servicing recently. But what was a man to do? His wife had closed the sex door so why shouldn't he find it elsewhere?

He clicked the remote to raise the garage door, grateful for a day off from looking at his clients' rotten teeth. God, where had it all gone so wrong? He'd been the king of college parties, had all the women and friends he needed and then Summer came into his life. But he'd fallen for her, head over heels and as soon as college was done, he went to dental school and immediately afterward, partnered up in a local practice which was now his, having bought out his aging partner.

He swung the Ford F-150 into the garage, even more pissed that his morning out shooting had yielded nothing much to write home about. Another wasted day, another wasted bag of ammo. He noticed Casey's Jeep parked out front and wondered what he was still doing at home. He should have started the drive back to school by now. Casey was another thorn in his side, just like Poppy was. When did these kids suddenly get minds of their own? Mind you, he wouldn't want to pick a fight with the kid, the boy was strong as an ox and towered over him now. Well, at least James had bred an athlete. He looked down at his ever-expanding paunch and realized that he'd never again be the athlete he once was himself. Fuck, fuck fuck.

He got down from the truck's cab and wrenched open the door leading from the garage to the house, still wearing his shooting jacket and carrying his rifle and headed to the gun safe in his office to stow it away. As he entered the kitchen, he saw Casey sitting on one of the bar stools, staring at him as though he was a stranger.

"What the fuck's up with you, Casey?" he said, his irritability surfacing as soon as he saw the boy.

"Nothing's up Dad, I'm just waiting around for you to deliver a message before I leave for Arizona."

"Message, what fucking message?"

James realized that his tone these days had become more and more aggressive and that his use of expletives was escalating in almost every conversation with his family.

"A message from Mom. And from Poppy too," said Casey.

"If your mom has something to tell me, I don't need a fucking kid messenger to tell me what it is. Goes for your sister too," he snarled, his anger rising as each second passed.

He put the rifle down on the countertop, acutely aware of the calmness that Casey displayed. The kid had certainly passed beyond the point of being scared of his father. When did that happen?

"Actually, I guess it's a message from all of us," said his son.

"Whatever it is, spit it out boy, I need to eat," replied James, opening the fridge door to find some eggs and bacon.

"It's over, Dad. They've gone."

"What the fuck are you talking about?"

"They've had enough of you, your redneck temper, your shitty attitude towards women and your total fucking selfish and vicious behavior. Actually, so have I," said Casey, still a picture of serenity as he sipped his coffee at the kitchen island.

"What? Have you lost your mind, you little fuck? When did anything you say have any relevance on anything? And what do you mean, they're gone?"

"Like I said, they're outta here, and they're not coming back. Mom finally told us about what you've been doing, how you enjoy letting your fists do the talking. She's scared that Poppy'll be your next target. So they left and they're not coming back. It's over, Dad."

Rage began to rush through James' whole body. He couldn't believe what Casey was telling him and the boy's calm was really pissing him off.

"Where've they gone, you little bastard, I'll bring them back even if I have to drag them here by their hair. This is where they belong, this is their home and I say what goes, not you, not your mom, not your sister!"

"You won't find them, they didn't leave a trail. And now I'm outta here too. I promised I'd deliver the message… oh, and here, Mom left a letter for you," replied Casey, handing an envelope to his father and picking up his Jeep keys from the counter as he started to leave.

"You ain't goin' nowhere, boy!" screamed James as he launched himself at Casey, the back of his fist delivering a sickening blow to the side of his son's head. But it had little effect, the punch bouncing off Casey, his concrete-like musculature impervious to his father's continued assault, the punches now raining down on him thick and fast.

"Is that all you've got? Is that what you dish out to Mom when no one's around?" he said, pushing his father away from him like a swatted fly.

"You think you're so clever, don't you? I haven't even started yet," replied James, rushing towards his son with another punch aimed at Casey's face.

But the punch never arrived, never made contact. Instead, his son planted his own fist straight into the center of James' face, the sound of cracking cartilage clear for them both to hear. His father's face was now a bloody mess from Casey's single blow and the unleashed torrent of angry punches that followed had James flailing around on the kitchen floor.

"I'm going now, Dad. You won't see me again. I wish you luck with your life but no one's going to miss you," said Casey, once again collecting his car keys from the counter.

James clasped onto the edge of the countertop, pulling himself up and reached for his gun, simultaneously chambering a round as he yelled at Casey who had already started to leave.

"Get your ass back here, boy, you ain't leavin' until I say you do!"

Casey turned back and slowly walked towards his father who was dripping blood from his face onto the kitchen floor, his eyes already beginning to close from the pummeling he'd taken from his son.

He was within six feet of his father now as James aimed the weapon at him but his rapidly closing eyes could barely make Casey out. He brought the gun stock to his shoulder, intent on stopping his son from coming any further but it was too late.

Casey grabbed the gun, unchambered the round, and clasping the rifle's barrel, he smashed the butt of the stock into his father's head, the fight finally ending with James now writhing semi-conscious on the floor. He then smashed the rifle down on the countertop, the granite cracking with the force and the gun breaking into pieces.

"Don't you ever point a gun at me."

The boy calmly pulled his phone from his pocket and dialed 911.

"Yes, hello… I'd like to report a domestic disturbance at 2805 Georgia Avenue in Green Hills," he said, his voice calm and even without a hint of a tremor.

"Yes, his name is James Larsen… yes, he's been hurt, probably needs an ambulance… Yes, he's breathing, but maybe for not much longer… You should probably hurry… My name? It doesn't matter… Thanks, goodbye," said Casey, ending the call.

He calmly walked over to where his father lay groaning from the searing pain caused by his son's final blow.

"It doesn't feel so good, does it, Dad? You know, to be on the receiving end? But let me tell you one last thing. If you ever go after Mom or Poppy, if you even get to within a thousand miles of them, I will kill you. That isn't a threat, Dad, that is a promise. By the way, you may want to have a dentist look at your teeth, they're not looking so good right now. Have a good day."

And without a look back, Casey walked out of the house, loaded up his luggage into the Jeep and began his journey to Arizona, never to return to Tennessee.

Chapter 114

It was four in the afternoon on the third day of driving after she'd said a tearful farewell to Poppy in Arizona when Summer had been forced to stop and put up the canvas roof of the Bronco because of the rain that had begun to fall. It always amazed her that Arizona had so much torrential rainfall at times, when most people regarded it as a dry state. It was in moments like this that she wished she could simply push a button and the roof would be in place in seconds because the Bronco's old canvas top was time-consuming to button into place. But finally, she was back on the road and still making good time.

For the long and sometimes monotonous cross country journey, she'd also made a selection of mix tapes for the Bronco's cassette player and somehow, the songs from her younger life helped the miles to pass more quickly. She touched the sea glass necklace that rested on her chest and smiled as one of her favorite songs began playing on her car stereo. ABC's "All Of My Heart" from 1982 was an old favorite and she sang along, knowing the words from singing it so often…

Once upon a time when we were friends

I gave you my heart, the story ends

No happy ever after now we're friends…

She'd been driving now for seven hours and even though Jake had urged her to leave the Bronco behind and simply take a plane to California, she could never leave this car, it meant too much to her. Anyway, he was just being silly, she was a good driver after all, and her dad had taught her well…

Wish upon a star if that might help

The stars collide if you decide…

The rain fell in sheets now, a blinding storm as the car's wipers worked overtime to keep up and she squinted to see through the windscreen…

What's it like to have loved and to lose her touch?

What's it like to have loved and to lose that much?

The Bronco's speedometer showed that she was doing sixty-five and she knew she should slow down but she wanted to get to her next hotel stop by seven that evening so she could have a good meal, call Jake, sleep for ten hours, get up and begin the next day's drive…

No, I won't be told there's a crock of gold

at the end of the rainbow…

But she also knew that it was foolish to take risks for the sake of a few minutes gained so she slowed down to fifty as impatient drivers behind her began to pass her on the two-lane highway…

Or that pleasure and pain, sunshine and rain

Might make this love grow…

The sky was black now as the heavens opened and the headlights from oncoming vehicles were dazzling as yet another impatient and angry driver tried to pass her in the insane weather conditions…

But I hope and I pray that maybe someday

You'll walk in the room with my heart...

There was no way the car behind her could get past in time when she realized the speed that the truck was traveling, hurtling towards her…

Add and subtract but as a matter of fact

Now that you're gone I still want you back...

She swerved wildly to avoid collision and in that moment, she ran out of asphalt…

Remembering, surrendering...

The car tumbled, over and over, finally stopping and landing on its roof at the bottom of the ravine, a crumpled mess of glass and metal…

The kindest cut's the cruelest part...

And in those last moments as the rain crashed down, and the blood poured in a torrent down her face, Summer closed her eyes for the last time as she felt her life ending…

All of my heart...

Chapter 115

For the second time in my life, Summer had disappeared from my world without explanation. I'd spent the last month searching online for her, calling her cell phone but I couldn't find her. The Bronco didn't have Bluetooth and I just thought that the car was dangerous enough without the distraction of talking on a cell phone so we'd agreed that we would call each evening once she'd arrived at a hotel for the night. And she'd called at 8pm like clockwork every night. Until she didn't.

My fear that James had discovered her plan was constantly in my mind. I fully realized that men like him were able to control their wives and everything in their wives' lives and that maybe Summer had been forced to return to Tennessee. Either that or she had decided at the last minute during the trip that she just couldn't do it, out of fear or guilt or loyalty. My biggest fear of all was that she had been involved in an accident in the Bronco but I searched everywhere online and couldn't find anything. I even asked Sammy to see if he could find anything out about any auto wrecks that had happened on the I-40 but he came up empty-handed for which I felt oddly grateful.

All of my calls to her cell phone went directly to voicemail and there was no response to texts or emails either. I wasn't even able to contact either of her children because I didn't know exactly what she'd told them about me. I knew they went to college somewhere in Arizona but I had no idea which one. I was alone once again and had a terrible feeling of déjà vu. The helplessness of not knowing, the misery of the unknown.

So now, as I spend my evenings and weekends walking the beach at Avila, I think back on a girl who could have been the one with whom I grew old and loved for the rest of my life. My only memory now is of that sparkling smile and that perfect face that will never grow old in my mind's eye. That one glorious summer of 1986 will be the only summer I ever want to remember, the last Summer…

As I came towards the end of my evening walk, my thoughts were interrupted by my iPhone and I reluctantly tugged it from my pocket and quizzically looked at the caller ID. I didn't recognize the number and I debated on whether to answer but seeing that it was an out of state call, I decided to touch the green phone icon.

"Hello?" I said.

No one there, just an empty void…

"Hello, is there anyone there?" I said again.

As I was about to hang up, the caller said something.

"Remember me?"

Summer?

I collapsed on the sand, my legs turning to jelly, no longer able to support my weight.

"Jake?" she said.

"Summer, is that you? Is it really you? Tell me I'm not dreaming," I whispered, no longer trusting my own mind.

"Jake, it's me. It's really me. It's me, my love!" she said.

Tears immediately began to stream down my face, I didn't know if this was real, didn't know if I was hallucinating, didn't even care if it was only my imagination. I'd just heard Summer's voice and it was heavenly.

"Oh Summer! I thought you had decided not to come, had second thoughts, turned back and returned to Tennessee. I even tried to see if you'd had an accident but couldn't find anything online about one," I blurted, barely able to string the words together and still not knowing if I was dreaming.

"I'm sorry, Jake, I can't even begin to understand how you must have felt all this time. I'd never turn back! But I *did* have a terrible accident and miraculously I survived but I only survived because my love for you kept me alive. I don't even remember anything about what happened, it's all such a blur. I made a mistake by taking a short cut on country roads instead of staying on the Interstate. It was foolish of me in that car. The last image I have in my head was driving on a rainy night and then I woke up in a hospital bed with tubes in my arms! I'm so sorry for what you must have gone through whilst I've been recovering."

"Oh my God, Summer, you could have been killed! How badly have you been injured? I've got so many questions but keep talking to me, all I need is to hear your voice, to know you're okay."

"We'll have lots of time to talk in the coming weeks so that I can explain everything but I was put into an induced coma to stabilize me while I was in the hospital because they didn't know what kind of head trauma I might have suffered in the crash. I'm still weary because it was only early yesterday morning when they finally brought me out of it. I'm so sorry."

"Oh Summer, I've missed you so much, are you really alive or am I dreaming again? I asked.

"I'm alive, Jake, I'm alive and I'm going to be with you very, very soon!" she answered.

"When? When? I need to see you now! I'll come to you right now, just tell me where you are, I'm going to get in my car and start driving," I said, my voice now breaking, realizing that this was her, that it wasn't a dream.

"Soon, Jake, I'm going to be with you the day after tomorrow," she said, "I'll be at San Luis Obispo airport by eleven o'clock. Pick me up!"

"Oh Summer, I thought I'd lost you, I thought I'd never get to share my life with you," I said.

"My lovely Jake Delaney, we'll share the rest of our lives together, everything's going to be perfect," she replied, "But where are you right now? Are you on the beach at Avila?"

"Yes, I am. It's where I come every day, it reminds me of you because I used to sometimes message you from here as the sun set, enjoying every moment as I walked along the shoreline."

"Whereabouts are you now? Exactly where are you?" she asked.

"I'm heading back from the far north end where the huge rock curves around the ocean, do you remember the photo I texted you?" I replied, "But… why do you need to know?"

"Jake, listen to me and trust me. I need to hang up now and make a call to someone. But I can't wait to have you in my arms in a couple of day's time so that we can start our new life together. Do you trust me? Will you? Please Jake, just trust me!" she said.

"I do, I do, I trust you with everything I have, I love you, you know that. I'll be waiting for you at the airport, I can't wait, I just can't wait to see you again."

We said goodbye to each other and as the call disconnected and I put the phone back in my pocket, I tried to unravel the events of the past few minutes. She was alive! We *were* finally going to be together. But in all honesty, I still didn't really know if I was dreaming. It felt real but I didn't trust myself to believe anything. But everything else felt real, even the squawking from the seagulls and the crashing of the waves felt real.

Looking down at my quivering hands though, I could see that I was visibly shaking and my heart felt like it wanted to rip free from my chest. My eyes were still blurred from the tears that kept running down my cheeks and I could still hear her voice in my head.

But as I walked back to the car parking area next to the beach, my head a maelstrom of whirling emotions and thoughts, I noticed a familiar figure walking towards me.

I rubbed my eyes to try and clear my vision as the girl continued to approach me. Summer? Was she here all along? Had she played a trick on me?

As she came to within a few yards, I recognized that familiar and captivating smile from so many years ago, it was unmistakable, forever etched in my mind. But I began to realize as she came closer that I was mistaken; this wasn't Summer… this wasn't Summer at all.

"Poppy?" I stammered, "Are you… Poppy?"

She held out her hands, offering them to me as she neared where I was now standing, my feet still planted in the sand, unable to move, barely able to breathe.

"Hello Daddy, I don't think we've met..."

Author's Note

The Sea Glass is my first novel, and I'm very proud of it, although it will probably be the longest novel I will ever write. There are reasons for this, firstly because a debut novelist invariably gets caught in the moment and it is difficult to rein in what I can only describe as an unleashed explosion of new thoughts. The other reason is that with any story that spans more than three decades, the story cannot be rushed to a finish line and is unlikely to fall within a publisher's limit of 100,000 words. Mostly, they want around 80,000 so you can understand that when *The Sea Glass* was completed at 130,000 words, no publisher was ever likely to embrace it. But that doesn't matter.

The writing of a novel, the painting of a picture and the composition of a song should initially be for just one purpose; the singular pleasure of the writer, the artist or the composer. Anyone who subsequently gains pleasure from the creator's achievements, is the icing on the cake. I decided to write *The Sea Glass* because I know that so many of us have stories to tell of lost and unrequited love, and that perhaps we wish sometimes that we could have changed what happened in the past. We read about people in their seventies, eighties and even their nineties, who somehow manage to rekindle a flame from decades earlier and for however many years remain in their lives, they finally find true love, true happiness and unbridled joy. For most of us who have distant memories of someone we loved, it is rarely the case. Time takes its toll and we take different journeys in our lives, the past no longer available to visit and love again.

But if after reading *The Sea Glass*, you have found something you can identify with, the distant passion that never died, or the stirring of a fractured and fragile but cherished moment from decades ago, or even just a beautiful thought from a moment in time, then it makes my efforts truly worthwhile and my time has been well spent. For me, the writing of this book was a life raft, when I found myself at a fairly low ebb, but it was a raft that I clung to and one that brought me happiness and also a resurgence in my own self-belief, that I had much still to offer and in fact, that I could actually write my first novel.

But as with the writing of any book, the process is a selfish and lonely existence. There are many days where you simply find yourself at a dead end or your mind doesn't function in the way you need it to. There are days when it would be so much easier to throw in the towel and admit defeat. And without the support, enthusiasm and encouragement from close friends and family, *The Sea Glass* would never have been completed and for that, I remain eternally grateful. So, a special 'thank you' goes out to a small group of lovely people for their advice, information, anecdotes, encouragement and kindness, and of course, ladies go first:

My wife and daughter, Jayne and Lucy Robson, for their love and support and for believing in me that I could write a novel.

Jodi Whitby, for her artistic and editorial contributions and exceptional talent for kicking my butt when I lost direction.

Lisa Holland, for her time, passion and patience as she waited for the next chapters to be finished for her brilliant scrutiny.

Cornelia Södergren, for interrupting her own precious writing time and giving me the thumbs up from a seasoned author.

My mum, Avril Robson, for having the courage to bring me into this world and for teaching me the benefits of buying good shoes.

My buddies, Craig Dallas and Glenn Greenspan, Craig for his endless optimism and Glenn for his fabulous eye for errors and detail.

But also without either of them, the characters of Perryman and Talbot would never have been created.

A big hug thank you goes to my lovely friend, Peter McGlasham, who helped immensely with the synopsis when he already had enough on his own plate.

And finally, to my only friend from the wee town of Glasgow, Matt Forrest, who gave it the rare and appreciated, Scottish Seal of Approval.

I thank you all.